The Man In The Twilight

by

Ridgwell Cullum

Double9 BOOKS

The Man In The Twilight

by Ridgwell Cullum

ISBN: 978-93-71817-25-7

Published by

DOUBLE 9 BOOKS

2/13-B, Ansari Road
Daryaganj, New Delhi – 110002
info@double9books.com
www.double9books.com
Tel. 011-40042856

ABOUT THE AUTHOR

Ridgwell Cullum was a British author known for his prolific output of adventure novels, often set in the sparsely populated regions of the United States and Canada. Born in London on August 13, 1867, Cullum developed a deep interest in frontier life and wilderness landscapes, which greatly influenced his literary works. His writing career spanned over 30 years, during which he created numerous novels that captured the spirit of adventure, exploration, and the challenges faced by people in remote and often harsh environments. Cullum's works were popular for their vivid descriptions of the landscapes and the characters that inhabited them, with many stories focusing on themes of survival, conflict, and personal growth. He passed away on November 3, 1943, in Newton Abbot, United Kingdom, leaving behind a legacy of adventure fiction that continues to be appreciated by readers of the genre. Cullum's parents were also from London, and while not much is known about his family background, his writing reflects a keen understanding of both human nature and the vast, untamed lands that he portrayed in his books.

CONTENTS

PART I

CHAPTER I
THE CRISIS

They sat squarely gazing into each other's eyes. Bat Marker had only one mood to express. It was a mood that suggested determination to fight to a finish, to fight with the last ounce of strength, the last gasp of breath. He was sitting at the desk, opposite his friend and employer, Leslie Standing, and his small grey eyes were shining coldly under his shaggy, black brows. His broad shoulders were squared aggressively.

There was far less display in the eyes of Leslie Standing. They were wide with a deep pre-occupation. But then Standing was of very different type. His pale face, his longish black hair, brushed straight back from an abnormally high forehead, suggested the face of a student, even a priest. Harker was something of the roused bull-dog, strong, rugged, furious; a product of earth's rough places.

"Give us that last bit again."

Bat's tone matched his attitude. It was abrupt, forceful, and he thrust out a hand pointing at the letter from which the other had been reading.

Standing's eyes lit with a shadow of a smile as he turned again to the letter.

> "There's just one thing more. It's less pleasant, so I've kept it till the last. Hellbeam is in Quebec. So is his agent—the man Idepski. My informant tells me he saw the latter leaving the steam-packet office. It suggests things are on the move your way again. However, my man is keeping tab. I'll get warning through at the first sign of danger."

Standing looked up. His half smile had gone. There was doubt in his eyes, and the hand grasping the letter was not quite steady. But when he spoke his tone was a flat denial of the physical sign that Bat had been quick to observe.

"Charlie Nisson's as keen as a needle," Standing said. "His whisper's a sight more than another fellow's shout."

Bat regarded the letter. He watched the other lay it aside on a pile of papers. He was thinking, thinking hard. And his thought was mostly of the man whose shaking hand betrayed him. Suddenly an explosive movement brought his clenched fist down on the table with a thud.

"Hell!" he cried, in a fury of impatience. "What's the use? The danger sign's hoisted. I know it. You know it. Nisson knows it. Well? Say, Hellbeam's been in Quebec a score of times since—since—. That don't worry a thing. No. He's got big finance in the Skandinavia bunch in Quebec. We know all about that. It's Idepski. Idepski ain't visiting the packet office for his health. He ain't figgerin' on a joy trip up the Labrador coast. No. That's the signal, sure. Idepski at the packet office. Their darn mud-scow mostly runs here, to Sachigo, and there ain't a thing along the way to interest Idepski—but Sachigo. We'll be getting word from Charlie Nisson in some hurry."

"Yes, we'll get it in a hurry."

Standing nodded. He was transparently perturbed. Bat watched him closely. Then, in a moment, his mind was made up.

"See right here, Les," he cried, in a tone he vainly endeavoured to restrain. "I've figgered right along this thing would need to happen sometime. You can't beat a feller like Hellbeam all the time and leave him without a kick. It don't need me to tell you that. But I want to get a square eye on the whole darn game. Maybe you don't get all you did to that guy when you cleaned him out of ten million dollars on Wall Street seven years ago.

"Say, you were a mathematical professor at a Scottish University before you reckoned to buck the game on Wall Street, weren't you?" he went on, more moderately. He forced a grin into eyes that were scarcely accustomed. "One of those guys who mostly make two and two into four, and by no sort of imagination can cypher 'em into five. I know. You figgered out that Persian Oil gamble to suit yourself, and forgot to figger that Hellbeam was at the other end of it. No. The other feller don't cut any ice with you while you're playing around with figgers. It's only afterwards you find that figgers ain't the whole game, and wrostling ten million dollars out of one of the biggest railroad kings and bank presidents in America has something to it liable to hand you nightmare. Well, you got that nightmare. So did I. You've had it for most the whole of the last seven years. But it ain't a nightmare now. It's dead real, which is only a way of sayin' Hellbeam's set his dogs on a hot trail, and we're the poor darn gophers huntin' our holes right up here on the Labrador coast.

"Oh, yes. I know what you'd say. You've said it all before. Hellbeam hasn't a kick comin'. You were both operators on Wall Street. You were both playing the financial game as all the world knows it. You beat him on a straight financial fight. It was just a matter of the figgers which it's your job to play around with.

"Now I'm just going to say the thing that's in my mind," he went on, his tone changing again to something clumsily persuasive. "You can take it easy from me. You see, you picked me up when I was down and out. You passed me a hand when there wasn't a hope left me but a stretch of penitentiary. I fought that darn lumber-jack to a finish, which is mostly my way in things. And it was plumb bad luck that he went out by accident. Well, it don't matter. It was you who got me clear away when they'd got the penitentiary gates wide open waiting for me, and it's a thing I can't never forget. I'm out for you all the time, and I want you to know it when I'm telling you the things in my mind. Hellbeam's got a mighty big kick coming. It's the biggest kick any feller of his sort can have. He's the money power of Sweden. He's one of the big money powers of the States. He lives for money and the power it hands him. Well? This is how I figger. Just how you played him up I can't say. But it's his job to juggle around with figgers same as it's yours, and if you beat him out of ten million dollars you must have played a slicker hand than him. All of which says you must have got more to windward of the law than him—and he knows it. Why, it's easy. The feller who has the money power to hold the crown jewels of Sweden from falling into the hands of yahoo politicians out to grab the things they haven't the brains to come by honestly, is mostly powerful enough to buy up the justice he needs, or any other old thing. Hellbeam means to get his hands on you. He's going to get you across the darn American border. And when he's got you there he's going to send you down, by hook or crook, to the worst hell an American penitentiary can show you. It's seven years since you hurt him. But that ain't a circumstance. If it takes him seventy-seven he'll never quit your trail."

Bat paused, and, for a moment, turned from the wide black eyes he had held seemingly fascinated while he was talking. It almost seemed that the emotions stirring in his broad bosom were too overpowering for him, and he needed respite from their pressure. But he came again. He was bound to. It was his nature to drive to the end at whatever cost to himself.

"I'm handing you this stuff, Les, because I got to," he went on. "It ain't because I'm liking it. No, sir. And if you've the horse sense I reckon you have, you'll locate my object easy. Those words of Nisson's have told us plain we got to fight. We got to fight like hell. And the time's right now. Oh, yes, we're going to fight. You an' me, just the same as we've fought a heap of times before. There ain't a feller I know who's got more fight in him than you—when you feel that way. But—well, say, you just need a boost to make you feel like it. You ain't like me who wants to fight most all the time. No. Well—I'm going to hand you that boost."

"How?"

Standing's unruffled interrogation was in sharp contrast with the other's earnestness. There was a calm tolerance in it. The tolerance of a temperament given to philosophy rather than passion. Perhaps it was a mask. Perhaps it was real. Whatever it was, Bat's next words sent the hot fire of a man's soul leaping into his eyes.

"When your boy's born, what then?"

"Ah!"

Bat's fists clenched at the sound of the other's ejaculation. It was the nervous clenching at a sound that threatened danger. Swift as a shot he followed up his challenge.

"Your pore gal's down there in Quebec hopin' and prayin' to hand you that boy child you reckon Providence is going to send you. Well, when he gets along, and Hellbeam's around—and—"

Bat broke off. Standing had risen from his chair. He had moved swiftly, his lean figure propelled towards the window by long, nervous strides. His voice came back to the man at the table, while his eyes gazed down upon the waters of Farewell Cove, over the widespread roofs of the great groundwood mill, the building of which was the result of his seven years' sojourn on the Labrador coast.

"You've handed it me, Bat," he said, in a quick, nervous way. "I'll fight. I know. You guess I'm scared at Nisson's news. Maybe I am, I don't know. I'm not a man of iron guts. Maybe I never shall be. It's hell to me to feel a shadow dogging my every step. Yes, you're right. It's been a nightmare, and now—why, now it's real. But get your mind at rest. I'm going to fight Hellbeam all I know. And with the thought of Nancy, and the boy she's going to give me, I don't need a thing else. No."

"That's how I figgered."

Bat's delight softened his hard eyes for the moment, and his attitude relaxed as Standing went on.

"You reckon I've no imagination," he said. "You reckon I'm just a calculating machine that can juggle figures better than any other machine." He shook his dark head. "I guess you don't do me full justice. When I quit the university on the other side it was because I had built myself up a big dream. I crossed to the United States with my imagination full of the things I hoped to do. It was the chance I looked for. And I found it in Hellbeam, and the Persian Oils it was his hobby to manipulate. I jumped in and grabbed it with both hands. And, as you say, I beat him at his own game. But that was only part of my dream. The next part you also know, though you choose to think it was only as a refuge from Hellbeam that I came here to Sachigo. I admit circumstances have modified my original dream, but then I dreamed my first dream as a man unmarried. Now I have added to it in the thought of the son my wife's going to present me with. After beating Hellbeam and making the fortune I desired, I didn't flee here to the coast of Labrador as a mere refuge from the man you tell me I robbed. No. This place served its purpose that way, it's true. But it was the place I selected long since for the fulfilment of the second part of my dream.

"Bat—Bat, old friend. It isn't I who lack imagination. It's you, with your bull-dog, fighting nature. Years ago, way back there in my rooms at the university, I took up a study that interested me mightily. It was when the European war was on, and was doing its best to unship the brains of half the world. I took it up to relieve myself of the strain of things. And it inspired me with a desire to achieve something that looked well-nigh impossible. I was watching the Swedes, the Skandinavians generally, and I saw them getting fat and rich by holding the rest of the world to ransom for paper and wood pulp—the stuff we call here groundwood. It was then that my dream was born. Oh, yes, it's changed a bit since then. But not so much. All I learned at that time told me there was only one country in the world that was due to hold the world's paper industry, and that country was yours—Canada. The illimitable forests of the country are one of the most amazing features of it. The water power—yes, and even the climate. But I saw all Skandinavia's advantage. Hitherto they've had a complete monopoly. Geographically they were in the thick of the world. The whole darn thing was in their lap. But they have a weakness which you could never find in this country. Their forests are being eaten into. Their lumber is receding farther and farther from their mills. Their labour is difficult. Well, I set to work with a map and those figures which you guess are my strong point. I played around with all the information of Quebec and Labrador I could get hold of. Then, after worrying around awhile, I realised that, with only eighteen hundred sea miles dividing Britain from Labrador, given the cheapness of power, sufficiently extensive plant and forest limits and adequate shipping, I could put groundwood on the European market in favourable competition with Skandinavia. By this means I could build up an industry which means the wealth of Canada for the Canadians, and establish the paper industry of the world within the heart of our British Empire. So it was Farewell Cove and

Sachigo on the coast of Labrador for me. And the locality had nothing to do with the man who guesses I robbed him."

It was Bat who was held silent now. He nodded his head at the narrow back that remained turned on him.

"Well, since then," Standing went on, "seven years have passed. Circumstances have forced modifications on my plans. Hellbeam is the circumstance. You say we are the gophers hunting our holes. Maybe you're right. Anyway Hellbeam's shadow is haunting me. It's haunting me in that I know—*I* feel—that the fulfilment of this dream is not for me. Why?"

He turned abruptly from the window. His pale face was even paler under the excitement burning in his dark eyes. He thrust out a hand, a delicate, long-fingered hand pointing at his friend and faithful servant.

"Say, you reckon I've no imagination. Listen. I see the time coming when all you say of Hellbeam's purpose will be fulfilled, and my dream shattered and tumbling about my head. If Hellbeam succeeds, can I let this thing happen? Can I sacrifice this great purpose in such a personal disaster? No. My hope is in my little wife, that dear woman who's given herself to me with the full knowledge of the threat hanging over my future. She and I have dreamed a fresh dream. And she's even now fulfilling her part of that dream. Yes, you're right. I'm going to fight for our dream with every ounce that's in me. I know my failings. I'm at heart a coward. But I'm out to fight though the gates of hell are agape waiting for me. And when I'm beaten, and Hellbeam's satisfied his kick, my boy, my little son, will step into my shoes and carry on the work till it's complete. Oh, yes, I say 'my son.' Nancy will see to it that she gives me a son. And, by God, how I will fight for him!"

Bat was silent before the tide of his friend's passion. He listened to the strange mixture of clear thinking and unreasoning faith with a feeling of something like awe of a man whom he had long since given up attempting to fathom. He was a rough lumberman, a mill-boss, who, by sheer force, had raised himself from the dregs of a lumber camp to a position where his skill and capacity had full play. And in his utter lack of education it was impossible that he should be able to fathom a nature so complex, so far removed from his sphere of culture.

His devotion to the ex-university professor was based on a splendid gratitude such as only the native generosity of his temper could bestow. The man had once served him in his extremity. Even to this day he never quite realised how the thing had come about, and Leslie Standing refused to talk of it. All he knew was that as mill-boss of an obscure mill, far in the interior of Quebec, away down south of Sachigo, he had fought one of those sudden battles with a lumber-jack which seem to spring up without any apparent reason. And in the desperateness of it, in the fierce height to which his battling temper had arisen, he had killed his man. Even so, these things were sufficiently common for little notice of the matter to have been taken. But it so happened that the dead man was the hero of the workers of the mill, and Bat Harker was their well-hated boss. Forthwith, in their numbers, the workers at once determined that Bat should pay the penalty. They seized and imprisoned him, while they sent down country to get him duly tried and condemned. It was then the miracle happened.

It happened in the night, with the appearance of a lean, tall man, with a high forehead, and smooth black hair, and the clothes of civilisation to which Bat Harker was little enough accustomed. He entered his prison room seemingly without question. He told Bat that if he cared to get away he had the means awaiting him outside. And the prisoner who had visions of hanging, or at best, a long term of imprisonment, snatched at the helping hand held out. And Leslie Standing had brought him in safety straight to Farewell Cove, where together, with the vast capital which the former had wrung from the Swedish financier, Nathaniel Hellbeam, they had undertaken the creation of the great mill of Sachigo.

Bat, in his wonder at the apparent ease of his rescue, had sought information. But little enough had been forthcoming. Leslie Standing had only smiled in his pensive fashion.

"Money," he had said calmly. "Just money. It can do most things."

That was all. And thenceforward the subject had been taboo. Even after seven years of intimate relations, Bat was still mystified on the subject, he was still guessing.

Now, as he listened to his friend's expressions of faith, so strangely jumbled with calculated purpose, he sat at the table groping helplessly. Suppose—suppose that faith were to be shattered. What then? His mind was concerned, deeply concerned. And he dared not put his fears into words.

Standing came back to his chair.

"Here, we've talked these things enough," he said. "You've got my word. Just don't worry a thing. If Hellbeam's dogs get around, well—we're here first. All I want is news of Nancy. And that'll be along any old time now. When I get that—."

The door of the office was thrust open, and an olive-hued face appeared. It was the clerk who worked in direct contact with the owner of the Sachigo mill. He was one-third nigger, another French Canadian, and the rest of him was Indian. It was a combination that appealed to the man who employed him.

"They've 'phoned it through from the wireless at the headland, Boss," the man said without preamble, pushing a sheet of paper into Leslie Standing's hand.

He had gone as swiftly and silently as he came, and the door was closed softly behind him.

Standing was gazing across at Bat. He had not even glanced at the message.

"I'd like to bet," he cried, his eyes alight with a smiling excitement. Then he shook his head. "No. I wouldn't bet on it. It's too sacred. Nancy—my Nancy—."

He broke off, and glanced down at the paper. In a moment the smile fell from his eyes. When he looked up it was to flash a keen glance at the rugged face beyond the desk.

"Here, listen," he cried, with a sharp intake of breath.

"Watch *Lizzie* for U.G.P. Signed—Nisson."

Bat nodded.

"U.G.P. That's Union Great Peninsular Railroad. That's Hellbeam's. It means—."

"It means Hellbeam's men are aboard. The packet *Lizzie* is due at our quay in less than an hour."

Standing tore the message into small fragments and dropped them into the wastepaper basket beside him. Only was his emotion displayed in the deliberate care with which he reduced the paper to the smallest possible fragments.

CHAPTER II
THE MAN WITH THE MAIL

The calm waters of Farewell Cove lay a-shimmer under the slanting rays of the sun. A wealth of racing white cloud filled the dome of the summer sky, speeding under the pressure of a strong top wind. Even the harsh world of Labrador was smiling under the beneficence of the brief summer season.

Leslie Standing stood for a moment before passing down the winding woodland trail on his way to the water-front below. The view of it all was irresistible to him in his present mood, and he feasted his eyes hungrily while the resolve he had taken yielded an inflexible hardening.

Bat Harker was less affected by the things spread out before him. He was concerned only for the mood of the man beside him. So he waited with such patience as his hasty nature could summon.

"It's all good, Bat, old friend," Standing said, after a moment's silent contemplation. "It's too good to lose. It's too good for us to stand for interference from—Nathaniel Hellbeam."

Bat grunted some sort of acquiescence. He was gazing steadily out over the spruce belt which covered the lower slopes of the hillside. His keen deep-set eyes were on the shipping lying out in the cove, watching the fussy approach of the bluff packet boat.

It was a scene of amazing natural splendour which the works of man had no power to destroy. Farewell Cove was a perfect natural harbour, deep-set amidst surrounding, lofty, forest-clad hills. It was wide and deep, a veritable sea-lake, backing inland some fifteen miles behind the wide headland gateway to the East, which guarded its entrance from the storming Atlantic. Its shores were of virgin forest, peopled with the delicate-hued spruce, and all the many other varieties of soft, white, long-fibred timber demanded in the manufacture of the groundwood pulp needed for the world's paper industry.

Far as the eye could see, in every direction, it was the same; forest and hill. And, in the heart of it all, the great watercourse of the Beaver River debouched upon the cove which linked it with the ocean beyond. It was a world of forest, seeming of limitless extent.

But the feast that had inspired Leslie Standing's words was less the banquet which Nature had spread than the things which expressed the labours he and his companion had expended during the past seven years. He was concerned for the endless forests. He appreciated the great waterfall to the west, where the Beaver River fell off the highlands of the interior and precipitated itself into the cove below. These were the two things in Nature he had demanded to make his work possible. For the rest, the rugged immensity of scenery, the mighty contours of the aged land about him, the vastness of the harsh primordial world, so inhospitable, so forbidding under the fierce climate which Nature had imposed, made no appeal. It served, and so it was sufficient. The lights and shades under the summer sunlight were full of splendour. No artist eye could have gazed upon it all and missed its appeal. But these men lived amidst it the year round, and they had learned something of the fear which the ruthless northland inspires. To them the beauty of the open season was a mockery, a sham, the cruel trap of a heartless mistress.

It was on the wide southern foreshore, just below where the falls of the Beaver River thundered into the chasm which the centuries of its flood had hewn in the granite rock, that Standing had founded his great mill. It lay there, in full view from the hillside, amidst a tangle of stoutly made roads, where seven years ago not even a game track had existed. He had set it up beside his water-power, and had given it the name which belonged to the ruined trading post he had found on the southern headland of the cove when first he had explored the region. Sachigo. A native, Labrador word which meant "Storm." The trading post had since been re-built into a modern wireless station, and so had become no longer the landmark it once had been. But Standing's whim had demanded the necessity for preserving the name, if only for the sake of its meaning.

In seven years the translation of the wilderness had been well-nigh complete. Its vast desolation remained. That could never change under human effort. It was one of the oldest regions of the earth's land, driven and beaten and desolated under a climate beyond words in its merciless severity. But now the place was peopled. Now human dwellings dotted the forest foreshore of the cove. And the latter were the homes of the workers who had come at the mill-owner's call to share in his great adventure.

Then there was shipping in the cove. A fleet of merchant shipping awaiting cargoes. There was a built inner harbour, with quays, and warehouses. There were travelling cranes, and every appliance for the loading of the great freighters with all possible dispatch. There were light railways running in every direction. There were sheltering "booms" in the river mouth crammed with logs, and dealt with by an army of river men equipped with their amazing peavys with which they thrust, and rolled, and shepherded the vast mass of hewn timber towards the slaughterhouse of saws. Then, immediately surrounding the mill, there was a veritable town of storehouses and offices and machine shops of every description. There were power-houses, there were buildings in the process of construction, and the laid foundations of others projected. It was a world of active human purpose lost in the heart of an immense solitude which it was nevertheless powerless to disturb.

"Yes, it's all too good to have things happen, Bat," Standing went on presently. "Hark at the roar of the falls. What is it? Five hundred thousand horsepower of water, summer and winter. Listen to the drone of the grinders." He shook his head. "It's a great song, boy, and they never get tired of singing it. There's only thirty-six of 'em at present. Thirty-six. We'll have a hundred and thirty-six some day. Look down there at the booms." He stood pointing, a tall, lean figure on the hillside. "Tens of thousands of logs, and hundreds of men. We'll multiply those again and again—one day. It's fine. The freighters lying at anchor awaiting their cargoes. Some day we'll have our own ships—a big fleet of 'em. See the smoke pennants floating from our smoke stacks. They're the triumphant pennants of successful industry, eh? We can't have too many such flags flying. One day we'll have trolley cars running along the shores of the cove to bring the workers in to the mill. It'll be like a veritable Atlantic City. Oh, it's a great big dream. There's nothing amiss. No."

"Only the *Lizzie* getting in."

Bat was without apparent appreciation. He was thinking only of the message they had received, and the threat it contained.

Standing glanced round at the sturdy figure beside him. A half smile lit his sallow features. Then he turned again and sought out the tubby vessel approaching the wharf below. But it was only for a moment. Some subtle thought impelled him, and he glanced back at the house on the hillside he had just left, the house he had erected for the woman whose devotion had taught him the real meaning of life.

It was a long, low, rambling, gabled building. It was an extensive timber-built home with a wide verandah and those many vanities and conceits of building that would never have been permitted had it been intended for bachelordom. He remembered how Nancy and he had designed it together. He remembered the delight with which they had looked forward to its completion, and ultimately their boundless joy in the task of its furnishing. He remembered how Nancy had insisted that it should contain not only their home, but his own private office, from which he could control the great work he had set his hand to. It had been her ardent desire to be always near him, always there to support him under the burden of his immense labours. And remembering these things a fierce desire leapt within him, and he turned again to the man at his side.

"Yes, she's getting in, Bat," he said. "But I just wanted to get a peek at things. Well, I've seen all I want, old friend. Now I'm ready. Fight? Oh, yes, I'm ready to fight. Come on." And he laughed as he hurried down the woodland trail to the water-side.

The two men had reached the quay-side, which was lined with bales of wood-pulp stacked ready for shipment. Farther down its length the cranes were rattling their chains, swinging their burdens out over the holds of the vessel taking in its moist cargo. The stevedores were vociferously busy, working against time. For, in the brief open season, time was the very essence of the success demanded for the mills. The noise, the babel of it all was usually the choicest music to Standing and his manager.

But just now they were less heeding. Their eyes were turned upon the small steamer plugging its deliberate way over the water towards them. It was a small, heavily-built tub of a vessel calculated to survive the worst Atlantic storms.

Bat's face was without any expression of undue emotion. But the hard lines about his clean-shaven mouth were sharply set. Standing was asurge with an excitement that fired his dark eyes. His wide-brimmed hat was thrust back from his forehead, and he stood with his hands thrust deeply in the pockets of his moleskin trousers. His nervous fingers were playing with loose coins and keys which they found irresistible.

The *Lizzie* came steadily on.

"We'll know the whole game in minutes now."

Standing could keep silent no longer. Bat nodded.

"Yep."

Orders from the bridge of the packet boat rang out over the water. Then Standing went on.

"I want to find Idepski aboard," he said. He was scarcely addressing his companion. "It would be good to get Master Walter here, fifty-three degrees north." A short, hard laugh punctuated his words. Then he turned abruptly. "Who's running No. 10 camp?"

Just for an instant Bat withdrew his gaze from the approaching vessel. He flashed a keen look of enquiry into the eyes of the questioner.

"Ole Porson," he said.

"I thought so. He's a good boy. He'll do."

Standing nodded. The cold significance of his tone was not lost on his companion. Maybe Bat understood the thing that was passing in the other's mind. At any rate he turned again to the broad-beamed tub steaming so busily towards them.

"I see old Hardy on the bridge," Standing went on a moment later. Then he added: "Fancy navigating the Labrador coast for forty years. No, I couldn't do it. I wouldn't have the—guts."

Bat still remained silent. He understood. The other was talking because it was impossible for him to refrain.

"They're standing ready to make fast," Standing said sharply. He drew a quick breath. Then his manner changed and his words came pensively. "Say, it's a queer life—a hell of a life. The sea folk, I mean. It's about the worst on earth. Think of it, cooped within those timbers that are never easy till they lie at anchor in the shelter of a harbour. I'd just hate it. Their life? What is it? It's not life at all. Hard work, hard food, hard times, and hard drinking—when they're ashore—most of them. I think I can understand. They surely need something to drown the memory of the threat they're always living under. No, they don't live. They exist. Here, let's stand clear. They're coming right in."

The bustle of landing was in full swing. Even with so small a craft as the *Lizzie* there was commotion. Orders flew from lip to lip. Creaking cables strained at unyielding bollards. Gangways clattered out from deck, and ran down on to the quay with a crash. Hatches were flung open and the steam winches rattled incessantly.

Standing and Harker were looking on from a vantage point well clear of the work of unloading. The captain of the vessel, "Old Man" Hardy, was with them. The seaman was beaming with that satisfaction which belongs to the master when his vessel is safely in port.

"Oh, I guess it ain't been too bad a trip," he was saying. "Takin' the 'ins' with the 'outs,' I'd say it was a fairish passage, which is mostly as it should be, seein' it's my last voyage in the old barge. Y'see, you folks are kind of robbing me of this blessed old kettle," he explained, with a grin that lit up the whole of his mahogany features. "Y'see we're loaded well-nigh rail under with stuff for your mill, which don't leave a dog's chance for the other folks along the coast. The Company guesses they got to put on a two thousand tonner. The *Myra*. I haven't a kick comin'. She's all a seaboat. Still, I'm kind of sorry, don't you know. I've known the *Lizzie* since she came off the stocks, which is mostly forty years, and we're mighty good friends, which ain't allus the way. I'd say, too, I'm getting old for a change. Still—."

Standing shook his head.

"What do they say? 'Hardy' by name, 'Hardy' by nature. The toughest and best sailorman on the Labrador coast! Well, I'm sorry you don't feel good about it. But," he added with a smile, "it means a good deal to us getting a bigger packet."

Captain Hardy nodded.

"Thankee kindly. It's good to know folks reckon a fellow something more than just part of a kettle of scrap like this old packet. But I'd have been glad to finish my job with her. Still, times don't stand around even in Labrador." He finished up with something in the nature of a sigh.

The work going forward was full of interest. But it was not the work that held Standing, or the watchful eyes of Bat Harker. Their sole interest was in the personality of the crew and the five passengers, mostly "drummers," from the great business houses of Quebec and Montreal, who were struggling to land their trunks of samples and get them off to the offices of the mill so as to complete their trade before the *Lizzie* put to sea again. Not one of these escaped their observation.

"You seem to keep much the same crew right along, Hardy," Standing said pleasantly. "I suppose they like shipping with a good skipper. I seem to recognise most of their faces."

"Oh, yes. They're mostly the same boys," Hardy agreed, obviously appreciating the compliment. "But I guess I lost four boys this trip. They skipped half an hour before putting to sea. It happens that way now and then, if they're only soused enough when they get aboard. They're a crazy lot with rye under their belts. I just had to replace 'em with some dockside loafers, or lie alongside another day."

Standing nodded. A man was moving down the gangway bearing a large, grey, official-looking sack on his shoulders. He was a slight, dark man with a curiously foreign cast about his features.

"The mail?" he enquired. And a curious sharpness flavoured his demand. Then he added, with studied indifference. "One of your—dockside loafers?"

Captain Hardy laughed. He continued to laugh as he watched the unhandiness of the man staggering down the gangway under his burden.

"Yep. The mail," he said. "And I'd hate to set that feller to work on a seaman's job. He's about as unhandy as a doped Chinaman. I'd say Masters is playing safe keeping him from messing up the running gear while we're discharging. Say, get a look at it."

A great laugh accompanied the old man's words as the foreign-looking creature tripped on the gangway, and only saved himself from a bad fall by precipitating his burden upon the quay. There was no responsive laughter in Standing. And Bat Harker's features remained rigidly unsmiling. Standing turned sharply.

"Maybe you can spare that boy to run those mails up to my office," he said. "It's a good healthy pull up the hill for him, and my folks are full to the neck with things. I'd be glad."

"Sure he can." Captain Hardy was only too delighted to be able to oblige so important a customer of his company. He promptly shouted at the landing officer.

"Ho, you! Masters! Just let that darn Dago tote them mails right up to Mr. Standing's office. He ain't no sort of use out of hell down here—anyway."

The mate's reply came back with an appreciative grin.

"Ay, sir," he cried, and forthwith hurled the order at the mail carrier with a plentiful accompaniment of appropriate adjectives.

"Thanks," Standing turned away. His smiling luminous eyes were shining. "I'll get right along up, Captain. There's liable to be things need seeing to in that mail before you pull out. You'd best come along, too, Bat," he added pointedly.

Standing hurried away. A sudden fierce passion was surging through his veins. Nisson was right. He knew it—now. And in a fever of impatience he was yearning to come to grips with those who would rob him of the hopes in which his whole being was bound up.

CHAPTER III
IDEPSKI

The two men reached the office on the hillside minutes before the mail carrier. They took the hill direct, passing hurriedly through the aisles of scented woods which shadowed its face. The other, the stranger, was left with no alternative but the roadway, zigzagging at an easier incline.

Standing passed into the house. His confidential man of many races looked up from his work. The quick, black eyes were questioning. He was perhaps startled at the swift return of the man whom he regarded above all others.

Standing spoke coldly, emphatically.

"There's a man coming along up. He's a sailorman, and he's dressed in dirty dungaree, and he's carrying a sack of mail. Now see and get this clearly, Loale. It's important. It's so important I can't stand for any sort of mistake. When he comes you've got to send him right into my room with the mail-bag. I want him to take it in *himself*. You get that?"

The half-breed's eyes blinked. It was rather the curious attitude of an attentive dog. But that was always his way when the master of the Sachigo Mill spoke to him.

Pete Loale was quite an unusual creature. He looked unkempt and unclean, with his yellow, pock-marked skin, and his clothes that would have disgraced a second-hand dealer's stores of waste. But for all his lack in these directions there was that in the man which was more than worth while. Out of his black eyes looked a world of intelligence. There was also a resource and initiative in him that Standing fully appreciated.

"Sure I get that," he said simply. Then he repeated in the manner of a child determined to make no mistake. "He's to take that mail-bag right into your office—*himself*."

"That's it. Don't knock on my door. Don't let him think there's a soul inside that room. Just boost him right in. You get that?"

The half-breed nodded.

"I'll just say: 'Here you! Just push that darn truck right inside that room, an' don't worry me with it, I'm busy.' That how?" The man hunched his slim shoulders into a shrug.

"See you do it—just that way," Standing said. Then he turned to Bat. "We'll get inside," he went on. "He'll be right along."

They passed into the office. The door closed behind them and Standing moved over to his seat at the crowded desk.

"Wal?"

Bat was still standing. He failed to grasp his friend's purpose. His wit was unequal to the rapid process of the other's swiftly calculating mind.

Standing littered his writing-pad with papers. He picked up a pen and jabbed it in the inkwell. Then he flung it aside and adopted a fountain-pen which he drew from his waistcoat pocket. His eyes lit with a half-smile as he finally raised them to the rugged face before him.

"You sit right over there by that window, Bat," he said easily. "If you get a look out of it you'll be amazed at the number of things to interest you." He nodded as Bat moved away with a grin and took the chair indicated. "That's it. Just sit around, and you won't see or even hear the fellow with the mail fall in through the door. And maybe, sitting there, you'll want to smoke your foul old pipe. Sort of pipe of peaceful meditation. Yes, I'd smoke that pipe, old friend, but you can cut out the peaceful meditation. You need to be ready to act quick when I pass the word. It's going to be easy. So easy I almost feel sorry for—Idepski."

"It *is*—Idepski?" Bat filled and lit his pipe.

"It surely is. No other. And—I'm glad. Now we'll quit talk, old friend. Just smoke, and look out of that window, and—think like hell."

Bat's understanding of his friend was well founded. The extreme nervous tension in Standing was obvious. It was in the wide, dark eyes. It was in the constant shifting of the feet which the table revealed. For the time, at least, the cowardice Standing claimed for himself was entirely swamped. He was stirred by the headlong excitement of battle in a manner that left Bat more than satisfied.

Once Bat turned from his contemplation of the piled-up country beyond the valley. It was at the sound of Standing's fiercely scratching pen. And his quick gaze took in the luxury of the setting for the little drama he felt was about to be enacted.

It was a wide, pleasant room, built wholly of red pine, and polished as only red pine will polish. There was a thick oriental carpet on the floor, and all the mahogany furniture was upholstered in red morocco. There were a few carefully selected pictures upon the walls, hung with an eye to the light upon each. But it was not an extravagant room. It suggested the homeland of Scotland, from which the owner of it all hailed. The Canadian atmosphere only found expression in the great steel stove which stood in one corner, and the splendid timber of which the walls of the room were built.

But Bat's eyes swiftly returned to their allotted task, and his reeking pipe did its duty with hearty goodwill. There was the sound of strident voices in the outer room, and the rattle of the door handle turning with a wrench.

The door swung open. The next moment there was the sound of a sack pitched upon the soft pile of the carpet. And through the open doorway the harsh voice of Loale pursued the intruder in sharp protest.

"Say, do you think you're stowing cargo in your darn, crazy old barge?" he cried. "If you fancy throwing things around you best get out an' do it. Guess you ain't used to a gent's office, you darn sailorman—"

But the door was closed with a slam and the rest of the protest was cut off. Bat swung about in his chair to discover a picture not easily to be forgotten.

Standing had left his desk. He was there with his back against the closed door, and his lean figure towered over the shorter sailorman in dungaree, who stood gazing up at him questioningly. The sight appealed to the grim humour of the manager. He wanted to laugh. But he refrained, though his eyes lit responsively as he watched the smile of irony that gleamed in the mill-owner's eyes.

"Well, well." Standing's tone lost none of the aggravation of his smile. "Say, I'd never have recognised you, Idepski, if it hadn't been that I was warned you'd shipped on the *Lizzie*." He laughed outright. "I can't help it. You wouldn't blame me laughing if you could see yourself. Last time I had the pleasure of encountering you was in Detroit. That's years ago. How many? Nearly seven. It seems to me I remember a bright-looking 'sleuth,' neat, clean, spruce, with a crease to his pant-legs like a razor edge, a fellow more concerned for his bath than his religion. Say, where did you raise all that junk? From old man Hardy's slop-chest? Hellbeam makes you work for your money when you're driven to wallowing in a muck-hole like the *Lizzie*. It isn't worth it. You see, you've run into the worst failure you've made in years. But I only wish you could see the sorry sort of sailorman you look."

Standing's right hand was behind him, and Bat heard the key turn in the lock of the door. He waited. But the trapped agent never opened his lips.

Idepski had seen Standing and the other down at the quay-side. He had left them there when he started up the hill. Yet—A bitter fury was driving him. He realised the trap that had been laid. He realised something of the deadly purpose lying behind it. So he remained silent under the scourge that was intended to hurt.

For all the filthy dungarees tucked into the clumsy legs of high leather sea boots, the dirty-coloured handkerchief knotted about his neck, the curious napless cloth cap with its peak pulled down over one eye, that curious cap which seems to be worn by no one else in the world but seafaring men, it was easy enough for Bat to visualise the dapper picture, that other picture of Walter Idepski that Standing had described. The man possessed a well-knit, sinuous figure which his dungarees could not disguise. His alert eyes were good-looking. And, cleaned of the black, stubbly growth of beard and whisker, an amazing transformation in his looks would surely have been achieved. But Bat's interest was less with these things than with the possible reaction the man might contemplate.

For the moment, however, the situation was entirely dominated by Standing, who displayed no sign of relaxing his hold upon it. He flung out a pointing hand, and Bat saw it was grasping the door key.

"You'd best take that chair, Idepski," he ordered. "You've opened war on me, but there's no need to keep you standing for it. You'll take that seat against my writing table. But first, Bat, here, is going to relieve you of the useless weapons I see you've got on you. Get those, Bat! There's a gun and a sheath knife, and they're clumsily showing their shape under his dungarees."

It was the word the mill-manager had awaited. He was on his feet in an instant. Idepski stirred to action. He turned to meet him.

"Keep your darn hands off!" he cried fiercely. "By—"

His hand had flown to his hip. But he was given no time. Bat was on him like an avalanche, an avalanche of furious purpose. The fighting spirit in him yearned, and in a moment his victim was caught up in a crushing embrace. There was a short, fierce struggle. But Idepski was no match for the super lumber-jack.

While Bat held on, the tenacious hands of Standing tore the weapons he had discovered from their hiding places. Then in a moment Idepski found himself sprawling in the chair he had been invited to take.

Standing's appreciation was evident as he watched the man draw a gold cigarette case from the breast pocket of his overalls as though nothing had occurred. It was an act of studied coolness that did not for a moment deceive, but it pleased. However, his next effrontery pleased the mill-owner still more.

"Say, boys," Idepski observed quietly, as he opened the case and extracted a cigarette. "I guess I'm kind o' glad you left me this. But I don't figger you're out for loot, anyway." Then he glanced up at the man watching him so interestedly. "Maybe you'll oblige me with a light," he demanded, and cocked up the cigarette he had thrust between his lips with an exaggerated impertinence.

The action was quite irresistible and Standing nodded.

"Sure," he said smilingly, and picked up the matchbox lying on his table.

He struck a match and held it while the other obtained the required light. Then he passed round the desk to the seat he had originally occupied.

Idepski leant back in his chair, and luxuriated in a deep inhalation of smoke. Bat watched him from his place at the window. Standing placed the revolver and sheath knife he had taken possession of in a drawer in the desk, and closed it carefully.

"Well, what's the play?" Idepski addressed himself solely to Standing. "I guess you've said a deal calculated to rile, and your pardner's done more," he went on. "Still—anyway we're mostly men and not school-kids. What's the play?"

Standing, too, was leaning back in his chair.

"It's easy," he said, after a moment's thoughtful regard. Suddenly he drew his chair up to the table, and, leaning forward, folded his arms upon the littered blotting pad in front of him. "It's seven years since Hellbeam—blazed the war trail," he said deliberately. "I know he's persistent. He's angry. And he's the sort of man who doesn't cool down easily. But it's taken him seven years to locate me here. And during all that time I've been looking on, watching his every move." He shook his head. "He's badly served, for all his wealth. He was badly served from the start. You should never have let me beat you in that first race across the border. I got away with every cent of the stuff, and—you shouldn't have let me. You certainly were at fault. However, it doesn't matter."

Idepski removed his cigarette from his lips and dropped the ash of it in the waste basket.

"No. It doesn't matter, because I'll get you—in the end," he retorted coldly.

"Perhaps."

Standing shrugged. But there was no indifference in his eyes. The acid sharpness of Idepski's retort had driven straight home. If the agent failed to detect it, the watchful eyes of Bat missed nothing. To him the danger signal lay in the curious flicker of his friend's eyelids. The sight impelled him. He jumped in and took up the challenge in the blunt fashion he best understood.

"Guess you've got nightmare, boy," he said, with a sneering laugh. "I ain't much at figgers, but it seems to me if it's taken you seven years to locate us here, it's going to take you seventy-seven gettin' Standing back across that border. Work it out."

Idepski had no intention of being drawn. He replied without turning.

"You think that?" he said easily. "Say, don't worry a thing; I'm satisfied. Just as sure as the sun'll rise to-morrow, Hellbeam'll get Leslie Martin, or Standing as he chooses to call himself now, just where he needs him. And if I know Hellbeam that'll be in the worst penitentiary the United States can produce. Guess you're going to wish you hadn't, Mister—Standing."

Perhaps Idepski knew his man, and understood the weakness of which Bat was so painfully aware. Perhaps he was just fencing, or even putting up a bluff in view of his own position. Whatever his purpose the effect of his added threat was instant.

Standing's luminous eyes hardened. The muscles of his jaws gripped. He sat up, and his whole attitude expressed again that fighting mood in which Bat rejoiced.

"That's all right," he said sharply. "That's just talk. You've come a hell of a long way with those boys of yours down at the *Lizzie* to worry out some body-snatching. That's all right. I don't just see how you've figgered to do it. But that's your affair. The point is, I'm going to do the body-snatching instead of you. And it's quite clear to me how I intend doing it. You're going a trip—right off. And it's a trip from which you won't get a chance of getting back to Quebec under this time next year. You see, winter's closing down in a month, and Labrador and Northern Quebec aren't wholesome territory for any man to set out to beat the trail in winter, especially with folks around anxious to stop him. You reckon I'm to pass a while in a States penitentiary. Well, meanwhile you're going to try what this country can show you in the way of a—prison ground. And you're going to try it for at least a year. You'll be treated white. But you'll need to work for your grub like other folks, and if you don't feel like working you won't eat. We're fifty-three degrees north here, and our ways are the tough ways of the tough country we live in. There's no sort of mercy in this country. Bat, here, is going to see you on your trip, and, if you take my advice, you won't rile Bat. He's got it in him, and in his hands, to make things darn unpleasant for you. You've a goodish nerve, and maybe you've goodish sense. You'll need 'em both for the next twelve months. After that it's up to you. But if you try kicking between now and then, why—God help you."

Standing beckoned Bat from his seat at the window. He held up the door key.

"You best take this," he said. "No. 10. And he starts out right away. He needs to be well on the road before the *Lizzie* puts to sea."

Bat took the key. He moved away and unlocked the door, and remained beside it grimly regarding the man who had listened without comment to the sentence passed on him, without the smallest display of emotion. Idepski was smoking his second cigarette.

"No. 10. I s'pose that's one of your lumber camps." Idepski looked up from his contemplation of the cigarette. His dark eyes were levelled at the man across the writing table. "A tough place, eh? or you wouldn't be sending me there." He laughed in a fashion that left his eyes coldly enquiring.

Standing inclined his head. He was without mercy, without pity.

"It's a tough camp in a tough country," he said deliberately. "It's a camp where you'll get just as good a time as you choose to earn. The boy who runs it learnt his job in the forests of Quebec, and you'll likely understand what that means. Well, you're going right off now. But there's this I want to tell you before I see the last of you—for a year. I know you, Idepski. I know you for all you are, and all you're ever likely to be. You're an unscrupulous blackmailer and crook. You're a parasite battening yourself on the weakness of human nature, taking your toll from whichever side of a dispute will pay you best. You're taking Hellbeam's money in the dispute between him and me, and you'll go on taking it till you pull off the play he's asking, or get broken in the work of it. That's all right as far as I'm concerned. You've nerve, you've courage, or you wouldn't be the crook you are. I guess you'll go on because I've no intention of competing with Hellbeam for your services. But I want you to understand clearly you've jumped into a mighty big fight. This is a country where a fight can go on without the prying eyes of the laws of civilisation peeking into things. And by that I take it you'll understand I reckon to make war to the knife. You came here prepared to use force. That's all right. We shan't hesitate to use force on our side. And we're going to use it to the limit. If peace is only to be gained at the cost of your life you're going to pay that cost—if it suits me. That's all I've to say at the moment. For the present, for a year, you'll be safely muzzled. You see, I don't need to worry with those boys you brought with you. You best go along with Bat now. He'll fix things ready for your trip."

The dismissal was complete, and Bat was prompt to accept his cue. He moved towards the man smoking at the table, much in the fashion of a warder advancing to take possession of his prisoner after sentence of the court.

It was at that moment that the cold mask of indifference fell from the agent. Hardy as he was, the contemplation of his momentary failure, which was about to cost him twelve months of hardship in one of the roughest lumber camps in Labrador, robbed him of something of that nerve which was his chief asset. He glanced for the first time at the burly figure of Bat. He contemplated the rugged features of the man whose battling instinct was his strongest characteristic. He read the purpose in the grim set of the square jaws, and in the unyielding light of the grey eyes peering out from under shaggy brows. And that which he read reduced him to a feeling of impotence. He flung a look of fury and hate at the man behind the desk.

"Maybe that's all you've to say," he cried, his jaws snapping viciously over his words, his eyes fiercely alight. "You think you've won when you've only gained a moment's respite. You can't win. You don't know. Oh, yes. I guess you can send me along out of the way. You can do just all you reckon. And if it suits you, you can shoot me up or any other old thing. You forget Hellbeam. You tell me I'm a crook and a blackmailer, you give me credit for nerve and courage. That's all right. You think these things, and I don't have to worry. But you've robbed Hellbeam. You've robbed him like any common 'hold-up'—of millions. It's not for you to talk of crooks and blackmailers. The laws of the States are going to find you the crook, and Hellbeam'll see they don't err for leniency. Hellbeam'll get you as sure as God. You've got months to think it over, and when you've done I reckon you won't fancy shouting. Well, I'm ready for this joy spot you call No. 10. I'm not going to kick. I've sense enough to know when the drop's on me. But you'll see me again. Oh, yes, you'll see me again because you're not going to shoot me up. For all your talk you haven't the nerve. You'll see me again, and when you do—well, don't forget Hellbeam's at the other end of this business. Guess I'm ready."

The man stood up. And as he stood his eyes looked squarely into those of Bat.

"Get on with it," he cried, and flung the remains of his lighted cigarette on the pile of the carpet, and trod it viciously underfoot with his heavy sea boot.

Standing was alone. He was alone with the thoughts his encounter with Idepski had inspired. Judging by the expression of his reflective eyes they were scarcely those of a man confident of victory. Had Bat been there to witness, the task he was at that moment engaged upon would surely have been robbed of half its satisfaction.

But Bat had gone. And with him had gone the man who was to learn the rigours of a Labrador winter under conditions of hardship he had not yet realised. Meanwhile Standing was free to think as his emotions guided him, with no watchful eyes to observe.

"You'll see me again, and when you do—well, don't forget Hellbeam's at the other end of this business."

The words haunted. The threat of them appealed to an imagination that was a-riot.

After a time Standing stirred restlessly. He sat up and brushed the litter of paper aside. Then he leant back in his chair and his fine eyes were lit with an agony of doubt and disquiet. The poisonous seed of the agent's retort had fallen upon fruitful soil.

But after awhile the tension seemed to relax, and his gaze wandered from the grey daylight beyond the window and was suddenly caught and held by the mail bag, still lying where the man had flung it. It was like the swift passing of a summer storm. The man's whole expression underwent a complete transformation. The mail! The mail from Quebec—unopened!

He sprang to his feet. For the moment Idepski, Hellbeam, everything was forgotten. His thought had bridged the miles between Farewell Cove and the ancient city of the early French, Nancy! That woman—that devoted wife who was striving with all the power of a frail body to serve him. There would be a letter in that mail from Nisson, telling him—Yes. There might even be a letter from Nancy herself.

The sack was in his hands. He had broken the seals. He shook out the contents upon the floor. A packet of less than half a hundred letters, and the rest was an assortment of parcels of all shapes and sizes. It was the letter packet that interested him, and he untied the string that held it.

A swift search produced the expected. Standing looked for the handwriting of Charles Nisson, the shrewd, obscure lawyer in the country town of Abercrombie. He had never yet failed him. He would not be likely to. A bulky letter remained in his hand. The others lay scattered broadcast upon the desk.

For some moments he held the letter unopened. The lean fingers felt the bulk of the envelope, while feverish eyes surveyed, and read over and over the address in the familiar small, cramped handwriting. The impulse of the moment was to tear open the letter forthwith, to snatch at the tidings he felt it to contain. But something deterred. Something left him doubting, hesitating. It was what Bat had called his "yellow streak." Suppose—suppose—But with all his might he thrust his fears aside. He tore off the outer cover and unfolded the closely written pages.

Long, silent moments passed, broken only by the shuffling of the sheets of the letter as he turned them. Not once did he look up from his reading. Right through to the end, the dreadful, bitter end, he read the hideous news his loyal friend had to impart. Twice, during the reading, the sharp intake of breath, that almost whistled in the silence of the room, told of an emotion he had no power to repress, and at the finish of it all the mechanically re-folded page's fell from shaking, nerveless fingers upon the littered desk.

His eyes remained lowered gazing at the fallen letter. His hands remained poised where the letter had fallen from them. His face had lost its healthful hue. It was grey, and drawn, and the lips that parted as he muttered had completely blanched.

"Dead!" he whispered without consciousness of articulation. "Dead! Nancy! My boy! Both! Oh, God!"

CHAPTER IV
THE "YELLOW STREAK"

The grey, evening light was significant of the passing season. A chilly breeze whipped about the faces of the men at the fringe of the woods. They were resting after a long tramp of inspection through the virgin forests. It was on a ledge, high up on the hillside of the northern shore of the cove, where the ground dropped away in front of them several hundreds of feet to the waters below. Behind them was a backing of standing timber which sheltered them from the full force of the biting wind.

It was nearly a week since Bat Harker had returned from his mission to No. 10 Camp. He had returned full of satisfaction at the completion of his task, and comforted by the knowledge that the horizon of the mill had been cleared of threatening clouds for at least the period of a year. Then he encountered the ricochet of the blow which Fate had dealt his friend and employer.

It had been within half an hour of his return, while yet the stains and dust of his journey remained upon him, while yet he was yearning for that rest for his body to which it was entitled.

Bat had concluded the report of his journey, and the two men were closeted together in the office on the hillside. The lumberman had had no suspicion of the thing that had happened in his absence, and Standing had given no indication. Standing seemed unchanged. There had been the customary smile of welcome in his eyes. There had been the cordial handshake of friendship. Maybe Standing had talked less, and the searching questions usual in him had not been forthcoming. Maybe there was a curiously tired, strained look in his eyes. But that was all.

At the conclusion of his report Bat had bent eagerly forward over the desk which stood between them. His hard eyes were smiling. His whole manner was that of a man anticipating something pleasant.

"Say, Les," he cried, "guess you've maybe some news for me, too. It's more than a month since—and you were expecting—Things all right?"

Standing reached towards the drawer beside him, and as he did so there was a sound. It was a curious, inarticulate sound that Bat interpreted into a laugh. The other opened the drawer and drew out the folded pages of a letter. These he passed across the table, and his eyes were without a shadow of the laugh which Bat thought he had heard.

"Best read it," he said. "Take your time. I'll just finish these figures I'm working on."

It was the curious, cold tone that stirred Bat to his first misgiving.

He took the letter. There were pages of it. He set them in order and commenced to read. And meanwhile Standing remained apparently engrossed in his figures.

He read the letter through. He read it slowly, carefully. Then, like the other had done, the man to whom it was addressed, he read it a second time. And as he read every vestige of his previous satisfaction passed from him. A cold constriction seemed to fasten upon his strong heart. And a terrible realisation of the tragedy of it all took possession of him. At the end of his second reading he handed the letter back to its owner without comment of any sort, without a word, but with a hand that, for once in his life, was unsteady.

"That was in the mail Idepski brought," Standing said, as he returned the letter to its place, and shut and locked the drawer.

"You remember?" he went on, pointing. "He flung it down there. Just by the door. Yes, it was just there, because I stood against the door, and was only just clear of it."

He paused and his hand remained pointing at the spot where the mail bag had lain. It was as if the spot held him fascinated. Then his arm lowered slowly, and his hand came to rest on the edge of the table, gripping it with unnecessary force.

"Seems queer," he went on, after a while. Then he shook his head. "Think of it. Nancy—my Nancy. Dead! She died giving birth to my boy. And he—he was stillborn. Why? I—I can't seem to realize it. I—don't—" He paused, and a strained, hunted look grew in his eyes. "No. It's easy. It's just Fate. That's it. There's no escape."

He drew a deep breath and one lean hand smoothed back his shining black hair. Then his eyes came back to the face of the man opposite, and the agony in them was beyond words. After a moment their terrible expression became lost as he bent over his work. "I'm glad you're back, Bat," he said, without looking up.

"There's a hell of a lot of orders to get out. We're running close up to winter."

The lumberman understood. At a single blow this man's every hope had been smashed and ground under the heel of an iron fate. The wife, the woman he had worshipped, had given her life to serve him, and with her had gone the man-child, about whom had been woven the entire network of a father's hopes and desires.

A week had passed since Bat had witnessed the voiceless agony of his friend. A week of endless labour and unspoken fears. He knew Standing as it is given to few to know the heart of another. His sympathy was real. It was of that quality which made him desire above all things to render the heartbroken man real physical and moral help. But no opening had been given him, and he feared to probe the wound that had been inflicted. During those first seven days Standing seemed to be obsessed with a desire to work, to work all day and every night, as though he dared not pause lest his disaster should overwhelm him.

Now it was Sunday. Night and day the work had gone on. No less than ten freighters had been loaded and dispatched since Bat's return, and only that morning two vessels had cast off, laden to the water-line, and passed down on the tide for the mouth of the cove. At the finish of the midday meal Standing had announced his intentions for the afternoon.

"We need to get a look into the lumber on the north side, Bat," he said. "You'd best come along with me. How do you think?"

And Bat had agreed on the instant.

"Sure," he said. "There's a heap to be done that way if we're to start layin' the penstocks down on that side next year."

So they had spent the hours before dusk in a prolonged tramp through the forests of the Northern shore. And never for one moment was their talk and apparent interest allowed to drift from the wealth of long-fibred timber they were inspecting.

But somehow to Bat the whole thing was unreal. It meant nothing. It could mean nothing. He felt like a man walking towards a precipice he could not avoid. He felt disaster, added disaster, was in the air and was closing in upon them. He knew in his heart that this long, weary inspection, all the stuff they talked, all the future plans they were making for the mill was the merest excuse. And he wondered when Standing would abandon it and reveal his actual purpose. The man, he knew, was consumed by a voiceless grief. His soul was tortured beyond endurance. And there was that "yellow streak," which Bat so feared. When, when would it reveal itself? How?

Now, at last, as they rested on the ledge overlooking the mill and the waters of the cove, he felt the moment of its revelation had arrived. He was propped against the stump of a storm-thrown tamarack. Standing was stretched prone upon the fallen trunk itself. Neither had spoken for some minutes. But the trend of thought was apparent in each. Bat's deep-set, troubled eyes were regarding the life and movement going on down at the mill, whose future was the greatest concern of his life. Standing, too, was gazing out over the waters. But his darkly brooding eyes were on the splendid house he had set up on the opposite hillside. It was the home about which his every earthly hope had centred. And even now, in his despair, it remained a magnet for his hopeless gaze.

Winter was already in the bite of the air and in the absence of the legions of flies and mosquitoes as well as in the chilly grey of the lapping waters below them. It was doubtless, too, searching the heart of these men whose faces gave no indication of the sunlight of summer shining within.

"Bat!"

The lumberman turned sharply. He spat out a stream of tobacco juice and waited.

"Bat, old friend, it's no use." Standing had swung himself into a sitting posture. He was leaning forward on the tree-trunk with his forearms folded across his knees. "We've done a lot of talk, and we've searched these forests good. And it's all no use. None at all. There's going to be no penstocks set up this side of the water next year—as far as I'm concerned. I've done. Finished. Plumb finished. I'm quitting. Quitting it all."

The lumberman ejected a masticated chew and took a fresh one.

"You see, old friend, I'll go crazy if I stop around," Standing went on. "I've been hit a pretty desperate punch, and I haven't the guts to stand up to it. When it came I set my teeth. I wanted to keep sane. I reminded myself of all I owed to the folks working for us. I thought of you. And I tried to bolster myself with the schemes we had for beating the Skandinavians out of this country's pulp-wood trade. Yes, I tried. God, how I tried! But my guts are weak, and I know what lies ahead. For nearly six weeks I've been working things out, and for a week I've been wondering how I should tell you. I brought you here to tell you.

"I want you to understand it good," he went on, after the briefest pause. "I can't stand to live on in the house that Nancy and I built up. Every room is haunted by her. By her happy laugh, and by memories of the hours we sat and talked of the boy-child we'd both set our hearts on. I just can't do it without going stark, staring, raving mad. I can't."

"That's how I figgered. I've watched it in you, Les. Tell me the rest."

Bat chewed steadily. It was a safety-valve for his feelings.

"The rest?" Standing turned to gaze out at the house across the water. "If it weren't for you, Bat, I'd close right down. I'd leave everything standing and—get out," he went on slowly. "The whole thing's a nightmare. Look at it. Look around. The forests of soft wood. The township we've set up. The harnessed water power. That—that house of mine. It's all nightmare, and I don't want it. I'm afraid. I'm scared to death of it."

Bat moved away from the stump he had been propped against. He passed across to the edge of the ledge and stood gazing down on the scenes below.

"You needn't worry for me," he said. "It don't matter a cuss where or how I hustle my dry hash. I was born that way. Fix things the way you feel. Cut me right out."

The man's generosity was a simple expression of his rugged nature. His love of that great work below him, in the creation of which he had taken so great a part, was nothing to him at that moment. He was concerned only for the man, who had held out a succouring hand, and led him, in his darkest moments, to safety and prosperity.

Standing shook his head at the broad back squared against the grey, wintry sky.

"I didn't mean it that way, old friend," he said.

Bat swung around. His grey eyes were wide. His face seemed to have softened out of its usual harsh cast.

"But I do, Les," he cried. "You don't need to figger a thing about me. You're hurt, boy. You're hurt mighty sore. Cut me right out of your figgers, and do the things that's goin' to heal that sore. If there's a thing I can do to help you, why, I guess I'd be glad to know it."

For a few moments Standing remained silent. Perhaps he was pondering upon what he had to say. Perhaps he was simply gaining time to suppress the emotions which the selflessness of the other had inspired.

"Here," he cried at last, "I best tell you the whole story that's in my mind. I told you I've been figuring it out. Well, it's figured to the last decimal. You think you know me. Maybe you do. Maybe you know only part of the things I know about myself. If you knew them all I'd hate to think of the contempt you'd have to hand me. You see, Bat, I'm a coward, a terrible moral coward. Oh, I'm not scared of any man living when it comes to a fight. But my mind's full of ghosts and nightmares ready to jump at me with every doubt, every new effort where I can't figure the end. Years ago, when I was a youngster, I yearned for fortune. And I realised that I had it in me to get it quick by means of that crazy talent for figures you reckon is so wonderful. I got the chance and jumped, for it. But every step I took left me scared to the verge of craziness. When I hit up against Hellbeam I got a desire to beat him that was irresistible, and I jumped into the fight with my heart in my mouth. It was easy—so easy. Hellbeam was a babe in my hands. I could play with him as a spider plays with its victim, and when, like a spider, I'd bound him with my figures, hand and foot, I was free to suck his blood till I was satiated. I did all that, and then my nightmare descended upon me again. You know how I fled with Hellbeam's hounds on my heels. I was terrified at the enormity of the thing I'd done. I could have stood my ground and beaten him—and them. But moral cowardice overwhelmed me and drove me to these outlands. God, what I suffered! And after all I haven't the certainty that I deserved it."

Bat came back to his stump and stood against it while Standing passed a weary hand across his forehead.

"The happenings since then you know as well as I do. I don't need to talk of them. I mean, how I met and married Nancy, when she was widow of that no-account McDonald feller, the editor of *The Abercrombie Herald!*"

Bat nodded.

"Yes, sure, I know, Les. When you married Nancy an' made her thirteen-year-old daughter—your daughter."

"Yes. I'd almost forgotten. Yes, there's her girl, Nancy. She's still at school. Well, anyway, you know, these things, all of 'em. But what you don't know is that you—you Bat, old friend, are solely responsible for all the work that's being done here. You, old friend, are responsible that I've enjoyed seven years of something approaching peace of mind. You, you with your bulldog fighting spirit, you with your hell-may-care manner of shouldering responsibility, and facing every threat, have been the staunch pillar on which I have always leant. Without you I'd have gone under years ago, a victim of my own mental ghosts. No, no, Bat," he went on quickly, as the lumberman shook his head in sharp denial, "it's useless. I know. Leaning on you I've built up around me the reality of that original dream, with the other things I've now lost, and with every ounce in me I've worked for its fulfilment.

"Well, what's the logic of it all?" he continued, after a moment's pause. "Yes, it is the logic of it. You may argue that for seven years I've been doing a big work and there's no reason, in spite of what's happened, that I should now abandon it all. But there is. And in your strong old heart you'll know the thing I say is true—if cowardly. During seven years, or part of them, I've known a happiness that's compensated for every terror I've endured. Nancy's been my guardian angel, and the boy, that was to be born, was the beacon light of my life. My poor little wife has gone, and that beacon light, the son we yearned for, has been snuffed right out. And in the shadows left I see only the groping hand of Hellbeam reaching out towards me. In the end that hand will get me, and crush the remains of my miserable life out. I know. Just as sure as God, Hellbeam's going to get me."

The sweat of terror stood on the man's high forehead, and he wiped it away.

Bat flung a clenched fist down upon the tree stump.

"You're wrong, Les. You're plumb wrong. If it means murder I swear before God Hellbeam'll never lay hands on you. Hellbeam? Gee! Let him set his nose north of 'fifty' and I'll promise him a welcome so hot that'll leave hell like a glacier. As for his darn agents? Why, say, I want to feel sorry for 'em 'fore they start. Idepski's hating himself right—"

"I know," cried Standing impatiently. "I know it all. Everything you've said you mean, but—it won't save me. But we can leave all that. There's the other things. Why should I go on living here, working, slaving, haunted by the terror of Hellbeam? With my boy, my wife, to fight for it was worth all the agony. But without them—why? Why in the name of sanity should I go on? To beat the Skandinavians out of Canada's trade, and claim it all for a country that doesn't care a curse? To build up a great name that in the end must be dragged in the mire of public estimation? Not on your life, Bat. No, no. I'm going to cut adrift. I'm going to quit. I'm going to lose myself in these forests, and live the remaining years of my life free to run to earth at the first shot of the hunter's gun. It's all that's left me—as I see it."

"And all this?" Bat said, reaching out one great hand in the direction of the Cove. "An' that school gal 'way down at Abercrombie, learning her knitting, an' letters, an' crying her dandy eyes out for the mother who had to leave her there when she passed over to you? Say, Les, you best go on. Jest go right on an' I'll say my piece after."

Standing sat up. A deep earnestness was in the dark eyes that looked fearlessly into Bat's. He took the other at his word and went on. He had nothing to conceal.

"The mill? Why, I want to pass it over to your care, Bat," he said, permitting one swift regretful glance in the direction of the grey waters below them. Then he spoke almost feverishly. "Here's the proposition. I'm going to hand you full powers—through Charles Nisson. You'll run this thing on the lines laid down. If you fancy carrying on the original proposition of extension, well and good. If not, just carry on and leave the rest for—later. You'll be manager for me through Nisson. I shan't remove one cent of capital. I don't want Hellbeam's money beyond the barest grub stake. It'll remain under Nisson's guardianship for your use in running this mill. You'll simply satisfy Nisson. For the rest I shan't interfere. You're drawing a big salary now. Well, seeing I go out of the work, that salary will be doubled. That's for the immediate. Then there's the future. I've a notion. Maybe it's a crazy notion. But it's mine and I mean to test it. Here. We reckon to build up this enterprise for one great, big purpose. It was my dream to break the Skandinavian ring governing the groundwood trade of this country. It was work that appealed to my imagination. I wanted to build this great thing and pass it on to my boy. It seemed to me fine. Worth while. It was a man's work, and it seemed to me a life well spent. I had the guts then—with your support, and the support the thought of my son gave me. I haven't the guts now. The notion fired you, too. It fired you, and it'll grieve you desperately to see it abandoned. It shan't be abandoned. Once in the woods of this queer country I found a man—such a man as is rarely found. He was a man into whose hands I could put my life. And I guess there's no greater trust one man can have in another. He was a man of immense capacity. A man of intellect for all he had no schooling but the schooling of Quebec's rough woods. That man was you, Bat. I'd like to say to you: 'Here's the property. You know the scheme. Go on. Carry it through.' But I can't. I can't because one man can't do it. Well, the woods gave me one man, and they're going to give me another to take the place of the weak-gutted creature who intends to 'rat.' I'm going to find you a partner, a man with brain and force like yourself. A man of iron guts. And when I've found him I'm going to send him on to you. And if you approve him he shall be full partner with you in this concern the day that sees the Canadian Groundwood Trust completed, and the breaking of the Skandinavian ring. Do you follow it all? You and this man will be equal partners in the mill, and every available cent of its capital—the capital I made Hellbeam provide. It'll be yours and his, solely and alone. I—I shall pass right out of it. Hellbeam has no score against you. He has no penitentiary preparing for you. You are not concerned with him. Whatever he may have in store for me he can do nothing to you, and the money I beat him out of will have passed beyond his reach."

"And this man you figger to locate? You reckon to take a chance on your judgment?"

Bat's challenge came on the instant.

"On mine, and—yours." Standing's eyes were full of a keen confidence. And Bat realised something of the sanity lying behind a seemingly mad proposition. "He'll own nothing until he and you have completed the work as we see it. To own his share in the thing he must prove his capacity. He'll be held by the tightest and strongest contract Charles Nisson can draw up."

Bat spat out his chew. He replaced it with a pipe, and prepared to flake off its filling from a plug of tobacco. Standing watched him with the anxious eyes of a prisoner awaiting sentence. With the cutting of the first flakes of tobacco, Bat looked up.

"And this little gal-child, with the same name as the mother who just meant the whole of everything life could hand you? This kiddie with her mother's blood running in innocent veins? She's your Nancy's daughter and I guess your marriage made her yours."

"She's another man's child."

Standing's retort was instant. And the tone of it cut like a knife.

Bat regarded him keenly. His knife had ceased from its work on the plug.

"That's so," he said after a while. Then his gaze drifted in the direction of the house across the water, and the expression in the grey depths of his eyes became lost to the man who could not forget that the remaining child of his wife was the offspring of another man. "It seems queer," he went on reflectively. "That woman, your Nancy, was about the best loved wife, a fellow could think of. She was all sorts of a woman to you. Guess she was mostly the sun, moon, an' stars of your life. Yet her kiddie, a pore, lonesome kiddie, was toted right off to school so she couldn't butt in on you. You've never seen her, have you? And she was blood of the woman that set you nigh crazy. Only her father was another feller. No, Les." He shook his head, and went on filling his pipe. "No, Les, this mill and all about it can go hang if that pore, lone kiddie is wiped out of your reckoning. Maybe I'm queer about things. Maybe I'm no account anyway when it comes to the things of life mostly belonging to Sunday School. But I'd as lief go back to the woods I came from, as handle a proposition for you that don't figger that little gal in it. You best take that as all I've to say. There's a heap more I could say. But it don't matter. You're feelin' bad. Things have hit you bad. And you reckon they're going to hit you worse. Maybe you're right. Maybe you're wrong. Anyway these things are for you, though I'd be mighty thankful to help you. You want to go out of it all. You want to follow up some queer notion you got. You reckon it's going to give you peace. I hope so. I do sure. The thing you've said goes with me without shouting one way or the other. It grieves me bad. But that's no account anyway. But there's that gal standing between us, and she's going to stand right there till you've finished the things you're maybe going to say."

For a moment the men looked into each other's eyes. It was a tense moment of sudden crisis between them.

"Well?"

Bat's unyielding interrogation came sharply. Standing nodded.

"I hadn't thought, Bat," he said. Then he drew a deep breath. "I surely hadn't, but I guess you're right. She's my stepdaughter. And I've a right to do the thing you say. Yes. It's queer when I think of it," he went on musingly. "When I married her mother the girl didn't seem to come into our reckoning. She was at school, and I never even saw her. Then her mother wanted her left there, anyway till her schooling was through. Everything was paid. I saw to that. But—yes, I guess you're right. It's up to me, and I'll fix it."

"The mill?"

"She shall have equal share when the time comes."

"When the whole work's put through?"

"Yes. And meanwhile she'll be amply provided for." Standing spread out his hands deprecatingly. "You see, we did things in a hurry, Bat. There was always Hellbeam. And my Nancy understood that. I wonder—"

Bat smoked on thoughtfully, and presently the other roused himself from the pre-occupation into which he had fallen.

"Does that satisfy?" he demanded.

Bat nodded.

"I'll do the darnedest I know, Les," he said in his sturdy fashion. Fix that pore gal right. Hand her the share she's a right to—when the time comes along. Do that an' I'll not rest till the Skandinavians are left hollerin'. That kid's your daughter, for all she ain't flesh and blood of yours, an' you ain't ever see her. And anyway she's flesh of your Nancy, which seems to me hands her even a bigger claim."

He moved away from his leaning post and his back was turned to hide that which looked out of his eyes.

"I'm grieved," he went on, in his simple fashion, "I'm so grieved about things I can't tell you, Les. I always guessed to drive this thing through with you. I always reckoned to make good to you for that thing you did by me. Well, there's no use in talkin'. You reckon this notion of yours'll make you feel better, it's goin' to hand you—peace. That goes with me. Oh, yes, all the time, seein' you feel that way. But—say, we best get right home—or I'll cry like a darn-fool kid."

CHAPTER V
NANCY MCDONALD

Charles Nisson was standing at the window. His eyes were deeply reflective as he watched the gently falling snow outside. He was a sturdy creature in his well-cut, well-cared-for black suit. For all he was past middle life there was little about him to emphasise the fact unless it were his trim, well-brushed snow-white hair, and the light covering of whisker and beard of a similar hue. He looked to be full of strength of purpose and physical energy.

His back was turned on the pleasant dining-room of his home in Abercrombie, a remote town in Ontario, where he and his wife had only just finished breakfast. Sarah Nisson was sitting beside the anthracite stove which radiated its pleasant warmth against the bitter chill of winter reigning outside. She was still consuming the pages of her bulky mail.

A clock chimed the hour, and the wife looked up from her letter. She turned a face that was still pretty for all her fifty odd years, in the direction of the man at the window.

"Ten o'clock, Charles," she reminded him. Then her enquiring look melted into a gentle smile. "The office has less attraction with the snow falling."

"It has less attraction to-day, anyway," the lawyer responded without turning. A short laugh punctuated his prompt reply.

"You mean the Nancy McDonald business?"

Sarah Nisson laid her mail aside.

"Yes." The lawyer sighed and turned from his contemplation of the snow. He moved across to the stove. "I'm a bit of a coward, Sally," he went on, holding out his hands to the warmth. "The lives of other people are nearly as interesting as they are exasperating. They seem just as foolishly ordered as we believe our own to be well and truly ordered. I don't know who it was said 'all men are fools,' or liars, or something, but I guess he was right. Yes, we're all fools. I really don't know how we manage to get through a day, let alone a lifetime, without absolute disaster. We spend most of our time abusing Providence for the result of our own shortcomings, when really we ought to be mighty polite and thankful to the blind good fortune that lets us dodge the results of our follies."

"All of which I suppose has to do with the way Leslie Martin, or Leslie Standing, as he calls himself now, is acting."

"Well, most of it."

The man's eyes had become seriously reflective again.

Sarah Nisson nodded her pretty head. She leant her ample proportions towards the stove and emulated her husband's attitude, warming her plump hands. Her brown eyes were twinkling, and her broad, unlined brow was calmly serene. Her iron-grey hair was as carefully dressed as though she were still in the twenties, moreover it was utterly untouched by any of the shams so beloved of the modern woman of advancing years.

"The death of his poor wife almost seems to have unhinged him," she said, with a troubled pucker of her brows. "But—but I don't wonder, I really don't. She was the sweetest girl. Poor soul. And that bonny wee boy. But there, I can't bear to think of it all. You mustn't blame him too much, Charles. I guess you don't in your heart. It's just as his attorney you feel mad about things. It's best to remember you were his friend first, and only his adviser, and man of business, after. The whole thing makes me feel I want to cry. And that poor girl coming to see you to-day. The other Nancy, I mean. I don't think I'd feel so bad about things if it wasn't for her. You know, I like Leslie. And I was as fond of his wife as I just could be, for all she made a fool of herself when she married that hateful James McDonald, who was no better than a revolutionary. Thank goodness he died and got out before he could do any harm. But I do think Leslie and poor Nancy were selfish about her child. I don't believe it was so much him as Nancy. From the moment Leslie came on the scene it was she who kept the poor child at college. She never even let him see her. And she's such a bonny girl, too. Do you know, I believe Nancy's death, and even the death of the baby boy, wouldn't have meant half so much to Leslie if he'd had Nancy's own girl with him. She'd have got herself right into his heart with her bonny ways, and her hazel eyes that look like great, big smiling flowers. Then her hair. She's a lovely, lovely child. I wish she was mine. I'd like to have her right here always. Couldn't you fix it that way?"

The man shook his head.

"I'd like to—but—"

"But what?"

"You see there's a whole lot to think about," the lawyer went on seriously. "Why, I don't even know how to get through my interview with her to-day without lying to her like a politician. Now just get a look at the position. Here's a girl, a beautiful, high-spirited girl of sixteen, straight out from college, at the beginning of life, with her, head full of 'whys,' and 'wherefores.' Sixteen's well-nigh grown up these days, mind you. Her mother's dead, and curiously the fact didn't seem to break her up as you'd have expected it to. Why?" The man shrugged. "It's not because she lacks feeling. Oh, no. Maybe it's because of the strength of those feelings. Remember her mother married Leslie when the child was thirteen. A good understanding age. She was never allowed to see her father. No. She was packed off to school and kept there—"

"Yes, I know," Sarah broke in, with impatient warmth. "And just at the time a girl most needs she never even saw her mother for over three years. God doesn't give us women our babies to treat them as if they weren't our own flesh and blood. Young Nancy was left to those maiden dames at college, who don't know more about a child than is laid down by highbrow officials in the text books they need to study to qualify for their posts. They haven't a notion beyond stuffing her poor wee head with the sort of view of life set down in fool history books. They say she's clever and bright. Well, that's all they care about. When they've done with her they'll have knocked all the girl out of her, and turned her adrift on the world behind a pair of disfiguring spectacles, with her beautiful hair all scratched back off her pretty face, and maybe 'bobbed,' and they'll fill her grips with pamphlets and literature enough to stock a patent med'cine factory, instead of the lawn, and lace, and silk a girl should think about, and leave her with as much chance of getting happily married as a queen mummy of the Egyptians. It's a shame, just a real shame. Why, if that poor, lonesome child came right along to me, I'd—"

"Teach her all the bright tricks of hunting down a husband and—hooking him." The lawyer shook his head and smiled. "You know, Sally, you're almost an outrage on the subject of marriage. Sometimes I wonder the sort of tricks I was up against when I—"

A plump warning finger and smiling threat interrupted the laughing charge.

"You were due at the office long ago, Charles," his wife admonished. "If you aren't careful I'll have to pack you off right away."

"That's all right, Sally," the man demurred. "I won't go further with that. I'll get back to the things I was saying before you interrupted." His pale blue eyes became serious again. "Do you think Nancy didn't understand why she was packed off to school—and kept there? Of course she did. She knew she wasn't wanted. She knew she was in the way. She must not be permitted to intrude on this stepfather, or her mother's new life. It was all a bit heartless, and if I know anything of the child, she understands it that way. I felt that when she came to see her mother, and went to her funeral. Now then, Nancy's coming to see me to-day. Remember she's sixteen. She's got to learn from me the settlement Leslie's made on her. She's got to learn further that she isn't likely to ever see her stepfather. She knows I'm his business man. She knows I'm his friend. Well, when she's financially independent, do you think she'll feel like rushing into our arms, here, for a home, feeling the way I believe she does about her parent? It's going to be difficult, and—damned unpleasant. And for all I'm ready to help Leslie anyway I know, I'd rather see anybody on his behalf than that kiddie, with her wide, honest, angry eyes and red hair. I'm not going to press our home on her, Sally, because, sooner or later, if she accepted it, which I don't believe she would, she'd have to learn things of Leslie, and—well, the affairs you know about. That must not be. She's not going to learn these things from us. I'm going to do the best I know for the child, and when it comes to the matter of a home she must choose for herself. There's always her mother's folk, or even James McDonald's folk—"

"God forbid! No. Oh, no." The woman's instant denial was horrified. "Not the McDonald lot. They're all revolutionaries. All of them. It's—it's unthinkable. It certainly is."

The man moved away.

"That's so," he agreed. "Well, anyway, I'll do the best I know for the child, Sally. You can trust me."

The woman's anxiety abated, and she rose from her chair.

"I know that, Charles," she said. "But the McDonalds! They're—"

"Sure they are." The man laughed. "Well, good-bye, my dear. I'll tell you all about it when I've fixed things. Thank goodness it's quit snowing and the sun's shining again. I wish I felt as good as it looks outside here."

Charles Nisson had become a lawyer without any marked inclination or enthusiasm for his profession. It had been simply a matter of following the father before him. It would have been much the same if his father had been a farmer, or a politician, or anything else. The son was patient, temperate, and of no great ambition. But he was also keenly intelligent. Without impulse, or striking originality, but with a tremendous capacity for hard work, he was bound to be moderately successful in any career. In his father's profession his temperament was particularly suited, and in spite of lacking enthusiasm he had become unquestionably a better lawyer than the country attorney he had succeeded.

Just now his mind was filled with unease. The matter of his forthcoming interview with a child of sixteen years had only small place in the affairs which disturbed him. His real concern was for his friend, Leslie Standing, and the disaster, which, in a seemingly overwhelming rush had befallen at far-off Sachigo. Again his trouble had no relation to these things as they affected his own worldly affairs. It was of the man himself he was thinking.

He knew it all now. He had painfully learned the complete story of disaster. And, to his sturdy mind, it was a deplorable example of almost unbelievable human weakness.

Standing had conveyed his final determination to abandon his Labrador enterprise in the correspondence which had passed between them during the three months which had elapsed since the funeral of his wife and stillborn child. And during that time their friendship had been sorely tested. There had been times when the lawyer's native patience had been unequal to the strain. There had been times when his temper had leapt from under the bonds which so strongly held it. But for all the ordeals of that prolonged correspondence, for all he deplored the pitiful weakness in the other, his friendship remained, and he finally accepted his instructions. But the whole thing left him very troubled.

As the hour of noon approached, his trouble showed no sign of abatement. It was the reverse. There were moments, as he sat in the generously upholstered chair before his desk, in the comfortable down-town office which overlooked Abercrombie's principal thoroughfare, that he felt like abandoning all responsibility in the chaos of his friend's affairs. But this was only the result of irritation, and had no relation to his intentions. He knew well enough that everything in his power would be done for the man who never so surely needed his help as now.

He refreshed his memory with the details of the deed of settlement for the abandoned stepdaughter. Then, as the hands of the clock approached the hour of his appointment, he sat back yielding his whole concentration upon those many problems confronting him.

What, he asked himself, was going to become of Standing now that he had cut himself adrift from that anchorage which had held him safe for the past seven years? He strove to follow the driving of the man's curiously haunted mind. He had declared his intention of going away. Where? Definite information had been withheld. He was going to devote himself to some purpose he claimed to have always lain at the back of his mind. What was that purpose? Again there had been no information forthcoming. Was it good, or—bad? The man who was endeavouring to solve the riddle of it all dared not trust himself to a decision. He felt that his friend's unstable soul might drive him in almost any direction after the shock it had sustained.

No. Speculation was useless. The crude facts were like a brick wall he had to face. Standing's wealth and the great mill at Sachigo were left to his administration with the trusting confidence of a child. The responsibility for the neglected stepdaughter had similarly been flung upon his shoulders. And, satisfied with this manner of disposing of his worldly concerns, Standing intended to fare forth, shorn of any possession but a bare pittance for his daily needs, to lose himself, and all the shadows of a haunted mind, in the dim, remote interior of the unexplored forests of Northern Quebec. The whole thing was mad—utterly—

The muffled electric bell on his table drubbed out its summons. One swift glance at the clock and the lawyer yielded to professional instinct. He became absorbed in the papers neatly spread out on his table as a bespectacled clerk thrust open the door.

"Miss McDonald to see you," he announced, in the modulated tone which was part of his professional make-up.

The lawyer rose at once. He moved toward the door with a smiling welcome. The sex and personality of his visitor demanded this departure from his custom.

Nancy McDonald stood just inside the doorway through which the clerk had departed. She was tall, beautifully tall, for all she was only sixteen. In her simple college girl's overcoat, with its muffling of fur about the neck, it was impossible to detect the graces of the youthful figure concealed. Her carriage was upright, and her bearing full of that confidence which is so earnestly taught in the schools of the newer countries.

But these things passed unnoticed by the white-haired lawyer. He was smiling into the radiant face under the low-pressed fur cap. It was the wide, hazel eyes, so deeply fringed with a wealth of curling, dark lashes, that inspired his smiling interest. It was the level brows, so delicately pencilled, and dark as were the eyelashes. It was the perfect nose, and lips, and chin, and the chiselled beauty of oval cheeks, all in such classic harmony with the girl's wealth of vivid hair.

Nancy returned his gaze without the shadow of a smile. She had come at this man's call from the coldly correct halls of Marypoint College, which was also the soulless home she had been condemned to for the three or four most impressionable years of her life. And she knew the purpose of the summons.

There was a deep abiding resentment in her heart. It was not against this man or his wife. From these two she had received only kindness and affection. It was directed against the stepfather whom she believed to be the cause of the banishment she had had to endure. Furthermore, she could never forget that her banishment was only terminated that she might gaze at last upon the dead features of her dearly loved mother before the cold earth hid them from view forever.

The lawyer understood. He had understood from her reply to his letter summoning her. There was no need for the confirmation he read now in her unsmiling eyes.

"You sent for me?" she said.

Nancy's voice was deep and rich for all her youth. Then with a display of some slight confusion, she suddenly realised the welcoming hand outheld. She took it hurriedly, and the brief hand clasp completely broke down the barrier she had deliberately set up.

"Oh, it's a shame, Uncle Charles," she cried, almost tearfully. "It's—it's a shame. I know. I'm just a kid—a fool kid who hasn't a notion, or a feeling, or—or anything. I'm to be treated that way. When he says 'listen,' why, I've just got to listen. And when he says 'obey,' I've got to obey, because the law says he's my stepfather. He's robbed me of my mother. Oh, it's cruel. Now he's going to rob me of everything else I s'pose. Who is he? What is he that he has the power to—to make me a sort of slave to his wishes? I've never seen him. I hate him, and he hates me, and yet—oh—I'm kind of sorry," she said, in swift contrition at the sight of the old man's evident distress. "I—I—didn't think. I—oh, I know it's not your fault, uncle. It's just nothing to do with you. You've always been so kind and good to me—you and Aunt Sally. You've got to send for me and tell me the things he says, because—"

"Because I'm his 'hired man.' But also because I'm his friend."

The lawyer spoke kindly, but very firmly. He knew the impulsive nature of this passionate child. He knew her unusual mentality. He realised, none better, that he was dealing with a strong woman's mind in a girl of childhood's years. He knew that Nancy had inherited largely from her father, that headstrong, headlong creature whose mentality had driven him to every length in a wild endeavour to upset civilisation that he might witness the birth of a millennium in the ashes of a world saturated with the blood of countless, helpless creatures. So he checked the impulsive flow of the child's protest. He held out his hands.

"You'd best let me take your coat, my dear," he said, with a smile the girl found it impossible to resist. "Maybe you'd like to remove your overshoes, too. There's a big talk to make, and I want to get things fixed so you can come right along up home and take food with us before you go back to Marypoint."

The child capitulated. But she needed no assistance. Her coat was removed in a moment and flung across a chair, and she stood before him, the slim, slightly angular schoolgirl she really was.

"Guess I'll keep my rubbers on," she said. Then she added with a laugh which a moment before must have been impossible. "That way I'll feel I can run away when I want to. What next?"

"Why, just sit right here."

The lawyer drew up a chair and set it beside his desk. His movements were swift now. He had no desire to lose the girl's change of mood.

And Nancy submitted. She took the chair set for her while the man she loved to call "Uncle Charlie" passed round to his. He gave her no time for further reflection, but plunged into his talk at once.

"Now, my dear," he said earnestly, "you came here feeling pretty bad about things, and maybe I don't blame you. But there isn't the sort of thing waiting on you you're guessing. Before we get to the real business I just want to tell you the things in my mind. Of course, as you say, you're a 'kid' yet—a school-kid, eh? That's all right. But I know you can get a grip of things that many much older girls could never hope to. That's why I want to tell you the things I'm going to. Now you've worked it out in your mind that your stepfather is just a heartless, selfish creature who has no sort of use for you, and just wants to forget your existence. He married your mother, but had no idea of taking on her burdens—that's you. It isn't so. It wasn't so. I know, because this man is my friend, and I know all there is to know about him. The whole thing has been deplorable. You've been the victim of circumstances that I may not explain even to you. But I promise you this, your stepfather is not the man to have desired to cut you out of your mother's life."

"Who did then? Mother?"

The girl's beautiful face flushed under her stirring emotions. The man shook his head.

"Circumstances. Yes, those circumstances I told you of. Those circumstances I can't explain." Charles Nisson picked up a typescript and held it out to the child.

"I want you to take this. It's not the deed, but a true copy. I want you to read it over and think about it, and when you get back to Marypoint, and feel like talking to those teachers you trust there, you can tell them what it contains, and hear what they have to say about it, and see if they won't think better of your stepfather than you do. You needn't read it now," as the girl turned the pages and glanced down the confusion of legal phraseology. "I'm going to tell you what it contains in plain words. But I want you to have it, and read it, and think over it, because I want you to try and get a real understanding of the man whose signature is set to the original deed."

"Yes," he went on, meditatively, and in a tone of real regret. "I'd be pretty glad to have you think better of him. I think just now he needs the kind thought of anyone who belongs to him. He's in pretty bad trouble—someways."

The girl looked up. A curious anxiety was shining in her eyes.

"Trouble?" she demanded. "You mean he's done wrong? What d'you mean? What sort of—trouble?"

The man shook his head.

"No. It's not that. It's—your mother. You know, Nancy, he loved your mother in a way that leaves a good man broken to pieces when he loses the object of his love. Every good thought he ever had was bound up in your mother. And your mother was his strong support, and literally his guiding star. You've lost your mother. You know how you felt. Well, I can't tell you, but think, try and think what it would be if you'd lost just every hope in life, too—the same as he has."

"I'd—I'd want to die," the girl cried impulsively.

"Yes. So would anyone. So does he. Just as far as the world's concerned he's dead now. You'll never see him, or hear from him. Nor will anyone else—except me. He'll never come into your life after this. He'll never claim his legal guardianship of you, beyond that document. To you he's dead, leaving you heir to what is contained in that deed. He's just a poor devil of a man hunted and haunted through the rest of his existence by the memory of a love that was more than life to him. Try and think better of him, Nancy, my dear. He's got enough to bear. I think he deserves far better than he's ever likely to get handed to him. I tell you solemnly, my dear, whatever sins he may have committed, and most of us have committed plenty," he added, with a gentle smile, "he's done you no real hurt. And now he's only doing that good by you I would expect from him."

Nancy sighed deeply, and it needed no words of hers to tell the man of law how well he had fought his friend's battle. A deep wave of childish pity had swept away the last of a resentment which had seemed so bitter, so implacable. It was the generous heart of the child, shorn, for the moment, of its inheritance from her father. Her even brows had puckered, and the man knew that tears, real tears of sympathy, were not far off.

"Tell me," she said, in a low voice. "Tell me some more."

But the man shook his head. "I can't tell you more," he said gently. "Where your stepfather is, or where he will be to-morrow, I may not tell you. Even when your mother was alive you were not permitted to know these things. That was due to the 'circumstances' I told you of. It just remains for me to tell you the contents of that document. They're as generous as only your stepfather knows how to make them. He's appointed me your trustee. And he's settled on you a life annuity of $10,000. There are a few simple conditions. You will remain at college till your education is complete, and, until you are twenty-one I shall have control of your income. That is," he explained, "I shall see that you don't handle it recklessly. During that time, subject to my approval, you can make your home with whom you like. After you've passed your twenty-first birthday you are as free as air to go or come, to live where you choose, and how you choose. And your income will be forthcoming from this office—every quarter. Do you understand all that, my dear? It's so very simple. Your stepfather has gone to the limit to show you how well he desires for you, and how free of his authority he wants you to be. There is another generous act of his that will be made clear to you when the time comes. But that is for the future—not now. His last word to me," he went on, picking up a letter, "when he sent me the deed duly signed, was: 'Tell this little girl when you hand her these things, it isn't my wish to trouble her with an authority which can have little enough appeal for her. Tell her that her mother was my whole world, and it is my earnest desire that her daughter should have all the good and comfort this world can bestow. If ever she needs further help she can have it without question, and that she only has to appeal to my friend and adviser, Charles Nisson, for anything she requires.'"

The man laid the letter aside and looked up.

"That's the last paragraph of the last communication I had from him. And they're not the words of a monstrous tyrant who is utterly heartless, eh?"

The girl made no answer. Her emotion was too strong for her. Two great tears rolled slowly down her beautiful cheeks.

The lawyer rose from his chair. He came round the desk and laid a gentle hand on the heaving shoulder, while Nancy strove to wipe her tears away with a wholly inadequate handkerchief.

"That's right, my dear," he said very gently. "Wipe them away. There's no need to cry. Leslie's done all a man in his peculiar position can do for you. You've got the whole wide world before you, and everything you can need for comfort—thanks to him. Now let's forget about it all. Just take that paper back to school with you. And maybe you'll write, or come and let me know what you think about it. If you feel like making your home with us, why, that way you'll just complete our happiness. If you feel like going to your mother's sister, Anna Scholes, I shan't refuse you. Anyway, think about it all. That's my big talk and it's finished. Just get your overcoat on, and we'll get right along home to food."

CHAPTER VI
NATHANIEL HELLBEAM

The room was furnished with extreme modern luxury. The man standing over against the window with his broad back turned, somehow looked to be in perfect keeping with the setting his personal tastes had inspired. He was broad, squat, fat. His head and neck were set low upon his shoulders, and the hair oil was obvious on the longish dark hair which seemed to grow low down under his shirt collar.

The other man, seated in one of the many easy chairs, was in strong contrast. His was the familiar face of the agent, Idepski, dark, keen, watchful. He was smoking the cigarette to which he had helped himself from the gold box standing near him on the ornate desk.

"You seem to have made a bad mess of things."

Nathaniel Hellbeam turned from the window and came back to his desk with quick, short, energetic strides.

He presented a picture of inflamed wrath. His fleshy, square face was flushed and almost purple. His small eyes were hot with anger. They snapped as he launched his harshly spoken verdict. His whole manner bristled with merciless intolerance.

He was enormously fat, and breathed heavily through clean shaven lips that protruded sensually. His age was doubtful, but suggested something under middle life. It was the gross bulk of the man that made it almost impossible to estimate closely. The only real youth about him was his dark, well oiled hair which possessed not a sign of greying in it.

He flung himself into the wide chair which gaped to receive him, and glared at the dark face of his visitor.

"What in the hell do I pay you for?" he cried brutally, lapsing, in his anger, into that gutteral Teutonic accent which it was his life's object to avoid. "A wild cat's scheme it was I tell you from the first. You go to this Sachigo with your men. You think to get this 'sharp' asleep, or what? You find him wide awake waiting for you to arrive. What then? He jumps quick. So quick you can't think. You a prisoner are. You go where he sends you.

You live like a swine in the woods. You are made to work for your food. And a year is gone. A year! Serve you darn right. Oh, yes. Bah! You quit. You understand? I pay you no more. You are a fool, a blundering fool. I wash my hands with you."

Idepski sat still, patient, as once before he had sat under the whip lash of a man's tongue. And he continued smoking till the great banker's last word was spoken.

Then he stirred, and removed his cigarette from his thin lips.

"That's all right, Mr. Hellbeam," he said coldly. "It seems like you've a right to all you've said. It seems, I said. But the 'fool' talk." He shook his head. "My best enemies don't reckon me that—generally. The game I'm playing has room enough for things that look like blunders. I allow that. It doesn't matter. You see, I know more of this feller Martin maybe than you do. I guess he's a mighty big coward, except when he's got the drop on a feller. I've given him the scare of a lifetime, and I've unshipped him from his safe anchorage on that darn Labrador coast. Do you know what's happened? I'll tell you. He's quit Sachigo. From what I can learn he's sold out his mill to that uncouth hoodlum, Harker, who was sort of his partner, and quit. Where? I don't know yet. Why has he quit? Why, because he knows we've located his hiding, and will get him if he remains. You reckon I've mussed things up." He shook his head. "He was well-nigh safe up there on Labrador—and I knew it. We had to get him out of it. Well, I've got him out. He's bolted like a gopher, and it's up to me to locate him. I shall locate him. I'm glad he's quit that hellish country. I've had a year of it, and it's put the fear of God into me. You needn't worry. I'm quite ready to quit your pay. But I'm going on with this thing, sure. You see, I owe him quite a piece for myself—now. I've been through the hell he intended me to go through when he sent me along up to be held prisoner by that skunk, Ole Porson. I'm going to pay him for that—good. I don't want your pay—now. One day I'll hand that feller over to you—and when you've doped him plenty—you'll have paid me." He rose leisurely from his comfortable chair. "May I take another of your good cigarettes?" he went on, with a half smile in his cold eyes. "You see, I won't get another, seeing I'm quitting you."

He deliberately helped himself without waiting for permission, while his eyes dwelt on the gold box containing them.

But the financier's mood had changed. The keen mind was busy behind his narrow eyes. Perhaps Idepski understood the man. Perhaps the coolness of the agent appealed to the implacable nature of the Swede. Whatever it was the hot eyes had cooled, and the fleshy cheeks had returned to their normal pasty hue. He raised a hand pointing.

"Sit down and smoke all you need," he said, in the sharp, autocratic fashion that was his habit. "We aren't through yet." Then, for a few moments, he regarded the slim figure as it lay back once more in the armchair. "Say," he began, abruptly, "you reckon to go on for—yourself? Yes? You're a good hater."

He went on as the other inclined his head.

"I like a good hater. Yes. Well, just cut out all I said. We'll go on. I guess you'll need to blunder some before we get this swine. You're bound to. But I want him. I want him bad. If it's good for you to go on for yourself, that's good for me. There's a lifetime ahead yet, and I don't care so I see him down—right down where I need him. Maybe I won't get the money, but we'll get him, and that'll do. Yes, cut out what I said, and go ahead. Tell me about it."

Idepski displayed neither enthusiasm nor added interest. He accepted the position with seeming indifference. Hellbeam to him was just an employer. A means to those ends which he had in view. If Hellbeam turned him down it would mean a setback, but not a disaster, and Idepski appraised setbacks at their simple value, without exaggeration. Besides, he knew that this Swede, powerful, wealthy as he was, could not afford to do without him in this matter. His intolerant, hectic temper mattered nothing at all. He paid for the privilege of its display, and he paid well. So—

"There's nothing much to tell," the agent returned, with a shrug. "I'm going to get him—that's all. See here, Mr. Hellbeam," he went on after a pause, with a sudden change to keen energy, "you're a mighty big power in the financial world, and to be that I guess you've had to be some judge of the other feller. That's so. You most generally know when he's beat before you begin. And when he squeals it don't come as a surprise. Well, that's how it is with me, only it's a bigger thing to me because it sometimes happens to mean the difference between life and death. Say, when you put up your bluff at a feller, and watch him square in the eyes, and you see 'em flicker and shift, do you reckon you've lit on the 'yellow streak,' that lies somewhere in most folk? I guess so. Well, that's how I know my man. I've seen it in this bum, Leslie Standing as he calls himself now. And when I saw it I knew he was beat, for all he'd the drop on me. Since then my notion's proved itself. He's lit out. He's cut from his gopher hole at Sachigo. An' when a gopher gets away from his hole, the man with the gun has him dead set. But say, that muss up you reckon I made doesn't look that way when you know the things it's taught me. While I was way up at that penitentiary camp on the Beaver River I kept all my ears and eyes wide, and I learned most of the things a feller's liable to learn in this world when he acts that way. I learned something of the notions lying back of this feller's work up there. Say, he hadn't finished with you when he took that ten millions out of you." An ironical smile lit the man's dark eyes as he thrust home his retaliation for the financier's insults. "Not by a lot," he went on, with a smiling display of teeth that conveyed nothing pleasant. "They've a slogan up there that means a whole heap, and it comes from him, and runs through the whole work going on, right down to the Chink camp cooks. Guess that mill is only beginning. It's the ground work of a mighty big notion. And the notion is to drive the Skandinavians out of Canada's pulp trade, and very particularly the Swedes, as represented by the interests of Nathaniel Hellbeam. Guess you sit right here in New York, but up there they've got you measured up to the last pant's button."

"They that think?"

The financier's bloated cheeks purpled as he put his clumsy interrogation.

"Oh, yes. This feller Standing reckons he's made a big start, and there are mighty big plans out. When he and that clownish partner of his, Harker, are through, Sachigo'll be the biggest proposition in the way of groundwood pulp in the world. They've forests such as you in Skandinavia dream about when your digestion's feeling good. They've a water power that leaves Niagara a summer trickle. They've got it all with a sea journey of less than eighteen hundred miles to Europe. But there's more than that. When Sachigo's complete it's to be the parent company of a mighty combine that's going to take in all the mills of Canada outside Nathaniel Hellbeam's group. And then—then, sir, the squeeze'll start right in. And it isn't going to stop till the sponge—that's Nathaniel Hellbeam—is wrung dry."

"You heard all this—when you were held prisoner and working like a swine in Martin's forests?"

The smile in Hellbeam's eyes was no less ironical than the agent's.

"When I was working like a swine."

"These lumber-jacks. They knew all that in Standing's mind is?"

"No. But I learned it all."

"How?"

The demand was instant, and a surge of force lay behind it.

"Because some I saw. Some I picked up from general talk. And the rest I pieced together because it's my job to think hard when the game's against me. But it don't matter. You know that the things I've told you are right. It's news to you, but you know it's right, because you're thinking hard, and the game's against—you."

"Yes."

The financier's admission was the act of a man who has no hesitation in looking facts in the face and acknowledging them. Idepski's deductions were irrefutable, because the Swede was a shrewd business man with a full appreciation of the man who had lightened his finances by ten million dollars.

For some moments the fleshy face was turned towards the window which yielded the hum of busy traffic many stories below them. His narrow eyes were earnestly reflective, but there was no concern in them. To the waiting man he was simply measuring the threat against him, and probing its possibilities for mischief.

"Yet this fellow. He on the run is—Yes?"

The eyes were smiling as they came back again to Idepski's face. The agent nodded, flinging his cigarette end into the porcelain cuspidore beside the desk.

"Which makes me all the more sure of the game," he said confidently. "He's rattled. He's so scared to death for himself, and for his purpose, he's getting out. It's as clear as daylight to me. He feels he's plumb against it if he stops around. He knows we've located him. He knows what he's done to me. He knows all he wants to know of you. Well, he reckons there's no sort of chance for him at Sachigo. And if he stops there's no sort of chance for this purpose of his. He reckons to call off the hounds on his own trail, while the feller Harker carries on the good work of squeezing the Swedes. That's how I see it. And I guess I'm right. Remember I had a year of hell up there to think in, and when I finally got clear away I had two months' solitary chasing of those woods to think in, and then, when I made the coast, I had the trip down with the folks on the boat to listen to. He's scared for his life, and of anything you hope to hand him. But he's more scared for the purpose that made him set up that mill at Sachigo."

Hellbeam leant back in his chair. His great paunch protruded invitingly and he clasped his hands over it.

"Maybe you're right," he said, with an air intended to conciliate. "Anyway you've picked up some pieces and set them together so they make a fancy shape. But—it isn't good. No. Here, I think, too. I see another, way from you. Without this fellow Sachigo is—nothing. See? I care nothing because of this Harker. No. The other—that's different. Yes. He the brain has. All this piece you make. He is capable of it. But he is on the run. Good. I still sleep well while he runs. Sachigo? Bah! It is nothing without Leslie Martin. Now, go you. Hunt this man. Maybe your year of the woods will help you," he said, with biting emphasis. "You know the woods? Well, don't quit his trail. Get him. Get him alive."

"Oh, I shall get him. Your urging ain't needed. I'll get him as you say—alive. And he knows it."

Idepski's cold eyes hardened with a frigid hatred as he spoke. He had only been paid for the work hitherto. Now he was implacable.

"But it's Sachigo I mean to watch," he went on, after a brief pause. "I mean to play in that direction. It's the home burrow where you lay your traps once your quarry's on the run."

Hellbeam nodded.

"That's good sense."

"Sure it is," retorted the agent. "I'm glad you see it that way," he added with a smile under which the financier grew restive once more.

"Yes. Well, see you get him. Money? It doesn't matter. Get him! Get him!" he reiterated fiercely. "You understand me? It doesn't matter how you get him. I can deal with the rest."

Suddenly he raised a clenched fist, fat, and strong, and white, and extended his thumb. He turned it downwards and pressed its extremity on the gold mounted blotting pad before him with a force that bent the knuckle backwards. "Get him so I can crush him—like that," he cried. "Get him alive. I want him alive. See?"

"I see. I'll get him—sure. You needn't worry a thing."

And as Walter Idepski rose to take his departure, for all his nerve, he felt glad that the passion of this Swede's hate was not directed against him.

PART II
EIGHT YEARS LATER

CHAPTER I
BULL STERNFORD

A great gathering thronged the heart of the clearing. There were men of every shade of colour, men of well-nigh every type. They stood about in a wide circle, whose regularity remained definite even under the stirring of fierce excitement. They had gathered for a fight, a great fight between two creatures, full human in shape and splendid manhood, but bestial in the method of the battle demanded. It was a battle with muscles of iron, and hearts that knew no mercy, and body and mind tuned only to endure and conquer. It was a battle that belonged to the savage out-world, acknowledging only the vicious laws of "rough and tough."

The rough creatures stood voiceless and well-nigh breathless. The combatants were well matched and redoubtable, even in a community whose only deity was physical might and courage and the skill of the wielded axe. The lust of it all was burning fiercely in every heart.

The sun poured out its flood of summer upon a world of virgin forest. The sky was without blemish. A dome of perfect azure roofed in the length and breadth of Nature's kingdom. Nevertheless the fairness of the summer day, with its ravishing accompaniment of soft, mystery sounds from an unseen world and the lavish beauty of shadowed woods were fit setting for the pulsing of savage emotions. It was far out in the lost world of Northern Quebec. It was far, far beyond the widest-flung frontiers of civilisation. It was out there where man soon learns to forget his birthright, and readily yields to the animal in him.

It was a scene of mighty slaughter amongst the giants of the forest. Hundreds sprawled in the path of man's gleaming axe. Giants they were, hoary with age, and gnarled with the sinews built up by Nature to resist her fiercest storms. They lay there, in every direction, reaching up with tattered arms outstretched, as though appealing for the light, the warmth, and the sweetness of life they would know no more.

Amidst this carnage a great camp was growing up. There were huts completed. There were huts only in the skeleton. They were dotted about in a fashion apparently without order or purpose. Yet long before the falling of the first snow, order would reign everywhere and man's purpose would be achieved.

The bunkhouses, the stores, the offices, the stables, they must all be ready before the coming of the "freeze-up." Summer is the time of preparation. Winter is the season when the lumber-jack's work must go forward without cessation or break of any sort. Not even the excuse of sickness can be accepted. There is no excuse. The lumber-jack must work, or sink to the dregs of a life that has already created in him a spirit of indifference to the laws of God and man. So the life of the forest is hard and fierce, and the battle of it all is long.

But the men who seek it are more than equal to the task. They are of all sorts, and all races. They drift to the forest from all ranks of life by reason of the spirit driving them. They come from the universities of the world. They come straight from the gates of the penitentiary. They come from the land, the sea, the office. They come from all countries, and they come for every reason. The call of the forest is deep with significance. Its appeal is profound. Its life is free, and shadowed, and afar.

For long moments the clinch of the fighting men remained unbroken. They lay there upon the ground locked in a deadly embrace. A spasmodic jolt, a violent, muscular heave. The result was changed position, while the clinch remained unrelaxed. There were movements of gripping hands. There were changes of position in the intertwined legs clad in their hard cord trousers. The heavily-booted feet stirred and stirred again in response to the impulse of the searching brains of the fighters, and every slight movement had deep meaning for the onlookers.

Yet none of these movements revealed the inspiration of passion. They were calculated and full of purpose. It was devilish purpose driving towards the objects of the fight. The stirring fingers yearned to reach the eyes of the adversary to blind him, and leave his organs of vision gouged from their sockets. The bared, strong teeth were only awaiting that dire chance to close upon the enemy's flesh, whether ear, or nose, or throat. Then the knee and foot. They were striving under ardent will for that inhuman maiming which would leave the victim crippled for life.

Each movement of the fighters was estimated by the onlookers at its due worth. They understood it all, the skill, the chance of it. Not one of them but had fought just such a battle in his time, and not a few carried the scars of it, and would continue to carry the scars of it for the rest of their days.

The moments of quiescence yielded to a spasmodic violence. There was a wild rolling, and the unlocking of mighty, clinging legs. One dishevelled head was raised threateningly. It remained poised for a fraction of time over the upturned face of the man lying in a position of disadvantage. Then it lunged downwards. And as it descended, a sound like the clipping of teeth came back to the taut strung senses of the onlookers. A sigh escaped from a hundred throats.

"Bull missed it that time."

Abe Kristin whispered his comment. The two men beside him had nothing to add at the moment. Their eyes were intent for the next development.

Suddenly the fair-haired giant who had missed his attack seemed to disengage himself from the under man's desperate hold. It was impossible to ascertain the means he employed. But he clearly released himself and one hammer fist swung up. It crashed sickeningly down on the upturned face, and a whistling breath escaped the emotional Abe.

"Gee! He's takin' a chance! That ain't the play in a 'rough and tough,'" he muttered.

"Nope. You're right, Abe," Luke Gats agreed without turning. "He's crazy. Gee! It's a chance. But he's maybe rattled. Bull's been fightin' over an hour."

"Here get it!" Tug Burke was pointing with a cant-hook in his excitement. "Get it quick. See? He's—"

The man's excitement found reflection in the whole concourse of onlookers. There was a furious movement in the human body crushed on the ground beneath the man they called Bull. Its knees came up under his adversary's body with a terrific jolt. The purpose of maiming was obvious.

"Gee! I'm glad."

Tug's relief found an echo in the sigh that escaped his companions. The intended victim had promptly swung his body clear and the threatened injury was averted. But his retaliation was instant. His great open hand spread over the man's face, smothering it; and it seemed the sought-for goal had been reached.

"Gouge! Gouge!"

The cry roared in hoarse, excited tones from every direction. Unanimity displayed the general feeling. The man whose face had been smothered was Arden Laval, the camp boss, the man they hated as only forest-men can hate. The other was a giant youngster, not long a member of the camp, the usual object for victimisation by such a man as the French Canadian boss.

The demand remained unsatisfied. The fingers remained spread out over the man's eyes, but the foul act was never perpetrated. The younger man's efforts were directed towards a deeper, more significant purpose, and perhaps less cruel. He could have blinded in a twinkling. But he refrained. Instead, he pressed up mightily with a fore-arm crooked under the back of the man's neck, his smothering hand pressed down with all his enormous strength.

"The darn fool! Why in hell don't he—?"

Abe was interrupted by the excited voice of the man with the cant-hook.

"God A'mighty!" Tug cried. "Do you get it? Gouge? It ain't good enough fer Master Bull. He's playin' bigger. He's playin' fer dollars while we was reck'nin' cents. Look! It'll crack sure! His gorl-darn neck! He means—!"

"To kill!"

Luke Gat's jubilation was dreadful to witness. His hard, be-whiskered features were alight with fiendish joy. This youngster had gone beyond all expectations. No less than the life of the greatest bully in the lumber world would satisfy him.

"Say, the nerve! He'll break the life out o' the skunk," he exulted. "The kid means crackin' his neck, sure as God!"

"Ken he do it?" Tug had thrust forward.

"Laval ain't the feller he was," mused Abe. "He shouldn't a let the boy get that holt. It's goin' back. It certainly is."

The men stood hushed before the terrible significance of what they beheld. In the abstract, a life-and-death struggle meant little enough to them. Witnessing it, however, violently stirred their deepest emotions. They hated the camp boss, the libertine, drunkard, bully, Arden Laval, who only held his position by reason of his fighting powers. They would be infinitely pleased to witness his end. All the more sure was their delight that it should come at the hands of this pleasant-voiced young giant, who had come amongst them out of the very lap of civilisation. Later on they would laugh at the thought of the redoubtable Laval in the hands of this "kid," as they considered him. But for the moment they were held enthralled by the excitement of it all.

The moments prolonged. The thrusting hand, and the crushing arm were forcing, forcing slowly, in their terrible strangle hold. The face of the camp boss was hidden from the spectators under the smothering hand. But the perilous angle at which his dark head was thrust back was there for all to see. His struggles, in that merciless hold, were becoming less violent. There was despair in their impotence.

The man called Bull was fighting with no less desperation. His youthful, resilient muscles were extended to the last ounce of their power, and an active, steely-tempered brain lay behind his every effort. The memory of months of brutal injustice and bullying, the bitterness of which had galled beyond endurance, supported this last mighty effort. Yes, for all he was bred in the gentle life of civilisation, for all ruthless cruelty had no place in his normal temper, his one desire now was to kill, to slay this brute-man who had made his life unendurable.

It was an awful moment. It was terrible even to these hardy men of the forests. The spectacle of a slow, deliberate killing was incomparable with the blood feuds to which they were used. There were those whose nerves prompted them to shout for haste. There were some even who welcomed the prolonged agony of the victim. But none shouted, none spoke or stirred. Furthermore, not one pair of shining eyes revealed the quality of mercy. Bull's right was his own. If he demanded death it was his due. Certainly it was the due of the bully, Laval.

On the far side of the circle a sudden commotion broke up the tense expectancy of the onlookers. Every eye responded, and the unanimity of the change of interest suggested the desire for relief. The commotion continued. There was some sort of struggle going on. Then, in a moment, it ceased. A tall, lean, dark-clad figure leapt into the arena and flung itself upon the combatants.

The circle had re-formed. Again were eyes fastened upon the point of fascination which had held them so long. But now a buzz of talk hummed on the summer air.

"What in hell!" demanded Luke, in the bitterness of disappointment.

"Here, I'm—"

Tug Burke made a move to break into the arena. But the powerful hand of Abe was fastened about one of his arms in a grip of iron.

"Say, quit, kid!" he cried hoarsely.

The man's harsh tones were stirred out of their usual quiet.

"Stop right here," he went on. "There's just one feller on this earth has a right to butt in when Death's flappin' his wings around. That's Father Adam. Maybe you're feeling sick to think Laval's going to get clear with his life. Maybe I am. Father Adam ain't buttin' in ordinary. He's savin' that hothead kid the blood of a killin' on his hands. Guess I'm glad."

The next moments were abounding with amazing incident. It seemed as though a flying, priestly figure had been absorbed in the life-and-death struggle. He seemed to become part of it. Then, with kaleidoscopic suddenness, the men lay apart, and the death strangle hold of Bull Sternford was broken. And the magic of it all lay in the fact that the stranger was standing over the prone combatants, his dark, bearded face, and wide, shining black eyes turned upon the living fury gazing up out of the eyes of the man who had been robbed of his prey.

"There's going to be no killing, Bull." Father Adam spoke quietly, deliberately, but with cold decision.

There was no yielding in his pale, ascetic features. One hand slipped quickly into a pocket of his short, black, semi-clerical coat, as he allowed his eyes to glance down at the still prostrate camp boss.

"And you, Laval," he cried, with more urgency, "get out quick. Get right out to your shanty and stop there. Later I'll come along and fix up your hurts."

Young Bull Sternford leapt to his feet. His youthful figure towered. His handsome blue eyes were ablaze with almost demoniac fury. His purpose was obvious. A voiceless passion surged as he started to rush again upon his victim.

But the priestly figure, with purpose no less, instantly barred the way.

"Quit," he cried sharply. "What I say, goes."

Bull halted. He halted within a yard of the automatic pistol whose muzzle was covering him. He stood for a second staring stupidly. And something of his madness seemed to pass out of his eyes. Then, in a moment, his voice rang out harshly.

"Get away. Let me get at him. Oh, God, I'll smash him! I'll—!"

"You'll quit right now!" Father Adam still barred the way with the threatening gun. He raised the muzzle the least shade. "There's this gun says you're not going to have murder on your hands, boy; and there's a man behind it knows how to make it stop your mad attempt. That's better," he went on, as, even in his fury the younger man drew back in face of the threat. "Say, you've done enough, boy. You've done all you need. He's deserved everything he's got, the same as most of us deserve the bad times we get. You've licked him like the good man you are. You've licked him without any filthy maiming, or unnecessary cruelty. Now leave him his life. He'll never trouble you again. Let it go at that."

The calm of the man, the gentleness of his tones were irresistible. The fury of the youth died hard, but it so lessened in face of the simple exhortation that it had passed below the point where insanity rules.

Suddenly a great, bleeding hand was raised to his mane of fair hair, and he smoothed it back off his forehead helplessly.

"Why? Why?" he demanded. Then spasmodically: "Why should—he—get away with it? He's handed me a dog's life He's—"

He broke off. His emotions were overwhelming.

Father Adam's dark eyes never wavered. They squarely held their grip on the stormy light shining in the other's. Laval had not stirred. He still lay sprawled on the ground. Quite abruptly the hand gripping the automatic pistol was thrust into the pocket of the black coat. When it was removed it was empty. The man took a quick step towards the half-dazed Bull.

"Come along, boy," he said persuasively, taking him by the arm. "Come right over to my shanty," he went on. "You'll feel better in a while. You'll feel better all ways, and glad you—didn't." Then he paused, holding the man's unresisting arm. He looked down at Laval who displayed belated signs of movement. "Get up, Laval," he ordered, returning to a coldness that displayed his inner feeling. "Get up, and—get out. Get away right now, and thank God your neck's still whole."

He waited for the obedience he demanded, and waiting he realised by the quiescence of the man beside him that all danger had passed.

Laval staggered to his feet. He stood up, a giant in the prime of early manhood, but bowed under the weight of physical hurt, and the knowledge of his first defeat. He stood for a moment as though uncertain. Then he moved slowly towards the crowding onlookers, finally passing through them on his way to his quarters pursued by a hundred contemptuous, unpitying glances, while busy tongues expressed regret at his escape. It was the scowl of the wolf pack in its merciless regard for a fallen leader.

Very different was the general attitude when Father Adam led the victor away. Hard faces were a-grin. The tongues that cursed the defeated camp boss hurled jubilant laudations at the unresponsive youth, who towered even amongst these great creatures. But for the presence of Father Adam, who seemed to exercise a miraculous restraining influence, these lumberjacks would have crowded in and forcibly borne their champion to the suttler's store for those copious libations, which, in their estimate, was the only fitting conclusion to the scene they had witnessed. As it was they made way. They stood aside in spontaneous and real respect, and the two men passed on in silence leaving the crowd to disperse to its labours.

CHAPTER II
FATHER ADAM

The hush of the forest was profound. For all the proximity of the busy lumber camp its calm was unbroken.

It was a break in the endless canopy of foliage, a narrow rift in the dark breadth of the shadowed woods.

It was one of those infinitesimal veins through which flows the life-blood of the forest.

A tiny streamlet trickled its way over a bed of decayed vegetation often meandering through a dense growth of wiry reeds in a channel set well below the general level. Banks of attenuated grass and rank foliage lined its course, and the welcome sunlight poured down upon its water in sharp contrast with the twilight of the forest.

Clear of the crowding trees a rough shanty stood out in the sunlight. It was a crazy affair constructed of logs laterally laid and held in place by uprights, with walls that looked to be just able to hold together while suffering under the constant threat of collapse. The place was roofed with a thatch of reeds taken from the adjacent stream-bed, and its doorway was protected by a sheet of tattered sacking. There was also a window covered with cotton, and a length of iron stove-pipe protruding through the thatch of the roof seemed to threaten the whole place with fire at its first use.

Inside there was no attempt to better the impression. There was no furnishing. A spread of blankets on a waterproof sheet laid on a bed of reeds formed the bed of its owner, with a canvas kit-bag stuffed with his limited wardrobe serving as a pillow. There were several upturned boxes to be used as seats, and a larger box served the purpose of a table and supported a tiny oil lamp. There was not even the usual wood stove connected up to the protruding stove-pipe. A smouldering fire was burning between two large sandstone blocks, which, in turn, supported a cooking pot. An uncultured Indian of the forests would have demanded greater comfort for his resting moments.

But Father Adam had no concern for comfort of body. He needed his blankets and his fire solely to support life against the bitterness of the night air. For the rest the barest, hardest food kept the fire of life burning in his lean body.

Squatting on his upturned box he gazed out upon the sunlit stream below him. His dark eyes were full of a pensive calm. His body was inclining forward, supported by arms folded across his knees. An unlit pipe thrust in the corner of his mouth was the one touch that defeated the efforts of his flowing hair and dark beard to suggest a youthful hermit meditating in the doorway of his retreat.

Bull Sternford was seated on another box at the opposite side of the doorway. He, too, had a pipe thrust between his strong jaws. But he was smoking. Beyond the dressings applied to a few abrasions he bore no signs of his recent battle. But there still burned a curiously fierce light in his handsome blue eyes.

"You shouldn't have butted in, Father," he said, in a tone which betrayed the emotion under which he was still labouring. "You just shouldn't." Then with a movement of irritation: "Oh, I'm not a feller yearning for homicide. No. It's not that. You know Arden Laval," he went on, his brows depressing. "Of course you do. You must know him a whole heap better than I do. Well? Say, I guess that feller hasn't a right to walk this earth. He boasts the boys he's smashed the life clean out of. He's killed more fool lumber-jacks than you could count on the fingers of two hands. He wanted my scalp to hang on his belt. That man's a murderer before God. But he's beyond the recall of law up here. And he stops around on the fringe looking for the poor fool suckers who don't know better than to get within his reach. Gee, it was tough! I'd a holt on him I wouldn't get in a thousand years, and I'd nearly got the life out of him. I'd stood for all his dirt weeks on end. He made his set at me because I'm green and college-bred. But he called me a 'son-of-a-bitch!' Think of it! Oh, I can't rest with that hitting my brain. It's no use. I'll have to break him. God, I'll break him yet. And I'll see you aren't around when I do it."

The man's voice had risen almost to a shout. His bandaged hands clenched into fists like limbs of mutton. He held them out at the man opposite, and in his agony of rage, it gave the impression he was threatening.

Father Adam stirred. He reached down into the box under him and picked up a pannikin. Then he produced a flask from an inner pocket. He unscrewed the top and poured out some of its contents. He held it out to the other.

"Drink it," he said quietly.

The blue eyes searched the dark face before them. In a moment excitement had begun to pass.

"What is it?" Bull demanded roughly.

"It's brandy, and there's dope in it."

"Dope?"

"Yes. Bromide. You'll feel better after you've swallowed it. You see I want to make a big talk with you. That's why I brought you here. That's why I stopped you killing that feller—that, and other reasons. But I can't talk with you acting like—like I'd guess Arden Laval would act. Drink that right up. And you needn't be scared of it. It'll just do you the good you need."

Father Adam watched while the other took the pannikin. He watched him raise it, and sniff suspiciously at its contents. And a shadowy smile lit his dark eyes.

"It's as I said," he prompted. Then he added: "I'm not a—Cæsar."

The youth glanced across at him, and for the first time since his battle a smile broke through the angry gleam of his eyes. He put the pannikin to his lips and gulped down the contents.

Father Adam drew a deep sigh. It was curious how this act of obedience and faith affected him. The weight of his responsibility seemed suddenly to have become enormous.

It was always the same. This man accepted him as did every other lumber-jack throughout the forests of Quebec. He was a father whose patient affection for his lawless children was never failing, a man of healing, with something of the gentleness of a woman. An adviser and spiritual guide who never worried them, and yet contrived, perhaps all unknown to themselves, to leave them better men for their knowledge of him. He came, and he departed. Whence he came and whither he went no one enquired, no one seemed to know. He just moved through the twilight forests like a ghostly, beneficent shadow, supreme in his command of their rugged hearts.

Bull set the pannikin on the ground beside him. His smile had deepened.

"You needn't to tell me that, Father," he said, almost humbly. "There isn't a feller back there in the camp," he added with a jerk of his head, "that would have hesitated like me when you handed him your dope. Thanks. Say, that darn stuff's made me feel easier."

"Good."

The missionary removed his empty pipe, and Bull hastily dragged his pouch from a pocket in his buckskin shirt. He held it out.

"Help yourself," he invited. And the other took it. For a moment Bull looked on at the thoughtful manner in which Father Adam filled his pipe. Then a curiosity he could no longer restrain prompted him.

"This big talk," he said. "What's it about?"

The missionary's preoccupation vanished. His eyes lit and he passed back the pouch.

"Thanks, boy," he said in his amiable way. "Guess I'll need to smoke, too—you see our talk needs some hard thinking. Pass me a stick from that fire."

Bull did as he was bid. And the missionary's eyes were on the fair head of the man as he leant down over the smouldering embers stewing his own meagre midday meal.

Bull Sternford was a creature of vast stature and muscular bulk. It was no wonder that the redoubtable Laval had run up against defeat. The camp boss had lived for twenty years the hard life of the forests. His body was no less great than this man's. His experience in physical battle was well-nigh unlimited. But so, too, was his debauchery.

Bull Sternford was younger. He was clean and fresh from one of the finest colleges of the world. He was an athlete by training and nature. Then, too, his mentality was of that amazing fighting quality which stirs youth to go out and seek the world rather than vegetate in the nursery of childhood. It was all there written in his keen, blue eyes, in the set of his jaws of even white teeth. It was all there in the muscular set of his great neck, and in the poise of his handsome head, and in the upright carriage of his breadth of shoulder. Even his walk was a thing to mark him out from his fellows. It was bold, perhaps even there was a suggestion of arrogance in it. But it was only the result of the military straightness of his body.

Little wonder, then, a man of Arden Laval's brutal nature should mark him down as desired victim. This man was "green." He was educated. He possessed a spirit worth breaking. Later he would learn. Later he would become a force in the calling of the woods. Now he would be easy.

The brute had sought every opportunity to bait and goad the man to his undoing. For months he had "camped on his trail," and Bull had endured.

Then came that moment of the filthy epithet, and Bull's spirit broke through the bonds of will that held it. The insult had been hurled at the moment and at the spot where the battle had been fought. Bull had flung himself forthwith at the throat of the French Canadian almost before the last syllable of the insult had passed the man's lips. And the end of nearly a two hours' battle had been the downfall of the bully, with the name of Bull Sternford hailed as a fighting man in his place.

The firebrand was passed to the waiting missionary. He sucked in the pleasant fumes of a lumberman's tobacco. Then the stick was flung back to its place in the fire.

Father Adam nursed one long leg, which he flung across the other, while his wide, intelligent eyes gazed squarely into the eyes of the man opposite.

"Tell me," he said. "What brought you into the life of the woods? What left you quitting the things I can see civilisation handed you? This is the life of the wastrel, the fallen, the man who knows no better. It's not for men starting out in possession of all those things—you have."

Bull sat for a moment without replying. Father Adam's "dope" had done its work. His passionate moments had vanished like an ugly dream. His turbulent spirit had attained peace. Suddenly he looked up with a frank laugh.

"Now, why in hell should I tell you?"

It was an irresistible challenge. The missionary nodded his approval.

"Yes. Why—in hell—should you?"

He, too, laughed. And his laugh miraculously lit up his ascetic features.

Instantly Bull flung out one bandaged hand in a sweeping gesture.

"Why shouldn't I—anyway?" he cried, with the abandon of a man impatient of all subterfuge. "Guess I ought to turn right around and ask who the devil you are to look into my affairs? Who are you to assume the right of inquisitor?" He shook his head. "But I'm not going to. Now I'm sane again I know just how much you did for me. I meant killing Laval. Oh, yes, there wasn't a thing going to break my hold until he was dead—dead. You got me in time to save me from wrecking my whole life. And you got in at—the risk of your own. If I'd killed him all the things and purposes I've worried with since I left college would have been just so much junk; and I'd have drifted into the life of a bum lumber-jack without any sort of notion beyond rye whiskey, and the camp women, and a well swung axe. You saved me from that. You saved me from myself. Well, you're real welcome to ask me any old thing, and I'll hand you all the truth there is in me. I'm an 'illegitimate.' I'm one of the world's friendless. I'm a product of a wealthy man's licence and unscruple. I'm an outcast amongst the world's honest born. But it's no matter. I'm not on the squeal. Those who're responsible for my being did their best to hand me the things a man most needs. Mind, and body, and will. Further, they gave me all that education, books, and college can hand a feller. More than that, my father, who seems to have had more honesty than you'd expect, handed me a settlement of a hundred thousand dollars the day I became twenty-one. I never knew him, and I never knew my mother. The circumstances of my birth were simply told me on my twenty-first birthday. I know no more. And I care nothing to hunt out those spectres that don't figger to hand a feller much comfort. The rest is easy. I hope I'm a feller of some guts—"

Father Adam nodded, and his eyes lit.

"Sure," was all he commented.

"Anyway, I feel like it," Bull laughed. "When I learned all these things I started right in to think. I thought like hell. I said to myself something like this: 'There's nothing to hold me where I am. There's no one around to care a curse. There's that feeling right inside the pit of my stomach makes me feel I want to make good. I want to build up around me all that my birth has refused me. A name, a life circle, a power, a—anyway, get right out and do things! Well, what was I going to do? It needed thinking. Then I hit the notion."

He laughed again. He was gazing in at himself and laughing at the conceits he knew were real, and strong, and vital.

"Say." He nodded at the prospect through the doorway. "There it is. This country's beginning. We don't know half it means to the world yet. Well, I hadn't enough capital to play with, so I resolved right away to start in and learn a trade from its first step to its topmost rung, and to earn my keep right through. Meanwhile my capital's lying invested against the time I open out. I'm going to jump right into the groundwood pulp business when the time comes. And out of that I mean to build a name that folks won't easily forget. Well, I guess you won't find much that's interesting in all this. It don't sound anything particularly bright or new. But for what it is it's my notion, and—I'm going to put it through. That's why I'm here. I'm learning my job from the bottom."

The decision and force of the man were remarkable. The conciseness of his story, and his indifference to the tragedy of his birth, indicated a level mind under powerful control. And Father Adam knew he had made no mistake.

"It's the best story I've heard in years," he replied, a whimsical smile lighting his dark eyes.

"Is it?"

Bull's smile was no less whimsical.

"Yes. You've guts of iron, boy. And I've been looking years for just such a man."

"That sounds—tough," Bull laughed, but he was interested. "What's the job you want him for? Are you yearning to hand out a killing? Is it a trip—a trip to some waste space of God's earth that 'ud freeze up a normal heart? Do you want a feller to beat the laws of God and man? Guts of iron! It certainly sounds tough, and I'm not sure you've found the feller you're needing."

"I am."

Father Adam was no longer smiling. The gravity of his expression gave emphasis to his words.

Bull was impressed. His laugh died out.

"I don't know I'm yearning," he said deliberately. "Anyway I don't quit the track I've marked out. That way there's nothing doing. It's a crank with me; I can't quit a notion."

"You don't have to."

"No?"

They were regarding each other steadily.

"Here, it's not my way to beat around," the missionary exclaimed suddenly. "When you find the thing you need you've got to act quick and straight. Just listen a while, while I make a talk. Ask all you need as I go along. And when I've done I'd thank you for a straight answer and quick. An answer that'll hold you, and bind you the way your own notions do."

"That's talk."

Bull nodded appreciatively. The missionary let his gaze wander to the pleasant sunlight through the doorway, where the flies and mosquitoes were basking.

"There was a fellow who started up a groundwood mill 'way out on the Labrador coast. He was bright enough, and a mighty rich man. And he'd got a notion—a big notion. Well, I know him. I know him intimately. I don't know if he's a friend to me or not. Sometimes I think he isn't. Anyway, that doesn't matter to you. The thing that does matter is, he set out to do something big. His notions were always big. Maybe too big. This notion was no less than to drive the Skandinavians out of the groundwood trade of this country. He figured his great mill was to be the nucleus of an all-Canadian and British combination, embracing the entire groundwood industry of this country. It was to be Canadian trade for Canada with the British Empire."

Bull emitted a low whistle.

"An elegant slogan," he commented.

He shifted his position. In his interest his pipe had gone out, and he leant forward on his upturned box.

"Yes," Father Adam went on. "And, like your notion, it was something not easily shifted from his mind. It was planned and figured to the last detail. It was so planned it could not fail. So he thought. So all concerned thought. You see, he had ten million dollars capital of his own; and he was something of a genius at figures and finance—his people reckoned. He was a man of some purpose, and enthusiasm, and—something else."

"Ah!"

Bull's alert brain was prompt to seize upon the reservation. But denial was instant.

"No. It wasn't drink, or women, or any foolishness of that sort," the missionary said. "The whole edifice of his purpose came tumbling about his ears from a totally unexpected cause. Something happened. Something happened to the man himself. It was disaster—personal disaster. And when it came a queer sort of weakness tripped him, a weakness he had always hitherto had strength to keep under, to stifle. His courage failed him, and the bottom of his purpose fell out like—that."

Father Adam clipped his fingers in the air and his regretful eyes conveyed the rest. Then, after a moment, he smiled.

"He'd no—iron guts," he said, with a sigh. "He had no stomach for battle in face of this—this disaster that hit him."

"It has no relation to his—undertaking?"

"None whatever. I know the whole thing. We were 'intimates.' I know his whole life story. It was a disaster to shake any man."

The missionary sighed profoundly.

"Yes, I knew him intimately," he went on. "I deplored his weakness. I censured it. Perhaps I went far beyond any right of mine to condemn. I don't know. I argued with him. I did all I could to support him. You see, I appreciated the splendid notion of the thing he contemplated. More than that, I knew it could be carried out."

He shook his head.

"It was useless. This taint—this yellow streak—was part of the man. He could no more help it than you could help fighting to the death."

"Queer."

A sort of pitying contempt shone in the younger man's eyes.

"Queer?" Father Adam nodded. "It was—crazy."

"It surely was."

The missionary turned back to the prospect beyond the doorway. But it was only for a moment. He turned again and went on with added urgency.

"But the scheme wasn't wholly to be abandoned. It was—say, here was the crazy proposition he put up. You see I was his most intimate friend. He said: 'The forests are wide. They're peopled with men of our craft. There must be a hundred and more men capable of doing this thing. Of putting it through. Well, the forests must provide the man, or the idea must die.' He said: 'We must find a man!' He said: 'You—you whose mission it is to roam the length and breadth of these forests—you may find such a man. If you do—when you do—if it's years hence—send him along here, and there's ten million dollars waiting for him, and all this great mill, and these timber limits inexhaustible waiting for him to go right ahead. It doesn't matter a thing who he is, or what he is, or where he comes from, so long as he gets this idea—sticks to it faithfully—and puts it through. I want nothing out of it for myself. And the day he succeeds in the great idea all that would have been mine shall be his.'"

As Father Adam finished, he looked into the earnest, wonder-filled eyes of the other.

"Well?" he demanded.

Bull cleared his throat.

"The mill? Where is it?" He demanded.

"Sachigo. Farewell Cove."

"Sachigo! Why it's—"

"The greatest groundwood mill in the world."

There was a note of pride and triumph in the missionary's tone. But it passed unheeded. Bull was struggling with recollection.

"This man? Wasn't it Leslie Standing who built it? Didn't it break him or something? That's the story going round. There was something—"

Father Adam shook his head.

"There's ten million dollars says it didn't. Ten millions you can handle yourself."

"Gee!"

Bull drew a sharp breath. Strong, forceful as he was the figure was overwhelming.

"This—all this you're saying—offering? It's all real, true?" Bull demanded at last.

"All of it."

"You want me to go and take possession of Sachigo, and ten—Say, where's the catch?"

"There's no 'catch'—anywhere."

The denial was cold. It was almost in the tone of affronted dignity. The missionary had thrust his hand in a pocket. Now he produced a large, sealed envelope. Bull's eyes watched the movement, but bewilderment was still apparent in them. Suddenly he raised a bandaged hand, and smoothed back his hair.

Father Adam held out the sealed letter. It was addressed to "Bat Harker," at Sachigo Mill.

"Here," he said quietly. "You're the man with iron guts Leslie Standing wants for his purpose. Take this. Go right off to Sachigo and take charge of the greatest enterprise in the world's paper industry. You're looking to make good. It's your set purpose to make good in the groundwood industry. Opportunities don't come twice in a lifetime. If you've the iron courage I believe, you'll grab this chance. You'll grab it right away. Will you? Can you do it? Have you the nerve?"

There was a taunt in the challenge. It was calculated. There was something else. The missionary's dark eyes were almost pleading.

Bull seized the letter. He almost snatched it.

"Will I do it? Can I do it? Have I the nerve?" he cried, in a tone of fierce exulting. "If there's a feller crazy enough to hand me ten million dollars and trust me with a job—if it was as big as a war between nations—I'd never squeal. Can I? Will I? Sure I will. And time'll answer the other for you. Iron guts, eh! I tell you in this thing they're chilled steel."

"Good!"

Father Adam was smiling. A great relief, a great happiness stirred his pulses as he stood up and moved over to the miserable fire with its burden of stewing food.

"Now we'll eat," he said. And he stooped down and stirred the contents of the pot.

CHAPTER III
BULL LEARNS CONDITIONS

The *Myra* ploughed her leisurely way up the cove. There was dignity in the steadiness with which she glided through the still waters. The cockleshell of the Atlantic billows had become a thing of pride in the shelter of Farewell Cove. Her predecessor, the *Lizzie*, had never risen above her humble station.

Her decks were wide and clean. Her smoke-stack had something purposeful in its proportions. The bridge was set high and possessed a spacious chart house. She had an air of importance not usual to the humble coasting packet.

"Old man" Hardy was at his post now. One of his officers occupied the starboard side of the bridge, while he and another looked out over the port bow.

"It's a deep water channel," the skipper said, with all a sailor's appreciation. "That's the merricle that makes this place. It'ud take a ten-thousand tonner with fathoms to spare right away up to the mooring berth. Guess Nature meant Sachigo for a real port, but got mussed fixing the climate."

Bull Sternford was leaning over the rail. For all summer was at its height the thick pea-jacket he was wearing was welcome enough. His keen eyes were searching, and no detail of the prospect escaped them. He was filled with something akin to amazement.

"It compares with the big harbours of the world," he replied. "And I'd say it's not without advantages many of the finest of 'em lack. Those headlands we passed away back. Why, the Atlantic couldn't blow a storm big enough to more than ripple the surface here inside." He laughed. "What a place to fortify. Think of this in war time, eh?"

The grizzled skipper grinned responsively.

"It's all you reckon," he said. "But she needs humouring. You need to get this place in winter when ice and snow make it tough. This cove freezes right around its shores. You'd maybe lay off days to get inside, only to find yourself snow or fog bound for weeks on end. We make it because we have to with mails. But you can't run cargo bottoms in winter. It's a coasting master's job in snow time. It's a life study. You can get in, and you can get out—if you've nerve. If you're short that way you'll pile up sure as hell."

He turned away to the chart room, and a moment later the engine-room telegraph chimed his orders to those below.

Bull was left with his busy thoughts.

It was a remarkable scene. The forest slopes came right down almost to the water's edge on either hand. They came down from heights that rose mountainously. And there, all along the foreshore were dotted timber-built habitations sufficient to shelter hundreds of workers. Their quality was staunch and picturesque, and pointed much of the climate rigour they were called upon to endure. But they only formed a background to, perhaps, the most wonderful sight of all. A road and trolley car line skirted each foreshore, and the mind behind the searching eyes was filled with admiration for the skill and enterprise that had transplanted one of civilisation's most advanced products here on the desperate coast of Labrador. Many of the forest whispers of Sachigo had been incredible. But this left the onlooker ready to believe anything of it.

The mill, and the township surrounding it, were already within view, a wide-scattered world of buildings, occupying all the lower levels of the territory on both sides of the mouth of the Beaver River before it rose to the heights from which its water power fell.

Bull was amazed. And as he gazed, his wonder and admiration were intensified a hundredfold by his self-interest. This place was to be in his control, possibly his possession if he made good. He thrust back the fur cap pressed low on his forehead.

His thought leapt back on the instant to the man who had sent him down to this Sachigo. Father Adam, with his thin, ascetic features, his long, dark hair and beard, his tall, spare figure. His patient kindliness and sympathy, and yet with the will and force behind it which could fling the muzzle of a gun into a man's face and force obedience. He had sent him. Why? Because—oh, it was all absurd, unreal. And yet here he was on the steamer; and there ahead lay the wonders of Sachigo. Well, time would prove the craziness of it all.

"Makes you wonder, eh?" The coasting skipper was at his side again. "You know these folks needed big nerve to set up this enterprise. It keeps me guessing at the limits where man has to quit. I've spent my life on this darn coast, an' never guessed to see the day when trolley cars 'ud run on Labrador, and the working folk 'ud sit around in their dandy houses, with electric light making things comfortable for them, and electric heat takin' the place of the cordwood stove it seemed to me folk never could do without. Can you beat it? No. You can't. Nor anyone else."

"Who is it? A corporation?" Bull asked, knowing full well the answer. He wanted to hear, he wanted to learn all that this man could tell him.

Hardy shook his head.

"Standing," he said. "That was the guy's name who started it all up. But," he added thoughtfully, "I never rightly knew which feller it was. If it was Standing, or that tough hoboe feller who calls himself Bat Harker. They never talk a heap. But since Leslie Standing passed out o' things eight years back—the time I was first handed command of this kettle—the mill's jumped out of all notion. Those trolleys," he pointed at the foreshore of the cove: "They started in to haul the 'hands' to their work only two years back. I'd say it's Bat Harker. But he looks more like a longshore tough than a—genius."

He shrugged expressively. Then he shook his head.

"No," he went on. "I don't know a thing but what any guy can learn who comes along up this coast. I've thought a heap. An', like you, I've ast questions all the time. But you don't learn a thing of this enterprise but the things you see. Bat Harker don't ever talk." He laughed in quiet enjoyment. "He's most like a clam mussed up in a cement bar'l. There don't seem any clear reason either. The only thing queer to me was Standing's 'get out.' There was talk then when that happened along. But it was jest talk. Canteen talk. Something sort of happened. No one seemed rightly to know. They guessed Bat was a tough guy who'd boosted him out—some way. Then I heard his wife had quit and he was all broke up. Then they said he'd made losses of millions on stock market gambles. But the yarns don't fit. You see, the mill's gone right ahead. The capital's there, sure. They've just built and built. There's more than twice the 'hands' there was eight years back. And get a look at the 'bottoms' loading at the wharves. No. Say, when I came aboard the *Myra* and they scrapped the *Lizzie*, I never guessed to get a full cargo. Well, I can load right down to the water line for this place alone all the time. No. Sachigo's a mighty big fixture in the trade of this coast. It's a swell proposition for us sea folk. It keeps our propellers moving all the time. They're bright folk, sure."

The old seaman laughed and moved off again to his telegraphs. The business of running in to the quayside was beginning in earnest.

The hawsers creaked and strained at the bollards. The vessel yawed. Then she settled at her berth. The engine-room telegraph chimed its final order, and the vessel's busy heart came to rest. Instantly activity reigned upon the deck, and the discharge of cargo was in full swing.

Bull Sternford was one of the first to pass down the gangway. Clad in the pleasant tweeds of civilisation, part hidden under a close-buttoned pea-jacket, he bulked enormously. His more than six feet of height was lost against his massive breadth of shoulder. Then, too, his keen face under a beaver cap, and his shapely head with its mane of hair, were things to deny his body that attention it might otherwise have attracted.

For all that, at least one pair of critical eyes lost no detail of his personality. Bat Harker was unobtrusively standing amongst the piled bales of groundwood that stacked the wharf from end to end. There was nothing about him to single him out from those who stood on the quay. The rough clothing of his original calling was very dear to him, and he clung to it tenaciously. He seemed to have aged not one whit in the added eight years. His iron-grey hair was just as thick and colourful as before. There was no added line in his hard face. His girth was no less and no more. And his eyes, penetrating, steady, had the same spirit shining in them.

He had laboured something desperately in the past eight years. With the passing of Leslie Standing from the life of Sachigo he had realized a terrible loss. His loss had more than embarrassed him. There was even a moment when it shook his purpose. But with him Sachigo was a religion, and his faith saved him. For a while, in both letter and spirit, he obeyed his orders, and Sachigo stood still. Then his philosophy carried the day. It was his dictum that no one could stand still on Labrador without freezing to death. He saw the application of it to his beloved mill. It must be "forward" or decay. So he scrapped his original orders, and drove with all his force.

Bull stared about him for the fascination of his journey up the cove was still on him. His pre-occupation left him watching the hurried, orderly movement going on about him.

"That all your baggage?"

The demand was harsh, and Bull swung round with a start. He was gazing down into the upturned face of Bat Harker, who was pointing at the suit case he was carrying.

"Guess I've a trunk back there in the hold somewhere," Bull replied indifferently, taking his interrogator for a quayside porter.

"That's all right. I'll have one of the boys tote it up. Best come right along. It's quite a piece up to the office. You've a letter for me?"

"I've a letter for Mr. Bat Harker."

The doubt in Bull's tone set a genuine grin in the other's eyes.

"Sure. That's me. Bat Harker. Maybe you don't guess I look it. Don't worry. Just pass it over."

Bull groped in an inner pocket, surprise affording him some amusement. His interest in Sachigo had abruptly focussed itself on this man.

"I'm kind of sorry," he said. "I surely took you for some sort of—porter."

Bat laughed outright, and glanced down at his work-stained clothing.

"Wal, that ain't new," he said. Then his eyes resumed their keen regard. "We don't need to wait around though. The skitters are mighty thick down here. Sachigo's gettin' a special breed I kind o' hate. That letter, an'—we'll get along."

Bull drew out Father Adam's letter and waited while the other tore it open. Bat glanced at the contents and jumped to the signature. Then he thrust out a gnarled and powerful hand.

"Shake," he cried. And there could be no doubting his good will. "Glad to have you around, Mr. Bull Sternford."

Bull Sternford was seated in the luxurious chair that had once known Leslie Standing. His pea-jacket was removed and his cap was gone. The room was warm, and the sun beyond the window was radiant. Beyond the desk Bat was seated, where his wandering gaze could drift to the one object of which it never tired. He was at the window which looked out upon the mill below.

He was reading Father Adam's letter. Sternford was silently regarding his squat figure. He was waiting and wondering, speculating as to the hard-faced, uncultured creature who had built up all the amazing details that made up an industrial city in a territory that was outlawed by Nature.

Bat thrust the letter away and looked up.

"Father Adam didn't write that letter for you? He just handed it out to you to bring along?"

"That's how," Bull nodded.

"Sure." Bat's tone became reflective. "He must have wrote that letter years, and held it against the time he located you. He's queer."

Bull laughed.

"Maybe he is," he said, "I don't know about that. But he's one hell of a good man," he went on warmly. "Do you know him? But of course you do. Say, he's just father and mother to every darn lumber-jack that haunts the forests of Quebec, and it don't worry him if his children are hellhound or honest. There's that to him sets me just crazy. I'd like to see his thin, tired face, always smiling." He stirred. And the warmth died abruptly out of his manner. "Say, you knew me—at the wharf?"

"Sure. I knew you before you came along. We've a wireless out on the headland."

"I see. Father Adam warned you I was coming. He told you—"

"The whole darn yarn. Sure."

Bull laughed grimly.

"That he guessed to shoot me to small meat if I didn't do as he said?"

"If you didn't cut out homicide from your notions of—sport."

"Yes. It was tough," Bull regretted. "But I'm glad—now."

"Yep. Guess any straight sort of feller would feel that way—after."

The lumberman's regret was unnoticed by the other.

Suddenly Bull leant forward in his chair. A smile, half whimsical, half incredulous, lit his eyes. He thrust his elbows on the desk and supported his face in his hands.

"It just beats hell!" he cried. "It certainly does. Oh, I'm awake all right. Sure, I am. One time I wasn't sure. Two months back I was lying around a lousy summer camp getting ready to take a hand in the winter cut for the Skandinavia Corporation. I was within two seconds of breaking a man's life—the rotten camp boss. And now? Why, now I'm sitting around in dandy tweeds in the boss chair of a swell office, with a crazy notion back of my head I'm here to beat the game with the greatest groundwood mill in the world, and ten million dollars capital behind me. Maybe there's folks wouldn't guess I'm awake, but I allow I am. But the whole thing sets me thinking of the fairy stories I used to read when I was a kid, and never could see the horse sense in wasting time over."

Bat helped himself to a chew from a fragment of plug tobacco.

"Here, listen," Bull went on, after the briefest pause. "It's my 'show down.' I don't understand a thing. I'm mostly a kid from college with a yearning for fight. So far I've learned some of the things the forest can teach the feller who wants to learn. They're the rough things. And I like rough things. I've some grip on groundwood. And the making of groundwood's the main object of my life. That, and the notion of licking hell out of the other feller. That's me, and those are the things made Father Adam send me along down to Sachigo. Well, it's up to you." He spread out his hands, "Where do I stand? How do I stand? And why in the name of all that's crazy am I sitting in this boss chair—right now?"

Bat swung one trunk-like leg across the other. His movement suggested an easing of mind and a measure of enjoyment. He pointed at the window and nodded in its direction.

"Quite a place," he said, in a tone and with a pride that had no relation to the other's demands. "Makes you feel man ain't the bum sort of inseck in the scheme of things some highbrows ain't happy not tellin' you. There's folks who guess it's Nature the proposition that matters. It's her does it all, an' keeps on doin' it all the time. But Nature's most like one mighty foolish, extravagant female. That sort o' woman who don't care but to please the notion of the moment. And when that's done, goes right on to please the next. Wal, anyway I guess she's got her uses if it's only to hand chances to the guy that's lookin' on. Take a look right down there below," he went on. "That's the truck the guy lookin' on has sweppen up in Nature's trail. It's taken most of fifteen years collectin' it. We've had to push that broom hard. And now I guess you're going to boost your weight behind it too. There's other things to collect, and that's what we want from you. You got nerve. You got big muscle, and education, too. Well, you'll handle the biggest sweeper of us all. Does it scare you?"

"Not a thing." Bull was smiling confidently.

Bat chuckled. His eyes were sparkling as he ruthlessly masticated his tobacco. This man pleased him mightily.

"That's all right," he said. Then he went on after a silent moment while he gazed thoughtfully out of the window. "It's right here," he exclaimed. "Here's a mill, a swell mill that don't lack for a thing to make it well-nigh perfect. I'll tell you about it. Its capacity. Its present limit is six thousand tons dry weight groundwood pulp to the week. That's runnin' full. There's a hundred and twenty grinders feeding a hundred and eighty sheetin' machines. And they're figgered to use up fifty-five thousand horse power of the five hundred thousand we got harnessed on this great little old river that falls off the highlands. That power is ours winter an' summer. It don't matter a shuck the 'freeze up.' It's there for us all the darn time. Then we've forest limits to hand us the cordage for that output that could give us three times what we're needing for a thousand years. Labour? We got it plenty. And later, by closing in our system of foresting, I figger to cut out present costs on a sight bigger output. The plans for all that are fixed in my head. Then we come to the market for our stuff, an' I guess that's the syrup in the pie. The world's market's waitin' on us. It's ours before we start. Why? Our power don't cost us one cent a unit. We're able to hand our folks a standard of living through the nature of things that leaves wages easy. The river's wide, and full, and it's *our own*. Then our sea passage to Europe's just eighteen hundred miles instead of three thousand. An' these things mean our costs leave us cutting right under other folks, and Skandinavia beat. There it is," he cried, with a wide gesture of his knotted hands. "It's pie!"

Something of the lumberman's enthusiasm found reflection in Sternford's eyes.

"But Nature's handed us a lemon in the basket of oranges," Bat went on, with a shake of his head. "It's that woman in her again. Y'see, she gives us just four months in the year to get our stuff out. Oh, she don't freeze the cove right up. No. That's the tough of it. The channel's mostly open. But storm, and fog, and ice, beats the ocean-going skipper's power to navigate it with any sort o' safety. The headlands are desperate narrow, and—well, there it is. We've four months in the year to get our stuff out. It's a sum. Figger it yourself. Set us goin' full. Six thousand tons in the week. What is it? Three hundred thousand in the year. How many trips at ten thousand tons? Or put the average tonnage lower. Say eight thousand. Forty trips. Four months. A vessel making two trips on an average turn round. We need a fleet of twenty 'bottoms,' to do it in the time. And they'll need to be our own. You can't help yourself to the world's market, and fix prices, and all the while fight for shipping in the open market. See?"

"Sure—I see."

Bat nodded approval.

"When we get that the rest can go through. Meanwhile there's sixty grinders idle, which leaves us workin' half capacity. As it stands it's a dandy enterprise. We're making a swell balance sheet. But profit ain't the whole purpose. There's the rest."

The super lumber-jack turned again to the window with that fascination that was almost pathetic.

"And the rest?"

Bull Sternford urged the other sharply, and Bat turned at once.

"Canada's groundwood for the Canadian, inside the Empire," he shot at him.

The other nodded.

"The world's market for the country that can and should supply it," he replied.

"The smashing of the darn Skandinavian ring," cried Bat, his deep-set eyes alight.

"And drive them—back over the sea."

Bat suddenly leant across the table.

"That's it, boy," he cried. "That's it! Hellbeam and all his gang. The Skandinavia Corporation. Smash 'em! Drive 'em to Hell! It ain't profit. It's the trade. The A'mighty made Canada an' built the Canadian. He set him right here to help himself to the things He gave him. It's being filched by these foreigners—his birthright. They're fat on it. Did we fight the world war for that? Not by a darn sight. We fought to hold a place on the map for ourselves. And that's a proposition we've all got to get our back teeth into."

"It sure is."

The mill manager sat back in his chair and chewed vigorously.

"That's it," he said. "How?" he went on. "Combination. Finance—and the interest of the little, great old country across the water. It's all planned and laid out by the feller that started up this proposition. It's scheduled for you. Guess you'll find the last word of it writ out in the locked book in this desk. It's clear and straight for the feller with the nerve. That's you. Wal?"

Bat was watching—searching. He was looking for that flicker of an eyelid he had learned to dread in the past. But he failed to discover it. The wide, clear eyes of the younger man returned his regard unwaveringly. The uncultured lumberman had stirred a responsive enthusiasm, and somehow the project no longer seemed the crazy thing it had once appeared to Bull Sternford.

"Guess my back teeth have got it," he said, with a smile. "You needn't worry I'll let go."

Bat drew a deep breath. He stood up and spat his mangled chew into the cuspidore.

"I'm glad. I'm real glad," he cried. "I'm a heap more glad you told me those words without askin' the other things you need to know. But you got to know 'em right away. Say, the day that fixes up the things we been talkin' sees you with me and another masters of this mill an' all it means. And while you're playin' your hand there's one big fat salary for you to draw. This house and office is yours, an' me an' the mill's ready to do all we know all the time, just the way you need it. Down in Abercrombie there's the attorney, Charles Nisson, who's got the outfit of papers that you're goin' to sign. And when you seen him, why you'll get busy. Shake, boy," he cried, thrusting out one knotted hand. "Father Adam sent you, and I don't guess he's made any mistake."

Bull had risen, and his height left him towering over the man across the table.

"Now for the mill," he cried, as their hands fell apart. "The *Myra* sails sundown to-morrow and I need to get a swift look around before then. Say, you folk have kind of taken me on a chance—well, that's all right. I'm glad."

CHAPTER IV
DRAWING THE NET

Nathaniel Hellbeam was contemplating the spiral of smoke rising from his long cigar. He was dreaming pleasantly. He was dreaming of those successful manipulations of finance it was his purpose to achieve. He had lunched, so his dream was of the things which most appealed.

In the midst of his reflections the drub of the muffled telephone beat its insistent tattoo. His dream vanished, and his senses became alert. He leant forward in his chair and picked up the receiver.

"Yes," he said shortly. And it sounded more like the Teutonic, "Ja!"

Putting up the receiver again he leant his clumsy body back in his chair. His small eyes no longer contained their dreaming light. They were turned expectantly upon the polished mahogany door.

The door swung silently open.

"Mr. Idepski!" The announcement was made in a carefully modulated tone.

The agent passed into the great man's presence, slim, dark, confident. Then the door closed without a sound.

"Well?"

There was no cordiality in the greeting. That was not Hellbeam's way with a paid agent.

Idepski walked across to the chair always waiting to receive a visitor and sat down.

"May I sit?" he inquired coolly, after the operation had been performed.

Hellbeam nodded.

"Well?" he repeated.

The agent laid his hat on the ornate desk, and removed his gloves with care and deliberation.

"I'm just back from Sachigo," he said.

"Hah!"

The financier settled himself more comfortably in his chair, and returned his cigar to his gross mouth.

"Tell me," he demanded.

"Easy. Things are moving our way."

The dark eyes glanced over the table for the gold cigarette box that always stood there.

"Help yourself," the banker ordered rather than invited.

Idepski needed no second bidding.

"You got all my code messages?" he asked. "Good," as the Swede nodded. "Then you know the position of the mill. Say, that feller Harker needs a sort of apology from me—also from you. The mill's a wonder. And he's the guy that's fixed it that way. You haven't a thing in Skandinavia comparable. I'd say you haven't a feller on your side capable of touching the fringe of that tough's genius for organisation. It's him. Not Martin—I mean Standing."

"And Standing?"

But Idepski was not to be deflected from his purpose.

"That's all right," he said easily. "I'm coming to him presently. I gave you, at times, the whole length and breadth, and size, and capacity of the Sachigo of to-day. You got all that stuff. But I've saved up the plum. There's a new man come into it. His name's Sternford—Bull Sternford. Guess it's him I need to tell you about before I pass on to the other. It's taken me a while to locate all I needed. And I guess I had luck or I wouldn't have got it all yet."

For once the man's smile reached his eyes.

"What's his position—in Sachigo?" Hellbeam demanded.

"Right on top of the business side of it."

"A financial man?"

The banker's interest was obviously stirred. But Idepski shook his dark head.

"That's the queer of it," he said. "He's a youngster straight out of the forest with no sort of record except as a pretty tough fighting proposition. Here, let me hand it to you in my own way, and I'll answer any sort of question after. I got men chasing up the forest camps. You know that. Well, I get their reports right here in this city at my office. They're read carefully, and anything that looks good is coded, and sent on to me wherever I am. Well, right after I located this feller, Sternford, coming into Sachigo, I got word of some stuff reported from one of your own camps way out northwest of Lake St. Anac. Guess it's about the farthest north in that direction, and it's cut off from any other camp by a hundred miles. On the face of it the stuff didn't seem to need more than a single thought. It was to say my man was quitting the camp. He'd sifted it right through, but there wasn't a 'jack' in the camp with any sort of story worth wasting paper on. There wasn't a trace of our man that way, and he proposed drawing another cover. At the end of his report was one of those notes these boys never seem able to resist mixing up with their official work. It told me of one of those scraps that happened in the camps, and he seemed mighty struck by it. It was between the camp boss, Arden Laval, and a kid called Sternford. Say, when I read that name I jumped. I felt like handing my feller promotion right away. Well, his story was good anyway. It seems this camp boss is about the biggest bluff in the scrap way known to that country. The kid licked him. They fought nearly two hours, 'rough and tough.' And the kid would have killed his man, but for the interference of a missionary feller called Father Adam. He broke 'em loose with a gun, and when he got 'em loose he took the kid right away so he shouldn't hand out the homicide he reckoned to. This report was more than two months old when I got it. Anyway I got it after a feller called Bull Sternford, a queer name by the way, had jumped in on the Sachigo proposition."

The agent flung away his cigarette and helped himself afresh.

"Well," he went on, smiling, "I guess it didn't take me thinking five seconds. I set the wires humming asking a description of this fighting kid. I got it. It was my man. The feller at Sachigo. Well?"

Idepski's smiling interrogation was full of satisfaction.

"Go on." The watchful eyes of the financier seemed to have narrowed.

"Now, by what chance does this feller, Bull Sternford, come straight from one hell of a scrap in a far-off camp belonging to Skandinavia to run the business end of Sachigo? What happened after that fool missionary got him away? And—"

Idepski broke off, pondering. He flicked his cigarette ash without regard for the carpet.

Hellbeam stirred in his chair impatiently. His lips seemed to become more prominent. His small eyes seemed to become smaller.

"You ask that, yes? You?" he snorted. "A child may answer that thing. You think? Oh, yes, you think." The hand supporting his cigar made a gesture that implied everything disparaging. "Our man—this Martin—has gone out of Sachigo because—of you? I tell you, no! Does a man give up the money, the big plan he makes, at the sight of an—agent? He took you in his hand and sent you to the swine life of the forest where he could have crushed you like that." He gripped the empty air. "Then he goes—where? You say he fears and quits. What does he fear? You?" The man shook his head till his cheeks were shaken by the violence of his movement. "He goes somewhere. But he does not quit. That is clear. Oh, yes. The mill goes on. It grows and prospers. The man Harker remains. Where comes the money for Sachigo to grow? Trade? Yes, some. But not all. I know these things. The mill goes on—the same as with Martin there. So Martin does not quit. He—just goes. Then who sets this Bull Sternford in the mill? Why? He says, 'This man can do the things I need.' Well? Say quick to your man, 'Do not leave this camp of Skandinavia.' Martin is there, or near by. He must know this Father Adam, too. He must be in touch with him. Maybe he watches the Skandinavia work. Maybe he plays his game so. Maybe he goes from Sachigo for that reason. Yes?"

The financier's undisguised contempt left the agent apparently undisturbed.

"That's the simple horse sense of it," Idepski retorted promptly. "I get all that. But you're wrong when you say, Martin's playing any other game than lying low because of one hell of a scare. I know him. You think you know him because you can't get away from judging a man from your end. However, that don't matter a shuck. I've told that man of mine to stop around. Don't worry. I told him that right away. I told him to watch this missionary." He shook his head. "Nothing doing. The missionary has quit. As I said, I'm right back from Sachigo. I didn't come back just to hand you this stuff. I'm on my way up to this camp of yours. We've been hunting this guy eight years—blind. Now there's a streak of daylight. I'm going for that streak myself. Anyway, it's liable to be pleasanter work than lumbering in the booms at Sachigo, and wondering when that feller Bat Harker, was going to locate me through a lumber-jack's outfit. And while I'm up there I mean to learn all I can of this Father Adam. I don't look for much that way. He's just a missioner that every feller in the forest's got a good word for, and anyway, it don't seem to me the feller who jumped in on you, and touched your bank roll is the sort to pass his time handlin' out tracts to the bums of the forest. I came in on my way to pass you these things. I go north again to-night. I'll be away quite a while, and, shut off up there, you'll not be likely to get word easy. But you'll hear things when I've got anything to hand you."

A sardonic light crept into Hellbeam's eyes as he listened to the final assurance.

"So," he ejaculated with a nod.

The agent rose to go.

"Meanwhile," he said, leaning over the desk, "it might be well for you to get a grip on the fact that Sachigo's going right on. It's the greatest groundwood proposition in the world. I know enough of Harker to realise his capacity to make it do just what he needs. And as for that other—this Sternford kid—why, I gather he's a pretty live wire that's set there for a reason. The slogan up there's much what it was, only the words are changed."

Hellbeam sucked his cigar and removed it from his lips.

"Changed? How?" he demanded, without suspicion.

"It was 'Canadian trade for the Canadians,'" Idepski said, his dark eyes snapping maliciously. "It's more personal since the fighting kid came along. It reminds me of the German slogans of the war. It's 'To hell with the Swedes, we'll drive 'em *into* the sea.'"

The financier nodded. His armour was impenetrable.

"The Germans said much," he said.

"That's all right, these folks aren't Germans," came the prompt retort, as Idepski picked up his hat and gloves.

"No." Hellbeam remained seated. It was not his way to speed a departing visitor. "I'm glad. Oh, yes." He smiled into the other's face, and his meaning was obvious. "You go to this camp. You find this missionary. That's work for you. The other—" his eyes dropped to the papers on the desk before him—"this mill, this Sachigo is for me. It is much nearer to the sea than the Skandinavia. Oh, yes."

CHAPTER V
THE PROGRESS OF NANCY

The girl reached out a hand in response to the ring of the telephone. It was slim and white; and her finger nails displayed that care which suggests a healthy regard for the niceties of a woman's life.

"Hullo! Yes?"

She remained silently intent upon the rapidly spoken message coming down to her over the wire. Her deep, hazel eyes were soberly regarding the blotting pad, upon which an idle pencil was describing a number of meaningless diagrams.

"Yes," she replied, after a while. "Oh, yes. All reports are in. I've gone through them all, and my summary is being prepared now. They're a pretty bad story. Yes. What's that? How? Oh, yes. Some of the camps are in pretty bad shape, I'd say. Output's fallen badly. Output! Yes. All sorts of reasons and—" she laughed, "—to me, none quite satisfactory. I think I've my finger on the real trouble, and fancy I've seen all this coming quite a while back. Very well. I'll be right up. Yes, I'll bring my rough notes if the summary isn't ready."

Nancy McDonald thrust the receiver back in its place and sat for a moment gazing at it. She knew she had committed herself. She had intended to. She knew that she had reached one of the important milestones in her career. In her youth, in the springtime energy abounding in her, she meant to pit her opinion against the considered policy of those who formed the management of the great Skandinavia Corporation she served. She understood her temerity. A surge of nervous anticipation thrilled her. But she was resolved. Her ambition was great, and her youthful courage was no less.

The brazen clack of typewriters beyond the glass partitions of her little private office left her unaffected. It was incessant. She would have missed it had it not been there. She would have lost that sense of rush which the tuneless chorus of modern commercialism inspired. And, to a woman of her temperament, that would have been a very real loss.

The great offices of the Skandinavia Corporation, in the heart of the city of Quebec, with their machine-like precision of life, their soulless method, their passionless progress towards the purpose of their organisation, meant the open road towards the fulfilment of her desires for independence and achievement.

All the promise of her earlier youth had been abundantly fulfilled. Tall, gracious of figure, her beauty had a charm and dignity which owed almost as much to mentality as it did to physical form. Yet, for all she had already passed her twenty-fourth birthday, she was amazingly innocent of those things which are counted as the governing factors of a woman's life. Certainly she knew and loved the Titian hue of her wealth of hair; her mirror was constantly telling her of the hazel depths of her wide, intelligent eyes, with their fringes of dark, curling, Celtic lashes. Then the almost classic moulding of her features. She could not escape realising these things. But they meant no more to her than the fact that her nose was not awry, and her lips were not misshapen, and her even, white teeth were perfectly competent for their proper function.

She was a happy blending of soul and mentality. Heredity seemed to have done its best for her. The Gaelic fire and the brilliance and irresponsibility of her misguided father seemed to have been balanced and tempered by the gentle woman soul of her mother. And through the eyes of both she gazed out upon the world, inspired and supported by a tireless nervous energy.

Since the memorable day of her interview with her appointed trustee, Charles Nisson, her development had been rapid. The events which had suddenly been flung into her life at the interview seemed to have unloosed a hundred latent, unguessed emotions in her child heart, and translated her at once into a thinking, high-spirited woman.

She honestly strove to banish bitterness against the man who had deprived her of that mother love which had been her childhood's treasure, but always a shadow of it remained to colour her thought, and influence her impulse. She had studied the deed of settlement as she had promised. She had studied it coldly, dispassionately. She had looked upon it as a mere document aimed to benefit her, without regard for her feelings for the man who had made it. She had thought over it at night when passion was less to be controlled. She had consulted those she had been bidden to consult, and had listened to, and had weighed their kindly advice. And when all was done she took her own decision as she was bound to do. It was a decision that had no relation to reason, only to passionate impulse.

She would not accept the things the deed offered her. She would not accept this reparation so coldly held out. She would not live a leisured, vegetable life, with no greater ambition than to marry and bear children. The simple prospect of marriage and motherhood could never satisfy in itself. That would be a happy incident, but not the whole, and acceptance of that deed would surely have robbed her of the rest.

There were times when she felt the disabilities of her sex. She knew she was deprived of the physical strength which the battle of life seemed to demand. But to her the world was wide, and big, and, in her girl's imagination, teeming with appealing adventure. The world alone could not satisfy her.

Once her decision was taken all the kindly efforts of her mentors at Marypoint were rallied in her support. They had advised out of their wisdom, but acted from their hearts. And the day on which the principal of the college notified her that the Skandinavia Corporation of Quebec had signified its willingness to absorb her into its service as typist and stenographer, at one hundred dollars per month, was the happiest she had known since her well-loved mother had been taken out of her life.

Now, after three years of unwearying effort, there was still no shadow to mar her happiness, or temper her enthusiasm. On the contrary, there was much to stimulate both. In that brief period she had succeeded almost beyond her dreams. Was she not already the trusted, confidential secretary to the ruling power in the great offices of the Skandinavia Corporation? Had she not been taken out of the ranks of the many capable stenographers, and been given a private office, a doubled salary, and work to do which left her wide scope for the play of those gifts with which she was so liberally endowed? Yes. All these things had been showered upon her in three years. She was a figure of authority in the great establishment. And furthermore, the man she served—this man, Elas Peterman—had hinted, and even definitely talked of, further rapid promotion.

She had worked hard for it all. Oh, yes. She had worked morning, noon, and night. When other girls had been content to study fashions and styles, and chatter "beaus" and husbands, she had given herself up to the study of the wood-pulp trade, and the world's market of the material she was interested in. She had saturated herself with the whole scheme, and purpose, and methods of her employers, till, as Peterman himself had once told her in admiration at her grasp of the business, she knew as much of the trade as he did himself. And even after that her mirror, that oracle of a woman's life, failed to yield her the real truth it is always ready to tell to its devotees.

The pre-occupation suddenly passed out of the girl's eyes. She stirred. Then she stood up and collected a number of papers into a small leather attaché case. A moment later she pressed the bell push on the desk.

Her summons was promptly answered by a slim figured girl, with fair hair, and "jumpered" in the latest style.

"I shall be away a while. See to the 'phone, Miss Webster," Nancy said, in a tone of quiet but definite authority. "I shall be with Mr. Peterman. Don't ring me unless it's something important. That summary. Is it ready?"

"It's being checked right now."

"Well, speed them up. You can send it up directly it's through. Mr. Peterman is needing it."

Nancy passed out of the room. Her discipline was strict. Sometimes it approached severity. But she understood its necessity for obtaining results. Her orders would be carried out.

Elas Peterman set the 'phone back in its place. His dark eyes were smiling. They were shining, too, in a curious, not altogether wholesome fashion. He had just finished talking to Nancy McDonald, and he was thinking of the vision of red hair, of the serious hazel eyes gazing out of their setting of fair, almost transparent complexion.

He took up his pen to continue the letter he had been writing. But he added no word. The girl he had been speaking with still occupied his thoughts to the exclusion of all else.

He was a good-looking man, clean cut and youthful. His profile was finely chiselled. But his Teutonic origin was clearly marked. It was in the straight square back of his head. It was in the prominent, heavily, rounded chin, and the squareness of his lower jaw. Furthermore, the high, mathematical forehead was quite unmistakable. There was power, force, in the personality of the man. But there was something else. It lay in his mouth, in his eyes. The former was gross, and definite sensuality looked out of the latter.

As the door opened to admit Nancy his pen promptly descended on his paper. But he did not write. He looked up with a smile.

"Come right in, my dear," he said cordially, with the patronising familiarity of a man conscious of his power. "Just sit right down while I finish this letter." Then he added gratuitously, "It's a rude letter to a feller I've no use for; and I don't guess to rob myself of the pleasure of passing it plenty to him—in my own handwriting."

Nancy smiled as she took the chair beside the desk which was usually assigned to her in her intercourse with her chief.

"I wish I felt that way writing a bad letter," she said. "But I don't. It just makes me madder with folks, and I go right on thinking things, and—and—it worries."

Elas Peterman shook his head.

"Guess you'll get over that, my dear," he said easily. "Sure you will. You're just a dandy-minded kid, learning the things of life. You feel good most all the time. That's how it is. You want to laff and see things happy all around you. Later you'll get so you see the other feller mostly thinks of himself, and don't care a hoot for the folks sitting around. Then you'll feel different; and you'll tell folks you don't like the things you feel about them."

He went on writing, smiling at his own cynicism.

Nancy leant back in her chair. His words left her unaffected. She was used to him. But, for a moment, she contemplated the dark head, supported on his hand, without any warmth of regard.

After awhile she glanced away, her gaze wandering over the luxurious furnishings of the room. And it occurred to her to wonder how much, if any, of the excellent taste of the decorations owed inception to the man at the desk. No. Not much. The cheque-book and the decorator's artist must have been responsible. This grossly Teutonic creature with his cynical, commercial mind, was something of an anachronism, and could never have inspired the perfect harmony of the palatial offices of his Corporation. It was rather a pity. He had been exceedingly good to her. She would have liked to think that he was the genius of the whole structure of the Skandinavia, even to the decorations of the office. But it was impossible.

The man blotted and folded his letter. He enclosed and sealed it. He even addressed it himself.

"I'm kind of sorry I had to break in on you while you were fixing those reports," he said, in his friendliest fashion. "But, you see, I'm just through with the Board, and we took a bunch of decisions that need handling right away. Tell me," he went on, an ironical light creeping into his smiling eyes, "you reckon you've set your finger on the real trouble with our dropping output. I want to know about it because the Board and I can't be sure we've located it right."

The sarcasm hurt. It was not intended to. Elas Peterman had no desire in the world to hurt this girl. A cleverer man would have avoided it. But this man had no refinement of thought or feeling. Cynicism and sarcasm were his substitutes for a humour he did not possess.

Nancy's cheeks flushed hotly. But she stifled her feelings. She was confident of herself, and despite the manner of the challenge, she knew the moment of her great opportunity had come.

With a quick movement she crossed her knees and leant forward. She smiled in response.

"Yet, it's easy," she said boldly, with bland retaliation. "The reports are not good. And the trouble stands out clear as daylight. I guess a big scale contour map is the key to it. We've 'hand-weeded' the Shagaunty Valley. It's picked bare to the bone. The folks have cleared the forests right away to the higher slopes of the river. We're moving farther and farther away from the river highway. Well, that's all right in its way. Ordinarily that would just mean our light railways are extending farther, and a few cents more are added to our transport costs. Owing to our concentration of organisation that wouldn't signify. No. It's Nature, it's the forest itself turning us down. And the map, and the reports show that. The camps are right out on the plateau surrounding the valley, which is unprotected from winter storms. The close, luxurious growth of the valley we have been accustomed to is gone. The standing cordage of lumber is no less, only in bulk, girth. The trees are mostly less than half the girth. The result? Why, they have to work farther out. Each camp cuts over four times the area. Instead of a proportion of, say, two trees in five, it's about one in, say, ten. It looks like a simple sum. I should say we've lumbered that valley at least one season too long."

The man's smile had passed. There was no longer derision in his keen eyes. He had invited this girl's talk for the sake of hearing it. Now he was caught in admiration of her clear perception.

"Do the reports bear out those facts?"

His question was sharp, and Nancy realised she had done well.

She shook her head.

"No. They do just the thing you'd expect them to do," she said. "They make every sort of excuse that couldn't possibly account for the drop. And avoid the real cause which their writers are perfectly aware of." She shrugged her pretty shoulders. "You wouldn't expect it otherwise. You want to remember those reports are written by bosses who're more interested in their own comfort than in the affairs of the Skandinavia."

"How?"

Again the girl's expressive shrug.

"To quit the Shagaunty and break new ground means the break up of those amenities and comforts they've accumulated in years. It means work, real hard work, and discomfort for at least two seasons. You see, we need to get into the skin of these folk. They can keep the booms full from these forests, and the kick only comes when the grinders get to work. Output falls automatically with the girth of the lumber sent down. It's a close calculation; but on the year it means a lot. I learned that from Mr. Osbert, at the mills on the Shagaunty. Well, so long as the booms are kept full, the camp bosses are satisfied. There's a limit below which the girth of logs may not go. They watch that limit, and are careful not to go below it. Well, our big output has been made up always, not by the minimum logs, but the maximum to which we have been hitherto accustomed. These boys know all about that; but they're satisfied with such bulk as doesn't fall below the minimum. And when asked, suggest fire, storm and sickness, anything rather than the real cause which drops our output. They'll not willingly face the discomfort and added work of opening a new territory. There's just one decision needed."

"What's that?"

The girl laughed. It was a low, pleasant, happy laugh. She felt glad. Her chief was serious. He was in deadly earnest, and it represented her revenge for his sarcasm.

"We've five other rivers running down to the lake. The Shagaunty isn't even the largest. Well, these boys will have to be shaken out of their dream. We ought to quit the Shagaunty right away and make a break for fresh 'limits.' It's simple."

The man had no responsive smile. He shook his head.

"That's what it isn't, my dear," he said.

For the time the girl's beauty, her personality were quite forgotten. Peterman was absorbed.

"It means the complete dislocation of our forest organisation," he went on. "Here, I'll tell you something. We've done a very great thing in the past. And it's been easy. Years ago we decided by concentration of all our forest work on a limited area we could cut costs to the lowest. That way we could jump in on the market cheaper than all the rest. Our forest limits were the finest in Canada. We had standing stuff practically inexhaustible, and of a size almost unheard of. What was the result? Why, one by one we've absorbed competitors at our own price till the Skandinavia stands head and shoulders above the world's groundwood industry. That's all right. That's fine," he went on, after a pause. "But like most easy trails, you're liable to keep on 'em longer than is good for you. We haven't had to worry a thing up to now. You see, we'd stifled competition, and we'd paid a steady thirty per cent dividend. Which left our Board in an unholy state of dope. I've tried to wake 'em. Oh, yes. I tried when that guy started up his outfit on Labrador. The Sachigo outfit. Then he seemed to fade away, and I couldn't rouse 'em again." He shook his head—"Nothing doing. Well, for something like fifteen years those guys of Sachigo have been doing and working; and now, to-day, they've jumped into the market with both feet. I haven't the full measure of things yet. But the play's a big thing. They're out for the game we've been playing. Say, they're combining every old mill we've left over. All the derelicts and moth-bounds. Their hands are out grabbing all over the country. Well, that wouldn't scare me worth a cent, only they've never let up in fifteen years, and there's talk about big British finance getting behind 'em."

The man broke off. His serious eyes remained steadily regarding the girl's interested face.

"You reckon this change is easy," he went on again. "I guess it would be easy if these folk hadn't jumped into the market. That makes all the difference. While we're changing they're busy. Their stuff's coming down in thousands of tons. And it's *better* groundwood than ours. If we change over we're going to leave the market short and these folk will get big contracts. You're right. We've been working the Shagaunty too long. But it's been by three or four seasons. Not one. The time's coming, if it hasn't already come, when we've got to fight these folks and smash 'em; or get right out of business."

Something of the girl's joy had passed in face of the man's statement.

"There's been talk of these Sachigo folk in the trade," she said thoughtfully, "but I didn't know it was as big as you say. Of course—"

"Sure you didn't. You haven't had to handle our stuff on the market." The man laughed. And something of his seriousness passed. "But you're a bright kid. And the Skandinavia's looking for bright kids all the time. It needs 'em to counter a doped Board. It's taken you five minutes to locate a trouble the Board's taken years to realise. And you've been talking one of the bunch of decisions we've taken. I mean quitting the Shagaunty. We didn't have your argument, but we had the 'drop.' So the decision was taken. We've got to move like hell. Sachigo has our measure, and it's going to be a big fight. How'd you fancy a trip up country? I mean up the Shagaunty?"

There was a change in the man's voice and manner as he put his demand. He was leaning forward in his chair. A hot light had suddenly leapt into his eyes, which left them shining unwholesomely. Nancy was startled at his words. And his attitude shocked her not a little out of her self-satisfaction.

"I don't know—. How do you mean?" she demanded awkwardly.

The man realised her astonishment and laughed. Then he reached out, and his hand patted the rounded shoulder nearest him. It was a touch that lingered unnecessarily, and the girl stirred restlessly under it.

"Why, it's the chance of a life—for you," he said boisterously. "You'll go right up through the camps. You'll take your notions with you and investigate. I'll hand you a written commission, and the folk'll lay their 'hands' down for you to see. When you've seen it all you'll get right back here, and I'll set you before the Board to tell your story. I don't need to tell a bright girl like you what that means to you. You'll get one dandy summer trip, and I'll lose one dandy secretary. But I'm not kicking. No. You see, Nancy, I'm out to help you all you need. Well?"

It was crude, clumsy. It was all so blatantly vulgar. It was not the thing he said. It was the manner of it and all that which was lying unspoken behind.

For the first time Nancy experienced a curious uncertainty in dealing with him. But here was real opportunity. She had dreamed of such. And she must take it. The touch of the man's hand upon her shoulder had disturbed her. But she smiled her gratitude at him.

"It's too good," she exclaimed, with apparent impulse. "It's just too good of you. Will I go? Why, yes. Surely. And I'll make good for you. I believe it's the best thing. Someone to go who'll bring back a dead right story. I'd be real glad."

"That's bully!" The man beamed as he leant back in his chair more than satisfied with himself. "But I don't fancy losing my dandy secretary," he went on. "No, sir. I'm going to hate this summer bad. I surely am. Still, there's next winter. Winter's not too bad with us. And a feller needs consolation in winter. There's theatres, and ice parties, and dances, and things. And I guess when the Board's fixed a big jump up for you, you'll feel like getting around some. Well, I'm mostly vacant. A feller can't live all the time at home with his wife and kids. I guess I could show you Quebec at night better than most—"

The telephone saved Nancy the rest of the man's rendering of his account and she breathed deeply her relief. But the interruption was by no means welcome to the man. And his irritation was promptly displayed by the vindictive "Well?" he flung at the unyielding receiver.

"Oh! What's that? Who? Hellbeam? Oh. Sure. Yes. Send him right up. Don't keep him waiting. Right up now. Yes."

He thrust up the instrument and sat back in his chair.

"Curse the man!"

Nancy had risen from her chair at the mention of Hellbeam's name. She was glad enough of the excuse. She understood Hellbeam was the great outstanding figure in the concern of the Skandinavia. His was the one personality that dwarfed everybody. He was the moving power of the whole concern.

"You'll let me know later?" she said. "I mean, just when I'm to start out. I'm ready when you like. I'll just go and see why those reports have not been sent up."

"Oh, don't worry with the reports. You've told me the things that matter."

The man's irritation was as swift as it was violent. But it passed as quickly as it came. He laughed.

"That's all right, my dear. Be off now. I'll let you know about things this afternoon."

Nancy gladly accepted her dismissal. She wanted to think. She wanted to get things into their proper focus. As she closed the door behind her her beautiful eyes had no joy in them. She had realised two things as a result of her interview. The opportunity she had looked forward to had materialised, and she had seized it with both hands. But the goodness of Elas Peterman to herself possessed none of that disinterested kindliness she had hitherto believed. Furthermore, there was dawning upon her that which her mirror should have told her long ago. She was beginning to understand that her work, her capacity, her application, counted far less in the favour of her chief than did those things with which nature had equipped her. She was shocked out of her youthful dream. And it left her so troubled, that, had she not been passing down the carpeted corridor of the Skandinavia offices, she would have burst into a flood of tears.

It was a different Elas Peterman who confronted the squat figure of Nathaniel Hellbeam. The master in the younger man was completely submerged. He possessed all the Teutonic capacity for self-abnegation in the presence of the power it is necessary to woo. There was only one master when the great financier was present. Elas Peterman knew that his part was to listen and obey with just that humility which he would have demanded had the position been reversed.

Another type than Hellbeam's would have despised the attitude. But the financier had no scruple. Nature had denied him qualities for inspiring affectionate regard, or even respect. But she had bestowed on him a lust for power, and a great vanity, and these he satisfied to the uttermost.

The financier drove straight to the object of his visit.

"I come for an important purpose," he said, in his guttural fashion. "There must be a special Board assemble. Skandinavia will buy the mill on Labrador. The Sachigo mill. I come on the night train, which is the worst thing I can think to do, to say this thing. If we do not buy this mill, then—" He broke off with an expressive gesture.

Elas nodded. He was startled, but his powers of dissimulation were profound.

"I understand," he said. "They have been approached?"

Hellbeam stirred his bulk in the chair Nancy had so recently occupied. It was a movement of irritation.

"That is for you. You represent Skandinavia. I—I say this thing. I the money find."

The face of Peterman was a study. His eyes were serious, his manner calmly considering. Amazement was struggling with a desire to laugh outright in the face of this grossly insolent money power.

"Nothing could suit us better, sir," he said, deferentially. "They've been handing us more trouble than I fancy talking about. And they look like handing us still more. These people have grown slowly, but very deliberately. There's something very like genius in their management. And seemingly they possess unlimited capital or credit. I guess I know something of their contemplated manoeuvres. They're assembling all the free mills outside our ring. I see a great big scrap coming. May I ask the price you're considering?"

Hellbeam produced a gold cigar case. A greater man would have been content with a certain modesty of appointment. His case was comparable in vulgarity with the size of his cigars. He thrust the pierced end of the cigar between his gross lips and spoke with the huge thing lolling.

"It does not matter. I say buy."

The tone, the snapping of the man's eyes forbade further probing in this direction. He lit his cigar.

"It will need careful handling," ventured Peterman.

Hellbeam snorted.

"It careful handling always needs. Eh?"

"Surely. I was thinking."

"So. You will think. Then you will act. You will communicate forthwith. See? You listen. I buy this Sachigo, yes. The price matters nothing. There is a reason. This fight. It is not that. Who is the head? I would know. I fancy this man to meet. He is what you call—bright. So."

Elas shook his head-

"There are two men in it we recognise. A man named Harker and another called Sternford—Bull Sternford. We know little of either. You see, it's kind of far away. Anyway, between them they're pretty—bright. I don't think they built the mill. I'm sure that's so. It was a man called Standing. But he seems to have gone out of active management. I might start by writing them and feel the way."

"Ach no!" Hellbeam shook his head in violent protest. "You write—no. You have your confidential man, yes? You send him. I give you the outline of terms. I give you alternative terms. Big terms. He will go. He will talk. He will hear. Then we will later come to terms. All men will sell—on terms. Your man. Where is he? I must see him. Then the Board. It meets. I will address it. I show them how this thing will serve."

"That's all right, sir," Elas was smiling. "You couldn't offer the Board a more welcome proposition than the purchase of Sachigo just now. We're changing our forest organisation right now, and that means temporary delays and drop in output. Sachigo's our worry while we're doing it. But with your permission I won't send a man up there. I think," he added deliberately, "I'd like to send a—woman."

Hellbeam's face was a study. His little eyes opened to their widest extent. His heavy lips parted, and he snatched his cigar into the safety of his white fingers.

"A—woman—for this thing? You crazy are!"

There was no restraint or pretence of restraint. The other's smile was more confident than might have been expected before such an intolerant outburst.

"Guess a woman has her limitations, sir. Maybe this one hasn't a wide experience. But she's clever. She's loyal to us, and she's got that which counts a whole heap when it comes to getting a man on her side. You reckon to buy Sachigo. If you send a man to deal he'll get short shrift. If there's anyone to put through this deal for Skandinavia it's the woman I'm thinking of. And she'll put it through because she's the woman she is, and not because of any talents. Your pardon, sir, if I speak frankly. But from all I know of Sachigo, if you—perhaps the king of financiers on this continent—went to these folk and offered them double what their enterprise is worth, I guess they'd chase you out of Labrador so quick you wouldn't have time to think the blasphemy suitable to the occasion."

Peterman's explanation caught the humour of his countryman. The bulk of the visitor shook under a suppressed laugh.

"Well," he retorted, "I do not go. This woman. A good-looker, eh? She is pleasant—to men? Where is she? Who is she?"

"She's my secretary, sir." Elas jumped at the change of his visitor's humour. "She's not much more than a kid. But she's quite a 'looker,' I'll send for her, if you'll permit me. She's getting some reports for me. I'll ask her to bring them up. You can see her then, sir, and, if you'll forgive me, I won't present her to you. If I do she'll guess something, and it's best she knows nothing of this contemplated deal—as regards you."

For a moment the banker made no reply. He sat, an adipose mass, breathing heavily, and sucking at his cigar. Then quite suddenly, he nodded.

"Send for her," he said sharply.

Elas reached the telephone and rang down.

"Hello! That you? Oh, will you step up a moment, Miss McDonald? Yes. Are they ready? Good. That's just what I want. Please. All of them."

Nancy knocked at the door and stepped into the room. She was carrying a large typescript of many pages. It represented many days and evenings of concentrated labour. It had been a labour not so much of love as of ambition. It was an exhaustive summary of the position of the Skandinavia's forestry in the Shagaunty Valley.

She missed the squat figure in the chair she usually occupied. She saw nothing of the stare of the narrow eyes concentrated upon her. She saw only the tall figure of Peterman, standing waiting for her beyond his desk in such a position that, to reach him, she must pass herself in review before the devouring gaze of the great banker.

She walked briskly towards him, her short skirt yielding the seductive rustle of the silk beneath it. Her movements were beyond words in grace. Her tall figure, so beautifully proportioned, and so daintily rounded, displayed the becoming coat-frock she usually wore in business to absolute perfection.

The banker's searching eyes realised all this to the last detail. He realised much more. For his was the regard that sought beneath the surface of things. It was that regard which every wholesome, good woman resents. But ultimately it was the girl's face and hair that held him. The rare beauty of the latter's colour sent a surge of appreciation running through his sensual veins. And the perfect beauty, and delicate charm of her pretty features, stirred him no less. Only her eyes, those pretty, confident, intelligent, hazel depths he missed. But he waited.

"These are the papers, Mr. Peterman."

Nancy held out the typescript to the waiting man whose eyes had none of the smiling welcome they would have had in Hellbeam's absence.

"Thank you." Elas glanced down at the neatly bound script.

"It's all complete?"

"Oh, yes. It's the whole story. It's in tabloid form. You will be able to take the whole close in half an hour."

A rough clearing of the throat interrupted her, and Nancy discovered the banker beside the desk. In something of a hurry she promptly turned to depart. But Elas claimed her.

"Will you come to me after lunch?" he said pleasantly.

"I want to go into the details of that trip I explained to you. You must get away as soon as possible."

"Directly after lunch?"

"Yes. Say three o'clock."

"Very well."

The girl again turned to go, but the banker anticipated her. As she reached the door he stood beside it, and opened it for her to pass out. He was holding something in his hand. It was an exquisitely formed gold fountain-pen.

"This yours is, I think," he said heavily, while his eyes searched those depths of hazel he had missed before.

The girl smiled as she gazed at the beautiful pen. She shook her head.

"No," she said. "I never possessed anything so beautiful in my life."

"But you drop it as you come, I think, yes?" The man's eyes were levelled at her devouringly. Quick as thought he turned to Elas watching the scene. "Is it yours? I see it on the carpet, yes?"

The manager was prompt to take his cue.

"It's not mine," he said. "It must be yours, Miss McDonald. If it isn't I guess you'd best have it till we find its owner."

The girl smiled from one to the other.

"Thanks ever so much," she said, with frank pleasure. "I'll keep it till we find the owner. It's a lovely thing."

She took the glittering pen from the fleshy fingers holding it. And just for an instant her hand encountered the banker's. It was only for an instant, however. A moment later the door was closed carefully behind her by the man who had thought Elas crazy to employ a woman.

"Well?"

Elas Peterman was seated behind his desk again. His challenging smile was directed at the heavily breathing figure of the banker who had hurried back to his chair.

The great man laughed. It was a curious, unpleasant laugh. His heavy cheeks were flushed, and his eyes glittered curiously.

"You're a judge, Elas, my boy," he exclaimed, with clumsy geniality. "Oh, yes. But you are a young man. There is power in that young woman's eyes." He laughed again. "Oh, no, I think of the young woman. It not her capability is. See you look to your place in Skandinavia. Let her go. She may not buy this Sachigo as I think to buy it. She will buy the men we would drive from our path."

CHAPTER VI
THE LONELY FIGURE

The girl was leaning against the storm-ripped bole of a fallen tree. The great figure of her companion was silhouetted against the brilliant sky-line. He was contemplating the distance at the brink of a sheer-cut ravine, which dropped away at his feet to giddying depths.

Nancy gazed out beyond him. For the moment he held no interest for her. She only had eyes for the splendid picture of Nature. They were on high ground, a great shoulder lifted them clear above their surroundings. Far as the eye could see was a lustreless green world of unbroken forest. It seemed to have neither beginning nor end. To the girl's imagination there could be no break in it until the eternal snows of the Arctic were reached.

The breadth of it all was a little overwhelming. Nancy was gazing upon just one portion of the Skandinavia's untouched forest limits, and somehow it left her with a feeling of protest.

She pointed with one gauntleted hand, stirred to an impulse she could not deny.

"It's too beautiful," she said. "It isn't fair: it's not right. To think it's all ours, and we have the right to destroy it."

The man turned. He gazed back at this unusual vision of a beautiful, well-gowned woman in the heart of the forests. He grinned ironically, this great, rough-bearded creature, in hard cord clothing, and with his well-worn fur cap pressed low over his lank hair that reached well-nigh to his shoulders.

"Why not?" he demanded roughly. "Oh, yes. It's Skandinavia's, every mile of it. An' I guess there's hundreds an' hundreds of 'em. Ain't that what Canada's forests are for? To feed us the stuff we're needin'? But you don't need to worry any. We ain't cuttin' that stuff for years. Guess the waterways out there are mostly a mean outfit that wouldn't raft a bunch of lucifers. We need to wait permanent railroad for haulage."

Nancy accepted the statement without reply. It was impossible to stir a man like Arden Laval to any sort of sympathy. He was hardened, crude, first, last and all the time. He was big and brutal. His limbs were like to the trees his men were accustomed to fell, and his hands reminded her of the hind limbs of the mutton. She felt he had a mind that matched his physical development.

Nancy McDonald was nearing the end of her third month of forest travel. The Shagaunty valley lay behind her, desolated by the fierce axe of the men who lived by their slaughter. She had seen it all. She had studied the re-afforestation which followed on the heels of the axemen. And the seeming puerility of this effort to salve the wounds inflicted upon Nature had filled her with pitying contempt.

She knew the whole process of the forest industry by heart now. It fascinated her. Oh, yes. It was picturesque, it was real, vital. The men on the river driving down to the booms had stirred her greatest admiration. These supermen with their muscles of iron, with the hearts of lions, and the tongues and habits of beasts of the forest. But they were men, wonderful men for all their savage crudity. So, too, with the transporters and freighters handling sixty-foot logs as though dealing with matchwood. But above all, and before all, the axemen made their appeal.

There was nothing comparable with the rough skill of these creatures, She had watched the flash and swing of the axe, with its edge like the finest razor. She had seen the standing muscles like whipcord writhing under sunburnt flesh as they served the lethal weapon. She had noted every blow, how it was calculated to a hair's-breadth, and fell without waste of one single ounce of power. And then the amazing result. The fallen tree stretched out on the exact spot and in the exact direction ready for the hauliers to bear straight away to the final transport station.

The summer days had been filled with vital interest. And at night, weary in body, Nancy still had time, lying in the amply, if crudely blanketed bed provided for her in some lumber-built shanty, to contemplate the lives of this strangely assorted race. She knew the pay of the forest men, from the haulier to the princely axeman and river-jack. She had seen their food, and their dwelling accommodation. She had heard such details as were possible of telling of their recreations, and had guessed the rest. And for all her admiration of their manhood she pitied, in her woman's way, and felt shame for the slavery of it all.

Oh, yes. She had no illusions. She was not weakly sentimental. She looked at it all with wide-open eyes. It was a well-paid animal life. It was a life of eating well, of sleeping well, of gambling, and drinking, and licence.

But it was a life of such labour that only perfect physical creatures could face.

She felt that these folks were wage slaves in the crudest meaning of the words. There was nothing for them beyond their daily life, which was wholly animal. Of spirituality there was none. Of future there was none. Their leisure was given over to their pastimes, while ahead the future lay always threatening. Stiffening muscles, disease, age. The king of them all in his youth, in age would be abandoned and driven forth, weary in body, aching in limbs, a derelict in the ranks of the world's labour.

She was gravely impressed by the things she saw, by the men she met.

Her summer had been an education which had stirred feelings and sympathies almost unguessed. It was the father, she could scarcely remember, making himself known to her. For all the ambitions firing her, the long, fascinating days in the forests of the Shagaunty had taught her of the existence of an "underdog," who, in himself, was the foundation upon which the personal ambition of the more fortunate was achieved. Without him to support the whole edifice of civilisation must crash to the ground, and life would go back again to the bosom of that Nature from which it sprang.

Her realisation inspired her with an added desire. It was a desire coming straight from an honest, unsophisticated heart. She registered a vow that whithersoever her ambitions might lead her, she would always remember the "underdog," and work for his betterment and greater happiness.

"So you can only cut the stuff here within reach of our light haulage system?" Nancy demanded at last. "The rest's gone. The real big stuff, I mean, down below in the valley. We're just driven to the plateau where the cut looks to me more like one in twenty than any better?"

Arden Laval left his position at the brink of the ravine. He came back to the girl in her modish costume that seemed so out of place beside the rough clothing that Covered his body.

"Why, I guess that's so," he said. "Still, it's a deal better than one in twenty." He laughed. "Sure. If it wasn't the darn booms 'ud need to go hungry."

The man's French temperament left him more than appreciative of the beauty he beheld. But he was wondering. He was searching his shrewd mind for the real explanation of Nancy's presence in these forests. To him it was amazing that the Skandinavia should send this girl, this good-looker, on a journey through their forests alone. He would willingly have asked the question. But he remembered her written commission, signed by Elas Peterman. So he was left with no alternative but to yield the utmost respect.

"Y'see, mam," he went on easily. "I guess I could talk quite a piece on this thing, but maybe you won't fancy my dope. Skandinavia's been badly spoilt by the cut in the Shagaunty Valley. You've seen it all. Guess you've come right through. Well, that being so, you'll understand the Shagaunty cut's been far above average. Now we're down to average. That's all. That's how the Skandinavia's been spoilt."

He thrust his cap back from his forehead. It was a movement of irritation. Then he produced a plug of tobacco from his hip-pocket, and bit off a chew.

"I've been twenty odd years lumbering," he went on a moment later. "I've lumbered most every forest in Ontario and Quebec. "There ain't more'n one bunch of plums like the Shagaunty. Mostly the forest's full of the sort of stuff we're handling here. These forests are average and I'd like to say to the Skandinavia, 'you've got to figger results on the average.' We're cutting down to the minimum because we've got to, to feed the booms right. Well, that's goin' on if I know my job. There's patch stuff better. I daresay there's new ground on our limits liable to hand us Shagaunty stuff. But that's just as I say, patch stuff, an' not average. If they want Shagaunty quality right through let 'em get out and get limits up on Labrador. I reckon there's a hundred years cutting up there that 'ud leave Shagaunty a bunch of weed grass. They say the folks out on the coast are worried to death there's so much stuff, an' so big, an' good, an' soft, an' long-fibred. The jacks out that way are up to the neck in a hell of a good time, sure. I get it they've time to sleep half the year, it's so easy. Well, it ain't that way here. We've no time singing hymns around this lay-out. It's hell, here, keeping the darn booms fed. Speakin' for my outfit I'd say they're a pretty bright lot of boys. What a feller can do they can do, I guess. But there are times I get mighty sick chasing to get even the minimum. An' it's all the time kick. The Skandinavia seems to have got a grouch about now you couldn't beat with a tank of rye whisky. You've seen it all as far as I can show you, mam, and I'd be glad to know if you're satisfied I've done the things you want. If I have, and you feel good about it, I'd be thankful if you'd report the way we're workin' this camp. And if you've a spare moment to talk other things, you might say that the boys of my camp are mighty hard put to get the stuff, and they're as tough a gang of jacks as ever heard tell of the dog's life of the forest."

The man spoke with the fluency of real protest. He somehow felt he was on his defence in the presence of this woman representative of his employers. This girl was not there enduring the discomforts of the forests for amusement. She came with authority, and she seemed to possess great understanding. Arden Laval knew his own value. His record was one of long service with his company. Furthermore, his outfit was trusted with the pioneering work of the forest where judgment and enterprise, and great experience were needed. He felt it was the moment to talk, and to talk straight to this woman with the red hair who had invaded his domain. So he gave full rope to his feelings.

It was some moments before the girl replied, and the man waited expectantly. He was studying the far-off gaze of the pretty hazel eyes, and wondering at the thought moving behind them. At length Nancy withdrew her gaze from the forest.

"I shall certainly report the things I've seen," she said with a smile that found prompt response in the man's dark eyes. "You've certainly done your best to show me, and tell me, the exact position. I shall make a point of reporting all that. Yes, I've seen it all, thank you very much."

Then her smile suddenly vanished. The shrewd gaze of commercial interest replaced it.

"But these Labrador folk?" she demanded. "Is that stuff just—hearsay?"

The man shook his head. He was feeling easier.

"It's God's truth, mam." He spat out a stream of tobacco juice. "I know them forests. Say," his eyes had lost their smile, "I don't guess I figger to know the business side of things, I don't calculate to know if the folks on Labrador work with, or against the Skandinavia. But I do know that if they're up against us they've got us plumb beat before we start. They got the sort of lumber the jacks dream about when they got their bellies full on a Saturday night, and they're going to wake up to find it Sunday mornin'. I'm just a lumberman, and if I hadn't fifteen years' record with the Skandinavia, and wasn't pouching two hundred and fifty bucks, and what I can make besides, a month, why, it 'ud be me for the coast where you can jamb the rivers in a three months' cut, and souse rye the rest of the year till the bugs look as big as mountains. Guess it's the summer rose garden of the lumber-jack, for all it's under snow eight months in the year, when you can't tell your guts from an iceflow, and the skitters, in summer, mostly reach the size of a gasoline tank. It's a dog's life, mam, lumberin' anywhere. But they're lap-dogs out that way."

The man's words brought the return of the girl's smile. "Yes, I spose it's—tough," she observed thoughtfully. Then quite suddenly she spread out her hands. "Oh, yes," she exclaimed, with a sudden vehemence, "it's worse than tough. It's hopeless. Utterly hopeless. I've seen it. I've watched it. I had to. I couldn't escape it. It's so desperately patent. But it's not the life as these folk live it. It's the future I'm thinking of. It's middle life and old age. These boys. They're wonders—now. How long does it last, and then—what happens? I'm here on business, hard business. But I guess this thing's got hold of me so I can't sometimes sleep at nights. Tell me about them."

Arden Laval, one of the hardest specimens of the lumber boss, turned away. His understanding of women was built up out of intimacy with the poor creatures who peopled the camps he knew. This girl's burst of feeling only stirred him to a cynical humour.

"Mam," he said, with a grin that was almost hateful, "if I was to start in to hand you the life history of a lumber-jack you'd feel like throwing up your kind heart, and any other old thing you hadn't use for in your stummick. But I guess I can say right here, a lumber-jack's a most disgustin' sort of vermin who hasn't more right than a louse to figger in your reckonin'. I guess he was born wrong, and he'll mostly die as he was born. And meanwhile he's lived a life that's mostly dirt, and no account anyway. There's a few things we ask of a lumber-jack, and if he fulfils 'em right he can go right on living. When he can't fulfil 'em, why, it's up to him to hit the trail for the pay box, an' get out. Guess you feel good when you see a boy swingin' an axe, or handlin' a peavy. Sure. That sort of thing don't come your way often. Neither does it come your way to see the rest. He's mostly a sink of filth in mind and body, and if he ain't all that at the start he gets it quick. He's a waster of God's pure air, and is mostly in his right surroundings when the forest does its best to hide him up from the eyes of the rest of the world. Guess he's the best man I know—dead."

For all his grin Arden Laval was in deadly earnest. Nancy stared at the broad back he had turned on her with his final word. And her indignation surged.

"I don't believe it," she cried. "I can't believe it. You're just talking out of years of experience of a life you've probably learned to hate. Man, if that's your opinion of your fellows, then it's you who ought never to leave the forest you claim does its best to hide up folk from the eyes of the rest of the world. You're a camp boss. You're our head man in these forests. You're trusted, and we know your skill. Well, it seems to me you've a duty that goes further than just feeding the booms right. You've a moral duty towards these men you condemn. You can help them. It should surely be your pride to lift them out of the desperate mire you claim they are floundering in. I'll not believe you mean it all."

The man turned away as a black-clothed figure emerged from the trees, and came to a stand at the brink of the ravine some hundred and more yards to the east of them. Nancy, too, beheld the lonely figure and she, too, became interested in its movements.

The lumber boss laughed shortly, roughly, and raised an arm, pointing as he turned a grinning face to the girl.

"See him, there?" he cried. "Say, mam, with all respect, I'd say to you, if you're feeling the way you talk, and look to get the sort of stuff you'd maybe fancy hearing, that's the guy you need to open out to. As you say, I'm the head camp-boss on the Skandinavia's limits. I've had nigh twenty years an' more experience of the lumber-jack. An' I'm tellin' you the things any camp-boss speakin' truth'll tell you. That's all, I don't hate the boys. I don't pity 'em. But I don't love 'em. They're just part of a machine to cut lumber, and it don't matter a hoot in hell to me what they are, or who they are, or what becomes of 'em. I ain't shepherdin' souls like that guy. It ain't in me, anyway. I just got to make good so that some day I ken quit these cursed forests and live easy the way I'd fancy. When that time comes maybe I'll change. Maybe I'll feel like that guy standin' doping over that spread of forest scene. I don't know. And just now I don't care—a curse."

But Nancy was no longer listening. The lonely, black-coated figure Laval had pointed out absorbed all her interest. His allusion to the man's calling had created in her an irresistible desire.

"Who is he? That man?" she demanded abruptly.

Laval laughed.

"Why, Father Adam," he replied. There was a curious softening in his harsh voice, which brought the girl's eyes swiftly back to him.

"Father Adam? A priest?" she questioned.

Laval shook his head. He had turned again, regarding the stranger. His face was hidden from the searching eyes of the girl.

"I just can't rightly say," he demurred. "Maybe he is, an' maybe he ain't. But," he added reflectively "he's just one hell of a good man. Makes me laff sometimes. Sometimes it makes me want to cry like a kid when I think of the things he's up against. He's out for the boys. He's out to hand 'em dope to make 'em better. Oh, it ain't Sunday School dope. No. He's the kind o' missioner who does things. He don't tell 'em they're a bum lot o' toughs who oughter to be in penitentiary. But he makes 'em feel that way—the way he acts. He's just a lone creature, sort of livin' in twilight, who comes along, an' we don't know when he's comin'. He passes out like a shadow in the forests, an' we don't see him again till he fancies. He's after the boys the whole darn time. It don't matter if they're sick in body or mind. He helps 'em the way he knows. An', mam, they just love him to death. There's just one man in these forests I wouldn't dare blaspheme, if I felt like it—which I don't. No, mam, my life wouldn't be worth a two seconds buy if I blasphemed—Father Adam. He's one of God's good men, an' I'd be mighty thankful to be like him—some. Gee, and I owe him a piece myself."

"How?"

Nancy's interest was consuming.

"Why, only he jumped in once when I was being scrapped to death. He jumped right in, when he looked like gettin' killed for it. And," he laughed cynically, "he gave me a few more years of the dog's life of the forest."

The girl moved away from her support.

"I want to thank you, Mr. Laval, for the trouble you've taken, and the time you've given up to me." The hazel eyes were smiling up into the man's hard face. "I don't agree with some of the things you've just been telling me; I should hate to, anyway. I don't even believe you feel the way you say about your men. Still, that's no account in the matters I came about. The things I've got to say when I get back are all to your credit. I'm going over now to talk to—Father Adam. And you needn't come along with me. You see, you've fired my curiosity. Yes, I want to hear the stuff I fancy about the—boys. So I'll go and talk to your—shepherd of souls. Good-bye."

Nancy's eyes were bright and smiling as she gazed up into the lean, ascetic face of the man in the black, semi-clerical coat. His garments were worn and almost threadbare. At close quarters she realised an even deeper interest in the man whose presence had wrought such a magical change in the harsh tones of the camp-boss. He was in the heyday of middle life, surely. His hair was long and black. His beard was of a similar hue, and it covered his mouth and chin in a long, but patchy mass. His eyes were keen but gentle. They, too, were very dark, and the whole cast of his pale face was curiously reminiscent.

"I just had to come along over, sir," she said. "I was with Mr. Laval, and he told me of the work—the great work you do in these camps. Maybe you'll forgive me intruding. But you see, I've come from our headquarters on business, and the folk of these camps interest me. I kind of feel the life the boys live around these forests is a pretty mean life. There's nothing much to it but work. And it seems to me that those employing them ought to be made to realise they've a greater responsibility than just handing them out a wage for work done. So when I saw you come out of the forest and stand here, and Mr. Laval told me about you, I made up my mind right away to come along and—speak to you. My name's McDonald—Nancy McDonald."

It was all a little hasty, a little timidly spoken. The dark eyes thoughtfully regarding the wonder of red hair under the close fitting hat were disconcerting, for all there was cordiality in their depths.

At Nancy's mention of her name, Father Adam instantly averted his gaze, and dropped the hand which he had taken possession of in greeting. It was almost as if the pronouncement had caused him to start. But the change, the movement, were unobserved by the girl.

"And you are—Father Adam?" she asked.

The man's gaze came quickly back.

"That's how I'm known. It—was kind of you to come along over."

In a moment all the girl's timidity was gone. If the man had been startled when she had announced her name, he displayed perfect ease now.

"Do you know," Nancy went on, with a happy laugh, "I almost got mad with Laval for his cynicism at the expense of the poor boys who work under his orders. But I think I understand him. He's a product of a life that moulds in pretty harsh form. He doesn't mean half he says."

"I'd say few of us do—when we let our feelings go." Father Adam smiled back into the eyes which seemed to hold him fascinated. "You see, Laval's much what we all are. He's got a tough job to put through, and he does his utmost. He's a big man, a brave man, a—yes, perhaps—a harsh man. But he couldn't do his job as he's paid to do it if he weren't all those things." He shook his head. "No, I guess we can't play with fire long without getting a heap of scars." He shrugged. "But after all I suppose it's just—life. We've got to eat, and we want to live. We don't need to judge too harshly."

"No. That's how I feel about the boys—he so condemned."

The girl turned away gazing pensively over the forest. Father Adam was free to regard her without restraint. With her turning the whole expression of his eyes had changed. Incredulous amazement had replaced his smiling ease.

"Would you care to come along through the woods to my shanty, Miss McDonald?" he said, almost diffidently, at last. "Maybe I've a cup of coffee there. And I'd say coffee's the most welcome thing on earth in these forests. It's a pretty humble shanty but, if you feel like talking things, why, I guess we can sit around there awhile."

The girl snatched at the invitation.

"I was just hoping you'd say something that way," she laughed readily. "I'd give worlds for a cup of coffee, and I guess the folks in the forests of Quebec know more about coffee in half a second than we city folk know in a year. Which way?"

"It's only a few yards. You'd best follow me."

The girl stood amazed. She was even horrified. She was gazing in through the opening of the merest shelter, a shelter built of green boughs with roof and sides of interlaced foliage. True it was densely interlaced, but no sort of distorted imagination could have translated the result into anything but a shelter. Habitation was out of the question. She stared at the primitive, less than aboriginal home, of the priestly man. She stared round her at the undergrowth upon which were spread his brown coarse blankets airing. She looked down at the smouldering fire between two granite stones upon which a tin of coffee was simmering and emitting its pleasant aroma upon the woodland air. It was too crude, too utterly lacking in comfort and even the bare necessites of existence.

The man emerged from the interior bearing two enamelled tin cups. He realised the amazement with which Nancy was regarding his home, and shook his head with a pleasant laugh as he indicated two upturned boxes beside the fire.

"You'd best sit, and I'll tell you about it," he said. "It's not exactly a swell hotel, is it? But it's sufficient."

The girl silently took her seat on one of the boxes. Father Adam took the other. Then he poured out two cups of coffee, and passed a tin of preserved milk across to the girl. There was a spoon in it. After that he produced a small tin of sugar and offered that.

You see, it's all I need," he said, in simple explanation. "When the rain comes I mostly get wet, except at nights when I get under my rubber sheet. But, anyway, there's plenty of sun to dry me. Oh, winter's different. I cut out a dug-out then, and burrow like the rest of the forest creatures. But, you see, this thing suits me well. I'm never long in one place. I've been here two weeks, and I pull out to-morrow."

"You pull out? Where to?"

"Why, I just pass on to some other camp. The boys are pretty widely scattered in these forests. You'd never guess the distances I sometimes make. Even Labrador. But it doesn't much matter. I've a good smattering of physic, and the boys are always getting hurt one way and another. I'd hate to feel I couldn't go to them wherever they are. Maybe if I built a better house I'd not want to leave it. It would be hard getting on the move. You see, I get their call any old time. Maybe it comes along on the forest breezes," he said whimsically. "Then I have to be quick to locate it, and read it right."

The girl had helped herself to milk and sugar, and sipped the steaming coffee. But she was listening with all her ears and thinking feverishly. This strange creature, with his deprecating manner, and smiling, sane eyes, filled her with a sense of shame at his utter selflessness.

She nodded.

"You mean they—always want help?"

"Sure. Same as we all do."

Father Adam sipped his coffee appreciatively.

"But tell me," he said. "It's kind of new the Skandinavia sending a woman along up here. It's your first trip?"

Nancy set her cup down.

"Yes."

"They're a great firm," Father Adam went on, reflectively. "I mean the—extent of their operations."

Nancy smiled.

"I like the distinction. Yes, they're big. You don't like their—methods?"

It was the man's turn for a smiling retort.

"Their methods?" he shook his head. "I don't know, I guess they pay well. And their boys are no worse treated than in other camps. They employ thousands. And that's all to the good."

"But you don't like them," Nancy persisted. "I can hear it in your voice. It's in your smile. Few people like the Skandinavia," she added regretfully.

"Do you?"

Like a shot the challenge came, and Nancy found herself replying almost before she was aware of it.

"Yes. Why shouldn't I? They've been good to me. More than good, when those who had a right to be completely deserted me. No. I mustn't say just that," she hurried on in some contrition. "They provided for me, but cut me out of their lives. Maybe you won't understand what that means to a girl. It meant so much to me that I wouldn't accept their charity. I wouldn't accept a thing. I'd make my own way with the small powers Providence handed me. So I went to the Skandinavia who have only shown me the best of kindness. Well, I'm frankly out for the Skandinavia and all their schemes and methods in consequence. It's not for me to look into the things that make folks hate them. That's theirs. My loyalty and gratitude are all for them for the thing they've done for me. Isn't that right?"

"Surely," the man concurred. "But your coffee. It's getting cold," he added.

Nancy hastily picked up her cup.

"Why am I telling you all this?" she laughed. "We were going to talk of the—boys."

"We surely were." Father Adam laughed responsively. "But personal interest I guess doesn't figure to be denied for long. We sort of get the notion we can shut it out. But we can't. We try to guess there's other things. Things more important. Things that matter a whole lot more." He shook his head. "It's no use. There aren't. I guess it doesn't matter where we look. Self's pushing out at every angle, and won't be denied. It would be hypocrisy to deny it, wouldn't it? It's the biggest thing in life. It's the whole thing."

"And it's such a pity," Nancy agreed slyly. "Just think," she went on, "I've got a hundred notions for the good of the world. These boys for instance. I'd like to make their lives what they ought to be. Full of comfort and security and—and everything to make it worth while. Instead of that my first and whole concern is to make good for Nancy McDonald. To do all those things for her. It's dreadful when you think of it, isn't it?" She sighed. "I want to do good to the—the 'underdog,' and all the time I'm planning for myself. I want to fight all the time for those who hold opportunity out to me. It doesn't really matter to me why the Skandinavia is disliked. They give me opportunity. I reckon they've been good to me. So I'm their slave to fight for them, and work for them, whatever their methods. Yes. It's too bad," she laughed frankly. "I can't deny it. I'd like to, but—I can't."

"No."

Father Adam set down his empty cup, and sat with his arms resting on his parted knees. His hands were clasped.

"You remind me of someone," he said, in his simple disarming fashion. "Queerly enough it's a man. A strong, hard, kindly, good-natured man.

I found him without a thought but to make good. And I knew he would make good. Then it came my way to show him how. I offered him a notion. The notion was fine. Oh, yes—though I say it. It was the sort of thing if it were carried to success would hand the fellow working it down to posterity as one of his country's benefactors. The notion appealed to him. It stirred something in him, and set fire to his enthusiasm. He jumped for it. Why? Was it the thought of doing a great act for his country? Was it for that something that was all good stirring in him? No. I guess it was because he was a strong, physical, and spiritual, and mental force concentrated on big things, primarily inspired by Self. Personal achievement. It seems to me the good man always does what's real and worth while in the way of helping himself."

"Yes. I think I understand." The girl nodded. "And this strong physical, and spiritual, and mental force? Have I heard of him? Is he known? Has he achieved?"

"He's carrying on. Oh, yes." Father Adam paused. Then he went on quickly. "You don't know him yet. But I think you will. He's out on the coast of Labrador. He's driving his great purpose with all his force through the agency of a groundwood mill that would fill your Skandinavia folk with envy and alarm if they saw it. He's master of forests such as would break your heart when compared with these of your Skandinavia. His name's Sternford. Bull Sternford, of Sachigo."

At the mention of Sachigo, Nancy's eyes widened. Then she laughed. It was a laugh of real amusement.

"Why, that's queer. It's—I'm going right on there from here. I'm going to meet this very man, Sternford. They tell me I've just time to get there and pull out again for home before winter freezes them up solid. So he is this great man, with this great—notion. Tell me, what is he like?"

"Oh, he's a big, strong man, as ready to laugh as to fight."

Father Adam smiled, and stooped over the fire to push the attenuated sticks of it together.

"May I ask why you're going to Sachigo?" he asked, without looking up.

Just for a moment Nancy hesitated. Then she laughed happily.

"I don't see why you shouldn't," she cried. "There's no secret. Skandinavia intends to buy him, or crush him."

The man sat up.

"And you—a girl—are the emissary?"

Incredulity robbed the man of the even calmness of' his manner.

"Yes. Why not?"

The challenge in the girls's eyes was unmistakable.

"You won't buy him," Father Adam said quietly. "And you certainly won't crush him."

"Because I'm a girl?"

"Oh, no. I was thinking of the Skandinavia." The man shook his head. "If I'm a judge of men, the crushing will be done from the other end of the line."

"This man will crush Skandinavia?"

The idea that Skandinavia could be crushed was quite unthinkable to Nancy. It was the great monopoly of the country. It was—but she felt that this lonely creature could have no real understanding of the power of her people.

"Surely," he returned quietly. "But that," he added, with a return of his pleasant smile, "is just the notion of one man. I should say it's no real account. Yes, you go there. You see this man. The battle of your people with him matters little. It will be good for you to see him. It—may help you. Who can tell? He's a white man, and a fighter. He's honest and clean. It's—in the meeting of kindred spirits that the great events of life are brought about. It should be good for you both."

"I wonder?" Nancy rose from her chair.

The man rose also.

"I think so," he said, very decidedly.

The girl laughed.

"I hope so. But—" She held out her hand. "Thank you, Father," she said. "I'll never be able to think of the things I'm set on achieving without remembering our talk—and the man I met in the forest. I wish—but what's the use? I've got to make good. I must. I must go on, and—do the thing I see. Good-bye."

Father Adam was holding the small gauntleted hand, and he seemed loth to release it. His eyes were very gentle, very earnest.

"Don't worry to remember, child. Don't ever think about—this time. It won't help you. You've set your goal. Make it. You will do the good things you fancy to do, though maybe not the way you think them. It seems to me that 'good' mostly has its own way all the time. You can't drive it. And the best of it is I don't think there's a human creature so bad in this world, but that in some way God's work has been furthered through his life. Good-bye."

For some moments the lonely figure stood gazing down the woodland aisles. The deep, shining light of a great hope was in his eyes. A wonderful tender smile had dispersed the shadows of his ascetic face. At length, as the girl's figure became completely swallowed up in the twilight of it all, he turned away and passed into the foliage shelter which was his home.

He was squatting on his box, and the small canvas bag containing his belongings was open beside him. Its contents were strewn about. He was writing a long letter. There was several pages of it. When he had finished he read it over carefully. Then he carefully folded it and placed it in an envelope, and addressed it. It was addressed:

MR. BULL STERNFORD,

Sachigo, Farewell Cove,

Labrador.

CHAPTER VII
THE SKANDINAVIA MOVES

Bat gazed up at the wooded ridge. They were standing in the marshy bottom of a natural hollow amidst a sparse scattering of pine and attenuated spruce. Beyond the ridge lay the waters of the cove. And to the left the broad waters of the river mouth flowed by. It was a desolate, damp spot, but its significance to the two men studying it was profound.

Skert Lawton, the chief engineer of Sachigo, tall, loose-limbed, raw-boned, watched his superior with somewhat mournful, unsmiling eyes. There was something of deadly earnest in his regard, something anxious. But that was always his way. Bat had once said of him: "Skert Lawton's one hell of a good boy. But I won't get no comfort in the grave if I ain't ever see him grin." There was not the smallest sign of a smile in him now.

"It's one big notion," Bat said, at last. Then he added doubtfully. "It comes mighty nigh being too big."

Lawton emitted a curious sound like a snort. It was mainly, however, an ejaculation of violent impatience. Bat turned with a twinkling grin, surveying the queer figure. His engineer was always a source of the profoundest interest for him. Just now, in his hard, rough clothing, he might have been a lumber-jack, or casual labourer. Anything, in fact, rather than the college-bred, brilliant engineer he really was.

Bat's doubt had been carefully calculated. He knew his man. And just now as he awaited the explosion he looked for, his thoughts went back to a scene he had once had with a half drunken machine-minder whom he had had to pay off. The man had epitomised the chief engineer's qualities and character, as those who encountered his authority understood them, in a few lurid, illuminating phrases. "You know," he had said, "that guy ain't a man. No, sir. He's the mush-fed image of a penitentiary boss. I guess he'd set the grease box of a driving shaft hot with a look. His temper 'ud burn holes in sheet iron. As for work—work? Holy Mackinaw! I've worked hired man to a French Canuk mossback which don't leave a feller the playtime of a nigger slave, but that hell-hired Scotch machine boss sets me yearnin' for that mossback's wage like a bull-pup chasin' offal. I tell you right here if that guy don't quit his notions there'll be murder done. Bloody murder! An' it's a God's sure thing when that happens he'll freeze to death in hell. It don't rile me a thing to be told the things he guesses my mother was. Maybe that's a matter of opinion, and, anyway, she's mixin' with a crop of angels who don't figger to have no truck with Scotch machine bosses. I guess a sight of his flea-bitten features 'ud set 'em seein' things so they wouldn't rec'nise their harps from frypans, and they'd moult feathers till you wouldn't know it from a snowfall on Labrador. But when he mixes his notions of my ma with 'lazy'! Lazy! Lazy! Gee! Why, if I signed in a half hour late from that bum suttler's canteen, I guess it was only the time it took me digestin' two quarts of the gut-wash they hand out there in the hope you won't know it from beer. No, sir, 'lazy son-of-a-bitch' from that guy is the talk no decent citizen with a bunch of guts is goin' to stand for."

Skert Lawton was known for a red-hot "burner," a "nigger driver." No doubt he was all this in addition to his brilliant attainments as an engineer. But the methods he applied to others he applied to himself. And the whole of him, brain and body, was for the enterprise they were all engaged in. Bat had intended to goad the demon of obstinate energy which possessed the man, and he succeeded.

Skert flung out his hand in a comprehensive gesture.

"Hell!" he cried. "That's no sort of talk anyway. I've been weeks on this thing. And I've got it to the last fraction. Big notion? Of course it is. Aren't we mostly concerned with big notions? Here, what are you asking? An inland boom with capacity for anything over a million cords. Well? It's damn ridiculous talking the size of the notion. This hollow is fixed right. Its bed is ten feet below the bed of the river. It's surrounded with a natural ridge on all sides a hundred and fifty feet high. There's a quarter mile below the hollow and the river bank, and the new mill extensions are just to the east of this ridge. It's well-nigh child's play. Nature's fixed it that way. Two cuttings, and a race-way on the river. We flood this. Feed it full of lumber in the summer with surplus from the cut and you've got that reserve for winter, so you can keep every darn machine grinding its guts out. What's the use talking? Big notion? Of course it is. We're out for big notions all the time. That's the whole proposition. Well?"

Bat grinned at the heated disgust in the man's tone.

"Sounds like eatin' pie," he retorted aggravatingly. "The cost? The labour? Time? You got those things?"

"It's right up at your office now." Skert's eyes widened in surprise at such a question. "It's not my way to play around."

"No." Bat's eyes refused seriousness.

"Oh, psha! This is no sort of time chewing these details. It's figgered to the last second, the last man, the last cent. I brought you to see things. Well, you've seen things. And if you're satisfied we'll quit right away. I've no spare play time."

There was no pretence of patience in Skert Lawton. He had looked for appreciation and only found doubt. He moved off.

Bat had done the thing intended. He had no intention of hurting the man. He understood the driving power of the mood he had stirred.

They moved off together.

"That's all right, Skert," he said kindly. "You've done one big thing. An' it's the thing Bull and I want—"

"Then why in hell didn't you say it instead of talking—notions?"

For all the sharpness of his retort, Skert was mollified. Bat shook his head and a shrewd light twinkled in his eyes.

"You're a pretty bright boy, Skert," he said. "But you're brightest when you're riled."

They had gained the river bank where booms lined the shore, and scores of men were rafting. They had left the water-logged hollow behind them, and debouched on the busy world of the mill. Ahead lay the new extensions where the saws were shrieking the song of their labours upon the feed for the rumbling grinders. It was a township of buildings of all sizes crowding about the great central machine house.

They crossed the light footbridge over the "cut in" from the river, and moved along down the main highway of the northern shore.

Both were pre-occupied. The engineer was listening to the note of his beloved machinery. Bat was concerned with any and every movement going on within the range of his vision. They walked briskly, the lean engineer setting a pace that kept the other stumping hurriedly beside him.

Abreast of the mill they approached a new-looking, long, low building. It was single storied and lumber built, with a succession of many windows down its length. The hour was noon. And men were hurrying towards its entrance from every direction.

Bat watched interestedly.

"They seem mighty keen for their new playground," he said at last, with a quick nod in the direction of the recreation house.

The engineer came out of his dream. His mournful eyes turned in the direction indicated and devoured the scene. Then he glanced down at the squat figure stumping beside him.

"Guess that's so. But not the way you figgered when you got that fool notion of handing 'em a playhouse," he said roughly. "If you pass a hog a feather bed, it's a sure thing he'll work out the best way to muss it quick."

"How? I don't get you?"

There was no humour in Bat's eyes now.

"They call it a 'Chapel'," Skert said dryly. "They've surely got preachers, but they don't talk religion. Maybe that's sort of new to you, here. It isn't across the water where I come from. Guess you think those boys are racing out to get a game of checkers, or billiards, or cards, or some other fool play you reckoned to hand 'em to make 'em feel good." He shook his head. "They're not. They've turned their 'Chapel' into a sort of parliament. Every dinner hour there's a feller, different fellers most all the time, gets up and hands 'em out an address. It's short, but red hot. The afternoon shift in the mill is given up to brightening up their fool brains on it. And when evening comes along, and they've their bellies full of supper and beer, they get along to the 'Chapel' and they debate the address, handing out opinions and notions just as bellies guide 'em."

"And the addresses. What are they mostly? On the work? The trade they're working at?"

A world of pity looked out of Skert's eyes as he surveyed the man he believed to be the greatest organiser the mill industry had ever seen. He shook his head.

"Work? Not on your life! Socialism, Communism—Revolution!"

Bat spat out a stream of tobacco juice. He was startled.

"But I ain't heard tell of any sort of unrest gettin' busy. We're payin' big money. It's bigger than the market. They got—"

"Best talk to Sternford when you get back up there to your office. He's got the boys sized right up to the last hair of their stupid heads. But I'll hand you something I've reckoned to hand you a while back, only I wanted to be sure. There's nothing of this truck about the 'hands' of the old mill. It's the new hands you've been collecting from the forests. We've grown by two thousand hands in the past year or so. And they're so darn mixed I wouldn't fancy trying to sort 'em. They come from all parts. The world's been talking revolution since ever these buzzy-headed Muscovites reckoned to start in grabbing the world's goods for themselves. Well, it's a hell of a long piece here to Labrador, but it's found its way, and the mutton-brained fools who're supposed to play around that shanty you handed 'em are recreating themselves talking about it in there. Here, come right over to that window. It's open."

Perhaps Skert was enjoying himself. Certainly his mournful eyes were less mournful as he led his chief over to the open window. Bat had had his innings with him. He was planning the game and hitting hard in his turn.

"The enemy of the world, of more particularly the worker is the—CAPITALIST!"

The words were hurled from the platform of the recreation room at the heads of the listening throng below and reached the open window just as Lawton and his chief came up to it. There was applause following this profound announcement, and Skert turned on his companion.

"Well?" he demanded, in a tone of biting triumph.

They had reached the window at the psychological moment. Nothing could have suited his purpose better.

Bat turned away abruptly. It was as if some fierce emotion made it impossible for him to remain another second. His heavy brows depressed, and his deep-set eyes narrowed to gimlet holes. Skert pursued him. Once clear of the window, and beyond earshot, Bat flung his reply with all the passionate force of his fighting nature.

"The lousy swine!" he cried. "I'll close that place sure as—hell."

Skert shook his head as they walked on.

"No, you won't," he said. "Guess you aren't crazy. You'll talk this over with Sternford. And when you've talked it some, you'll keep that place running, and let them talk. It's best that way. But I've got tab of most of the speakers, and I've located where they come from. Most of them have sometime worked for the Skandinavia. Maybe that's the reason of their talk. Maybe even Skandinavia's glad they're talking that way here on Labrador. I don't know. But—well, I'll have to quit you here. They're setting up the two big new machines, and it don't do leaving them long. So long. Anything else you need to know about that recreation room, why, I guess I can hand it to you."

Bull Sternford laid the telegram aside while a shadowy smile hovered about his firm lips. Then he settled himself back in his chair, and gave himself up to the thoughtful contemplation of the brilliant sunlight, and the perfect, steely azure of the sky beyond the window opposite him.

The change in the man was almost magical. The hot-headed, determined, fighting lumber-jack whom Father Adam had rescued from furious homicide had hidden himself under something deeper than the veneer which the modest suit of conventional life provides. It was the subtle change that comes from within which had transformed him. It was in his eyes. In the set of his jaws. It was in the man's whole poise. His resources of spiritual power; his mental force; his virility of personality. All these things were concentrated. They were no longer sprawling, groping, seeking the great purpose of his life as they had been in the lumber camp of the Skandinavia.

A feeling akin to triumph filled the man's heart as he gazed out upon the pleasant light of Labrador's late summer day. In something like twelve months he had thrust leagues along the road he meant to travel. And his progress had been of a whirlwind nature. It had been work, desperate, strenuous work. It had been the double labour of intensive study combined with the necessary progress in the schemes laid down for the future of Sachigo. It had only been possible to a man of his amazing faculties, combined with the fact that Bat Harker and the mournful Skert Lawton had left him free from the clogging detail of the mill organisation and routine.

In twelve months he had crystallised the dreams and projects of his predecessor in the chair he was now occupying. In twelve months he had built up the shell of the great combination of groundwood and paper mills which was to have such far-reaching effect upon the paper trade of the world. And now, ahead of him was spread out the sea of finance upon which he must next embark. He felt that already giant's work had been done. But his yearning could never be satisfied by a mere measure of completion. He must embrace it all, complete it all.

Already he seemed to have lived with bankers and financial specialists, but he felt it was only the beginning of that which he had yet to do. He was unappalled. He was more than confident. He had discovered unguessed faculties for finance in himself. He had surprised himself as well as those others with whom he had come in contact. They had discovered in him all that which Father Adam had been so prompt to realise. They had found in him a young, untrained mind, untrained in their own calling, whose natural aptitude was amazing, and whose courage and confidence were beyond words. But greatest of all was the perception he displayed. They realised he never required the telling of more than half the story. Intuition and inspiration completed it for him without the labour of their words. The result of those twelve months was there for all to see. The lumberman had been translated into a hard, fighting, business man.

The train of the man's thought was broken by the unceremonious entry of Bat Harker. Bull turned. One swift glance into the grizzled face warned him his associate's mood was by no means easy. He, like everyone who came into contact with Bat, had learned to appreciate the volcanic fires burning under the lumberman's exterior.

Bull promptly fended any storm that might possibly be brewing. He held up his telegram and his eyes were smiling.

"The Skandinavia's on the move," he cried. And Bat recognised the battle note in the tone.

"How?"

Bull flung the message across the desk.

"The Skandinavia's representative is arriving on the *Myra*," he said. Then he added, "Elas Peterman says so."

"What for?"

Bat had picked up the message and stood reading it.

The other searched amongst his papers.

"I kind of forgot putting you wise before," he said. "There were two letters came along a week back. One was from Elas Peterman, of the Skandinavia folk, and the other from Father Adam. That message was 'phoned on from the headland. The letters didn't just concern a deal, so I set 'em aside. This message is different."

For the moment the affairs down at the recreation room were forgotten, and Bat contented himself with the interest of the moment.

"How?" he demanded again in his sharp way.

Bull laughed.

"Here," he cried, holding out the letters he had found. "I best pass you these. That's from Peterman. There's not much written, but a deal lies under the writing. You'll see he asks permission for a representative of the Skandinavia to wait on us. I wirelessed back, 'I'd just love to death meeting him.' By the same mail came Father Adam's yarn. An' I guess that's where the soup thickens. He says some woman's coming along from the Skandinavia folk. He guesses they're going to put up some proposition that looks like butting in on the plans laid out for Sachigo. But that don't seem to worry him a thing. I guess his letter wasn't written to hand us warning. He seems concerned for the woman. You'll see. He asks me to treat her gently. Firmly, yes. But also, 'very, very gently.' He says, 'you see, she's a woman'."

Bull waited while the other perused both letters. Then, as Bat looked up questioningly, he went on:

"That telegram got here half an hour back," he said. Then he shrugged. "The woman's on the *Myra,* and the vessel's been sighted off the headland. She'll be along in two hours."

"And what're you doin' about it?"

Bat's eyes were searching. Perhaps Father Adam's letter had told him something it had failed to tell the other.

"I'll see her right away," Bull laughed. "If she feels like stopping around and getting a sight of the things we're doin' she's welcome. She can put up at the visitor's house. It 'ud do me good for her to pass the news on to the folk she comes from."

But Bat's manner had none of the light confidence of the other. Bitter hatred of the Skandinavia was deeply ingrained in him. He shook his head.

"Keep 'em guessin'," he said. "It'll worry 'em—that way."

Then he passed the letters back, and dropped into the chair that was always his.

"But this woman," he went on, in obvious puzzlement. "It's—it's kind of new, I guess. Then there's Father Adam's message. That don't hand us much."

Bull's lightness passed.

"No," he said, "that message is queer. He knows about it. Yet he hasn't given her name or said a thing. Say—I like that phrase though. What is it? He says, 'treat her very, very gently—you see, she's a woman.' That's Father Adam right thro'—sure. But—well it's a pity he don't say more."

Bat nodded.

"You'll go along down an' meet her?"

"No." Bull shook his head decidedly. "You will."

Bat's eyes twinkled with a better humour than they had hitherto displayed.

"Why—me?"

"She comes from the Skandinavia. Guess Skandinavia would fancy me meeting their representative at the quay—quite a lot."

The argument met with Bat's entire approval. He pulled out a silver timepiece and consulted it.

"That's all right," he said, "I'll quit you in ha'f an hour. Say—I'm kind of guessin' there's other representatives of the Skandinavia around. I didn't guess ther' was much to Sachigo that I wasn't wise to. But that boy, Skert Lawton, showed me a play I hadn't a notion about. It's that darn play shanty I set up for the boys. I feel that mad about it I got a notion closing it right down. It worried me startin' it. It worries me more now. You see, I guess it's come of me lappin' up the ha'f-baked notions you find wrote in the news-sheets. Folks seem to be guessin' the worker needs somethin' more than his wage. They guess he's gotten some sort of queer soul needin' things he can't pay for. I allow I hadn't seen it that way myself. It mostly seemed to me a hell of a good wage and a full belly was mostly the need of a lumber-jack, and a dead sure thing all he deserved. But I fell for the news-sheet dope, an' set up that cursed recreation shanty. Now we're goin' to git trouble."

"How?"

Bull's ejaculation was sharp.

"They hold meetings there. They dope out Capital and Labour stuff there, instead of pushing games at each other. Guess they got the bug of politics an' are scratching themselves bad. It ain't the old Labrador guys, Skert says. It's mostly new hands passin' their stuff on. Skert reckons we got a whole heap of the Skandinavia 'throw-outs,' around here now. That don't say Skandinavia's workin' monkey tricks. Though they might be. You see, this sort of dope's been talked most everywhere, except on Labrador, years now. I guess we need to go through the bunch with a louse comb. But maybe the mischief's done. I'm dead crazy to shut that darn place down."

"Don't!" Bull was emphatic. "Shut it down and you'll make it a thousand times worse. No, sir. Let 'em shout. Let 'em blow off any old steam they need. Just sit tight. If it's the usual hot air there's nothing much coming of it up here on Labrador. There's this to remember. We're a thousand miles of hell's own winter, and a pretty tough sea, from the politicians who spend their lives befooling a crowd of unthinking muttons. Pay 'em well, and feed 'em well, and they've the horse sense to know there ain't no electric stoves out in the Labrador forests in winter. That way we don't need to worry. If it's the Skandinavia tricks it's different. They'll play the game to the finish. It don't signify a curse if you close down the recreation shanty or not. We've got to meet it as a competition, and fight it the way we'd fight any other."

Bat's eyes snapped.

"That's the kind of dope Skert Lawton's handed me," he protested.

"And Skert's a wise guy," came the prompt retort.

Quite suddenly Bat flung out his gnarled hands.

"Hell!" he cried violently. "Have we got to sit around like mush-men, while the rats are chawin' our vitals. Fifteen or sixteen year I've handled this lay-out without a growl I couldn't kick plumb out o' the feller who made it. Now—now, because of a fool play I made, I've got to set the kid gloves on my hands, sayin' 'thank you,' while the boys git up and plug me between the eyes. No, sir. It ain't my way. It's me for the shot gun in the stern of the gopher all the time. It's me to mush up the features of any hoboe who don't know better than to grin when I'm throwin' the hot air. I can't stand for the politics of labour where I hand out the wage. A man's a man to me, not one darn slobber of policy. I'm goin' to jump in on that talk. And when I'm thro'—"

"You'll get all the trouble in the world plumb on your neck." Bull's fine eyes were alight with humour. He revelled in the fighting spirit of the older man. "Here, Bat," he cried, "I'm a fool kid beside you. I don't begin to know my job when I think of you. But I'm up sides with all the politics games. Politics are ideals, notions. They haven't real horse sense within a mile. They're just the fool thoughts of folk who haven't better to do than sit around and think, and talk, an' see how they can make other folk conform to the things they think. That's all right. It's human nature in its biggest conceit, or it's another way of helping themselves without pushing a shovel. It don't matter which it is. But what I want to impress on you is, it's the biggest thing in life. It's the whole thing in life. Get a notion and think it hard enough, and talk it hard enough, and you'll hypnotise a hundred brains bigger than your own, and sweep the crowd with you. You'll even hypnotise yourself into believing the truth of a thing your better sense knows isn't true, never was true, an' couldn't be true anyway. And when you're fixed that way you'll die for your notion. Oh, a politician ain't yearning for any old grave. He wouldn't get an audience there. Politicians 'ud hate to die worse than a condemned man. But that's the queer of it; he'd die rather than give up a notion he's built up. He'd hate to death to push a blue pencil through it and—try again. All of which means, bar the doors of this recreation room parliament, and you'll start up a hundred such parliaments, and worse, throughout your enterprise here on Labrador, and you'll finish by wrecking the whole blessed concern."

If Bull looked for yielding he was disappointed. But he appreciated the twinkle that had crept into the lumberman's stern eyes. The answer he received was a curiously expressive grunt as the man took out his timepiece and consulted it. When he saw him rise abruptly from his chair, Bull felt that if his talk had not had the effect he desired it had not been wholly wasted.

"Guess I'll git goin'," Bat said shortly. Then he glanced out of the window, where he could plainly see the stream of the *Myra's* smoke as she came down the cove. "I'll bring your lady friend right up. Maybe she'll fancy the dope, which I 'low you can hand out good an' plenty."

With this parting shot he hurried from the room, and Bull fancied he detected the sound of a chuckle as the man departed.

CHAPTER VIII
AN AFFAIR OF OUTPOSTS

The business of making fast the vessel had no interest for Nancy McDonald. The thing that was about her, the thing that had leapt at her out of the haze hanging over the waters of Farewell Cove, as the *Myra* steamed to her haven, pre-occupied her to the exclusion of everything else. Her feelings were something of those of the explorer suddenly coming upon a new, unguessed world.

"Old Man" Hardy was at her side, waiting for the adjustment of the gangway. He was quietly observing her with a sense of enjoyment at the obvious surprise and interest she displayed. Besides, her beauty charmed him for all his years. And then had she not been entrusted to his especial care by those people who held powerful influence in all concerning the coastal trade upon which he was engaged?

Sachigo was not only a mill. It was a—city. This was the sum of Nancy's astonishing discovery. And the picture of it held her fascinated. She commented little, she had questioned little of the old skipper at her elbow. The thing she saw was too overwhelming. Besides, reticence was impressed upon her by the nature of her visit.

"It's a mighty elegant place," the seaman said at last.

The girl nodded. Then she smiled.

"I've seen trolley cars on the seashore. I've seen electric standards for lighting. What am I to see next on—Labrador?" she asked.

Captain Hardy laughed.

"You've to see the folks who've done it all," he replied. "And—there's one of 'em."

He indicated the squat figure of Bat Harker leaning against some bales piled on the quay. Nancy turned in that direction.

She discovered the rough-clad, almost uncouth figure of Bat. She noted his moving jaws as he chewed vigorously. She saw that a short stubble of beard was growing on a normally clean-shaven face, and that the man's clothing might have been the clothing of any labourer. But the iron cast of his face left her with sudden qualms. It was so hard. To her imagination it suggested complete failure for her mission.

"Is he the—owner? Is he—Mr. Sternford?" Her questions came in a hushed tone that was almost awed.

"No. That's Bat—Bat Harker. He's mill-boss."

"I see." There was relief in Nancy's tone. But it passed as the seaman continued.

"Maybe he's waiting for you though. Are they wise you're coming along? You don't see Bat around this quay without he's lookin' for some folk to come along on the *Myra*."

The gangway clattered out on to the quay, and the man moved toward it.

We best get ashore," he said. "You see, mam, my orders are to pass you over to the folks waiting for you. That'll be—Bat. He'll pass you on to Sternford. I take it you'll sleep aboard to-night. Your stateroom's booked that way. We sail to-morrow sundown, which will give you plenty time looking around if you fancy that way. I allow Sachigo's worth it. One day it'll be a big city, if I'm a judge. Will you step this way?"

The seaman's deference was obvious. But Nancy remained oblivious to it. To her it was just kindliness, and she was more than grateful. But his final remark about Sachigo left her pathetically disquieted. For the first time in her life she doubted the all-powerful position of the people to whom she had sold her services.

"Yes, thanks," she returned, smiling to disguise her feelings. Then she added, "I'm glad we don't sail till to-morrow evening. You see, I couldn't leave—this, without a big look around."

The ship-master had hurried away.

Bat's deep-set eyes were steadily regarding the beautiful face before him. He was gazing into the hazel depths of Nancy's eyes without a sign. He had noted everything as the girl had come down the gangway. The height, the graceful carriage in the long plucked-beaver coat which terminated just above the trim ankles in their silken, almost transparent, hose. Not even at Captain Hardy's pronouncement of her name had he yielded a sign. And yet—

"Miss—Nancy McDonald?"

Bat's tone had lost its usual roughness. His mind had leapt back over many years to a time when he had been concerned for that name in a way that had stirred him to great warmth. He smiled. It was a baffling, somewhat derisive smile.

"You're the lady representing the—Skandinavia?" he added.

"Why, yes," Nancy cried, "and I feel I want to thank you for the privilege of obtaining even an outside view of your wonderful, wonderful place here."

Bat raked thoughtfully at the stubble on his chin.

"If you feel that way, Miss, it'll hand me pleasure to show you and tell you about things," he said. "You come right out of what the folks around here like to call the enemy camp, but it don't matter a little bit. Not a little bit. The whole of Sachigo's standin' wide open for you to walk through." Then he dashed his hand across his face to clear the voracious mosquitoes. "But if we stop around here mor'n ha'f another minute, the memory you'll mostly carry away with you from Labrador'll be skitters—an' nothing much else. Will you come right along up to Mr. Sternford's office? It's quite a piece up the hill, which helps to keep it clear of skitters an' things?"

Nancy laughed. Her early impression of the super-lumberjack had passed. The man's smile was beyond words in its kindliness. His deep, twinkling eyes were full of appeal.

"Why, surely," she assented. "If you'll show me the way I'll be glad. The flies and things are certainly thick, and as I intend leaving Sachigo with happy memories, well—"

"Come right along. I'm here for just that purpose."

As they made their way up the woodland trail they talked together with an easy intimacy. Nancy was young. She was full of the joy of life, full of real enthusiasm. And this rough creature with his ready smile appealed to her. His frank, open way was something so far removed from that which prevailed under the Skandinavia's rule.

For Bat, the walk up from the quayside was one of the many milestones in his chequered life. He talked readily. He listened, too. But under it all his thought was busy. The mystery of Father Adam's letter was no longer a mystery. He understood. But he was also puzzled. How had this thing come about? How had Father Adam learned of this visit? How had this girl become representative of the Skandinavia? A hundred questions flashed through his mind, for none of which he could find a satisfactory answer. But he smiled to himself as he thought of that last line in Father Adam's letter. "Treat her gently—firmly, yes—but very gently. You see, she's a—woman."

It was a moment likely to live with both in the years to come. For Nancy it was at least the final stage of her apprenticeship, the passing of the portal beyond which opened out the world she so completely desired to take her place in. Did it not mean the moment of shouldering the great burden of responsibility she had so steadfastly trained herself to bear? For Bull Sternford it had no such meaning. His powers had long since been tested. As a meeting with the representative of a rival enterprise it was merely an incident in the life to which he had become completely accustomed. Its significance lay in quite another direction.

Bat had taken his departure. He had witnessed the meeting of Nancy with this protégé Father Adam had sent him from the dark world of the forests. And his witness of it had been with twinkling eyes, and the happy sense of an amusement he had never looked to discover in the presence of a representative of the Skandinavia. In an unexpressed fashion he realised he was gazing upon something in the nature of a stage play.

He had found Bull transformed. The office suit was gone. The man's hair was carefully brushed. He even suspected the liberal use of soap and water. And then, too, the heavy, rough boots had given place to shining patent leather. The youth and human nature of it pleased him. So he had departed to the workshops below with a voiceless chuckle, and a greater appreciation of the inevitability of the things of life.

Apart from Nancy's appreciation of that meeting, the woman in her sought to appraise the man she beheld. Her impression was far deeper than she knew. The height and muscular girth she beheld left her with a feeling that she was gazing upon one of the pictures her school-girl mind had created for the great men of Greek and Roman history. The clean-shaven, clear-cut face, with its fine eyes and broad brow, its purposeful mouth; these were details that had to be there, and were there. And somehow, as she realised them, and the sense of the man's power and personality forced itself upon her, her original confidence still further lessened, and she wondered not a little anxiously as to the outcome of this interview she had sought.

As for the man, his eyes had calmly smiled his spoken greeting. His handshake had been conventionally firm. But behind the mask of it all was one great surge of feeling. The vision of a beautiful, fur-coated figure, with the peeping lure of pretty ankles, the warm cap pressed low on the girl's head as though endeavouring to hide up the radiant framing of the sweetest, most beautiful face he felt he had ever seen, dealt all his preconceived purpose for the interview one final, smashing blow.

"I'm real glad to welcome you to Sachigo," he had begun. Then in a moment, the conventional gave place to the man in him. "But say," he added with a pleasant laugh, "we've a big piece of talk to make. You best let me help you remove that coat. The stove we always need to keep going here on Labrador makes this shanty hot as—very hot."

The manner of it sent convention, caution, business pose, scattering to the winds. The girl laughed and yielded.

"Why, thanks," she said readily. "I'm glad you reckon we're to make a big talk. You see," she added slyly, "I've been looking out of the window, and there's quite a drop below. Up to now I felt my fur might—be useful."

Bull laughed as he laid the coat aside. He had drawn up a comfortable lounging chair which Nancy was prompt to accept. For himself he stood at the window.

"Why, yes." He smiled. "I'd say it's a wise general who looks to his retreat before the encounter. I'd sort of half forgotten you come from the—Skandinavia."

"But I hadn't."

"No."

They both laughed. Nancy leant back in her chair. Her pose was all unconscious. She had toiled hard to keep pace with the sturdy gait of Bat in the ascent from the quay. Now she was glad of the ease the chair afforded.

"Why did you say that?" Nancy asked a moment later.

Bull spread out his great hands.

"The Skandinavia don't usually let folks forget they're behind them."

"Now that's just too bad. It—it isn't generous," the girl said half seriously.

"Isn't it?"

Bull left the window and took the chair that was usually Bat's. He set it so that he could feast his eyes on the beauty he found so irresistible.

"You see," he went on, "I've got a right to say that all the same. It's not the—the challenge of a—what'll I say—competitor? I once had the honour of drawing a few bucks a month on the paysheets of the Skandinavia. And folks reckoned, and I guess I was amongst 'em, that Skandinavia said to its people: 'Make good or—beat it.' That being so it makes it a sure thing they're not liable to leave you forgetting who's behind you."

His smile had gone. He was simply serious. This man had worked for her people, and Nancy felt he was entitled to his opinion.

"That's going to make my talk harder," she said. "I'm sorry. But there," she went on. "It doesn't really matter, does it? Anyway I want to tell you right away of the craze the sight of your splendid Sachigo has started buzzing in my head. Say, Mr. Sternford, it beats anything I ever dreamed, and I want to say that there's no one in the Skandinavia, from Mr. Peterman downwards, has the littlest notion of it. It's not a mill. It's a world of real, civilised enterprise. And it's set here where you'd look for the roughest of forest life. I just had no idea."

It was all said spontaneously. And the pleasure it gave was obvious in the man's eyes. He nodded.

"Yes," he said. "The construction of this mill, here on Labrador, isn't short of genius by a yard. And the genius of it lies where you won't guess."

Nancy's pretty eyes were mildly searching.

"You're the head of Sachigo," she suggested.

Bull's eyes lit.

"Sure," he cried, "an' I'm mighty proud that's so. But I'm not the genius of this great mill. No. That grizzled, tough old lumberman who toted you along up from the quayside is the brain of this organisation. He's a—wonder. There's times I want to laff when I think of it. There's times I'm most ready to cry. You see, you don't know that great feller. I'm just beginning to guess I do. He's a heart as big as a house, and the manner to scare a 'hold-up.' He's the grit of a reg'ment of soldiers and the mutton softness of a kid girl. He's the brain of a Solomon, and the illiteracy of a one day school kid. He's all those things, and he's the biggest proposition in men I've ever heard tell about. It's kind of tough. Don't you feel that way? He'll suck a pint of tobacco juice in the day, and blaspheme till your ears get on edge. And while your folks are guessing he'll put through a proposition that 'ud leave ha'f the world gasping."

Nancy stirred. This man's whole-hearted appreciation of another was something rather fine in her simple philosophy. The last thing she had contemplated in approaching the head of a rival enterprise was such talk as this. But somehow it seemed to fit the man. Somehow as she noted the squarely gazing eyes, and the power in every line of his features, she realised that whatever lines he chose to talk on, nothing could change the decision lying behind it all. She liked him all the better for that, and found herself drawing comparison between him and Elas Peterman to the latter's detriment.

"I like that," she cried impulsively. Then the colour rose in her cheeks at the thought of her temerity. "I guess he's all you say. Maybe some day I'll hear his side of things. I'd like to. You see—I felt I'd known him years when he brought me in here. Maybe you won't understand what that implies."

"I think I do."

Bull stood up from his chair and passed round his desk.

"Here, say, Miss McDonald," he went on, in his keen fashion. "You come from Skandinavia. And I guess you come on a pretty stiff proposition. It's going to be difficult for you to hand it me. Maybe you're young in the game. Well, it doesn't matter a thing. Now we're going to start right in talking that proposition, and I'm going to help you. But before that starts I just want to say this. You, I guess, are going right back on the *Myra* and she sails to-morrow, sundown. That means you'll stay a night in Sachigo—"

"I'm stopping on the vessel. It's all fixed."

Bull sat down at his desk.

"I'm kind of glad," he said, with a shade of relief. "It isn't that you aren't welcome to all the old hospitality Sachigo can hand you. You're just more than welcome. But Bat hasn't built his swell hotel yet," he laughed. "And as for us here, why, we 'batch' it. There isn't a thing in skirts around this place, only a Chink cook, a half-breed secretary, and a clerk or two, and a bum sort of decrepit lumber-jack who does my chores. So you see I'm—kind of relieved. Anyway you sleeping on the *Myra* makes it easy. Now there's a mighty big conceit to me, and it's all for this mill in our country's wilderness. And I just can't let you quit to-morrow night without showing you all it means. You've simply got to see the thing that's going to make the whole world's groundwood trade holler before we're through. You're my prisoner until you've seen the things I'm going to show you. Is it anyway agreeable?"

Nancy smiled delightedly.

"You couldn't drive me out of Sachigo till I've peeked into all your secrets down there," she said.

Bull leant forward with his arms outspread across the desk.

"Great!" he cried. "And," he added, "you shall see them all. The things I can't show you Bat will. And if I'm a judge that old rascal'll be tickled to death handing his dope out to you. But—let's get to business."

Nancy sat up. In a moment all ease was banished. She knew the great moment had come when she must prove herself to those who had entrusted her with her mission.

"Yes," she said, almost hurriedly. "I don't know the word Mr. Peterman sent you. And anyway it doesn't matter. I must put things my way. You are a great enterprise here. We are a great enterprise. It looks to us a pretty tough clash is bound to come between us in the near future, and—there should be no necessity for it. There's room—plenty of room—for both of us in our trade—"

She paused. The keen eyes of Bull were closely observing. He realised her attitude. Her words and tone were almost mechanical, as though she had schooled herself and rehearsed her lesson. And her voice was not quite steady. He jumped in with the swift impulse of a man whose rivalry could not withstand that sign of a beautiful girl's distress.

"Here," he cried, with that command so natural to him. "Just don't say another word. Let me talk. I guess I can tell you the things it's up to you to hand me. It'll save you a deal, and it'll hand me a chance to blow off the hot air that's mostly my way. This is the position. Peterman's wise to the things doing right here. The Skandinavia's up against years of cutting on the Shagaunty. The Shagaunty's played right out. You folks have got to open new stuff. It's my job to know all this. Very well. As I said, Peterman's at last got wise to us. He knows we look like flooding the market, and jumping right in on him. So—you're a mighty wealthy corporation—he figures to recognise us, and embrace us—with a business arrangement. That so?"

"Yes. A business arrangement."

The girl's relief was almost pathetic. Bull smiled.

"That's so. A business arrangement. Should I entertain one, eh? That's the question you're right here to ask. And you want to take back my answer." He paused. "Well, you're going to take back my answer. And I kind of feel it's the answer you'll like taking back. Say, Miss McDonald, I'm only a youngster, myself, but I guess I know what it means to set out on a work hoping and yearning to make good. Will it make good for you to go back to Elas Peterman and say the feller at Sachigo is coming right along down by the *Myra* to-morrow, and would be pleased to death to talk this proposition right out in the offices of the Skandinavia? Will it?"

Nancy's eyes lit. Their hazel depths were wells of thankfulness.

"Why, surely," she said. "You mean you're going to sail to-morrow?"

Bull laughed and his laugh was infectious. The girl was smiling her delight.

"That's so. I need to cross the Atlantic. I wasn't going till the *Myra's* next trip. I'll go to-morrow an' stop over in Quebec to see your people. It just means hurrying my choreman packing my stuff while I show you around to-morrow. That kind of fixes things, and if you'll hand me that pleasure I'd just love to show you around some this afternoon. There's a heap to see, and I don't fancy you missing any of it." He passed round the desk, and picked up the girl's coat and held it out invitingly. "Will you come right along?"

There was no denying him. Nancy looked up into his smiling eyes. She felt there was a lot she wanted to say, ought to say, on the business matter in hand. But it was impossible. And in her heart she was thankful.

"Why, I'd just love to," she said, and stood up from her chair.

Very tenderly, very carefully the man's hands helped her into her coat. And somehow Nancy was very glad the hands were big, and strong, and—yes—clumsy.

CHAPTER IX
ON THE OPEN SEA

The *Myra* laboured heavily. With every rise and fall of her high bows a whipping spray lashed the faces of those on deck. The bitter north-easterly gale churned the ocean into a white fury, and the sky was a-race with leaden masses of cloud. There was no break anywhere. Sky and sea alike were fiercely threatening, and the wind howled through the vessel's top gear.

Bull Sternford had been sharing the storm with the sturdy skipper on the bridge. He had been listening to the old man's talk of fierce experience on the coast of Labrador. It had all been interesting to the landsman in view of the present storm, but at last he could no longer endure the exposure of the shelterless bridge.

"It's me for the deck and a sheltered corner," he finally declared, preparing to pass down the iron "companion."

And the Captain grinned.

"I don't blame you," he bellowed in the shriek of the gale. "But I guess I'd as lief have it this way. It's better than a flat sea an' fog, which is mostly the alternative this time o' year. The Atlantic don't offer much choice about now. She's like a shrew woman. Her smile ain't ever easy. An' when you get it you've most always got to pay good. She can blow herself sick with this homeward bound breeze for all I care."

"That's all right," Bull shouted back at him. "Guess you've lost your sense of the ease of things working this coast so long. It 'ud be me for the flat sea and fog all the time. I like my chances taken standing square on two feet. So long."

He passed below, beating his hands for warmth. And as he went he glanced back at the sturdy, oil-skinned figure clinging to the rail of the bridge. The man's far-off gaze was fixed on the storm-swept sky, reading every sign with the intimate knowledge of long years of experience. It was a reassuring figure that must have put heart into the veriest weakling. But Bull Sternford needed no such support. In matters of life and death he was without emotion.

He scrambled his way to the leeward side of the engines where a certain warmth and shelter was to be had, and where a number of hardly tested deck chairs were securely lashed. It was the resting place of those few beset passengers who could endure no longer the indifferent, odorous accommodation of the *Myra's* saloon. Only one chair was occupied. For the rest the deck was completely deserted.

Bull's first glance at the solitary passenger was sufficient. The gleam of red hair under the fur cap told him all he wanted to know, and he groped his way along the slippery deck, and deposited his bulk safely into the chair beside Nancy McDonald.

"Say," he cried, with a cheerful grin, as he struggled with his rug, "this sort of thing's just about calculated to leave a feller feeling sympathy with the boy who hasn't more sense than to spend his time trying to climb outside more Rye whisky than he was built to hold. It makes you wonder at the fool thing that lies back of it all. I mean the fuss going on out yonder."

Nancy smiled round from amidst her furs.

"It does seem like useless mischief," she agreed readily. Then she laughed outright. "But to see you crawling along the deck just now, grabbing any old thing for support, and often missing it, was a sight to leave one wondering how much dignity owes to personality, and how much to environment. Guess environment's an easy win."

"Did I look so darn foolish?"

Bull's eyes were smiling, and Nancy laughed again.

"Just about as foolish as that fellow with the Rye whisky you were talking about."

The man settled himself comfortably.

"That's tough. And I guess I was doing my best, too. Say," he went on with a laugh, "just look at those flapping sea-gulls, or whatever they are out there. Makes you wonder to see 'em racing along over this fool waste of water. Look at 'em fighting, struggling, and using up a whole heap of good energy to keep level with this old tub. You know they've only to turn away westward to find land and shelter where they could build nests and make things mighty comfortable for themselves. I don't get it. You know it seems to me Nature got in a bad muss handing out ordinary sense. I'd say She never heard of a card index. Maybe Her bookkeeper was a drunken guy who didn't know a ledger from a scrap book. Now if She'd engaged you an' me to keep tab of things for Her, we'd have done a deal better. Those poor blamed sea-gulls, or whatever they are, would have been squatting around on elegant beds of moulted feathers, laid out on steam-heat radiators, feeding on oyster cocktails and things, and handing out the instructive dope of a highbrow politician working up a press reputation, and learning their kids the decent habits of folk who're yearning to keep out of penitentiary as long as the police'll let 'em. No. It's no use. Nature got busy. Look at the result. Those fool birds'll follow us till they're tired, in the hope that some guy'll dump the contents of the *Myra's* swill barrel their way. Then they'll have one disgusting orgy on the things other folks don't fancy, and start right in to fly again to ease their digestions. It's a crazy game anyway. And it leaves me with a mighty big slump in Nature's stock."

Nancy listened delightedly to the man's pleasant fooling.

"It's worse than that," she cried, falling in with his humour. "Look at some of them taking a rest, swimming about in that terribly cold water. Ugh! No, if we'd fixed their sense we'd have made it so they'd have had enough to get on dry land, like any other reasonable folk yearning for a rest."

The man studied the girl's pretty profile, and a great sense of regret stirred him that the Skandinavia had been able to buy her services. What a perfect creature to have been supported by in the work he was engaged on.

"That sounds good," he said. "Reasonable folks!" He shook his head. "Nature again. Guess we're all reasonable till we're found out. No. Even the greatest men and women on earth are fools at heart, you know."

The girl sat up as the vessel lurched more heavily and flung their chairs forward, straining dangerously.

"How?" she questioned, glancing down anxiously at the moorings of her chair.

"They're safe—so far," Bull reassured her. Then he leant back again, and produced and lit a cigar. "Guess I'll smoke," he said. "Maybe that'll help me tell you—'how.'"

The girl watched him light his cigar and her eyes were full of laughter.

"It's a real pity women can't sit themselves behind a cigar," she said at last, with a pretence of regret. "It's the wisest looking thing a man does. A cigarette kind of makes him seem pleasantly undependable. A pipe makes you feel he's full of just everyday notions. But a cigar! My! It sort of dazzles me when I see a man with a big cigar. I feel like a lowgrade earthworm, don't you know. Say," she cried, with an indescribable gesture of her gloved hands, "he handles that cigar, he sort of fondles it. He cocks it. He depresses it. He rolls it across his lips to the opposite corner of his mouth, and finally blows a thin, thoughtful stream of smoke gently between his pursed lips.

And that stream is immeasurable in its suggestion of wise thought and keen calculation. I'd say a man's cigar is his best disguise."

Bull nodded.

"That's fine," he cried. "But you've forgotten the other feller. The man who 'chews.'"

Nancy laughed happily.

"Easy," she cried promptly. "When he of the bulged cheek gets around just watch your defences. He's mostly tough. He's on the jump, and hasn't much fancy for the decencies of life. The harder he chews the more he's figgering up his adversary. And when he spits, get your weapons ready. When the chewing man succeeds in life I guess he's dangerous. And it's because his force and character have generally lifted him from the bottom of things."

Bull shook his head in mock despair.

Nancy settled herself back in her chair.

"That's fixed it. Guess you'll need to tell *me* 'how.'"

"No, sir," she cried. "You can't go back. 'The greatest men and women in the world are fools at heart.' That's what you said."

"Yes. I seem to remember."

The man stirred and sat up. He folded the rug more closely about his feet. Then he turned with a whimsical smile in his eyes.

"Well?" he cried. "And isn't it so? What do we work, and fight, and hate for? What do we spend our lives worrying to beat the other feller for? Why do we set our noses into other folks' affairs and worry them to death to think, and act, and feel the way we do? And all the while it don't matter a thing. Of course we're fools. We'll hand over when the time comes, and the old world'll roll on, and it's not been shifted a hair's-breadth for our having lived, in spite of the obituaries the news-sheets hand out like a Sunday School mam at prize time. Say, here, it's no use fooling ourselves. Life's one great big thing that don't take shape by reason of our acts. What's the civilisation we love to pat ourselves on the back for? I'll tell you. It's just a thing we've invented, like—wireless telegraphy, or soap, or steam-heat; and it hands us a cloak to cover up the evil that man and woman'll never quit doing. Before we made civilisation a feller got up on to his hind legs and hit the other feller over the head with a club; and if he was hungry he used him as a lunch. Now we don't do that. We break him for his dollars and leave him and his poor wife and kids hungry, while we buy a lunch with the stuff we beat out of him. Why do we work? For one of two elegant notions. It's either to fill ourselves up with the things we've dreamt about when appetite was sharp set, and hate to death when we get, or it's to satisfy a conceit that leaves us hoping and believing the rest of the world'll hand us an epitaph like it handed no other feller since ever it got to be a habit burying up the garbage death produces. Why do we fight and hate? Because we're poor darn fools that don't know better, and don't know the easy thing life would be without those things. And as for settin' our noses into the affairs of other folk, that's mostly disease. But it isn't all. No, sir. There's more to it than that," he laughed. "If it was just disease it wouldn't matter a lot, but it isn't. There isn't a fool man or woman born into this world that doesn't reckon he or she can put right the fool notions and acts of other fools. And when the other feller persuades them the game's not the one-sided racket they guessed it was, then they get mad, and start groping and scheming how to boost their notions on to a world that's spent a whole heap of time fixing things, mostly foolish, to its own mighty good satisfaction. I say right here we're fools if we aren't crooks, which is the exception. There's a dandy world around us full of sun to warm us and food to eat, and birds to sing to us, and flowers and things to make us feel good. If we needed more I guess Providence would have handed it out. But it didn't. And so we got busy with our own notions till we've turned God's elegant creation into a home for crazes and cranks. I could almost fancy the Archangels hovering around, like those silly sea-gulls, with a bunch of straight-jackets to wrap about us when we jump the limit they figger we've a right to. Fools, yes? Why, I guess so—sure."

Nancy breathed a deep sigh.

"My, but that's a big say."

Then she broke into a laugh which found prompt response in the other. It was cut short, however. A sea thundered against the staunch side of the vessel and left her staggering. The girl's eyes became seriously anxious. The straining chairs held, and presently the deck swung up to a comparative level.

"I had visions of the—"

"Scuppers?" Bull laughed. "Yes. That sea's one of the elegant things Providence handed out for our happiness."

Nancy nodded.

"So man built things like the *Myra*, which, of course, was—foolish?"

"An' set out sailing around in a winter storm off Labrador, instead of basking in a pleasant tropical sun, which hasn't any—sense."

Bull chuckled.

"All because two mighty fine enterprises reckoned they'd common interests which were jeopardised by rivalry, which was also—foolishly?"

Bull's cigar ash tumbled into his lap.

"But not ha'f so foolish as the notion that a girl has to suffer the worries and dangers of one hell of a trip on the worst sea that God ever made to try and square the things between them."

Nancy shook her head.

"I can't grant that," she cried quickly.

"No?"

"I mean—oh, psha! Don't you see, or does your cynical philosophy blind you? We're fools, maybe. The things Providence sends us aren't the things we've got a notion for. Maybe we know better than Providence, and can't find happiness in the things it's handed us. What then? As you say, we start right in chasing happiness in the way we fancy. It seems to me the only real happiness in life is in doing. Ease, wealth, love, all the things folk talk and write about are just dreams of happiness that aren't real. Work, achievement, even if it's wrong-headed—that's life; that's happiness. That's why I'd say there's nothing foolish in a girl putting up with dangers and discomforts to bring two enterprises to an understanding, calculated to promote a greater achievement for both. It's my little notion of snatching a bunch of happiness for myself."

There was no laughter in Nancy's eyes now. They were quite serious. Her words were alive with vehemence. Bull was watching her intently, probing, in his searching way, the depths which her hazel eyes hinted at. The things she said pleased him. Her tone thrilled him. He wanted more.

"I wonder," he said, as he rolled the cigar across his lips in the way Nancy had laughingly pointed. "You reckon it's handed you happiness—this thing?"

The girl was stirred.

"Surely," she cried. "Later, when things get fixed up between the Skandinavia and Sachigo, I'll get a focus of my little share in the business of it—the achievement. Then I'll get warm all through with a glow of happiness because I—helped it along."

Bull nodded as he watched the rising colour in the perfect cheeks. The girl was very, very beautiful.

"Yes, I suppose you will," he said. Then he went on provocatively. "But do you guess it's always so? I mean that always happens? Isn't it to do with temperament? Now, take the forest-jacks. Do you guess they feel happiness in a tree dropped right? Do you guess there's happiness for the poor fool who don't know better than to spend his days in a forest risking his life boosting logs on the river jamb? Do you guess there's any sort of old joy for the feller turned adrift, when he's getting old in the tooth, and there's no room for him on the pay roll of the camp, in the thought that he *was* the best axeman the forest ever bred? It seems like a crazy sort of happiness that way. Happiness in achievement's great while the achieving's going on. But at the finish we get right back to Nature. And when that time comes Nature doesn't do much to help us out."

Nancy sat up.

"What are you doing? That great Sachigo!" she demanded challengingly. "You're building, building one magnificent enterprise. Is there happiness in it for you?"

"Sure," Bull admitted frankly. "Oh, yes. But I've no illusions," he said. "I don't go back on the things I said. Nature as she dopes out life couldn't hand me a hundredth part of the happiness I get that way. But when I'm through, like that lumber-jack who's struck off the pay roll, how's it going to be with me? A trained mind without the bodily ability to thrust on in the game of life. It'll be hell—just hell. The one hope is to die in harness. Like the forest-jack who drowns under the logs on the river, or who gets up against the other feller's knife in a drunken scrap. That way lies happiness. The rest is a sort of passing dream with the years of old age for regret."

The girl spread out her hands.

"I can't believe you feel that way," she cried, with something very like distress. "Oh, if I had your power, your ability. Why, I'd say there's no end to the things you could achieve, not only now, but right through, right through that time when you're old in body, but still strong in brain. A limited goal for achievement isn't the notion in my foolish head. Why, if I'd only the strength to knit socks for the folks who need them, there'd still be happiness and to spare. But let's keep to our own ground. The forest-jack. I guess you're one big man who employs thousands. What of those boys when they're struck off the—pay roll. Is there nothing to be achieved that way—nothing to last you to your last living moment? Think of their needs. Think of the happiness you could hand yourself in handing them comfort and happiness when they're—through. It's a thing I've promised myself, if luck ever hands me the chance. You've got the pity of their lives. Your words tell that. Well?"

The man had forgotten the storm. He had forgotten everything but the charm of the girl's hot enthusiasm. And the picture of superlative beauty she made in her animation.

He shook his head.

"It's a bully notion," he demurred, "but it's not for me. No. You see, I'm just a tough sort of man who's big for a scrap. I haven't patience or sympathy for the feller who don't feel the same. You've seen the forest boys?"

"I've been through the Shagaunty."

"Ah!"

Bull Sternford's ejaculation was sharp. The problem of Father Adam's letter was partially solved.

"Well, I guess you're a woman," he went on. "And I'd like to say right here a woman's sympathy is just about the best thing on this old earth. That's why I'd like to cry like a kid when I see it going out to the things that haven't any sort of excuse for getting it. It's good to hear you talk for those boys. It isn't they deserve it, but—as I said, you're a woman. Talk it all you fancy, but leave it at talk. Don't let it get a holt. Don't waste one moment of your hard earned happiness on 'em. I was a forest-jack. I know 'em. I know it—the life. And if you knew the thing I know you wouldn't harden all up as you listen to the things I'm saying:—"

"But—"

Bull flung his cigar away with vicious force.

"Let me say this thing out," he went on. "There's a man in the forest I know, every jack knows. He's a feller who sort of lives in the twilight. You see, he sort of comes and goes; and no one knows a thing about him, except he haunts the forests like a shadow. Well, he's settin' the notion you feel into practice—in a way. He's out for the boys. To help 'em, physically, spiritually, the whole time. They love him. We all love him to death. Well, ask him how far he gets. Maybe he'd tell you, and I guess his story 'ud break the heart of a stone image. He'll tell you—and he speaks the truth—there isn't a thing to be done but heal 'em, and feed 'em, and just help 'em how you can. The rest's a dream. You see, these jacks come from nowhere particular. They take to the forests because it's far off; and it's dark, and covers most things up. And they go nowhere particular, except it's to the hell waiting on most of us if we don't live life the way that's intended for us. No. Quit worrying for the forest-jack. Maybe life's going to hand you all sorts of queer feelings as you go along. And the good heart that sees suffering and injustice is going to ache mighty bad. The forest wasn't built for daylight, and the folks living there don't fancy it. And there isn't a broom big enough in the world to clean up the muck you'll find there."

"You're talking of Father Adam?"

Nancy's interest had redoubled. It had instantly centred itself on the man she had met in the Shagaunty forests. The lumber-jacks were forgotten.

"Yes." Bull nodded. "Do you know him?" There was eagerness in his question.

"I met him on the Shagaunty."

The man had produced a fresh cigar. But the renewed heavy rolling of the vessel delayed its lighting. Nancy gazed out to sea in some concern.

"It's getting worse," she said.

Bull struck a match and covered it with both hands.

"It seems that way," he replied indifferently. Then after a moment he looked up. His cigar was alight. "He's a great fellow—Father Adam," he said reflectively.

"He's just—splendid."

The girl's enthusiasm told Bull something of the thing he wanted to know.

"Yes," he said. "He's the best man I know. The world doesn't mean a thing to him. Why he's there I don't know, and I guess it's not my business anyway. But if God's mercy's to be handed to any human creature it seems to me it won't come amiss—Say!"

He broke off, startled. He sat up with a jump. A great gust of wind broke down upon the vessel. It came with a shriek that rose in a fierce crescendo. His startled eyes were riveted upon a new development in the sky. An inky cloud bank was sweeping down upon them out of the north-east, and the wind seemed to roar its way out of its very heart.

The vessel heeled over. Again the wind tore at the creaking gear. It was a moment of breathless suspense for those seated helplessly looking on. Then something crashed. A vast sea beat on the quarter and deluged the decks, and the chairs were torn from their moorings.

Bull Sternford was sprawling in the race of water. Nancy, too, was hurled floundering in the scuppers. They were flung and beaten, crashing about in the swirling sea that swept over the vessel's submerged rail.

Bull struggled furiously. Every muscle was straining with the effort of it. A fierce anxiety was in his eyes as he fought his way foot by foot towards the saloon companion. The handicap was terrible. There was practically no foothold, for the vessel was riding at an angle of something like forty-five degrees. Then, too, he had but one hand with which to help himself along. The other was supporting the dead-weight of the body of the unconscious girl.

At last, breathless and nearly beaten, he reached his goal and clutched desperately at the door-casing of the companion. He staggered within. And as he did so relief found expression in one fierce exclamation.

"Hell!" he cried. And clambered down, bearing his unconscious burden into the safety of the vessel's interior.

CHAPTER X
IN QUEBEC

It was the final stage of her journey. Nancy was on her way up from the docks, where she had left the staunch *Myra* discharging her cargo.

It was that triumphant return to which she had always looked forward, for which she had hoped and prayed. Her work was completed. It had been crowned with greater success than she had dared to believe possible. Yet her triumph somehow found her unelated, even a shade depressed.

A belated sense of humour battled with her mood. There were moments when she wanted to laugh at herself. There were others when she had no such desire. So she sat gazing out of the limousine window, as though all her interest were in the drab houses lining the way, and the heavy-coated pedestrians moving along the sidewalks of the narrow streets through which they were passing.

It was winter all right, for all no snow had as yet fallen, and the girl felt glad that it was so. It suited her mood.

Once or twice she took a sidelong glance at the man seated beside her; but Bull Sternford's mood was no less reticent than her own. Once she encountered the glance of his eyes, and it was just as the vehicle bumped heavily over the badly paved road.

"We can do better in the way of roads up at Sachigo," he said with a belated smile.

"You surely can," Nancy admitted readily. "The roads down here in the old town are terrible. This old city of ours could fill pages of history. It's got beauties, too, you couldn't find anywhere else in the world. But it seems to need most of the things a city needs to make it the place we folk reckon it is."

She went on at random.

"Do you always keep an automobile in Quebec?" she asked.

Bull shook his head.

"Hired," he said.

"I see."

Bull's eyes twinkled.

"Yes," he went on, "when I make this old city it's with the purpose of driving twenty-four hours work into twelve. An automobile helps that way."

"And you're wasting all this time driving me up to my apartments?" Nancy smiled. "I'm more indebted than I guessed."

The man's denial was instant.

"No," he said. "Your apartments are about two blocks from the Château. But tell me, when'll you be through making your report to Peterman?"

Nancy's depression passed. She was caught again in the interest of everything.

"Why, to-day—surely," she said. "You see, I want to get word to you right away."

Bull nodded.

"That's fine," he said. "It's not my way leaving things lying around either. I'll be on the jump to get through before sailing time to that little old country across the water. But tell me. That report. After it's in you'll have made all the good you reckon to? And then you, personally, cut right out of this thing?"

His manner gave no indication of the thing in his mind.

"Oh, yes," Nancy replied happily. "You see, I've bearded you—only you've no beard—in your fierce den up in Sachigo. And I've—and you've come right down here to Quebec with me to discuss with my people the thing they want to discuss with you. They didn't think I—they didn't hope that. Maybe I've done better than they expected. Why, when I hand the news to Mr. Peterman he'll—he'll—oh, I'm just dying to see his face when I tell him."

"You—haven't wired him already?"

"No. The news was too good to send by wire."

For a moment the man contemplated the simple radiant creature beside him. She was so transparently happy. And the sight of her happiness satisfied him.

"It'll—astonish him, eh?"

"Astonish him?" Nancy laughed. "That doesn't say a thing. I shouldn't wonder if he refused to believe me."

"And you'll get—promotion? Promotion—in Skandinavia?"

The girl's eyes sobered on the instant.

"Surely. Why not?"

"Yes. Why not?"

Just for a moment Nancy hesitated. Then her challenge came incisively

"What do you mean?"

But the man smilingly shook his head.

"You want promotion under Peterman—in the Skandinavia?"

Nancy's eyes widened.

"Why shouldn't I? The Skandinavia's everything to me. It ought to be everything. Isn't that so? Now, I wonder what you mean?" she went on, after the briefest pause. "Are you talking that way just because you are a rival concern?" She shook her head. "That's no affair of mine. But wait while I tell you. Try and think yourself a young girl without folks that count, with a pretty tough world laid out in front of her, and with a healthy desire to dress, and eat the same as any other girl of her age. She's given a chance in life to make good, to gather round her all those things she needs by—the Skandinavia. Well, how would you feel? Wouldn't you want that—promotion? Yes. I want it. I want it with all my heart. The Skandinavia gave me my first start. They've been very, very good to me. I've big room in my heart for them. Their work's my work all the time. I've nothing but gratitude for Mr. Peterman."

"Yes." Bull's smile had passed. He was thinking of Nancy's feeling of gratitude towards the Swede—Peterman.

He turned away, and the grey wintry daylight beyond the window seemed to absorb him. He was possessed by a mad desire to fling prudence to the winds and then and there point out the wrong he felt she was committing against the country that had bred her in spending her life in the service of these foreigners. But he knew he must refrain. It was not the moment. And somehow he felt she was not the girl to listen patiently to such ethics as he preached when their force was directed against those who claimed her whole loyalty and gratitude.

To Nancy it seemed as though some shadow had arisen between them. She was a little troubled at the thing she had said. But somehow she had no desire to withdraw a single word of it.

The car had passed out of the old part of the city. And Nancy realised it was ascending the great hill where the Château Hotel looked out over the old citadel and the wide waters of the busy St. Lawrence river. In a few minutes the happy companionship of the past few days would be only a memory.

It was only a little way to her apartments now. Such a very little way. Yes. The porter would be there. He would take her trunks and baggage, and then her door would close behind her, and—She remembered that moment at which she had awakened to consciousness in this man's strong arms in the poor little saloon of the storm-beaten *Myra*. She remembered the embracing strength of them, and the way she had thrilled under their pressure. It had been all very wonderful.

"Say!"

Bull Sternford had turned back from the window. He was smiling again.

"Yes?" The girl was all eager attention.

"I was wondering," Bull went on. "Maybe you'll' fancy hearing how things are fixed after I see Peterman?"

"I'll be ever so glad. There's the 'phone. You can get me most any time after business hours. I don't go out much. I—"

Nancy broke off to glance out of the window. The automobile had slowed.

"Why, we're at my place," she cried. And the man fancied he detected disappointment in her tone.

The car stopped before the apartment house, and Bull hurled himself at the litter of the girl's belongings strewn about their feet. A few moments later they were standing together on the sidewalk surrounded by the baggage.

Bull gazed up at the building.

"You live here?" he asked at random.

Nancy nodded.

"Yes. It isn't much. But some day, maybe, I'll be able to afford a swell apartment with—"

"Sure you will," Bull agreed, as they passed up the steps to the entrance doors. "But meanwhile I mostly need your 'phone number of this," he added with a laugh.

The baggage was left to the porter's care, and they stood together in the hallway. Bull's youthful stature was overshadowing for all Nancy was tall. Somehow the girl was glad of it. She liked his height, and the breadth of his great shoulders, and the power of limbs his tweed suit was powerless to disguise.

She moved across to the porter's office and wrote down her 'phone number while the man looked on. But he only had eyes for the girl herself. At that moment her telephone number was the last thing he desired to think about.

She stood up and offered him the paper.

"You won't forget it that way," she said, with a smile.

"No."

Bull glanced down at it. Then he looked again into the smiling eyes.

"Thanks," he said. "I'll ring up." Then he held out a hand. "So long."

He was gone. The glass door had swung to behind him. Nancy watched him pass into the waiting automobile, and responded to his final wave of the hand. Then she turned to the porter, and her smile had completely vanished.

Nathaniel Hellbeam stood up. He had been seated at Elas Peterman's desk studying the papers which his managing director had set out for his perusal. His gross body hung over the table for a moment as he reached towards his hat. He took his gloves from inside it and commenced to put them on.

"The *Myra*? You say she is in?" he asked in his guttural fashion. "This girl? This girl who is to buy up this—this Sachigo man," he laughed. "Is she arrived?"

The man's eyes were alight with unpleasant derision. Peterman gave no heed. The man's arrogance was all too familiar to him.

"I've not heard—yet," he said. "She should be."

"You not have heard—yet?" The challenge was superlatively offensive. "You a beautiful secretary have. You lose her for weeks—months. Yet you do not know of her return—yet? Sho! You are not the man for this beautiful secretary. She for me is—yes? Hah!"

Peterman smiled as was his duty.

"I shall be glad to get her back," he said quietly. "But I haven't heard from her at all. And—well, she's not the sort of woman to bombard with telegrams. She's out on a difficult job and I felt it best to leave her to it. I shall hear when she's ready, I guess she'll be right along in to tell me personally. Maybe—"

He broke off and picked up the telephone whose buzzer was rattling impatiently on the desk.

"Hullo!" he said softly. "Oh, yes. Oh, how are you? So glad you've got back. What sort of passage did—oh, bad, eh? Well, well; I'm sorry. Oh, you're a good sailor. That's fine. Right away? You'll be over right away? Wouldn't you like to rest awhile? All right, I see. Yes, surely I'll be glad. I just thought—oh, not at all. You see, if you were a man I wouldn't be concerned at all. Yes, come right along whenever you choose. Eh? Successful? You have been? Why, that's just fine. Well, I'm dying to hear your news. Splendid. I shall be here. G'bye."

Peterman set the 'phone down. His smiling eyes challenged those of the man who a moment before had derided him.

"Well?"

Hellbeam's impatience was without scruple at any time.

"She's got back all right, and she's succeeded far better than you hoped. Better than she hoped herself. But—no better than I expected."

The other's eyes snapped under the quiet satisfaction of the man's reply.

"Ah, she has. Does she say—yes?"

Elas shook his dark head.

"No. She's coming right over to tell me the whole story."

"Now?"

"In a while."

Elas Peterman knew his position to the last fraction when dealing with Nathaniel Hellbeam. He knew it was for him to obey, almost without question. But somehow, for the moment, his Teutonic self-abnegation had become obscured. He was yielding nothing in the matter of this woman to anyone. Not even to Nathaniel Hellbeam whom he regarded almost as the master of his destiny.

Perhaps the gross nature of the financier possessed a certain sympathy. Perhaps even there was a lurking sense of honour in him, where a woman, whom he regarded as another man's property, was concerned. Again it may simply have been that he understood the other's reticence, and it suited him for the moment to restrain his grosser inclinations. He laughed. And it was not an hilarious effort.

"Oh, yes," he said. "You will see her first. That is as it should be. Later, we both will talk with her. Well—good luck my friend."

Hellbeam thrust his hat on his great head and strutted his way across to the door.

"These people must be bought. Or—" he said, pausing before passing out—

"Smashed!"

Hellbeam nodded.

"It suits me better to—buy."

"Yes. You want to come into touch with—the owner."

"Yes."

The gross figure disappeared through the doorway.

Peterman did not return to his desk. He crossed to the window and stood gazing out of it. His hands were thrust deep into his pockets. And his fingers moved nervously, rattling the contents of them. He was a goodly specimen of manhood. He was tall, and squarely erect, and carried himself with that military bearing which seems to belong to all the races of Teutonic origin. It was only in the study of the man's face that exception could be taken. Just now there was none to observe and he was free from all restraint.

His dark eyes were smiling, for his thoughts were streaming along the channel that most appealed. He was thinking of the beauty of the girl who was about to return to him, and it seemed to him a pity she was so simply honest, so very young in the world as he understood it. Then her ambition. It was—but he was rather glad of her ambition. Ambition might prove his best friend in the end. In his philosophy an ambitious woman could have no scruple. Anyway it seemed to him that ambition pitted against scruple was an easy winner. He could play on that, and he felt he knew how to play on it, and was in a position to do so. She had come back to him successful. He wondered how successful.

He moved from the window and passed over to the desk, where he picked up his 'phone and asked for a number.

"Hullo! Oh, that Bennetts? Oh, yes. This is Peterman—Elas Peterman speaking. Did you send that fruit, and the flowers I ordered to the address I gave you? Yes? Oh, you did? They were there before eleven o'clock. Good. Thanks—"

He set the 'phone down and turned away. But in a moment he was recalled. It was a message from downstairs. Nancy McDonald wished to see him.

Peterman was leaning back in his chair. Nancy was occupying the chair beside the desk which had not known her for several months.

It was a moment of stirring emotions. For the girl it was that moment to which she had so long looked forward. To her it seemed she was about to vindicate this man's confidence in her, and offer him an adequate return such as her gratitude desired to make. And deep down in her heart, where the flame of ambition steadily burned, she felt she had earned the promised reward, all of it.

The man was concerned with none of these things. He was not even concerned for the girl's completed mission. It was Nancy herself. It was the charming face with its halo of red hair, and the delightful figure so rounded, so full of warmth and charm, which concerned him.

He had no scruple as he feasted his eyes upon her. He did nothing to disguise his admiration, and Nancy, full of her news and the thrilling joy of her success, saw nothing of that which a less absorbed woman, a more experienced woman, must unfailingly have observed.

"You've a big story for me," Peterman said, with a light laugh. "Have you completed an option on—Sachigo? You look well. You're looking fine. Travelling in Labrador seems to have done you good."

Nancy's smiling eyes were alight with delight.

"Oh, yes," she said. "It's done me good. But then I've had a success I didn't reckon on. Maybe it's made all the difference. It was a real tough journey. I'm not sure you'd have seen me back at all if it hadn't been for Mr. Sternford."

"How?"

The man's smiling eyes had changed. Their dark depths were full of sharp enquiry. Nancy read only anxiety.

"Why, we were sitting on deck, and it was storming. It was just terrible. We lurched heavily and shipped a great sea. Our chairs were flung into the scuppers by the rush of water, and I—why, I guess I was beaten unconscious and drowning when he got hold of me. He just fought his way to safety. I didn't know about it till I was safe down in the saloon. I woke up then, and he was carrying me—"

"Sternford?"

The change in the man's eyes had deepened. Then his smile came back to them. But that, too, was different. It was curiously fixed and hard.

"You've gone a bit too fast for me," he said. "I don't get things right. Sternford, the man running Sachigo was with you on the *Myra*? He's here—in Quebec?"

It was Nancy's great moment.

"Yes," she said, with a restraint that failed to disguise her feelings. "He's come down to discuss a business arrangement between the Skandinavia and his enterprise. That's what you wanted—isn't it?"

The man leant forward in his chair. He set his elbows on the desk and supported his chin in both hands. His smile was still there, and his eyes were steadily regarding her. But they expressed none of the surprise and delight Nancy looked for. They were smiling as he literally forced them to smile.

"You brought him down with you—to meet us?" he asked slowly.

The girl nodded.

"You did your work so well that he entertained the notion sufficiently to come along down—with you?"

"I—I—he's come down for that purpose."

The man's eyes were searching.

"Where is he?"

"At the Chateau. He's waiting to hear from you for an appointment."

Peterman flung himself back in his chair with a great laugh. Nancy missed the mirthless tone of it.

"Say, my dear," he cried at last. "How did you do it? How in—You're just as bright and smart as I reckoned. You've done one big thing and I guess you've earned all the Skandinavia can hand you. But—"

He broke off, and his gaze drifted away from the face with its vivid halo. The wintry daylight beyond the window claimed him, and Nancy waited.

"How did you persuade him to ship down on the *Myra* with you?" he asked, after a moment's thought.

"I didn't persuade him. He volunteered."

"Volunteered?"

"Yes. He was coming down on her next trip. You see, he's making England right away. He guessed he'd come along down with me instead. He seemed keen set to discuss this thing with you."

"I see. Keen set, eh? Keen set to talk with me?"

The man shook his head. It was not denial. It was the questioning of something left unspoken.

The girl became anxious. Somehow a sense of disappointment was stirring.

"Is there anything wrong?" she asked at last, as the man remained silent.

Peterman shook his head again.

"Not a thing, my dear," he said. "No. You've done everything. You couldn't have done more if—if you'd been the most experienced woman schemer in big business. You went up to prepare the ground for our business. Well, you prepared it in a way I'd never have guessed. You've brought this hard business head, Bull Sternford, right down out of his fortress to meet us on our business proposition. Guess only you could have done that." He laughed. "And this man saved your life, eh? And he carried you in his arms to—safety. Say he was lucky. That's something any man would be crazy to do. Well, well, I—"

He rose from his chair and passed round to the window where he stood with back turned. Nancy's gaze followed him. For all his praise she was disturbed.

The man at the window saw nothing of that upon which he gazed. His eyes were unsmiling now that the girl could no longer observe them. They were the eyes of a man of unbridled jealous fury. They were burning with an insensate hatred for the man who had hitherto been only a stranger rival in business.

Oh, he understood. Was it likely that this Bull Sternford was going to yield for a business proposition in this fashion at the request of a formidable rival? Was he going to change all his plans at the bidding of the Skandinavia, and seize the first boat to come and tell them he was prepared to fall for any plans they might design to beat him? Not likely. No. It was the girl he had fallen for. He had changed his plans for her, and for his nerve he had reaped a harvest such as he, Peterman, had never reaped. He had held this beautiful creature in his arms, this innocent, red-haired child, whom he,

Peterman, had marked down for his own. For how long? And she was all unconscious. Oh, it was maddening, infuriating. And—

Suddenly he came back to the desk. Nancy was relieved as she beheld the familiar smiling kindness in his eyes.

"Well, my dear. I can't tell you how delighted I am to get you back," he said, pausing at her side. "My work's not been by any means satisfactory with you away. There's just no one suits me in this house like you. But the thing I'm most glad about is your success. That's been wonderful. I felt you would make good, but I didn't know how good. Now I'm going to ring this fellow up and fix things to see him. Meanwhile you get your big report of the camps ready for the Board. Then, when you're ready, I'm going to let them see you, and hear it all from you first hand, and I'm going to get them to give you the head of the forestry department right here. It'll be a mighty jump, but—well—"

Nancy was on her feet and her eyes were shining a gratitude which words could never express. Impulsively she held out a hand in ardent thanks.

"Why, say—" she began.

The man had seized the delicate tapering fingers and held them warmly in the palms of both of his.

"Now just don't say a thing," he said. "I know. I know just how you feel, and the things you want to say. But don't. You've earned the best, and I'm going to see you get it. I'm going to lose a smart secretary, but I don't care if I make one good little friend. Now, Nancy, what about to-night? I think we ought to celebrate your triumphant return with a little dinner up at the Chateau. What say? Will you—honour me? Eight o'clock. Thank goodness we're not a dry country yet, and it's still possible to enjoy our successful moments properly. Will you?"

Nancy longed to withdraw the hand the man still held. It was curious. Every word he said expressed just those things and tributes which her girlish vanity had desired. There was not a word in all of it to give offence. But for the second time she experienced a sense of trouble which her woman's instinct prompted, and a feeling akin to panic stirred. But she resisted it, as she knew she must, and her mind was quite made up.

"You're—very kind," she said, with all the earnestness she could summon, and with a gentleness that was intended to disarm. "But I'm so very—very tired. You don't know what it was like on the *Myra*. We were battered and beaten almost to death. I feel as if I needed sleep for a week."

The man released her hand lingeringly. His disappointment was intense, but he smiled.

"Why, sure," he said, "if you feel that way. I hadn't thought."

Then he turned abruptly back to his desk. "That's all right. Guess we'll leave it. You go right home and get your rest."

For a moment Nancy hesitated. She was fearful of giving offence. She felt the man's disappointment in his tone, and in the manner of his turning away. But she dared not yield to his request. Suddenly she remembered, and all hesitation passed.

"I—I just want to thank you for your kind thought sending me those flowers and fruit," she exclaimed. "I wanted to thank you before, but I was too excited with my news. I—"

The man cut her short.

"That's all right, my dear," he said. Then he nodded and deliberately turned to his work. "I'm glad. Now—just run right along home and—rest."

CHAPTER XI
DRAWN SWORDS

The palatial halls and public rooms of the hotel were crowded. Everywhere was the hum of voices, which penetrated even to the intended quiet of the writing rooms. Every now and then the monotony of it all was broken by the high-pitched, youthful voices of the messenger boys seeking out their victims.

Bull Sternford was at work. Within an hour of his arrival he was plunged in the affairs connected with the great business organisation he projected. The earlier date of his visit to Quebec had necessitated considerable changes in plans already prepared. He had entailed for himself endless added work for the pleasure of the companionship of a beautiful girl on the journey down the coast, and begrudged no detail of it. Just now he was writing to a number of important people, bankers and financial men, re-arranging appointments to suit his change of plans.

There was something tremendously purposeful in the poise of the man's body as he sat at one of the many writing tables scattered about the smoking lounge. There were few passers-by who did not glance a second time in his direction with that curiosity which is unfailing in human nature at sight of an unusual specimen of their kind.

Twice a name was called by a uniformed boy in that unintelligible fashion which seems to be the habit of his species. The boy hovered round. Then he came up behind the chair on which Bull was seated and hurled his final challenge.

"Sternford, sir?" he asked curtly.

His victim turned.

"Yes."

"Wanted on the 'phone, sir."

The boy was gone on the run. He had hunted his quarry down. There were still fresh victories to be achieved.

Bull was at the 'phone, and his eyes were smiling at an insurance advertisement set up for the edification and interest of those whose use of the instrument prevented their escape.

"Yes. Oh, yes. Got in this morning. What's that? Oh, pretty rough. Yes. It's a bad sea most all the time. Why, that's good of you, Mr. Peterman." His smile broadened. "Yes. You sent an excellent ambassador. A charming girl. Well, there's no time like the present. Yes. I've lunched. I'm just through with my mail. Four o'clock would suit me admirably. Why sure I'd like to. All right. G'bye."

He stood for a moment after replacing the receiver. Then, becoming aware of another wanting to use the instrument, he moved away.

Returning to the smoking lounge he finished off his correspondence and took possession of one of the couches and lit a cigar.

For a time the hang-over of business pre-occupied him. But it was not for long. His whole thought swiftly became absorbed in Nancy McDonald, with her wonderful halo of vivid hair. It had been the same during the whole of his journey down from Sachigo, in fact, from the moment he had first set eyes on her when she entered his office on that memorable day of her visit. She pre-occupied all his leisure.

He had thought deeply on the meaning of her visit to him, and his thought had had little to do with the mission she had come upon. Swift decision had dealt with that. No, it was the girl herself who claimed him.

He understood the sheer design of the Skandinavia in sending so perfect a creature to him. That was easy. It only helped to prove their desire—their urgent desire—to free themselves from the threat of his competition. But he wondered at their selection.

Somehow he felt that the Skandinavia should have chosen, if their choice fell upon a woman, a clever, brilliant, unscrupulous creature who knew her every asset, and was capable of playing every one of them in the game of commercial warfare. Instead of that they had sent Nancy, with her sweetly beautiful face and perfect hair, to be their unthinking tool. He realised her simplicity, her splendid loyalty to those she served. He knew she was without design or subterfuge. She was just the most beautiful, desirable creature he had ever beheld in his life.

He told himself it was all wrong. This wonderful child should never have been sent on such a journey, on such an errand. She was fit only for the shelter of a happy home life, protection from every roughness, every taint with which the sordid world of commerce could besmirch her. His chivalry was stirred to its depths, and the wrong of it all, as he saw it, only the more surely deepened his purpose for his dealings with an unscrupulous rival who could commit so egregious an outrage.

Bull Sternford's existence, until now had always been a joyous heart-whole striving which had no more in it than the calmly conceived ideals of a heart undisturbed by sexual emotions. Now—now that had been completely changed. Perhaps he was not yet wholly aware of the thing that had come to him. He saw a woman, a perfect creature who had come to him out of the forest world in which his whole life was bound up, and a passionate excitement had taken possession of him. There could be no denial of that. But so far the full measure of his feelings had not revealed itself. All he wanted was to think of nothing and nobody just now, but this girl who had stirred him so deeply. So he stretched himself out on the well-sprung couch and yielded to the delight of it all.

But the hour he had been free to dispose of thus was swiftly used up with his pleasant dreaming. And it was with a feeling of real irritation that he finally flung away his cigar and bestirred himself. His irritation did not last long, however, and his consolation was found in the fact that Elas Peterman was awaiting him, and Elas Peterman was the man who had so outrageously offended against his ideas of chivalry.

He stood up and brushed the fallen cigar ash from his clothing. His one desire now was to get through with the business once and for all, to do the thing that should leave Nancy McDonald with the reward of her labours. Yes, he wanted to do that. Afterwards—well, he must leave the "afterwards" to itself.

He hurried away in search of his heavy winter overcoat.

Elas Peterman looked up as the door opened to admit his visitor. His first impression startled him not a little.

It was the first time he had encountered the man from Sachigo.

Bull moved into the room with that large ease which big men so often display. And he paused and frankly gripped the carefully manicured hand Peterman held out to him.

"I'm real glad to meet you, Mr. Peterman," he said quietly. Then he dropped into the chair set for him, while his eyes responded unsmilingly to the measuring gaze of the other.

"It's queer we've never met before," Bull said, leaning back in his chair.

Peterman laughed. He pushed a large box of cigars close to the visitor's hand.

"It's mostly that way with the high command in—war," he said easily. "The opposing generals don't meet except at the—peace table. Those are Bolivars. Try one?"

Bull helped himself with a laugh that was about as real as the other's.

"The pipe of—peace, eh?" he said.

"That's how I hope," Peterman replied.

Bull nodded as he lit his cigar.

"Most of us hope for peace, and do our best to aggravate war. That so?"

"It's damn fool human nature."

Peterman sat back in his chair, and laughed a little boisterously. Then he turned to the window while Bull silently consulted the white ash of his cigar.

"You're projecting a big thing in pulp," the Swede said a moment later. "You figger to split the Canadian pulp trade into two opposing camps. The Skandinavia and the Labrador enterprises. It means one great, big prolonged battle in which one or the other is to be beaten. Guess it's liable to be a battle in which the public'll get temporary benefit, while we—who fight it—look like losing all along the line. It seems a pity, eh?"

"War's a tough proposition, anyway," Bull replied slowly. "Its only excuse is it's Nature's way of wiping out the fool mistakes and crimes human nature spends most of its time committing. If two sets of criminals set out to grab, it's odds they'll do hurt to each other, and end by leaving the world easier when they're completely despoiled."

Peterman laughed.

"Sure," he said. "And these fool criminals? Is there need for them to fall out?"

"None."

"That's how we of the Skandinavia feel. That's the notion always in my mind. Say—"

"Yep?"

Bull's eyes were squarely gazing. Their clear depths looked straight into the dark eyes of the man at the desk. Their regard was intense. It was almost disconcerting.

"What's the proposition?" he went on. And his firm lips closed over the last word and contrived to transform the simple question into a definite challenge.

Peterman stirred uneasily. At that moment he beheld more clearly than ever the picture of this man with his great arms about the body of the woman he coveted, and feeling lent sharpness to his tone.

"What's the price you set on your enterprise up at Labrador?" he said.

Bull removed his cigar. He emitted a pensive stream of smoke. His eyes were again pre-occupied with the white ash, so firm and clean on its tip. Then quite suddenly he looked up.

"If you'll tell me the price you set on the whole of the Skandinavia, I'll talk."

"What d'you mean?"

The Swede had less command of his feelings than the other. He had never learnt the methods of the forest as Bull had learned them.

"Why, I can't set a price on Sachigo till I know the price you set on the Skandinavia," Bull's eyes were smiling. "You see I should need to double it for—Sachigo."

The man from Labrador had driven home to the quick, and the Teutonic vanity of the Swede was instantly aflame. Peterman had committed the one offence which the younger man could not forgive. He had dared, in his vanity, to believe that the situation between them was a question of price.

"I didn't invite you here to sell you—the Skandinavia," Peterman blustered, giving way to anger he could not restrain.

"No. And I didn't accept your invitation for the purpose of selling—Sachigo. If there's any buying and selling going on you'd best understand quite clearly I am the buyer."

There was a dangerous light in Bull's eyes levelled so steadily on the angry face of the Swede.

"Then—it's war?"

Bull shrugged at the challenge.

"I'm quite indifferent," he said coldly.

There was a moment of tense silence. Then the Swede smiled.

"You're ready then to let the fool public benefit at your expense?"

"No." A smile of real humor flashed in Bull's eyes. "At yours."

"You mean—you think to—smash us?"

"Just as sure as the sun'll rise to-morrow. Just as sure as Providence set up forest and water powers on Labrador such as you've never dreamed of since you forgot your boyhood. Just as sure as your Shagaunty's played out and you need to start in on fresh limits you aren't sure of yet. Just as sure as they're going to cost you a heap more than when you were busy treating the fortune that Shagaunty handed you like the worst fool-head spendthrift who ever broke a bank at the gambling tables."

Bull rose abruptly from his chair.

"I'm obliged for this interview, Mr. Peterman," he went on. "It's suited me. That's why I came along down in a hurry. You're fortunate in that lady representative. Her tact and persuasion left me feeling you had a real proposition that was worth considering. I guess she'll go a long way for you, and if there's any live person can help your ship along, she's that live person. But you can't buy me, and you can't smash me. I mean that. You see, I know your position. It's my job to know the position of any possible competitor, and naturally I know yours. Your Shagaunty's run dry, and, well, I don't need to tell you all that means to you." He dropped the stump of his cigar into an ash tray. "That's a good cigar," he went on with a derisive smile. "Thanks. Good-bye."

Bull was at the telephone again. He was again smiling at the insurance advertisement. But now his smile was of a different quality. It was full of delighted anticipation.

"Oh, yes," he was saying. "I spent quite a pleasant ha'f hour with him. I enjoyed it immensely. Yes. He seems to be the man to run an enterprise like yours. He certainly has both initiative and confidence. A little hasty in judgment, I think. But—yes, I'd like to tell you all about it. What are you doing this evening? Oh, resting. I suppose you eat while resting. Yes. It's necessary, isn't it? Anyway I find it so. Eh? Oh, yes. You see, I've a big frame to support. Will you help me to support it this evening? I mean dinner here? Will you? Oh, that's fine. I'd love to tell you about it all. Fine. Right. Eight o'clock then. I'll go and arrange it all now. It shall be a very special dinner, I promise you. Good-bye."

He put up the receiver and turned away. His smile remained, and it had no relation to anything but his delight that Nancy McDonald had consented to dine with him.

CHAPTER XII
AT THE CHATEAU

Nancy was standing before the mirror which occupied the whole length of the door of the dress-closet with which her modest bedroom had been provided by a thoughtful architect.

She was studying the results of her preparations. She was to dine with Bull Sternford, the man who had caught and held her interest for all she knew that they belonged to camps that were sternly opposed to each other. She wanted to look her best, whatever that best might be, and she was haunted by a fear that her best could never rank in its due place amongst the superlatives.

However, she had arrayed herself in her newest and smartest party frock. She had spent hours, she believed, on her unruly masses of hair, and furthermore, she had assiduously applied herself to obliterating the weather stain which the fierce journey from Labrador had inflicted upon the beautiful oval of her cheeks. Now, at last, the final touches had been given, and she was critically surveying the result.

The longer she studied her reflection the deeper grew the discontent in her pretty, hazel eyes. It was the same old reflection, she told herself. It was a bit tricked out; a bit less real. It was a tiresome thing which gave her no satisfaction at all. There was the red hair that looked so very red. There were the eyes, which, at times, she was convinced were really green. There was the stupid nose that always seemed to her to occupy too much of her face. And as for her cheeks, the wind and sea had left them looking more healthy, but—She sighed and hurriedly turned away. She felt that mirrors were an invention calculated to upset the conceit of any girl.

She moved quickly round the little room. Her gloves, her wrap. She picked them up. The gloves she was painfully aware had already been cleaned twice, and her cloak had no greater merits than the modest-priced frock which had strained her limited bank roll. Then she consulted the clock on her bureau, and, picked up her scent-spray. This was the last, the final touch she could not resist.

In the midst of using it she set it down with a feeling of sudden panic.

She had remembered. She stood staring down at the dressing table with a light of trouble in her eyes. The whole incident had been forgotten till that moment. She remembered she had refused to dine with Elas Peterman that night on a plea of weariness, and without a thought had unhesitatingly accepted the invitation of the man whom the Skandinavia had marked down for its victim.

For some seconds the enormity of the thing she had done overwhelmed her. Then a belated humour came to her rescue and a shadowy smile drove the trouble from her eyes.

Suppose—but no. Her chief would be dining at home, as was his habit. Then, anyway, there could be no harm. She was concerned in this thing. She had a right. She even told herself it was imperative she should know what had transpired at the interview she had brought about. Besides, was there not the possibility of certain rougnnesses occurring between the two men which it might be within her power to smooth down? That was surely so. She had no right to miss any opportunity of furthering the ends of her own people.

Then she laughed outright. Oh, it was excuse. She knew. She was looking forward to the evening. Of course she was. Then, just as suddenly all desire to laugh expired. Why? Why was she looking forward to dining with Bull Sternford?

Bull! What a quaint name. She had thought of it before. She had thought of it at the time when the lonely missionary of the forest had told her of him.

Swiftly her thought passed on to her meeting with the man himself. She remembered her nervousness when she had first looked into his big, wholesome face, with its clear, searching eyes. Yes, she had realised then the truth of Father Adam's description. He would as soon fight as laugh. There could be no doubt of it.

And then those days on the *Myra*. She recalled their talk of the sea-gulls, and of the men of the forests, and she remembered the almost brutal contempt for them he had so downrightly expressed. Then the moment of disaster to herself. It was he who had saved her, he who had fought for her, although he had been in little better case himself.

What was it they had told her? He must be bought or smashed. She wondered if they realised the man they were dealing with. She wondered what they would have felt and thought if they had listened to the confident assurance of Father Adam. If they had listened to Bull Sternford himself, and learned to know him as she had already learned to know him. The Skandinavia was powerful, but was it powerful enough to deal as they desired with this man who was as ready to fight as to laugh?

She shook her head. And it was a negative movement she was unaware of. Well, anyway, the game had begun, and she was in it. Her duty was clear enough. And meanwhile she would miss no opportunity to pull her whole weight for her side, even when she knew that was not the whole thought in her mind.

But somehow there were things she regretted when she remembered the fight ahead. She regretted the moment when this man had saved her from almost certain death against the iron stanchions and sides of the *Myra*. She regretted his fine eyes, and he had fine eyes which looked so squarely out of their setting. Then, too, he had been so kindly concerned that she should achieve the mission upon which she had embarked. It would have been so easy and even exacting had he been a man of less generous impulse. A man whom she could have thoroughly disliked. But he was the reverse of all those things which make it a joy to hurt. He was—

She pulled herself up and seized the pretty beaded vanity bag lying ready to her hand. Then the telephone rang.

It was the cab which the porter had ordered, and she hastily switched off the lights.

On the way down in the elevator her train of thought persisted. And long before she reached the Chateau, a feeling that she was playing something of the part of Delilah took hold of her and depressed her.

But she was determined. Whatever happened her service and loyalty was in support of her early benefactors, and no act of hers should betray them.

The scene was pleasantly seductive. There was no doubt or anxiety in Nancy McDonald's mind now. How should there be? She was young. She was beautiful. The man with whom she was dining was remarkable amongst the well-dressed throng that filled the great dining-room. Then the dinner had been carefully considered.

But it was the delightful surroundings, the little excitement of it all that left the girl's thought care-free. The shaded table lights. The wonderful flowers. The dark panelling of the great room constructed and designed in imitation of an old French Chateau. Then the throng of beautifully gowned women, and the men who purposed an evening of enjoyment. The soft music of the distant string band and—oh, it was all dashed with a touch of Babylonic splendour with due regard for the decorum required by modern civilisation, and Nancy was sufficiently young and unused to delight in every moment of it.

The first excitement of it all had spent itself, and laughing comment had given place to those things with which the girl was most concerned.

"Folks can't accuse us of dilatoriness," she said. "Let's see. Why, we made land this morning after every sort of a bad passage, battered and worn, and in less than how many hours?—eight?—nine?—" she laughed. "Why, I guess a sewing bee wouldn't have got through their preliminary talk in that time."

"No." Bull too was in the mood for laughter. "A sewing bee's mighty well named. There's a big buzz mostly all the time, and the tally of work only needs to be figgered when the season closes. We've settled up the future of two enterprises liable to cut big ice in this country's history in record time."

"You've settled with Mr. Peterman?"

"Roughly."

The man's eyes were shining with a smile of keen enjoyment.

Nancy experienced a thrill of added excitement as she disposed of her last oyster.

"I haven't a right to butt in asking too many questions," she suggested.

Bull tasted his wine and thoughtfully set his glass down. Then he looked across at the eager face alight with every question woman's curiosity and interest could inspire. He smiled into it. And somehow his smile was very, very gentle.

"That's pretty well why we're here now though," he said. "You can just ask all you fancy to know, and I'll tell you. But maybe I can save you worry by telling you first."

"Why, yes," Nancy said eagerly. "You see, I'm only a secretary. I'm not one of the heads of the Skandinavia. I sort of feel this is high policy which doesn't really concern me. You're sure you feel like telling me? Was Mr. Peterman—friendly?"

"As amiable as a tame—shark."

"That's pretty fierce."

Bull shook his head.

"It's just a way of putting it. Y'see even a tame shark don't get over a lifetime habit of swallowing most things that come his way. Peterman figures to swallow me—whole."

Nancy's eyes widened. But the man's tone had been undisturbed. There was a contented smile in his eyes, and an atmosphere of unruffled confidence about him that was rather inspiring. The girl felt its influence.

"You mean he figures to have you join up with the Skandinavia?"

Bull shook his head as the waiter set the next course on the table.

"No. He guesses the Skandinavia can buy me."

"I—see."

Nancy waited. She remembered this man was as ready to fight as to laugh. Somehow she scented the battle in him now, for all the ease in his manner.

"I told him it couldn't. I pointed out if there was any buying to be done I figgered to do it."

"You mean you would buy up—the Skandinavia?"

Bull's smile deepened. The girl's incredulity amused him. He understood. To her the Skandinavia Corporation was the beginning and end of all things. In her eyes it was the last word in power and influence and wealth. She knew nothing beyond—the Skandinavia. A man in her place would have received prompt and biting retort. But she was a girl, and Bull was young, and strong, and at the beginning of a great manhood. He shook his head.

"Well, not just that," he said. "But say, let's get it right. How'd a woman feel if she'd an elegant baby child, thoroughbred from the crown of his dandy bald head to the pretty pink soles of his feet? Just a small bit of her, of her own creation. Then along comes some big, swell woman, who's only been able to raise a no account, sickly kid, an' wants to buy up the first mother's bit of sheer love. Wouldn't she hear the sort of things a woman of that sort ought to? Wouldn't she get hell raised with her?"

"But the Skandinavia's no—sickly kid."

The girl's eyes were challenging. There was warmth, too, in her retort. His words had stirred her as he intended them to stir her.

"You think that?" he said. "You think that they have the right to demand my—child? You approve? That was your desire when you came to me—that they should buy me up?"

Bull's smile still remained. There was no shadow of change in it. But his questions came in headlong succession.

Just for an instant a feeling of helplessness surged through the girl's heart. Then it passed, leaving her quite firm and decided. She looked squarely into the smiling eyes, and hers were unsmiling but earnestly honest.

"My approval isn't of any concern. I knew that was the Skandinavia's purpose when I came to you."

"And you called it a business arrangement?"

"No. You did."

The man broke into a laugh. It was a laugh of sheer amusement.

"That's so," he said. "You were going to hand me the story of your mission, and I—and I butted in and told it to you—myself."

The girl nodded.

"You were very good to me," she said. "You saw I was going to flounder, and you took pity on me."

Bull's denial was prompt.

"I just short-circuited things. That's all," he said. Then he laughed again. "And I'm going to do it again right now. Here, I want you to hear things the way they seem to me. You think the Skandinavia's no sickly kid. Well, I tell you it is. Anyway, in this thing. Peterman wants to buy me. Why? Don't you know? I think you do. The Skandinavia's got a mighty bad scare right now. The Shagaunty's played out. And I'm jumping the market. For the practical purposes of the moment the Skandinavia's mighty sick. So Peterman and his friends reckon to buy me. You're wise to it all?"

Bull's eyes were levelled squarely at the girl's. There was a challenge in them. But there was no roughness. It was his purpose to arrive at the full measure of the girl's feelings and attitude, so far as this effort on the part of his rivals was concerned.

Nancy was swift to understand. In an ordinary way her reply would have been prompt. There would have been no hesitation. But, somehow, there was reluctance in her now. She made no attempt to analyse her feelings. All she knew was that this man had a great appeal for her. He was so big, he was so strongly direct and fearless. Then, too, his manner was so very gentle, and his expressive eyes so kindly smiling, while all the while she felt the fierce resentment against her people going on behind them.

After a moment decision came to her rescue. She was of the opposing camp. She could not, and would not, pretend. It was clear that war lay ahead, and her position must be that of an honest enemy.

"Yes," she said simply. "I think I know all there is to know about the position."

She hesitated again. Then she went on in a fashion that displayed the effort her words were costing.

"We're out to buy you or break you, and I shall play the part they assign me in the game. Oh, I've nothing to hide. I've no excuse to make. You will fight your battle, and we shall fight ours. Maybe we shall learn to hate each other in the course of it. I don't know. Yet there's nothing personal in the fight. That's the queer thing in commercial warfare, isn't it? I'd be glad for our two concerns to run right along side by side. But they can't. They just can't. And, as I understand, one or the other's got to go right to the wall before we're through. Can't all this be saved? Must all this sort of—bloodshed—go on? We're two great enterprises, and, combined, we'd be just that much greater. Together we'd rule the whole world's markets and dictate our own terms. And then, and then—"

"We'd be doing the thing I'm out to stop—if it costs me all I have or am in this world."

For a moment the man's eyes forgot to smile, and Nancy was permitted to gaze on the great, absorbing purpose his manner had hitherto held concealed. She was startled at the passionate denial, and robbed of all desire to reply.

"Here!" Bull set his elbows on the table and supported his chin on his hands. "Get this. Get it good, and all the time. I wouldn't work with the Skandinavia for all the dollars this country's presses could print. I'm not going to hand you the reason. Some day, maybe when your folks have smashed me, or I've smashed them, I'll tell you about it. But I tell you this now, there's no sort of business arrangement I ever figgered to enter into with Elas Peterman, and there's no sort of thing in God's world ever could, or would, induce me to come to any terms of his."

Then his manner changed again, and his passionate moment became lost in a great laugh.

"Maybe you'll want to know why I changed my plans so easily, and came along down in a hurry to see Peterman. Why I seemed ready to fall for his proposition. Well, I guess I won't hand you the reason of that, either. I'd like to, but I won't." He shook his head and his laugh had gone again. "Anyway, it served my purpose, and Peterman knows just how things stand—and are going to stand—between us."

"Then it's war? Ruthless, implacable—war?" There was awe in the girl's tone and her lips were dry. She sipped her wine quickly to moisten them, and set the glass down with a hand that was not quite steady. Bull saw the signs of distress.

"Oh, yes, it's war all right," he said quietly. "Maybe it's ruthless, implacable. But it's part of the game. Don't worry a thing. You're in the enemy lines. You've got your duty. So far you've done your duty; and you've made good, and will get the reward you need. Well, go right on doing that duty, and there isn't a just creature on God's earth that'll have right to blame you. I won't blame you. Go right on; and when it's all through, I'll be ready to sit here with you again, and talk and laugh over it, as we've been doing—"

He broke off. A frightened look had leapt into Nancy's eyes. She was no longer attending to him. She was watching the tall, squarely military figure of a man moving down one of the aisles between the softly lit tables. The man's dark eyes were searching over the room, as he followed the head waiter conducting him to the table that had been reserved for him. Bull turned and followed the direction of the girl's gaze. And as he did so he encountered the cold, unsmiling glance of the other man's eyes. It was only for an instant. Then he turned back to the girl.

"Friend Peterman," he said.

Nancy made a pretence of eating.

"Yes," she said, without raising her eyes.

Nancy's emotion was painfully obvious. Bull realised it. She was afraid. Why? A swift thought flashed through the man's mind, to be followed by a feeling such as he had never known before. Hitherto Elas Peterman had represented only a sufficiently worthy adversary who must be encountered and defeated. Now, all in a moment, that was changed into something fiercer, more furiously human and abiding.

"Does it matter?" he asked very quietly.

Nancy looked up from her plate. There was a flicker of a smile in the eyes that a moment before had expressed only apprehension. She shook her head.

"I don't know—yet," she said. Her smile deepened. "You see, I refused to dine with him here to-night. I excused myself on a plea of weariness. I really did want rest. But—well, I didn't want to dine with him, anyway. He's seen me—with you."

"Do you often dine with him?"

The man had no smile in response, and his question came swiftly.

"I've never dined with him."

Bull sat back. His eyes were smiling.

"Well, I guess the answer's easy. You're here fighting for the Skandinavia. And I'd say you've been doing it mighty well. Maybe Peterman'll feel sore, but he'll see it that way after—awhile."

CHAPTER XIII
DEEPENING WATERS

Nancy thought long and earnestly over her breakfast. She thought deeply as she proceeded to her office. Even the business of again taking up the thread of her work failed to absorb her.

Apprehension disturbed, and a certain sense of guilt weighed upon her. The vision of the tall figure of Elas Peterman as it moved down the dining-room at the Chateau remained with her. She had caught the glance of his dark eyes. She knew he had recognised her; and there had been neither smile nor recognition in the swift exchange that had passed between them.

So she answered the usual morning summons of her chief without any pleasant anticipation. She expected a bad time, and strove to prepare herself for it.

But alarm vanished the moment she ushered herself into the man's presence. He was not at his desk poring over his littered correspondence. She found him standing before his favourite window, gazing out reflectively upon the grey light of the early winter day. He turned at the sound of her entry, and his smile of greeting lacked nothing of its usual cordiality.

Had she observed him a moment before it must have been different. But she had been spared all sight of the mood that had driven him to abandon urgent correspondence in favour of the drab outlook beyond the window. It was a bad expression. It was the expression of a man of fierce cruelty. It was not an expression of open, hot anger, which flares up, passes, and is forgotten like the fury of a summer storm. It was rather the slowly banking clouds of winter, piling up for a climax that should be devastating. And through it all he had smiled, smiled with angry eyes that seemed to grow colder and harder every moment.

Nancy knew little of the world, and less of men and women. It could not have been otherwise. Vital with a youthful optimism and strong purpose, she had devoted herself to work to the exclusion of everything else. And before that there had only been the scrupulous care of the good matrons of Marypoint. A wider experience, a maturer mind would have yielded her doubt as she beheld the man's smiling greeting now. She would have reminded herself of her offence, and understood its enormity in the eyes of a man. She would have had a better appreciation of her own attractions, and would have long since understood this man's regard for her.

As it was she snatched at the relief his smile inspired.

The man laughingly shook his head as the girl approached.

"Nancy, my dear, I hope Mr. Bull Sternford gave you as good a dinner as I would have given you, and—as good a time generally. You look well rested, anyway."

There was a sting in the words that all the man's care could not quite shut out. But the tone was of intended good-nature. In a moment Nancy was explaining.

"Oh, I know you must think me terribly mean," she cried impulsively. "You must think I was just lying to you when you asked me to dine yesterday. But it wasn't so. It surely wasn't. May I tell you about it?"

The man came back to his desk, and indicated the empty chair beside it.

"Sure, if you feel that way," he said, dropping into his seat while Nancy took hers. "But I'm not angry. Truth I'm not." For a moment he gazed smilingly into the girl's troubled eyes. "Here," he went on. "I'll tell you just how I think. Maybe you won't figger it flattering, but it's just plain truth. Now I'm a married man and you're a young girl. Well, the Chateau isn't the sort of place for you and me to be seen together in. I didn't think of it when I asked you. I just wanted to hand you a good time for the good work you've done. Sort of prize for a good girl, eh? I hadn't another thought about it. And when you refused me, and I thought it over, I was kind of glad—I might have compromised you, and I certainly would have compromised myself. You get that? You understand me? Of course you do. That's what I like. You're so darn sensible. Now you tell me—if you fancy to?"

Nancy sighed her relief. Her last cloud had passed away.

"Oh, yes," she began at once. "I do want to tell you. You see I think it's all-important."

"Yes."

The man's smile was unchanged. But there was a dryness in his monosyllable that only Nancy could have missed.

"Mr. Sternford 'phoned me after his interview with you."

"He had your 'phone number?"

"Surely, I gave him that before he left me after driving up from the docks."

"I see. Of course. You drove up together after landing. I forgot."

Nancy laughed.

"I don't think I told you," she said. "But it doesn't matter, anyway. Yes, he drove me up. And the whole of this affair was so interesting I just had to hear the result of the interview with you. So I told him my 'phone number. Well, right after he'd seen you he rang me up. He told me he couldn't speak over the 'phone the things that passed, and asked me to dine. I just had to fall for that. You see, this thing meant so much to me. It was the first big thing I'd handled, and—and I was so crazy to make good for you. So I promised. And it wasn't till after it was all fixed I realised the mean way I'd acted. You'll forgive me, won't you, Mr. Peterman? I just hadn't a notion to be mean, and I was all tired to death. But I had to hear about the things you'd fixed."

"And you heard?"

The man was leaning on the desk with one hand supporting his head. Not one shadow of condemnation or resentment was permitted in voice or look. And the girl was completely disarmed. But her smile died out and a swift apprehension, that had no relation to herself, replaced it. In a moment her mind had gone back to the declaration of war which was to involve the two enterprises.

"Yes. He told me."

"And—?"

"Oh, it's all wrong. It's all foolish, and wrong, and just terrible," she broke in impulsively. Then she became calmly thoughtful, and her even brows drew together in an effort to straighten out the things she wanted to say. She shook her head. "I'm sure he can be handled," she went on deliberately. "Oh, yes. In spite of the things they say of him."

"What's that?"

"Why he's as ready to fight as to laugh."

"Who says that?"

"That's the way they speak of him."

"Who speaks that way?"

Nancy laughed.

"It was just a queer sort of missionary who told me. I met him when I was at Arden Laval's camp. A man they call Father Adam."

Peterman nodded.

"And you guess he can be handled?"

"I think so." Nancy spread out her hands. "Oh, it's not for me to talk this way to you, Mr. Peterman, but—but—"

"Go on." The man was patiently reassuring as the girl hesitated. "It's good to hear you talk. And then it was you who got him to listen to our proposal at all."

The compliment had prompt effect. The girl's cheeks flushed, and a light of something approaching delight shone in the hazel depths of her eyes.

"I don't know," she cried. "But it seems to me he's sort of reasonable. He's kind of full of ideals and that sort of notion. He's out for a big purpose and all that. But I don't believe he'd turn down any business arrangement that would hand him the thing he wants—"

"Business arrangement?" Peterman sat up. The laugh accompanying his words was full of amiable derision. He shook his head. "If he won't sell he's got to be smashed. That's the only business arrangement that suits us. We're far too big for compromise. No, my dear. He won't sell. He asked to buy us. He—this darn fool man from Sachigo. He thinks to buy the Skandinavia like he's buying up all the mills he can lay hands on. But he bit off a chunk when he handed that stuff to me. He's as ready to fight as to laugh. Well, I guess he's going to get all the fight he needs. He'll get it plenty."

"Then you mean to—smash him?"

"Just as sure as it's started to snow right now," the man exclaimed, pointing at the window.

Nancy's gaze followed the pointing finger. But it was not the snow she was thinking of. It was the man whom she beheld staggering under the tremendous weight of the Skandinavia's might. She felt pity for him. And incautiously she permitted Elas Peterman to realise her pity.

"Can't anything be done?" she ventured gently. "Have you handled him? I mean—Oh, I'm sure he's reasonable. Can't the offer be made—more suitable? More—?"

Peterman's eyes suddenly hardened.

"What do you mean? I haven't handled him right? I've blundered? I—" He laughed without any mirth. "See here, Nancy, my dear, you're a bright girl, but don't hand me your worry for this darn fool. You're kind of tender-hearted. You guess it's a pretty tough thing to see a good-looker boy go down in a big commercial fight. That's because you're a woman. This sort of thing's part of business. It's harsher, more ruthless than even war on the battlefield with guns, and bombs, and stinking gas. We're going to fight this thing just that way. There's no mercy for Mr. Bull Sternford. He'll get all I can hand him just the way I know best how to hand it. And the tougher I can make it the better it'll please me. See? Now you just run right along and see to those things that are going to make you big in the Skandinavia, and don't give a thought for the feller who's handed me stuff I don't stand for in any man. There's liable to be big work for you in this fight, and I'd say you'll make as good in fight as in peace. You've got my goodwill anyway, my dear, just for all it's worth. That's all."

The door had closed behind the girl. Elas Peterman was on his feet pacing the thickly carpeted floor. There was no longer any attempt at disguise. A surge of jealous fury was raging through his hot heart and drove him mercilessly.

The picture of Nancy, radiantly beautiful, seated at dinner with Bull Sternford had lit a fire of bitter hatred in his Teutonic heart. So he paced the room and permitted the fierce tide to flood the channels of sanity and set them awash with the ready evil of his impulse.

From the first moment of the girl's story of her successful effort with this man, Sternford, this vaunting rival, Peterman had been bitterly stirred. The man's change of plans at her bidding he had understood on the instant. The man from Labrador had not changed his plans at the bidding of the Skandinavia. It was the girl who had induced him. It was she who had attracted him. Then the boat trip, and the girl's confession of his having, perhaps, saved her life. What had preceded that incident? What had followed it? And when Elas Peterman asked himself such questions it was simple for him to find the answer. He had seen Sternford, and had judged the position. He knew what would have happened had he been in this man's place. Sternford wasn't the man to throw away such chances, either. He had fallen for the girl, and she doubtless had—The picture he had witnessed at the Chateau had left him without any doubt. The driving up together from the docks, the telephone. Sternford had taken her to her apartment. Oh, it was all as clear as daylight. Then the girl's pity for the man who was to feel the weight of the Skandinavia's wrathful might. She had said he was reasonable. She had hinted that he, Peterman, had blundered. There was only one reasonable interpretation to the position. And it did not leave him guessing for one single moment.

Once he passed a fleshy hand up over his forehead and brushed back his dark hair. Once he came to a pause before his window and stood gazing out at the falling snow with hot eyes. No such fury of jealousy had ever entered into his life before. Never had he dreamed before of the tremendous hold this girl had obtained upon him. His claim on her had all seemed so natural, so easy. He had looked upon her as property that was indisputably his. He might have learned something from his feelings when he had paraded her before Hellbeam. But he had not done so. Now he knew. Now he knew the whole measure of them. And the bitterness of his awakening was maddening.

Well, Bull Sternford should get away with no play of that sort at his expense. He warned himself that he was no simple fool to be played with. And if Nancy wanted the man— But he broke away from under the lash of impotent fury, and turned to a channel of thought which was bound to serve a nature such as his in his present mood.

He returned to his desk and flung himself into the chair. And after a while his mind settled itself to the task his mood demanded. He sat staring straight ahead of him, and presently the heat passed out of his eyes, and they grew cold, and hard. Later, they began to smile again—but it was a smile of cruelty, of evil purpose. It was a smile more unrelenting in its cruelty than any frown could have expressed.

For the first time Nancy's eyes were open to the things of life as they really were. She had tasted a certain bitterness in the early days of her girlhood. But up till now the world had seemed something of a rose garden in which it was a delight to labour. Up till now she had seen no reverse to the picture of life as youth had painted it for her. Now, however, it was borne in upon her that there was a reverse, a reverse that was ugly and painfully distressing. It was this declaration of war between her own people and the man from Labrador.

She lay in her bed that night thinking, thinking, and without any desire for sleep. Strive as she would to search the position out logically, to estimate the true meaning of it all, to fathom the chances of this war, and to grasp the necessity for it, all these efforts only resulted in a tangle of thought revolving about the picture of a youthful man of vast stature, with eyes that were always clear-searching or smiling, and with a head of hair that reminded her of a lion's mane. And as she gazed upon this mental picture there were moments when it seemed to her there was grave trouble in the clear depths which so appealed to her. The smile in her eyes seemed to fade out, to be replaced by a look that seemed to express the hurtful knowledge of a man disheartened, defeated, crushed. They were in rival camps. They were at war. Each desired victory. And yet the sight she beheld, the signs of defeat she discovered in the man's eyes gave her no joy, no satisfaction.

She felt that the battle could end only one way. The might of the Skandinavia was too great for anything but its complete victory. She was sure, quite sure. Oh, yes. And she knew she would not have it otherwise. But the pity of it. This creature of splendid manhood. To think that he must go down—smashed. That was the word they used—smashed.

How she hated the word. The big soul of him with his ready kindliness. Oh, it was a pity. It was a distracting thought. And why should it be? For the life of her she could see no need. A little yielding on his part. Just a shade less iron stubbornness. The whole thing could have been avoided she was sure. The olive branch had been held out by the Skandinavia. But he had deliberately refused it.

No. He had made himself their enemy. Then surely there could be no complaint at the disaster that would overtake him. He was clearly to blame. So why let the contemplation of it distract her?

She strove a hundred times to dismiss the whole thing from her mind. She courted sleep in every conceivable way. But it was all useless. The man's fine eyes and great body haunted her. They pursued her to her last waking thought. And, at last, she fell asleep, thinking of the strong supporting arms that had held her safe from the fury of Atlantic waves.

CHAPTER XIV
THE PLANNING OF CAMPAIGN

Nathaniel Hellbeam sat ominously calm and unruffled while Elas Peterman told of his meeting with Bull Sternford. He gave no sign whatever. There was just the flicker of a smile of appreciation of Bull's effrontery when he heard of his response to Peterman's invitation to sell. That alone of the whole story seemed to afford him interest. For the rest, it had only been the sort of thing he expected.

He waited until the other had finished. Then he stirred in his chair. It was an expression of relief that his long, silent sitting had ended.

"So," he said. "We do not buy him. No. We smash him."

There was obvious satisfaction that the more peaceful process was to be set aside.

He sat blinking at his subordinate in the fashion of a man who is thinking hard, and has no interest in the object upon which he is gazing.

"It is as I think—all the time," he said at last. "That is all right. I make no cry out. It is easy to fight. I would fight always with an enemy. It is good. Now my friend, you have acted so. You bring the man from Sachigo to tell you to go to hell. Eh? Well you have thought much? You have planned for the fight? How is it you make this fight?"

Elas was standing before the desk. He had, yielded his place to this man who was master of the Skandinavia. Now he looked down at the square-headed creature with his gross, squat body. It was a figure and face bristling with venom and purpose; and somehow he was conscious of a sudden lack of his usual assurance.

"Oh, yes," he replied thoughtfully. "I've planned—sure. But I guess I'm in the dark a bit. It's going to cost a deal. It's not going to be easy. You were ready to buy. It was not necessarily to be the Skandinavia who bought. Well, are you—going to vote the credit for this fight?" He smiled uncertainly. "And to what extent?"

"The limit. Go on."

Peterman nodded.

"There's no commercial enterprise that can stand idleness. His work must stop. His—"

"That is the A.B.C. of it."

There was sharp impatience in the financier's biting tone.

"Just so. It is the A.B.C. of it."

Hellbeam set back in his chair. He clasped his hands across his stomach.

"I will tell you," he said, a wicked smile lighting his deep-set eyes, his cheeks rounding themselves in his satisfaction. "His work will stop. His mill is far away. There is no protection from attack except that which he can set up himself. He is going away. He will have eighteen hundred miles of water between him and his mill. It should be easy with a good plan and all the money. Listen.

"His work must stop. How? There are ways. His mill may burn. His forests may burn. His men may revolt. They may refuse to work for him. All, or any of these things may serve. There are men at all times ready to carry out these things. You can tell them, or you need not, the way they must act." He shook his head. "You say to them his work must stop; and you pay them more than he can pay them. So his work will stop. That is so? Yes? Very well. There is ha'f a million dollars that will pay for his work to stop. I say that."

Peterman was startled. He had not been prepared for so sweeping a proposal. He had understood that the man had been prepared to stand at almost nothing in his desire to achieve some end, the nature of which still remained somewhat obscure to him. For all his own lack of scruple in his dealings with those who offended, the calm, fiendish purpose of this man shocked him not a little.

He took the chair usually occupied by his visitors.

"You will pay ha'f a million dollars for this thing?" he demanded, to re-assure himself.

Self-satisfaction looked out of the eyes of the man behind the desk.

"More—if necessary."

"By God! You must hate this boy, Sternford."

Peterman's feelings had broken from under his control.

"Sternford? Psha! It is not Sternford. No."

The smile had gone from Hellbeam's eyes. They were fiercely burning. They were the hot, passionate eyes of a man obsessed, of a man possessed of a monomania. Peterman, watching, beheld the sudden change in him. He shrank before the insanity he had so deeply probed.

Hellbeam sat forward in his chair. His forearms were resting on the desk, and his hands were clenched so that the finger-nails almost cut into the flesh of their palms. His massive face was flushed, and the coarse veins at his temples stood out like cords.

"Here, I tell you," he cried gutturally, returning in his fury to the native Teuton in him. "Can you hate—yes? Have you known hate? Eh? No. You the white liver have. You cannot hate. It is not in you. Oh, no. It is for me. Yes. It has been so for years. And I tell you it is the only thing in life. Woman? No. I have known them. They mean little. They are a pleasure that passes. Money? What is it when you play the market as you choose? The day comes when you can help yourself. And you no longer desire so to do. Hate? That lives. That feeds on body and brain. That consumes till there is only a dead carcase left. Ah! Hate is for the lifetime. It can leave all those others as nothing. In it there is joy, despair, all the time, every hour of life."

He held up one hand and opened his fingers. Then he slowly closed them with a curious expressive movement of ruthless destruction.

"You hate and you think. You see your vengeance in operation. You see him there in your hand; and you see the blood sweat as you squeeze and crush out the life that has offended. Man, it is a joy that never leaves you till you accomplish this thing. Then, after, you have the memory. And while you think, even though he is dead, smashed in your grip, he still suffers as you think. Oh, yes."

"And you hate—that way?"

A feeling of sudden fear had taken possession of Peterman. This gross squat man had become something terrible to him.

"Ja!"

The Teuton leapt in the furious emphasis hurled.

"Oh, ja! I hate. I tell you of it."

The man with the insane eyes picked up a pen. He turned it about in his fingers. Then, suddenly, but slowly, the fingers began to break it. The wood split under their pressure, and the pieces littered the table. He gazed at them for a moment. Then one hand clenched and came down with a crash on the blotting pad. Then he sat back in his chair again, with his cruel eyes gazing straight out at the window opposite.

"It is years now. Oh, yes." A deep breath escaped from between the man's coarse lips. "I ruled the markets. I ruled them so that they obeyed me. I was the money power of this continent. I did as I chose. So I thought. Then he came. This man. He did not disturb me. Oh, no. I slept good all the time. Then I woke. I woke to find I was beaten of ten million dollars; and that Wall Street, the markets of the world, were laughing that this schoolmaster, this fool Scotsman from over the water, had picked my pocket while I slept. It was not the money. It was the laugh. And he got away. Oh, yes. I tell it now. The market knew of it then. They laughed. How they laughed. So I sat and thought. I had all. There was nothing more to have. And then I learned to hate."

The narrowed eyes came back to the face of the man beside the desk. There was a sharp intake of breath.

"This mill, this Sachigo, was built out of my money. And the man who built it was the man who robbed me while I slept."

A world of fierce bitterness lay in the final words, and the man listening realised the enormity of the offence, as this man saw it. But he was left puzzled.

"But you would have—bought this Sachigo?" he said, said.

Hellbeam's eyes were again turned to the window.

"Oh, yes," he said. "I would have bought. It would bring me to meet this man. It is that I ask. That only. My hands would close upon him. And I would see the blood sweat of his heart ooze under them."

Hellbeam had finished. Peterman understood that. The passion had passed out of his eyes and the veins of his forehead were no longer distended. He remained gazing at the window.

For some moments the younger man made no attempt to intrude further. He had little desire to, anyway. Without scruple himself, he still found little pleasure in probing the heart of this man, who was so powerful in his own destiny. That which he had witnessed had served only to show him the delicacy of his own position. He knew that the story had been told for one reason only. It was to convince him, for the sake of his own wellbeing in the Skandinavia, that he must make no mistake in the warfare he must wage against the people of Sachigo. It was for him to wage the battle with every faculty that was in him; and any failure of his would mean disaster for himself. This was no commercial warfare. It was the insane purpose of a monomaniac.

In those silent moments Elas Peterman thought with a rapidity inspired by the urgency he felt to be driving him. And the fertility of his imagination served him unfailingly. Oh yes. Necessity was driving. But so, too, was his own personal feelings. He saw in the position that this man had revealed an advantage to himself he had never looked for. With the necessary money forthcoming, and no directors to concern himself with, literally a free hand, he could employ a power which, in these days of unrest and hatred between capital and labour, would be well-nigh overwhelming. The morality of it, the ultimate consequence of it mattered nothing. The smashing of Sachigo would mean the smashing of Bull Sternford. And he saw a way whereby the smashing of Bull Sternford could be achieved through—

His mind focused itself, as it was bound to do, upon this thing as it affected his own desires. He, too, was a passionate hater, for all Hellbeam's denial. His thought leapt at once to Nancy McDonald and the man who had thrust himself between him and his desires. Whatever insane hatred lay behind Hellbeam's purpose, it was not one whit more insensate than Elas Peterman's feelings against the man who had come down from Sachigo at Nancy's bidding.

Suddenly he looked up and glanced at the man occupying the chair that was his. Hellbeam was still gazing at the window, pre-occupied with his own thoughts.

"You can leave this thing in my hands, sir," he said. "Our organisation has been working steadily to undermine the Sachigo people for months past. That has always been part of our policy. I'd say the whole thing's going to fit very well. You say, if necessary, you'll find half a million dollars for the business. We shan't need a tithe of that. However, it's well to know it. And none of it needs to worry our directors. I'll set about it right away—in my own fashion—and I'll promise you a quick result. We'll smash these folk all right. But how it's to hand you the man you need I'm not wise—"

"No." Hellbeam's eyes were certainly derisive as they turned back from the window. "This man, Martin, will show himself when he sees the—destruction. My people will do the rest."

"Unless he leaves it—to Sternford. They tell us this man would as soon fight as laugh. That's how Miss McDonald said the missionary, Father Adam, told her."

"Father Adam?" The derision in the financier's eyes had deepened. "That's the man that other fool talks of."

Peterman shrugged. The sting in the financier's words stirred him to resentment.

"I don't know about that. Anyway—"

"How is it you say? Get busy. Yes."

Hellbeam rose stiffly from his seat and picked up his hat. He was quite untouched by the other's change of tone.

"Do it how you please. Break that mill. I care nothing for the means. Smash 'em, and leave the rest to me. And when you that have done you can do the thing you please. You will have my good will. I say that. Now I go."

Peterman picked up the 'phone the moment the door had closed behind the one man in all the world he really feared, and at the other end of it Nancy took the message summoning her to his presence. The man spoke with unusual urgency. But his tone was pleasant, and more than conciliatory. He wanted her at once. She could leave her reports. She could leave everything. He had some news for her of the pleasantest nature. Oh, yes. He had determined big things for her. She had earned them all. But a thing had happened whereby there need be no limit to her advancement if she would take the chance of a big work offered her. Would she kindly come up right away.

Nancy listened to this message with a stirring of heart. What was the great work that was to place no limit on her advancement? It was a feeling rather than a thought. For a moment she stood in her glass-partitioned office after she had received the message and a smile of great happiness lit her eyes.

She was desperately earnest with a singleness of purpose which had in it something of the recklessness of the father before her. She was a child in all else. A wide vision of achievement was spread out before her. She could see nothing beyond. She could see nothing to give her pause, nothing even to bestir a belated caution. So she left her office for the interview Peterman had demanded without suspicion, and with a heart and mind ready to plunge her headlong into any labours which the Skandinavia demanded of her.

She had completely forgotten, in that moment of exultation, the squarely military figure that had passed down the dining-room of the Chateau, and the coldly unsmiling eyes with which it had regarded her as she sat with her companion over their memorable meal.

CHAPTER XV
THE SAILING OF THE EMPRESS

Bull Sternford was reading over the telegram he had just written. Its phraseology was curious. But it expressed the things he wanted to say, and he knew it would be understood by the man to whom it was addressed.

> "HARKER, SACHIGO, LABRADOR.
>
> "Sailing to-morrow. War. Pass mill through hair sieve. Clear all refuse. Watch fireguard. Look around. Plums otherwise ripe. Return earliest date.
>
> "BULL."

He smiled as he looked up from his reading. An acquaintance passed through the hall of the hotel. He nodded to him. Then the smile died out of his eyes, and it was like the passing of a gleam of sunshine. He passed the message across the counter to the attendant and paid for it.

War! It was only an added development in the course of the ceaseless work of life. The thought of it disturbed him not one whit. It was the element in which he thrived. But for all that his mood had lost much of its usual equanimity.

For two weeks he had applied himself assiduously to the work upon which he was engaged. He had travelled hundreds of miles to the other capital cities of the country in pursuit of his affairs. He had worked in that express fashion which was characteristic of him. But under it all, through it all, a depressing disappointment hung like a shadow over every successful effort he put forth. The memory of an evening at the Chateau haunted him. The vision of smiling hazel eyes and a radiant crowning of vivid hair filled every moment of his waking dreaming. He had not seen or heard of Nancy McDonald since that first night in Quebec.

To-morrow he sailed for England. The thought of it afforded him none of the satisfaction with which he had always looked forward to that journey. Yet it meant no less to him now. On the contrary. It really meant more. It meant that his work was marching forward to the great completion which was to crown his labours, and the work of those others who had conceived the task.

It should have been a wonderful moment for him. The house of Leader and Company of London had thrown its doors open to him in welcome. Sir Frank Leader with his millions, his shipping, his great power, and the confidence which his name inspired in British commercial circles, would not fail. The prospect lying ahead, for all the threatened war, should have stirred him to a keen enthusiasm that achievement was within his grasp. But none of these emotions were stirring.

He felt if he could only see Nancy McDonald, that perfect creature with her amazing beauty and splendid courage, just to exchange a few words, just to receive her smiling "bon voyage," and even to hear her laughing declaration of her frank enmity, why—it would—But there was no chance now—none at all. He sailed to-morrow.

He had dreamed a wonderful dream since first he had beheld the charming fur-clad figure enter his office at Sachigo. He had realised, even in those first moments, the impish act of Fate. Nancy McDonald was the one woman in the world who could mean life—real life to him, and they were definitely arrayed against each other in the battle for commercial supremacy in which they were both engaged.

But Fate's act had only added to his desire. The whole thing had appealed to his combative instinct. It had left him feeling there was not alone the storming of the Skandinavia's stronghold to be achieved. There was also a captive, a fair, innocent captive held bound and prisoned within the citadel for him to set free. He wanted Nancy as he wanted nothing else in the world. Sachigo? Canada for the Canadians? These things were cold, meaningless words. He only thought of the dawning of the day that should see Nancy his wife, his everything in life.

He betook himself out on to the Terraces overlooking the slowly freezing waterway of the great St. Lawrence river. It was keenly cold, and the white carpet of winter's first snow remained unmelted on the ground. But the sun was shining, and the crisp air was sparkling, and the terraces were filled with fur-clad folk who, like himself, had found leisure for a half hour of one of the finest views in the world.

He paced leisurely down the great promenade towards the old Citadel with all its memories of great men, and the old time Buccaneers who had made history about its walls. He gazed upon it and wondered. Were they such bad old days? Were the men who lived in those times great men? Were they scoundrelly Buccaneers? Were their scruples and morals any more lax than those of to-day? Were they any different from those who walked under the shadow of the old walls? They were the questions doubtless asked a thousand times in as many minutes by those who paused to think as they contemplated this fine old landmark.

Bull found his own prompt answers. There was no difference, he told himself. The men and women of to-day were doing the same things, enduring the same emotions, fighting the same battles, living and loving, and hating and dying, just as life had ordained from the beginning of time. And as he stood there he wondered how long this round of human effort and passion must continue. How long this—

"Why, I hadn't an idea you were so interested in our old history as to be wasting precious time out here in the snow, Mr. Sternford."

The challenge was full of pleasant, even delighted greeting. And Bull snatched his cigar from his lips and bared his head.

It was the voice he had longed to hear for many days. And it rang with an added charm in his delighted ears. He had turned on the instant, and stood smiling down into eyes that had never ceased from their haunting.

He shook his head.

"If you'll believe me I wasn't wasting time," he said. "I came out here for a very definite purpose. I've done the thing I hoped. Do you know I guessed I'd have to sail to-morrow without seeing you again?"

Nancy's eyes sobered. And without their smile Bull thought he detected a cloud of trouble in them.

"I didn't know you were sailing to-morrow," she said. "It's just a chance I couldn't help that let me meet you now."

"You mean you avoided me—deliberately?"

Bull's smile had passed. But there was no umbrage in his manner. The girl's appeal for him was never so great as at that moment. She had never been more beautiful to him. He had first seen her in that same long fur coat, and had gazed into her pretty eyes under the same fur cap. He was glad she was so clad now. To his mind no other costume could have so much charm for him.

"Yes."

The simple downrightness of the admission might have disconcerted another. But its honesty and lack of subterfuge only pleased the man.

"That's what I thought. It's this business standing between your folk and me?"

Nancy nodded.

"Yes. We are enemies."

"That's so," Bull agreed. "That's the pity of it. If you were on my side—"

"But I'm not. No." Nancy's denial was almost sharp. It certainly was hurried. "I'm kind of glad I've seen you, though," she went on. "I've had it in mind I wanted to say things to you." A smile came back to her eyes. "You see, there are enemies and enemies. There's the enemy you can regard well. There's the enemy you can hate and despise. Well, I just want to say we're enemies who don't need to hate and despise—yet. I don't know how things'll be later. Maybe you'll learn to hate me good before we're through. But that's as maybe. I'm going to do my work for all I know for my folks. I'm going to be in this fight right up to my neck. I've been warned that way. Well, that being so, I'm going to fight without looking for quarter, and I shall give none. That sounds tough, doesn't it? But I mean it. And I wanted to say it before things start. I'm glad I've had the chance—against my notions of things."

Bull laughed. He was in the mood to laugh—now.

"It sounds fine. Say—"

"Are you laughing at me?"

"There isn't a thing further from my thoughts." Bull's denial was sincere and prompt. "I'm glad you happened along. I'm glad you said those things. Fight this war—as I shall—with all that's in you. It don't matter a thing if you're right or wrong. Fight it square and hard for your folk, and there isn't a right man or woman, but who'll respect you, and think the better of you for it. A good fight's no crime when you're convinced you're right."

The girl drew a deep breath, and, to the man, it seemed in the nature of relief. A great anxiety for her stirred him.

"I'm glad you said that," she said. Then she gazed reflectively up at the old ramparts. "No. It's no crime to fight when you're convinced. Besides it's right, too, to fight for your side at any time. That's how I see it. You'll fight for yours—"

"Any old how." Bull's eyes were deeply regarding. They were very gentle. "Here," he went on, "fight has a clear, definite meaning for me. I fight to win. I'll stop at nothing. It's always a game of 'rough and tough' with me. Gouge, chew, and all the rest of it. Frankly, there's a devil inside me, when it's fight. I want you to know this, so your scruples needn't worry you."

"Yes."

Nancy's gaze was turned seawards.

"And you sail—to-morrow? When do you return?" she asked a moment later.

Bull smilingly shook his head.

"We are at war," he said.

The girl's eyes came back. She, too, smiled.

"I forgot." Then she added: "You go by the *Empress*?"

"Yes."

They had both contrived to make it difficult. The barrier was growing. Both realised it, and Nancy was stirred more than she knew. She had seen this man and hurried over to him. She had purposely denied him for two weeks, but the sight of him on the promenade had been irresistible. Now—now she hardly knew what to say; and yet there were a hundred things struggling in her mind to find expression. She was paralysed by the memory of the recent interview she had had with her employers—the great financial head of her house included—wherein she had learned all that the coming war meant personally to herself. She would have given worlds at that moment to have been able to blot out that memory. But she had no power to do so. It loomed almost tragically in its significance in the presence of this man.

Bull found it no less difficult. He had striven to make things easy for her. He had no second thought. And now he realised the thing he had done. His words had only served to fling an irrevocable challenge, and thus, finally and definitely, made the longed-for approach between them impossible.

He drew a deep breath.

"Yes. I sail on the *Empress*."

"And you are glad—of course?"

Bull laughed.

"Some ways."

"You mean—?"

"Why, I shouldn't be sailing if things weren't going my way," he said. Then he turned about and his movement was an invitation. "But let's quit it," he said. "Let's forget—for the moment. You don't know what this meeting has meant to me. I wanted to see you, if only to say 'good-bye.' I thought I wasn't going to."

They moved down the promenade together.

Nancy did her best. They talked of everything but the impending war, and the meaning of it. But the barrier had grown out of all proportion. And a great unease tugged at the heart of each. At length, as they came back towards the hotel, Nancy felt it impossible to go on. And with downright truth she said so.

"It must be 'good-bye'—now," she said. "This is all unreal. It must be so. We're at war. We shall be at each other's throats presently. Well, I just can't pretend. I don't want to think about it. I hate to remember it. But it's there in my mind the whole time; and it worries so I don't know the things I'm saying. It's best to say 'good-bye' and 'bon voyage' right here. And whatever the future has for us I just mean that."

She held out her hand. It was bare, and soft, and warm, as the man took possession of it.

"I feel that way, too," he said. "But—" he broke off and shook his head. "No. It's no use. You've the right notion of this. Until this war's fought out there is nothing else for it. You'll go right back to your camp and I'll go to mine. And we'll both work out how we can best beat the other. But let's make a compact. We'll do the thing we know to hurt the other side the most we can. If need be we'll neither show the other mercy. And we'll promise each to take our med'cine as it comes, and cut out the personal hate and resentment it's likely to try and inspire. We'll be fighting machines without soul or feeling till peace comes. Then we'll be just as we are now—friends. Can you do it? I can."

For all the feeling of the moment Nancy laughed.

"It sounds crazy," she exclaimed.

"It is crazy. But so is the whole thing."

"Yes. Oh, it surely is. It's worst than crazy." Passion rang in the girl's voice. Then the hazel depths smiled and set the man's pulses hammering afresh. "But I'll make that compact, and I'll keep it. Yes. Now, 'good-bye,' and a happy and pleasant trip."

Their hands fell apart. Bull had held that hand, so soft and warm and appealing to him, till he dared hold it no longer.

"Thanks," he said. "Good-bye. I can set out with a good heart—now."

It was again the luncheon hour. It was also the hour at which the *Empress* was scheduled to sail. Nancy was again on the Terrace. But now she was standing on the edge of the promenade—alone. She was gazing down at the grey waters of the great river, searching with eager eyes, and listening for the "hoot" of the vessel's siren. This was the last departure the *Empress* would make from Quebec for the season. By the time she returned across the ocean the ice would deny her approach, and she would make port farther seawards.

Nancy had come there in her leisure just out of simple interest, she told herself. The man was nothing to her. Oh, no. She felt a certain regret that they were at war. She felt a certain pity that it was necessary that so brave a man's hopes must be crushed and all his plans broken, but that was all. She told herself these things very deliberately.

And so she had hurried over her mid-day meal, lest she should miss the sight of the *Empress* steaming out, with Bull Sternford aboard.

The day was cold and grey. There was snow in the heavy clouds, and the north wind was bitter. But it mattered nothing. Waiting there the girl's feet in their overshoes grew cold. Her hands were cold. Even her slim, graceful body under its outer covering of fur was none too warm. But her whole interest was absorbed and she remained so till the appointed time.

Oh, yes. It was simply interest in the departure of the vessel that held her. Just the same, as it was simply interest that stirred her heart and set it a-flutter, as the sound of the ship's siren came up to her from below. And surely it was only a 'God-speed' to the departing vessel that was conveyed in the fluttering handkerchief she held out and waved, as the graceful giant passed out into the distant mid-channel.

CHAPTER XVI
ON BOARD THE EMPRESS

It was the second day out and the passengers on the *Empress* had already settled down to their week's trip.

The sea was calm, with just that pleasant, lazy swell which the Atlantic never really loses. The decks were thronged with a happy company of men and women determined not to lose one single moment of the bodily ease which the clemency of the weather vouchsafed to them.

Bull Sternford was amongst them. Engulfed in a heavy fur overcoat, he stood lounging against the lee rail of the wide promenade deck, contemplating the oily swell of the waters. His great stature was somewhat magnified by his voluminous coat, with its deep, upturned storm-collar. There was that about him to attract considerable attention. But he remained unconscious of it, and his aloofness was by no means studied.

Deep emotion was stirring. A man of iron nerve and purpose, a man of cool deliberation under the harshest circumstances, just now Bull was afflicted like the veriest weakling with alternating hope and doubt, and something approaching indecision. The youth in him was plunged in that agony of desire which maddens with delight and drives headlong to despair. His whole horizon of life had changed. Old scenes, old dreams, had been suddenly blotted out. And in their place was the wonderful vision of a girl with vivid hair and gentle eyes. Nancy—Nancy McDonald. The name was always with him now, unspoken, unwhispered even; but occupying every waking thought.

It was a time of reckless resolve, of hot-headed planning. He knew in his sober moments how almost impossible was the position. But these were not sober moments. He told himself, in his headlong way, that if Nancy was chained in the heart of Hell he would seek her out, and claim her. She should be his even though every infernal power were arrayed against him. His eyes were alight with a fierce smile, as he contemplated the grey waters. It was a smile of conscious strength, of reckless purpose. Well, he was ready. He was—

"Guess we'll git this sort of stuff all the way."

Bull started and swung around. A fur-coated man with a dark close-cropped beard was leaning over the rail beside him. He was expensively clad. His astrachan collar was turned up about his neck to shut out something of the biting winter air; and a cap of similar fur was pressed low down over his dark head. Bull noted the man's appearance, and his reply was promptly forthcoming.

"Maybe," he admitted without interest.

"Sure we will. It's always that way with the *Empress's* last trip of the season from Quebec. I most generally make it for that reason. Your first trip?"

"No."

"It's my nineteenth. You see," the stranger went on, "I can't spare summer time. I'm too full gettin' orders out. I'm in the lumber business. It's only with the freeze up I can quit my mills. Have a cigar?"

Bull had no alternative. The man was there to talk, and his desire to do so was frankly displayed.

"I won't smoke, thanks," Bull replied without offense. "It's too near dinner."

"Dinner? There's a ha'f hour to the dressing bugle." The stranger returned the elaborate case stuffed full of large, expensive cigars to his pocket, and drew out a gold cigarette case instead. "Still I don't blame you a thing. Cigars? Me for a cigarette all the time. I don't guess any feller ever heard tell of tobacco, till he'd inhaled a good, plain Virginia Cigarette."

Bull looked on while the man wasted half-a-dozen matches lighting his beloved cigarette. He was not without interest. There was a slightly Jewish caste about his face which was frankly smiling, and lit with shrewd, twinkling dark eyes. He conveyed, too, somewhat blatantly, an atmosphere of abounding prosperity.

Bull laughed as the cigarette was finally lighted.

"That's better," he said. "Now—you can inhale."

"Sure I can." The man's smile was full of amiability. "Inhale anything. Say, up in the camps I've inhaled tea-leaves rolled in cracker paper before now. Ever hit a lumber camp?"

"Yes."

"But not out West? British Columbia?"

"No. Only Quebec."

The stranger shook his head disparagingly.

"Quebec! Psha! Quebec ain't a thing. It ain't a circumstance," he said complacently. "No, sir. The West. That's the place for lumbering. B.C. West of the Rockies. Man, it's the world's greatest proposition. The place you can spend a lifetime cutting ninety foot baulks, and lose track of where you cut. Quebec's mostly small stuff," he went on contemptuously, "pulp-wood an' that." He shook his head. "It's no place for capital. And, anyway, the Frenchies have got the whole darn place taped out. Oh, they're wise—the Frenchies. If a feller's lookin' to get ahead of 'em he needs to stake out the Arctic, where you'd freeze the ears of a brass image. The Frenchies got it all. The only big stuff lies on Labrador, anyway. I know. I prospected. No, it's me for the big hills, West. The big hills and the big waterways that 'ud leave Quebec rivers looking like a leak in a bone dry bar'l. My name's Aylin P. Cantor, Vancouver, B.C. Maybe you know the name?"

Bull shook his head.

"I'm not—"

"Oh, it don't matter," interjected Mr. Cantor. "You see, the West's one hell of a long way—west. I just didn't get your—"

"Oh, my name's Sternford."

Mr. Cantor's face beamed.

"Why I'm glad to know you, Mr. Sternford," he exclaimed. Then a quick, enquiring upward glance of his shrewd eyes suggested recollection. "But say—you ain't Sternford of Labrador? The groundwood outfit up at—up at—"

"Sachigo?"

"That's it, sure. Guess I'd lost the name a moment."

Bull nodded amusedly.

"Yes. That's where I hail from. And, as you say, there's big stuff up there, too."

"Big? Why I'd say. Well, now! That's fine! I've heard tell big yarns of Labrador. It's just great meeting—"

The man broke off at the sound of the first blast of the dressing bugle.

"Why, it's later than I guessed," he said. "Anyway, you'll take a cocktail with me? This vessel's good and wet, thanks be to Providence, and the high seas being peopled with fish instead of cranks. I hadn't a notion I was goin' to run into a real lumberman on this trip. It's done me a power of good."

Aylin P. Cantor was a diverting creature for all his appearance of ostentatious prosperity. Good fortune had undoubtedly been his, and his whole being seemed to have become absorbed in the trade which had so generously treated him. Before the cocktail was consumed Bull had listened to a long story of British Columbia, and forests of incomparable extent. He had also learned that a country estate, miles in extent, outside the city of Vancouver, and the luxuries associated with the multi-millionaire had fallen to the lot of Aylin P. Cantor. But somehow there was no offence in it all. The man was just a bubbling fount of enthusiasm and delight that this was so. He simply had to talk of it.

But the acquaintance was not to terminate over a cocktail. Shipboard offers few avenues of escape to the man seeking to avoid another. So it came that Bull found himself sipping a brandy, reputed to be one hundred years old, over his coffee after dinner, while Aylin P. Cantor told him the story of how it came into his possession at something far below its market value.

Later, again, while the auction pool was being sold, he found himself ensconced on a lounge in a far corner of the smokeroom beside his fellow craftsman, still listening chiefly, and absorbing fact and anecdote pertaining to a successful lumberman's life. And it was nearly eleven o'clock, and the pool had been sold, and the bulk of the occupants of the smoking-room were contemplating their last rubber of Auction Bridge, when the busy-minded westerner consented to abandon his particular venue for a brief contemplation of the despised East.

"Oh, I guess there's money in your territory, too," he condescended at last. "I ain't a word to say against the stuff I've heard tell of Labrador. But you're froze up more'n ha'f the year. That's your trouble."

"Yes."

Bull nodded over the latter portion of his third cigar which Mr. Cantor had not permitted him to escape.

"Sure," the man laughed. "Oh, the stuff's there. I know that. But Labrador needs a mighty big nerve to exploit. I heard it all from a feller I met when I was prospecting Quebec. You see, I had the notion of playing a million dollars in the Quebec forests once. But I weakened. I kind of fancied my chance against the Frenchies didn't amount to cold water on a red hot cookstove. I cut it out and hunted my own patch, West, again. But I guess

I'd have fallen for the stories of Labrador, if it hadn't been for the feller who put me wise."

"Who was that?" Bull had lost interest, but the man invited the enquiry.

"Oh, a sort of missionary crank," Cantor returned indifferently. "You know the sort. We got 'em out West, too. They hound the boys around, chasin' them heavenwards by a through route they guess they know about." He laughed. "But the boys bein' just boys, the round up don't ever seem to make good; and that through trip looks most like a bum sort of freight in the wash-out season. Outside his missioner business I guess the guy was pretty wise, though. And his knowledge of the lumber play left me without a word. He knew it all—an' I guess he told it to me."

Bull laughed. But the laugh was inspired by the thought that there could be found in the world a man who could leave Aylin P. Cantor without a word on the subject of lumber.

"I'd like to make a guess at that feller," he said. "There's just one man I know who's a missionary in Quebec who knows anything about Labrador. Did he call himself, 'Father Adam?'"

"That's the thing he did."

"Ah, I thought so." Bull's smile had passed. "Where did you meet him?" he went on after a moment.

"On the Shagaunty. The Skandinavia Corporation territory. He told me he'd just come along through from Labrador."

"Oh, yes?"

Mr. Cantor laughed.

"Why he took me to his crazy shanty and handed me coffee. And he talked. My, how he talked."

"Did he know you were—prospecting?"

There was no lack of interest in Bull now. His steady eyes were alight, as he watched the stewards moving amongst the tables, setting the place straight for the night.

"Yes. I told him."

Cantor's dark eyes were questioning. As Bull remained silent he went on.

"Why? Is he interested for the Skandinavia to keep folk out?"

Bull shook his head.

"No. It isn't that. He's a queer feller. No, I'd say he's got just one concern in life. It's the boys. But you're right, he knows the whole thing—the whole game of lumbering in Eastern Canada. And if he told you and warned you, I'd say it was for your good as he saw it. No. He's no axe to grind, and though you found him on the Skandinavia's territory, I don't think he likes them. I'm sure he doesn't. Still, he's not concerned for any employer. He just comes and goes handing out his dope to the boys, and—You know the forest-jacks. They're a mighty tough proposition. Well, it's said they feel about Father Adam so if a hair of his head was hurt they'd get the feller who did it, and they'd cut the liver out of him, and pass what was left feed for the coyotes."

Mr. Cantor nodded.

"Yes, I sort of gathered something of that from the folks I hit up against. It seems queer a feller devoting his life to bumming through the forests and seekin' shelter where you couldn't find shelter from a summer dew. He's got no fixed home. Maybe he's sort of crazed."

Bull was prompt in his denial.

"Saner than you or me," he said. "You know I'd want to smile if I didn't know the man. But I know him, and—but there we all owe him a deal, we forest men. And maybe I owe him more than anyone."

"How's that?"

Mr. Cantor's question came sharply. Even Bull, tired as he was, noted the keenly incisive tone of it. He turned, and his steady eyes regarded the dark face of the lumberman speculatively. Then he smiled, and picked up his glass and drained the remains of his whisky and soda.

"Why, he's more power for peace with the lumber-jacks of Quebec than if he was their trade leader," he said, setting his empty glass down on the table. "We employers owe him there's never any sort of trouble with the boys."

"I see." Mr. Cantor gazed out across the nearly empty room, and a shadowy smile haunted his eyes. "And if there was trouble? Could you locate him in time?"

"We shouldn't need to. He'd be there."

The lumberman stirred, and persisted with curious interest.

"But he must have a place where you folks can get him? This coming and going. It's fine—but—"

Bull stood up and stretched himself.

"Oh, he's got a home, all right. It's the forests."

Mr. Cantor threw up his hands and laughed.

"Who is he, anyway? A sort of Wandering Jew? A ghost? A spook? That sort of thing beats me. He's got to be one of the two things. He's either a crank—you say he ain't—or he's dodging daylight."

But Bull had had enough. Deep in his heart was a feeling that no man had any right to pry into the life of Father Adam. Father Adam had changed the whole course of his life. It was Father Adam who had made possible everything he was to-day—even his association with Nancy McDonald. He shook his head unsmilingly.

Father Adam's one good man," he said. "And I wouldn't recommend anyone to hand out anything to the contrary within hearing of the men of the Quebec forests. Good-night."

He strode away. And Mr. Cantor followed him, slight and bediamonded in his evening clothes. And somehow the dark eyes gazing on the broad back of the man from Labrador had none of the twinkling shrewdness the other had originally observed in them. They were quite cold and very hard. And there was that in them which suggested the annoyance inspired by a long evening of effort that had ended in complete failure.

The man's dark, foreign-looking features had lost every semblance of their recent good-natured enthusiasm.

CHAPTER XVII
THE LONELY FIGURE AGAIN

The laden sled stood ready for the moment of starting on the day's long run. Five train dogs, lean, powerful huskies, crouched down upon the snow. They gave no sign beyond the alertness of their pose and the watchfulness of their furtive eyes. Their haunches were tucked under them. And their long, wolfish muzzles, so indicative of their parentage, were pressed down between great, outstretched forepaws.

The man studied every detail of his outfit. He knew the chances, the desperate nature of the long winter trail. He had no desire to increase the hardship of it all by any act of carelessness.

Behind him lay the mockery of a camping ground. It was a minute, isolated bluff of stunted, windswept trees, set in a white, wide wilderness of barren land. Perhaps there was some half a hundred of them. But that was all. They had served, but only by reason that their shelter had satisfied habit, which, even in the men of the long trail, will not be denied.

He turned away. Everything was to his satisfaction. So his tall, fur-clad figure passed in amongst the dwarf trees.

The dogs remained crouching, their fierce eyes gazing out over the desolate expanse of winter's playground. It lay at a great altitude, several thousands of feet above the level of the sea. The sky was drab. It was bitter with threat. It was unrelieved by any break in the menacing winter cloud. It was a snow sky which only refrained from releasing its burden by reason of the high, top wind that drove the heavy masses relentlessly. The earthly prospect was no more inviting. It was wide, and flat, and devoid of vegetation. There were no hills anywhere, and the skyline was just a vanishing point similar to the horizon of the open sea. One vast, wide field of snow and ice spread out in every direction, and made desolation complete.

When the man re-appeared he was armed with a sturdy "gee-pole," and at his belt was coiled a heavy-thonged, short-stocked driving whip.

Without a word he thrust the pole under the front of the sled runners, and a sharp command broke from his lips. The effect was instantaneous. Each dog sprang at his "tug." The man heaved on his pole. There was a moment of straining, then the holding ice gave up its grip, and the sled shot forward.

The man stood for a moment beating his mitted hands. Then he took his place on the sled, buried his legs and feet under the heavy seal robes set ready, and so the long-waited command to "mush" was hurled at the waiting beasts.

The dogs leapt at their work and the sled swept forward with a rush. A blinding flurry of snow dust rose in its wake, enveloping it, and the dogs raced on, yelping with the joy of activity. Their great muscles were aquiver with the eager spirit which is bred of the wild. And so they would continue to run, for their load was light, and the heavy-thonged whip was playing in skilful hands, and they knew, and feared, and obeyed its constant threat.

The way lay across the frozen bosom of a great lake, no less than an inland sea, and a hundred miles must be travelled before night, or the snow, overtook them. It was a hard run. But it must be accomplished. Failure? But failure must not be considered. No man could contemplate failure and face the winter trail in the barren desolation of the lofty interior of Labrador's untracked wild.

The austerity of the country was well-nigh overwhelming. The nakedness of it all suggested a skeleton world robbed of everything that could make existence possible. It suggested a world that was sick, and aged, and too unfruitful to harbour aught but the fierce elemental storms of the northern winter. And the cold of it ate into the bones of the lonely figure passing through the great silence like a ghost.

The night was deathly still. A thermometer would have registered something colder than sixty degrees below zero. Not a breath of wind stirred. The only sound that came was the doleful note of a prowling wolf in the forest belt near by, and the booming protest of the trees against the bitterness of winter.

The sky was ablaze with a myriad jewels in a velvet setting. And a cold wealth of aurora lit the northern heavens. Camp had been pitched well wide of the nearby forests, and three men sat crouching over the fire. There was little enough to differentiate between them. They were white men, and all were clad, from their heads to the soles of their seal hide moccasins, in heavy furs. The dark outlines of two sleds showed up a few yards away, but the dogs, themselves, were not visible. Weary with their day's run they had betaken themselves to their nightly snow burrows to dream over past battles, past labours.

The men were talking earnestly in the low, slow tones which the silence of the forests seems to inspire. Three pairs of bare hands were outheld to the welcome blaze of the fire. Three pairs of clear gazing eyes searched the heart of it. None were smoking. It would have been a burden to keep the pipe stem from freezing even in the vicinity of the fire, and none of them were in any mood to accept any added burden.

A blue-eyed, beardless youth shifted his gaze to the dark face directly opposite him beyond the fire.

"Oh, we got that guy—good," he said. There was laughter in his eyes but not in his tone. "We got him plumb at the game. He was chock full of kerosene and tinder, and he'd fired the patch in several places. We were on it quick. We beat the fire in seconds. As for him, why, I guess his Ma's going to forget him right away. Leastways I hope so. He went out like the snuff of a lucifer, and his body's likely handed plenty feed to any wolf straying around."

The dark man across the fire nodded.

"Did he hand a squeal before—he went?"

"Not a word. Hadn't time. Peter here didn't ast a thing either."

The youth laughed softly, and the man called Peter took up the story.

"Tain't no use arguin' with a feller loaded with kerosene in these forests," he said, in a low grumbling way. Then he reached down and snatched a brand from the fire and flung it out on the snow. His action was followed swiftly by a wolfish howl of dismay. Then he again turned his grizzled, whiskered face to the dark man beyond the fire. "You see, Father, it's our job keeping these forests from fire, an' it ain't easy. It don't much concern us who's out to fire 'em. That's for other folks. The feller with kerosene in these forests is goin' to get the stuff we ken hand him. That's all. Bob an' me got our own way fer actin'."

Bob laughed

"We sure have," he said. "But we don't allers pull it off. No. We've had ten fires on our range in two weeks. We've beat the fires, but we ain't smashed the 'bugs' that set 'em."

"Would they be all one feller? The feller that got it?" The dark man's eyes were serious. His tone was troubled.

Peter shook his head.

"No, sir. There's more'n one, sure. An' from the things I've heerd tell from the boys on the neighbourin' ranges it's happening all along through our limits. They tell me there's queer things doin' an' no one seems to locate the meaning right."

"What sort of things?"

The dark man spoke sharply. Peter's reply came after profound deliberation.

"Oh, things," he said. Then he thrust a gnarled brown hand up under his fur hood, and scratched his head. "There's our forest 'phones. They're bein' cut. It's the same everywhere. There's most always things to break 'em happenin', but a break aint a cut. No. They're cut. Who's cuttin' 'em, and why? Fire-bugs. It ain't grouchy jacks. No. I've heerd the jacks are on the buck in parts, but that ain't their play. There ain't a jack who'd see these forests afire, or do a thing to help that way. You see, it's their living, it's their whole life. We got so we can't depend a thing on the 'phones. An' cut our forests 'phones and we're gropin' like blind men."

"Yes."

The leaping flames were dropping, and Bob moved out to the store of fuel. He returned laden, and packed the wood carefully to give the maximum blaze. Then he squatted again, and again his hands were thrust out to the warmth which meant luxury.

Peter had no more to add. His grey eyes searched the heart of the fire as he reflected on the things which were agitating his mind.

"I want to get word down, but I can't depend on the 'phones," he said presently. "If they ain't cut I can't tell who's gettin' the message anyway. Maybe the wires are bein' tapped."

The man across the fire nodded.

"I'm going down," he said.

"I'm glad." Peter's acknowledgment came with an air of relief. "I'll hand you a written report before you pull out."

"It's best that way."

The fire was leaping again. Its beneficent warmth was very pleasant. Bob turned his eyes skyward.

"You'll get a good trip, Father," he said. "That snow's cleared out of the sky. It 'ud ha' been hell if it had caught you out on the lake."

"Yes. I wouldn't have made here. I wouldn't have made anywhere if that had happened." The dark man laughed.

Peter shook his head.

"No. You took a big chance."

"I had to."

"So?"

"Yes. I had to get through. There's a big piece of trouble coming."

"To do with these fires?"

"I guess so."

"I see."

Peter's comment was full of understanding. After awhile the other looked up.

"Guess I need a big sleep," he said. "I've got to pull out with daylight. Anything you want besides that written report passed on down?"

Peter shook his head and sat on awhile blinking silently at the firelight. Then the dark man scrambled to his feet. He stood for a moment, very tall, very bulky in his fur clothing, and nodded down at the others.

"So long," he said. And he moved off to his sleeping bag which was laid out to receive his tired body.

The man stood just within the shelter of the twilit forests. He was a powerful creature of sturdy build, hall-marked with the forest craft which was his life. He was clad in tough buckskin from head to foot. Even his hands, which he frequently beat in a desire for warmth, were similarly clad. His weatherbeaten face was hard set, and his eyes were narrowed to confront the merciless snow fog which the rage of the blizzard outside hurled at him.

The cold was almost unendurable even here in the wooded shelter. Outside, where the storm raged unrestrainedly over its fierce playground only blind hopelessness prevailed.

There was nothing to be done. He could only wait.

He could only wait, and hope, or abandon his vigil, and return to his camp which was far back in the heart of the forests. Away out there, somewhere lost in the blinding fog of the blizzard, which had only sprung up within the last hour, a lonely fellow creature was making for the shelter in which he stood. He was driving headlong towards him. Oh, yes. He knew that. He had seen the moving outfit far off, several miles away, over the snowy plains, before the storm had arisen. Now—where was he? He could not tell. He could not even guess at what might have happened. Blinded, freezing, weary, how long could the lonely traveller endure and retain any sense of direction?

To the forest man the position was well-nigh tragic. Had he not experience of the terror of a northern blizzard? Had he not many a time had to grope his way along a life-line lest the slightest deviation in direction should carry him out into the storm to perish of cold, blinded and lost?" Oh, yes. This understanding was the alphabet of his life.

As he stood there watching and wiping the snow from his eyes, he reminded himself not only of his own experience but of every story of disaster in a blizzard he had ever listened to. And so he saw no hope for the poor wretch he had seen struggling to make the shelter.

But he could not bring himself to abandon his post. How could he with a fellow creature out there in peril? Besides, there was other reason, although it needed none. He had urgent news for this man, news which must be imparted without delay, news which his employers must hear at the earliest possible moment.

His trouble grew as he waited. He searched his mind for anything calculated to aid the doomed traveller. He could find nothing. He thought to call out, to burst his lungs in a series of shouts on the chance of being heard in the chaos of the storm. But he realised the uselessness of it all, and abandoned the impulse. No puny human voice could hope to make impression on the din of the elemental battle being fought out on the plain. No. His only service must be to stand there beating life into his numbing hands, ready to act on the instant should opportunity serve.

He was eaten up by anxiety, and so took no cognisance of time. He had forgotten the passing of daylight. Therefore sudden realisation flung him into headlong panic. The forest about him was growing dark. The snow fog outside had changed to a deeper hue. Night was coming on. The man in the storm was beyond all aid, human or otherwise.

The impulse of the moment was irresistible. He moved. He passed out from behind the long limbs of his leafless shelter. He went at a run shouting with all the power of his lungs. Again and again his prolonged cry went up. And with each effort he waited listening, listening, only to receive the mocking reply of the howling storm. But he persisted. He persisted for the simple human reason that his desire outran his power to serve. And in the end exhaustion forced him to abandon his hopeless task.

It was then the miracle happened. Far away, it seemed, a sound like the faintest echo of his own voice came back to him, but it came from a direction all utterly unexpected. For a moment he hesitated, bewildered, uncertain. Then he sent up another shout, and waited listening. Yes. There it was. Again came the faintly echoing cry through the trees. It came not from the open battle ground of the storm, but from the shelter of the forests somewhere away to the north of him.

A tall, fur-clad figure stood nearby to the sled which was already partly unloaded. A yard or two away a fire had been kindled, and it blazed comfortingly in the growing dusk of the forest. It was the moment when the forest man came up somewhat breathlessly and flung out a mitted hand in greeting.

"I guessed you were makin' your last run for shelter, Father," he cried. "I just hadn't a hope you'd make through that storm. You beat it—fine."

The tall man nodded. His dark eyes were smiling a cordiality no less than the other's.

"I guessed that way, too," he said quietly. "Then I didn't." He shrugged his fur-clad shoulders. "No. It's not a northern trail that's going to see the end of me. But it's your yarn I need to hear. How is it?"

"Bad."

The two men looked squarely into each others eyes, and the gravity of the forest man was intense. The man who had just come out of the storm was no less serious, but presently he turned away, and for a second his gaze rested on the group of sprawling dogs. The beasts looked utterly spent as they blinked at the fire which they were never permitted to approach. He indicated the fire.

"Let's sit," he said. "It's cold—damnably cold."

The other needed no second invitation. They both moved back to the fire and squatted over it, and the forest man pointed at the dogs.

"Beat?" he said.

"Yes. But they hauled me through. They're a great outfit. I fed 'em right away and now they need rest. They'll be ready for the trail again by morning. Anyway I can't delay."

"No. You've got to get through quick."

Both were holding outspread hands to the fire. Both were luxuriating in the friendly warmth.

"Well?" The tall man turned his head so that his dark eyes searched the other's face again. "You'd best tell it me, Jean. If the storm lets up I pull out with daylight. I've come through every camp, and this is the last. Maybe I know the stuff you've got to tell. It's been the same most all the way."

Jean looked up from the heart of the fire.

"Trouble?" he enquired.

"Every sort." The tall man's eyes were smiling. "There's jacks quitting and pulling out, and nobody seems to know how they're getting, seeing it's winter. Others are going slow. There's others grumbling for things you never heard tell of before. There's fire-bugs at work, and the forest 'phones are being cut or otherwise tampered with all the time. We've lost hundreds of acres by fire already."

"My yarn's the same." Jean nodded and turned back to the fire. "Say," he went on, "have you heard of the things going on? The thing that's happening?"

"You mean the outfit working it?"

"Yes. It's a political labour gang. Leastways that's the talk of 'em. They call 'em 'Bolshies,' whatever that means. They're chasing these forests through. They make the camps by night, and get hold of the boys right away. They throw a hurricane of hot air at them, preachin' the sort of dope that sets those darn fools lyin' around when they need to be makin' the winter cut. And when they're through, and started the bug the way they want it, they pull out right away before the daylight comes. We never get a chance at 'em. Our boys are all plumb on the buck. I was just crazy for you to come along, Father. Guess you're the one man to fix the boys right. An' when I see you caught up in that darn storm—"

"I'll do the thing I know," the dark man replied. "I've been doing it right along. But it's not enough. That's why I'm chasing down to the coast. We've got to lay this spook that worries the boys at night. It's no Bolshie outfit." He shook his head. "Anyway if it is it's got another thing behind it. It's the Skandinavia."

He sat on for a few minutes in silence. He squatted there, hugging his knees. He was weary. He was weary almost to death with the incessant travel that had already occupied him weeks.

Quite abruptly his hands parted and he stood up. Jean followed his movements with anxious eyes.

"You goin' down to talk to the boys?" he asked at last.

The man nodded.

"Yes. Right away. I'll do all I know."

"They'll listen to you."

The other smiled.

"Yes. Till the spook comes back."

Jean brushed the icicles from about his eyes.

"That's just it," he said. "An' meanwhile the cut's right plumb down. If this thing don't quit the mill's going to starve when the ice breaks. I've lost nigh three weeks' full cut already. It's—it's hell!"

"Yes."

The dark man moved away, and Jean sat on over the fire. But his troubled eyes watched the curious figure as it passed over to its outfit. He saw the man stoop over the litter of his goods. He saw him disentangle some garment from the rest. When he came back the furs he had been clad in were either abandoned or hidden under fresh raiment. The man towered an awesome figure in the firelight. He was clad in black from head to foot, and his garment possessed the flowing skirts of a priest.

"I'm going right down to the boys now," he said. "You best stop around here. Just have an eye to the dogs. It's best you not being with me."

Jean nodded. He understood. Accompanied by the camp boss this man's influence with the boys would have been seriously affected. Alone he was well-nigh all powerful.

"Good," he said. "For God's sake do what you can, Father," he cried. "I'll stop right here till you get back. So long."

CHAPTER XVIII
BULL STERNFORD'S VISION OF SUCCESS

"I'd say it's best story I've listened to since—since—Say, those fellers are pretty big. They surely are."

Bat Harker stirred. He shifted his feet on the rail of the stove, where the heavy leather soles of his boots were beginning to burn.

Bull's shining eyes were raised to his.

"Big?" he echoed. "I tell you that feller, Leader, has the widest vision of any man I know."

He leant back in his chair and imitated his companion's luxurious attitude. And so they sat silent, each regarding the thing between them from his own angle.

It was the night of Bull's return from his journey to England. He had completed the final stage only that afternoon. He had travelled overland from the south headland, where he had been forced to disembark from the *Myra* under stress of weather. It was storming outside now, one of those fierce wind storms of Labrador's winter, liable to blow for days or only for a few hours.

He and Harker were closeted together in the warm comfort of the office on the hill. Here, without fear of interruption, in the soft lamplight, lounging at their ease, they were free to talk of those things so dear to them, and upon which hung the destiny of their enterprise.

Winter was more than half spent. Christmas and New Year were already seasons which only helped to swell the store of memory. Labrador was frozen to the bone, and would remain so. But there were still two months and more of snow and ice, and storm, to be endured before the flies and mosquitoes did their best to make life unendurable.

Bull's return home had been a time of great looking forward. Life to him had become full of every alluring possibility. He saw the approaching fulfilment of his hopes and aims. The contemplation of the pending war with the Skandinavia only afforded his fighting instincts satisfaction. Then there was that other. That great, new sensation which stirred him so deeply—Nancy McDonald. So he had returned home full of enthusiasm and ready to tackle any and every problem that presented itself.

He had just completed the telling of the story he had brought back with him. It was a story of success that had stirred even the cast-iron emotions of Bat Harker. Nor had it lost anything in the telling, for Bull was more deeply moved than he knew.

The recounting of his dealings in London with the man, Sir Frank Leader, had been coloured by the enthusiasm with which the Englishman had inspired him. Sir Frank Leader was known as the uncrowned king of the world's pulp-wood trade. But Bull felt, and declared, that the appellation did not come within measurable distance of expressing the man's real genius. Then there were those others: Stanton Brothers, and Lord Downtree, and the virile, youthful creature, Ray Birchall. All of them were strong pillars of support for the ruling genius of the house of Leader & Company. But it was the man himself, the head of it, who claimed all Bull's admiration for his intensity of national spirit, and the wide generosity of his enterprise.

The story he had had to tell was simple in its completeness. Before setting out on his journey he had spent months in preparation of the ground by means of voluminous correspondence and documentary evidence. It was a preparation that left it only necessary to convince through personal appeal on his arrival in London. This had been achieved in the broad fashion that appealed to the men he encountered. His "hand" had been laid down. Every card of it was offered for their closest scrutiny, even to the baring of the last reservation which his intimate knowledge of the merciless climate of Labrador might have inspired.

The appeal of this method had been instant to Sir Frank Leader. And the appeal had been as much the man himself as the thing he offered. The result of it all was Bull's early return home with the man's whole organisation fathering his enterprise, and with a guarantee of his incomparable fleet of freighters being flung into the pool. Leader had swept up the whole proposition into his widely embracing arms, and taken it to himself. Subject to Ray Birchall's ultimate report, after personal inspection on the spot of the properties involved, the flotation was to be launched for some seventy million dollars, and thus the consummation of Sachigo's original inspiration would be achieved.

Bat had listened to the story almost without comment. He had missed nothing of it. Neither had he failed to observe the man telling it. The story itself was all so tremendous, so far removed from the work that pre-occupied him that he had little desire to probe deeper into it. But the success of it all stirred him. Oh, yes. It had stirred him deeply, and his mind had immediately flown to that other who had laboured for just this achievement and had staggered under the burden of it all.

Bull removed his pipe and gazed across the stove.

"And now for your news, Bat," he said, like a man anticipating a pleasant continuation of his own good news.

Bat shook his head decidedly.

"No," he said, in his brusque fashion. "Not to-night, boy. Guess I ain't got a thing to tell to match your stuff. We just carried on, and we've worked big. We're in good shape for the darn scrap with the Skandinavia you told me about. Guess I'll hand you my stuff to-morrow, when I'm goin' to show you things. This night's your night—sure."

His twinkling eyes were full of kindly regard, for all the brusqueness of his denial. And Bull smiled back his content.

"Well, it's your 'hand' Bat," he said easily. "You'll play it your way."

His eyes turned to the comforting stove again, as the howl of the storm outside shook the framing of the house.

Presently the other raised a pair of smiling eyes.

"You know, boy," the lumberman said, ejecting a worn-out chew of tobacco, "all this means one mighty big thing your way. You see, you got life before you. Maybe I've years to run, too. But it ain't the same. No," he shook his grizzled head, "you can't never make nuthin' of me but a lumber-boss. You'll never be a thing but a college-bred fighter all your life. There's a third share in this thing for both of us. Well, that's goin' to be one a' mighty pile. I was wonderin'. Shall you quit? Shall you cut right out with the boodle? What'll you do?"

Bull sat up and laughed. And his answer came on the instant.

"Why, marry," he said.

Bat nodded.

"That's queer," he said. "I guessed you'd answer that way."

"Why?"

Bat folded his arms across his broad chest.

"You're young," he replied.

Bull laughed again.

"Better say it," he cried. "An' darn foolish."

"No, I hadn't that in mind. No, Bull. If I had your years I guess I'd feel that way, too. I wonder—"

"You're guessing to know who I'd marry, eh?" Bull's pipe was knocked out into the cuspidore. Then he sat up again and his eyes were full of reckless delight. "Here," he cried, "I guess it's mostly school-kids who shout the things they reckon to do—or a fool man. It doesn't matter. Maybe I'm both. Anyway, I'm just crazy for—for—"

"Red hair, an'—an' a pair of mighty pretty eyes?"

"Sure."

Bat nodded. A deep satisfaction stirred him.

"I reckoned that way, ever since— Say, I'm glad."

But Bull's mood had sobered.

"She's in the enemy camp though," he demurred.

"It'll hand you another scrap—haulin' her out."

"Yes."

Bat rose from his chair and stretched his trunk-like body.

"Well," he said, "it's me for the blankets." Then he emitted a deep-throated chuckle. "You get at it, boy," he went on. "An' if you're needin' any help I can pass, why, count on it. If you mean marryin' I'd sooner see you hook up team with that red-haired gal than anything in the world I ever set two eyes on. Guess I'll hand you my stuff in the morning if the storm quits."

The dynamos were revolving at terrific speed. There were some eighteen in all, and their dull roar was racking upon ears unused. Bat was regarding them without enthusiasm. All he knew was the thing they represented. Skert Lawton had told him. They represented the harnessing of five hundred thousand horse power of the Beaver River water. The engineer had assured him, in his unsmiling fashion, that he had secured enough power to supply the whole Province of Quebec with electricity. All of which, in Bat's estimation, seemed to be an unnecessary feat.

Bull was gazing in frank wonder on the engineer's completed work. It was his first sight of it. The place had been long in building. But the sight of it in full running, the sense of enormous power, the thought and labour this new power-house represented, filled him with nothing but admiration for the author of it all.

Bat hailed one of the electricians serving the machines.

"Where's Mr. Lawton?" he shouted.

"He went out. He ain't here," the man shouted back.

Bat regarded the man for a moment without favour. Then he turned away. He beckoned Bull to follow, and moved over to the sound-proof door which shut off the engineer's office. They passed to the quiet beyond it.

It was quite a small room without any elaborate pretensions. There was a desk supporting a drawing board, with a chair set before it. There was also a rocker-chair which accommodated the lean body of Skert Lawton at such infrequent moments as it desired repose. Beyond that there was little enough furniture. The place was mainly bare boards and bare walls. Bat sat himself at the desk and left Bull the rocker-chair.

"I'd fixed it so Skert was to meet us here," he said. "All this is his stuff. I couldn't tell you an' amp from a buck louse."

Bull nodded.

"That's all right," he said. "Maybe he's held up down at the mill. He'll get—"

"Held up—nuthin'!"

The lumberman was angry. But his anger was not at the failure of his arrangements. Back of his head he was wondering at the thing that claimed the engineer. He felt that only real urgency would have kept him from his appointment. And he knew that urgency just now had a more or less ugly meaning.

"Lawton's a pretty bright boy—" Bull began. But the other caught him up roughly.

"Bright? That don't say a thing," Bat cried. "Guess he's a whole darn engineering college rolled into the worst shape of the ghost of a man it's been my misfortune ever to locate. He's a highbrow of an elegant natur'. He calls this thing 'co-ordination,' which is another way of sayin' he's beat nigh a hundred thousand dollars out of our bank roll to hand us more power than we could use if we took in Broadway, New York, at night. But it's elegant plannin' and looks good to me. Your folks over the water'll maybe see things in it, too. It's them blast furnaces we set up for him last year made this play possible. Them, and the swell outfit of machine shops he squeezed us for. He figgers to raise all sorts of hell around. An' his latest notion's to build every darn machine from rough-castin' to a shackle pin, so we don't have to worry with the world outside. He's got a long view of things. But—"

He pulled out his timepiece, and the clouds of volcanic anger swept down again upon his rugged brow. But it was given no play. The door of the office was thrust open, and the lean figure of the engineer, clad in greasy overalls, came hurriedly into the room.

Bat challenged him on the instant.

"What's the trouble, boy?" he demanded in his uncompromising fashion.

"Trouble?" Skert's eyes were wide, and his tone was savage. "That's just it. I reckoned to show Sternford all this stuff," he went on, indicating the machine hall with a jerk of his head. "But we'll have to let it pass. Say," he glanced from one to the other, his expression developing to something like white fury. "They started. It's business this time. I got a message up they were stopping the grinders. It's the 'heads' gave the order. Oh, they're all in it. They got a meeting on in that darn recreation parliament place of theirs, and every mother's son on the machines was called to it. They've shut down! You get that? There isn't even a greaser left at the machines. It's set me with a feeling I'm plumb crazy. I've been down, and they're right there crowding out that hall. And—"

"I guessed something that way," Bat interrupted with ominous calm. He turned to Bull, who was closely regarding his lieutenants.

"It's mutiny first and then a sheer strike," he said. "Here, listen. I'll hand you just what's happenin'. There's been Bolshie agitators workin' the boys months, and I guess they got a holt on 'em good. It started with us openin' the new mill on this north shore. We were forced to collect our labour just where we could. An' they got in like the miser'ble rats they are. Gee! It makes me hot—hot as hell! The leaders of this thing ain't workers. I don't guess they done a day's work with anything but their yahoo mouths in their dirty lives. They're part of the crowd that's paid from Europe to get around and heave up this blazin' world of ours just anyway they know. The only thing I don't get is their coming along here, which is outside most all the rest of the world. If Labrador can hand 'em loot I'd like to know the sort it is. And it's just loot they're out for. If I'm a judge there's one hell of a scrap comin,' and if we're beat it looks like leaving Sachigo a thing forgotten."

Bull stood up. He laughed without the least mirth.

"It's the Skandinavia," he said decidedly. "War's begun. I'm going right down to that meeting."

Bat leapt to his feet.

"No," he said. "This is for Skert an' me—"

"Is it?"

Bull brushed his protest aside almost fiercely. Then he turned as the door opened and a small man hurried in. The fellow snatched his cap from his head and his eyes settled on Skert Lawton, the man he knew best.

"It ees a document," he cried, in the broken English of a French Canadian. "They sign him, oh, yes. You no more are the boss. They say the mill it ees for the 'worker.' All dis big mill, all dis big money. Oh, yes. Dey sign him."

"Who's this?" Bull demanded.

"One of my machine-minders. He's a good boy," the engineer explained.

Bull nodded.

"That's all right We want all we can get of his sort." He turned to Bat. "Are there others? I mean boys we can trust?"

"Quite a bunch."

"Can we get them together?"

"Sure."

"Right. This is going to be the real thing. The sort of thing I'd rather have it."

He turned to Skert who stood by, watching the light of battle in his chief's eyes.

"Here, shut down the dynamos. Set them clean out of action. Do you get me? Leave the machines for the time being so they're just so much scrap. Then, if you got the bunch you can rely on, leave 'em guard. We'll get on down, an' sign that damned document for 'em."

The recreation room was crowded to suffocation. Men of every degree in the work of the mill had foregathered. A hubbub of talk was going on. Voices were raised. There was anger. There was argument, harsh-voiced argument which mainly expressed feeling. At the far end of the hall, on the raised platform designed for those who fancied their vocal attainments, a group of men were gathered about a table upon which was outspread the folios of an extensive document. The men at the table were talking eagerly.

The gathering had listened to the furious oratory of a pale-faced man, with long black hair and a foreign accent. It had listened, and agreed, and applauded. For he had talked Communism, and the overthrow of the Capitalists, and the possession of the wealth creating mills for those who operated them. It had listened to an appeal to the latent instinct in every human creature, freedom from everything that could be claimed as servitude, freedom, and possession, and independence for those who would once and for all rid themselves of the shackles which the pay-roll and time-sheet imposed upon them.

They had been called together to witness the iniquity of spending their lives in the degrading operation of filling the pockets of those who laboured not, by the toil in which their lives were spent. They had been told every flowery fairy tale of the modern communistic doctrine, which possesses as much truth and sanity in it as is to be found in an asylum for the mentally deficient. And they had swallowed the bait whole. The talk had been by the tongue of a skilled fanatic, who was well paid for his work, and who kept in the forefront of his talk that alluring promise of ease, and affluence, and luxury, which never fails in its appeal to those who have never known it.

But something approaching an impasse had been reached when the would-be benefactors passed over the demand that their deluded victims should sign the roll of Communal Brotherhood. The bait that had been offered had been all to the taste of these rough creatures who had never known better than an existence with a threat of possible unemployment overshadowing their lives. But in the signature to the elaborate document they scented the concealed poison in the honeyed potion. There was hesitation, reluctance. There was argument in a confusion of tongues well-nigh bewildering. A surge of voices filled the great building.

The agents were at work, men who posed as workers to attain their ends. And the pale, long-haired creature and his satellites waited at the table. They understood. It was their business to understand. They knew the minds they were dealing with, and their agents were skilled in their craft. The process they relied on was the unthinking stupidity of the sheep. Every man that could be persuaded had his friends, and each friend had his friend. They knew friend would follow friend well-nigh blindly, and, having signed, native obstinacy and fear of ridicule would hold them fast to their pledge.

Presently the signing began. It began with a burly river-jack who laughed stupidly to cover his doubt. He was followed by a machine-minder, who hurled taunts at those who still held back. Then came others, others whose failure to think for themselves left them content to follow the lead of their comrades.

The stream of signatures grew. A pale youth, whose foolish grin revealed only his fitness for the heavy, unskilled work he was engaged upon, came up. The pen was handed him, and the name of Adolph Mars was scrawled on the sheet. The long-haired man at the table looked up at him. He smiled with his lips, and patted the boy's hand. Then something happened.

It was movement. Sudden movement on the platform. The babel in the body of the hall went on. But the long-haired man and his supporters at the table turned with eyes that were concerned and anxious. A dozen men had entered swiftly through the door in rear of the platform. Bull Sternford led them. And he moved over to the table, with the swift, noiseless strides of a panther, and looked into the unwholesome face of the Bolshevist leader.

It was only for the fraction of a second. The man made a movement which needed no interpretation. His hand went to a hip pocket. Instantly Bull's great hands descended. The man was picked up like a child. He was lifted out of his seat and raised aloft. He was borne towards the window where he was held while the master of the mill crashed a foot against its wooden sash. The next moment the black-clothed body was hurled with terrific force out into the snowdrift waiting to receive it. It was all so swiftly done. The whole thing was a matter of seconds only. Then Bull Sternford was back at the table, while his comrades, Bat and Lawton, and the men of loyalty they relied on, lined the platform.

As Bull snatched up the document and held it aloft, a deathly silence reigned throughout the hall, and every eye was turned angrily upon the intruders. Bull yielded not a moment for those witless minds to recover from their shock. His voice rang out fiercely.

"Here," he cried, "d'you know what you're doing, listening to that fool guy I've thrown through that window, and signing this crazy paper he's set out for you? No. You don't unless you're just as crazy yourselves. You're declaring war. You're starting a great fight to steal the property that hands you your living. You reckon you've got all you need of our brains, and your own brute force and darnation foolishness can run these great mills which are to hand you the big money you reckon it hands us. That means war. Maybe you fancy it's the one-sided war you'd like to have it. Maybe you fancy there's about a dozen of us, and we're going to be made to work for the wage you figger to hand us. You're dead wrong. It's going to be a hell of a war if you swallow the dope these fellows hand you. You've begun it, and we're taking up the challenge. We've fired the first shot, too. It's not gun-play yet. No. Maybe it'll come to that and you'll find we can hand you shot for shot. No. We're quicker than that. The mill's closed down! Wages have ceased! And all power has been cut off! There's not a spark of light or heat, for the whole of Sachigo. The vital parts of the power station have been removed, and you can't get 'em back. I've only to give the word and the *penstocks on the river will be cut so you can't repair them.* It's forty degrees below Zero out there, where I've shot that crazy Bolshie, and so you know just how you stand here on Labrador with no means of gettin' away until the thaw comes. You and your wives and kiddies'll have to pay in the cold for the crime of theft you reckon to put through. We're ready for you, whether it's gun-play or any other sort of war you want to start. That's the thing I've come here to tell you."

He paused for a moment to watch the effect of his words. It was there on the instant. A furious hubbub arose. There was not a man in the room who did not understand the dire threat which the *coup* of the master mind imposed. Power cut off! Light! Heat! Power! Forty degrees below Zero! The terror of the Labrador winter was in every man's mind. Life would be unendurable without heat. There were the forests. Oh, yes. They could get heat of sorts. The sort of heat which the men on a winter trail were accustomed to. *Their electrically-heated houses were without stoves in which they could burn wood.*

Bull listened to the babel of tongues while his men watched for any act that might come. Every man on the platform was armed ready.

"Here!"

Bull's voice rang out again, but he was interrupted.

A man shouted at him from the back of the hall.

"Who the hell are you, anyway? You ain't the guy owning these mills. We know where you come from—"

Like lightning Bull took him up.

"Do you?" he shouted back. "Then we know where you come from. The man who knew me before I became boss here must belong to the Skandinavia. That's the only place any lumber-jack could have known me. Here. Come up here. Stand out. Show yourself. And I'll hand the boys your pedigree. It'll be easy. It's the trouble with us just now, we've got too many stiffs from the Skandinavia, and you've got our own good boys paralysed. They haven't the guts to stand on the notions that have handed them the best wages in the pulp trade these fifteen years. Guess you've persuaded them they ain't got swell houses, and good food, and cheap heat and light, and, instead are living like all sorts of swine in their hogpens. It's the way of the Skandinavia just now. The Skandinavia's out for our blood. They want to smash us. Do you know why? Because they're an alien firm who wants to steal these forests from the Canadians to fill their own pockets with our wealth. We're for the Canadians, and we've built up a proposition that's going to beat the foreigner right out into the sea. But that don't matter now.

These guys, these long-haired, unwashed guys, that reckon to hand you boys these mills, are sent by the Skandinavia to wreck us. Well, go right over to 'em. Help 'em. Sign every darn document they hand you. They'll be your own death warrants, anyway. You want war. You can have it. I'm here to fight. Meanwhile you best get home to your cold houses, for the mills are closed down. You're locked out."

He turned without waiting a second and passed through the back door by which he had entered. And his men followed on his heels.

Bull was in his office. For all the storm of the morning the rest of the day had passed quietly. Now it was late at night. His stove was radiating a luxurious heat. He was quite unconcerned that the electrically-heated steam radiators were cold. He was alone. Harker and the engineer were still down at the mill. He was awaiting the report they would bring him later.

He had passed some time in reading the pledge of Communal Brotherhood which he had brought away with him from the recreation room, and he had read the signatures that had been affixed to it. The latter were few, and every name inscribed was of foreign origin. But it was the document itself which concerned him most. If it were honest he felt that its authors were wild people who should be kept under restraint. If it were not honest, then hanging or shooting was far too lenient a fate to be meted out to them. It was Communism in its wildest, most unrestrained form.

In his final disgust he flung the papers on his desk. And as he did so a sound reached him from the outer office, which had long since been closed for the night by the half-breed, Loale.

He leapt to his feet. Without a second thought he moved over to the door and flung it wide.

"What the—?" He broke off. "Good God!" he cried. "You, Father?" He laughed. "Why I thought it was some of the Bolshies from down at the mill."

He withdrew the gun from his coat pocket in explanation. Then he stood aside.

"Will you come right in?"

The man Bull had discovered made no answer. But as he stood aside, tall, clad in heavy fur from head to foot, Father Adam strode into the room.

Bull watched him with questioning eyes. Then he closed the door and his visitor turned confronting him in the yellow lamplight.

"I've made more than a hundred miles to get you to-night," Father Adam said.

Then he flung back the fur hood from his head, and ran a hand over his long black hair, smoothing it thoughtfully.

"Yes?"

Bull's eyes were still questioning.

"Won't you shed your furs and sit?" he went on. "The Chink's abed, but I'll dig him out. You must get food."

The other glanced round the pleasant office, and his eyes paused for a moment at the chair at the desk.

"Food don't worry, thanks," he said, his mildly smiling eyes coming back to his host's face. "I've eaten—ten miles back. I rested the dogs there, too. I've maybe a ha'f hour to tell you the thing I came for. There's trouble in the woods. Bad trouble. If it's not straightened out, why, it looks like all work at your mills'll quit, and you're going to get your forest limits burnt out stark."

CHAPTER XIX
THE HOLD-UP

Ole Porson took a final glance round his shanty. The last of the daylight was rapidly fading. There was still sufficient penetrating the begrimed double window, however, to reveal the littered, unswept condition of the place. But he saw none of it. It was the place he knew and understood. It was at once his office, and his living quarters; a shanty with a tumbled sleeping bunk, a wood stove, and a table littered with the books and papers of his No. 10 camp. He was a rough creature, as hard of soul as he was of head, who could never have found joy in surroundings of better condition.

He solemnly loaded the chambers of a pair of heavy guns. Then he bestowed them in the capacious pockets of his fur pea-jacket. He also dropped in beside them a handful of spare cartridges. In his lighter moments he was apt to say that these weapons were his only friends. And those who knew him best readily agreed. Drawing up the storm-collar about his face, he passed out into the snow which was falling in flakes the size of autumn leaves. There was not a breath of wind to disturb the deathly stillness of the winter night.

Minutes later he was lounging heavily against the rough planked counter of Abe Risdon's store. He was talking to the suttler over a deep "four-fingers" of neat Rye, while his searching eyes scanned the body of the ill-lit room. The place was usually crowded with drinkers when the daylight passed, but just now it was almost empty.

"Who's that guy in the tweed pea-jacket an' looks like a city man?" he asked his host in an undertone, pointing at one of the tables where a stranger sat surrounded by four of the forest men.

Abe's powerful arms were folded as he leant on the counter.

"Blew in about noon," he said. "Filled his belly with good hash an' sat around since."

"He's a bunch o' the boys about him now, anyway. An' I guess he's talking quite a lot, an' they're doing most o' the listening. Seems like he's mostly enjoying hisself."

Abe shrugged. But the glance he flung at the man sitting at the far-off table was without approval.

"It's mostly that way now," he said, with an air of indifference his thoughtful eyes denied. "There's too many guys come along an' sell truck, an' set around, an' talk, an' then pass along. Things are changing around this lay out, an' I don't get its meanin'. Time was I had a bunch of boys ready most all the time to hand me the news going round. Time was you'd see a stranger once in a month come along in an' buy our food. Time was they mostly had faces we knew by heart, and we knew their business, and where they came from. Tain't that way now. You couldn't open the boys' faces fer news of the forest with a can-opener. These darn guys are always about now. They come, an' feed the boys' drink, an' talk with 'em most all the time. An' they're mostly strangers, an' the boys mostly sit around with their faces open like fool men listenin' to fairy tales. How's the cut goin'?"

Porson laughed. There was no light in his hard eyes.

"At a gait you couldn't change with a trail whip."

The other nodded.

'"That's how 'nigger' Pilling said. He guessed the cut was down by fifty. What is it? A buck? Wages?"

Porson's hand was fingering one of the guns in his pocket. His eyes were snapping.

"Curse 'em," he cried at last. "I just don't get it. They're goin' slow."

He pushed his empty glass at the suttler who promptly re-filled it.

"Young Pete Cust," Abe went on confidentially, "handed me a good guess only this mornin'. He'd had his sixth Rye before startin' out to work. Maybe he was rattled and didn't figger the things he said. He was astin' fer word up from the mills. I didn't worry to think, and just said I hadn't got. I ast 'why'? The boy took a quick look round, kind o' scared. He said, 'jest nothin'.' He reckoned he'd a dame somewhere around Sachigo. She'd wrote him things wer' kind of bad with the mills. They were beat fer dollars, and looked like a crash. He'd heard the same right there, an' it had him rattled. He thought of quittin' and goin' over to the Skandinavia. Maybe it's the sort o' talk that's got 'em all rattled. Maybe they're goin' slow on the cut, worryin' for their pay-roll. You can't tell. They don't say a thing. Seems to me we want Sternford right here to queer these yarns. Father Adam's around an' talked some. But—"

Porson drank down his liquor, and his glass hit the counter with angry force.

"They're mush-faced hoodlams anyway," he cried fiercely. "Ther' ain't a thing wrong with the mills. I'd bet a million on it."

He stood up from the counter and thrust his hands deep in the pockets of his coat. He was a powerful figure with legs like the tree trunks it was his work to see cut. Quite abruptly he moved away, and Abe's questioning eyes followed him.

He strode down amongst the scattered tables and came to a halt before the tweed-coated stranger. All the men looked up, and their talk died out.

"Say, what's your bizness around here?"

Ole Person's manner was threatening as he made his demand. The stranger dived at the bag lying on the floor beside his chair. He picked it up and flung it open.

"Why, I got right here the dandiest outfit of swell jewellery," he cried, grinning amiably up at the man's threatening eyes. "There's just everything here," he went on, with irrepressible volubility, "to suit you gents of the forest, an' make you the envy of every jack way down at Sachigo. Here, there's a be-autiful Prince Albert for your watch. This ring. It's full o' diamonds calculated to set Kimberly hollerin'. Maybe you fancy a locket with it. It'll take a whole bunch of your dame's—"

"You'll light right out of this camp with daylight to-morrow!"

The tone of the camp-boss banished the last shadow of the pedlar's cast-iron smile.

"Oh, yes?" he said, his eyes hardening.

"That's wot I said. This camp's private property an' you'll light out. You get that? Daylight. If you don't, we've a way of dealing with Jew drummers that'll likely worry you. Get it. An' get it good."

For a moment they looked into each other's eyes. There was not the flicker of an eyelid between them. Then Porson turned and strode away.

He passed down the store re-fastening his coat. He paused at the door as a chorus of rough laughter reached him from the little gathering at the table. But it was only for an instant. He looked back. No face was turned in his direction. So he passed out.

The night outside was inky black. The heavy falling snow made progress almost a blind groping. But Porson knew every inch of the way. He passed down the lines of huts and paused outside each bunkhouse. His reason was obvious. There was a question in his mind as to the whereabouts of the crowd of his men who usually thronged the liquor store at this hour of the evening.

It was at the last bunkhouse he paused longest. He stood for quite a while listening under the double glassed window. Then he passed on and stood beside the tightly closed storm-door. The signs and sounds he heard were apparently sufficient. For, after a while, he turned back and set out to return to his quarters.

For many minutes he groped his way through the blinding snow, his mind completely given up to the things his secret watch had revealed. His brutish nature, being what it was, left him concerned only for the forceful manner by which he could restore that authority which he felt to be slipping away from him under the curious change which had come over the camp. His position depended on the adequate output of his winter's cut and on nothing else. That, he knew, was desperately falling, and—

But in a moment, all concern was swept from his mind. A sound leapt at him out of the stillness of the night. It was the whimper of dogs and the sharp command of a man's voice. He shouted a challenge and waited. And presently a dog train pulled up beside him.

Bull Sternford was standing before the wood stove in the camp-boss's shanty. He had removed his snow-laden fur coat. He had kicked the damp snow from his moccasins. Now he was wiping the moisture out of his eyes, and the chill in his limbs was easing under the warmth which the stove radiated.

Ole Porson's grim face was alight with a smile of genuine welcome, as he stood surveying his visitor across the roaring stove.

"It's surely the best thing happened in years, Mr. Sternford," he was saying. "I'm more glad you made our camp this night than any other. Maybe I'd ha' got through someways, but I don't know just how. We're down over fifty on our cut, an', by the holy snakes, I can't hand you why."

Bull put his coloured handkerchief away, and removed the pea-jacket which he had worn under his furs.

"Don't worry," he said with apparent unconcern. "I can hand it you. That's why I'm here."

The camp-boss waited. He eyed his chief with no little anxiety. He had looked for an angry outburst.

Bull pulled up a chair. He flung the litter of books it supported on to the already crowded table and sat down. Then he filled his pipe and lit it with a hot coal from the stove.

"Here," he said, "I'll tell you. I've been the round of four camps. I've been over a month on the trail, and I've heard just the same tale from every camp-boss we employ. I've three more camps to visit besides yours, and when I've made them maybe I'll get the sleep I'm about crazy for. Night and day I've been on the dead jump for a month following the trail of a red-hot gang that's going through our forests. If I come up with them there's going to be murder."

He spoke quietly without a sign of emotion. But the light in his hot eyes was almost desperate.

"I want to hand you the story so you'll get it all clear," he went on after a moment. "So I'll start by telling you how we stand at the mill. Get this, an' hold it tight in your head, and the rest'll come clear as day. Sachigo's right on top. We've boosted it sky high on to the top of the world's pulp trade. In less than twelve months we'll have grabbed well-nigh the whole of this country's pulp industry, and we'll beat the foreigners right back over the sea to their own country. The Skandinavia folk are rattled. They know all about us and they've done their best to buy us out of the game. We turned 'em down cold, and they're mad—mad as hell. It means they're in for the fight of their lives. So are we. And we know Peterman an' his gang well enough to know what that means. It's 'rough an' tough.' Everything goes. If they can't gouge our eyes they'll do their best to chew us to small meat. But we've got 'em every way. This forest gang is sent by the Skandinavia. If they can't smash us by fire or labour trouble next year'll see us floated into a seventy million dollar corporation with the whole Canadian wood-pulp industry lying right in the palms of our hands. That's the reason for the things doing."

He paused, and the camp-boss nodded his rough head. It was a story he could clearly understand. Then there were those figures. Seventy million dollars! They swept the last shadow of doubt from his mind.

"That's the position," Bull went on. "Now for the trouble as it is in the forests right now. The thing that's had me travelling night an' day for a month. There's an outfit going right through these forests. I can't locate its extent. Only the way it works. There's two objects in view. One is to fire our limits. The other reckons to paralyse our cut. So far these folks have failed against the fire-guard organisation, and I guess they'll likely miss most of their fire-bugs when they call the roll. The other's different."

Bull knocked out his pipe on the stove and gazed thoughtfully at the streak of brilliant light under the edge of the front damper.

"I've a notion there's an outfit of pedlars at work, as well as others," he went on presently.

The camp-boss nodded.

"Sure," he said.

Bull looked up.

"You think that way?" he asked. Then he nodded. "Yes, I guess we're right. They're handing the boys dope to keep 'em guessing—worrying. They're telling 'em we're on the edge of a big smash at Sachigo. That we can't see the winter through. We're cleaned out for cash, and the mill folk are shouting for their wages and starting in to riot. It's a swell yarn. It's the sort of yarn I'd tell 'em myself if I was working for the Skandinavia. It's the sort of dope these crazy forest-jacks are ready to swallow the same as if it was Rye. Do you see? These fools are being told they won't get their pay for their winter's cut. So, being what they are, the boys are going slow. They're going slow, and drawing goods at the store against each cord they cut. Well, do you see what's going to happen if the game succeeds? With our forests ablaze, and our cut fifty down, and the whole outfit on the buck, when spring comes, Skandinavia reckons our British financiers, when they come along to look our land over will turn the whole proposition of the flotation down, and quit us cold. But that's not just all. No, sir. Elas Peterman isn't the boy to leave it that way. He's handing out the story that when Sachigo smashes the Skandinavia's going to jump right in and collect the wreckage cheap. Then they'll start up the mill, and sign on all hands on their own pay-roll, only stipulating that they won't pay one single cent of what Sachigo owes for their cut. So, if they're such almighty fools as to cut, it's going to be their dead loss and the Skandinavia's gain. Do you get it? It's smart. I guess there's a bigger brain behind it than Peterman's."

The camp-boss spat into the stove. It was his one expression of disgust.

Bull rose from his chair.

"Here, I need food. So does my boy out there with the dogs. We'll take it after I'm through with the men. It's snowing like hell, but I pull out two hours from now. You see, I'm on a hot trail, an' don't fancy losing a minute."

"You're goin' to talk to 'em—the boys?" Porson's eyes lit with a gleam of satisfaction. "Can you—twist 'em?"

Bull thrust a hand into his breast pocket and drew out a sealed packet. He held it up before the other's questioning eyes.

"I haven't failed yet," he said quietly. "In nine of our camps back on the river the work's running full already. I've a whole big yarn for our boys.

But right here I've got what's better. It's the only thing that'll clinch the yarn I'm going to hand 'em. This," he went on, indicating the parcel in his hand, "is the bunch of dollars representing the price of this camp's full winter cut, and the price of a bonus for making up all leeway already lost. I'm going to have the boys count it. Then I'm going to have them hand it right over to Abe Risdon to set in his safe, with a written order from me to pay out in full the moment the winter cut is complete. Is it good? Can the Skandinavia's junk stand in face of it? No, sir. And so I've proved right along. I don't hold much of a brief for the intelligence of the forest-jack, but his belly rules him all the time. You see, he's human, and no more dishonest than the rest of us. Have him guessing and worried and you'll get trouble right along. Show him the lies the Skandinavia's been doping him with, and he'll work out of sheer spite to beat their game. You get right out and collect the gang."

The snowfall had ceased. And with its passing the temperature had fallen to something far below its average winter level. The clouds had vanished miraculously, and in their place was a night sky ablaze with the light of myriad stars, and the soft splendour of a brilliant moon.

It was a scene of frigid desolation. Away on the southern horizon lay the black line which marked the tremendous forest limits of the Beaver River. For the rest it was a world of snow that hid up the rugged undulations of a sterile territory.

The dog train was moving at a reckless gait over the untracked, hardening snow. The man Gouter was driving under imperative orders such as he loved. Bull Sternford had told him when he left the shelter of No. 10 Camp: "Get there! Get there quick! There's dogs and to spare at all our camps, and I don't care a curse if you run the outfit to death."

To a man of Gouter's breed the order was sufficient. Half Eskimo, half white man, he was a savage of the wild, born and bred to the fierce northern trail, one of Labrador's hereditary fur hunters by sea and land. Speed on the fiercest trail was the dream of his vanity. Relays of dogs, such as he could never afford, and something accomplished which he could tell of over the camp fire to his less fortunate brethren. So he accepted the white man's order and drove accordingly.

Bull Sternford sat huddled in the back of the sled under the fur robes which alone made life possible. His work at No. 10 Camp had left him satisfied, but every nerve in his body was alert for the final coup he contemplated. He was weary in mind as well as body. And in his heart he knew that the need of his physical resources was not so very far off. But he was beyond care. He had said he was crazy for sleep, but the words gave no indication of his real condition. His eyes ached. His head throbbed. There were moments, even, when the things he beheld, the things he thought became distorted. But he knew that somewhere ahead a ghostly outfit of strangers was pursuing its evil work against him, and he meant to come up with it, and to wreak his vengeance in merciless, summary fashion. His purpose had become an obsession in the long sleepless days and nights he had endured.

It was war. It was bitter ruthless war on the barren hinterland of Labrador, where civilisation was unknown. Mercy? Nature never designed that terrible wilderness as a setting for mercy.

The dogs had been running for hours when Gouter's voice came sharply back over his shoulder.

"Dog!" he cried, in the laconic fashion habitual to him.

Bull knelt up. His movement suggested the nervous strain he was enduring. It was almost electrical.

"Where?" he demanded, peering out into the shining night over the man's furry shoulder.

The half-breed raised a pointing whip ahead and to the south.

"Sure," he said. "I hear him."

Bull had heard nothing. Nothing but the hiss of the snow under their own runners, and the whimper of their own dogs.

"It wouldn't be a wolf or fox?" he demurred.

The half-breed clucked his tongue. His vanity was outraged.

Bull gazed intently in the direction the whip had pointed. He could see only the far-off forest line, and the soft whiteness of the world of snow.

"Hark!"

The half-breed again held up his whip. This time it was for attention. Bull listened. Still he could hear nothing, nothing at all but the sounds of their own progress.

"Man! Him speak with dog. Oh, yes."

Gouter had turned. His beady black eyes were shining with a smile of triumph into the white man's face.

"By the forest?"

"Oh, yes."

"Then in God's name swing over and run to head them off!"

Gouter obeyed with alacrity. He had impressed his white chief. It was good. A series of unintelligible ejaculations and the dogs swung away to the south. Then the whip rolled out and fell with cruel accuracy. The rawhide tugs strained under a mighty effort, as the great dogs were set racing with their lean bellies low to the ground.

Bull wiped the icicles from about his mouth and nose.

"Now have your guns ready," he cried. "The driver of that team is your man. The other's mine. If he shows fight kill him. There's five hundred dollars for you if you get 'em."

"I get 'em."

The half-breed's confidence was supreme. Bull dropped back into the sled. He sat with a pair of automatic pistols ready to his hand and gazed out over the sled rail.

It was a terrific race and all feeling of weariness had passed under the excitement of it. The dogs were silent now. Every nerve in their muscular bodies were straining. The pace seemed to increase with every passing moment, and up out of the horizon the dark line of the forest leapt at them, deepening and broadening as it came.

For some time the less practised white man saw and heard nothing of his enemies. He was forced to rely on the half-breed. He observed the man closely. He noted his every sign and read it as best he could. Presently Gouter leant forward peering. Then he straightened up and his voice came back triumphantly.

"I see dem," he exclaimed. And pointed almost abreast. "Dogs. One—two—five. Yes. Two man. Now we get him sure."

Down fell the whip on the racing dogs. The man shouted his jargon at them. The sled lurched and swayed with the added spurt, and Bull held fast to the rail. A glad thrill surged through his senses.

It was a moment of tremendous uplift. Bull had yearned for it for weeks. But the short days and long nights of deferred hope had had their effect. He had almost come to feel that this thing that was now at hand was something impossible.

Yes. There was the outfit growing plainer and plainer with every moment. He could see it clearly. He could even count its details as the other's sharper eyes had counted them minutes before. There were five dogs. And they were running hard. They, too, were being flogged, and the man driving them was shouting furiously in his urgency.

Suddenly there was a leap of flame and a shot rang out. It came from the driver of the fleeing dog train. It was replied to on the instant by Gouter who lost not a second. His own shot sped even as the enemy's bullet whistled somewhere past his head. He fired again. A third shot split the air. And with that last shot the enemy's sled seemed to leap in the air. There was a moment of hideous confusion. Then the wreckage dropped away behind the pursuers, sprawled and still in the snow.

A fierce shout from Gouter and his dogs swung round. The sled under him heeled over, and took a desperate chance on a single runner. But the half-breed's skill saved them from catastrophe. It righted itself, and the dogs slowed to a trot. Then they halted. And the occupants of the sled flung themselves prone, with their guns ready for the first sign of movement in the tangled mass of their adversary's outfit.

Two of the dogs lay buried under the overturned sled. Three others were sprawling at the end of their rawhide tugs. They were alive. They were unhurt. They lay there taking full advantage of the situation for rest.

But for the moment interest centred round the body of a white man lying some yards away. A groan of pain came up to the two men standing over him.

Bull dropped on his knees. He reached down and turned the body over. The eyes of the man were visible between the sides of his fur hood. But that was all.

There was a moment of silent contemplation. Then the injured man struggled desperately to rise.

"Sternford?" he ejaculated

Gouter was on him in a moment. He heard the tone of voice, and interpreted the man's movement in his own savage fashion. He knew the man to be the driver of the team, whom his boss had told him was his man. So he threw him back and held him.

Bull stood up. The man's voice told him all he wanted to know.

"Laval, eh?" he said quietly. "A second time. I didn't expect it. No."

Then he laughed and turned away. And the sound of his laugh possessed something terribly mocking in the night silence of the wilderness.

He passed back to the sled. There had been two men in it. He had seen that for himself.

The wreckage looked hopeless. The sled was completely overturned and its gleaming runners caught and reflected the white rays of the moon. It had been thrown by reason of the fallen bodies of the dogs which lay under it, pinned by its weight, and additionally held fast by their own tangled harness.

Bull had no thought for anything but the purpose in his mind. So he reached out and caught the steel runners in his mitted hands and flung the vehicle aside.

Yes, it was there in the midst of a confusion of baggage and lying cheek by jowl with the mangled remains of the dogs. He cleared the debris, and dragged the dogs aside. Then he stood and gazed down at the figure that remained.

It was clad in a voluminous beaver coat. It was hooded, as was every man who faced the fierce Labrador trail. But—

The figure moved. It stirred, and deliberately sat up. Bull's hands had been on his guns at the first movement. But he released them, as the hood fell back from the face which was ghastly pale in the moonlight.

He flung himself on his knees, and tenderly supported the swaying figure.

"God in Heaven!" he cried. "Nancy! You?"

CHAPTER XX
ON THE HOME TRAIL

Nancy's eyes were desperately troubled as she gazed out across the great valley of the Beaver River. Somewhere behind her, in the shelter of the woods, a mid-day camp had been pitched, and the men who had captured her red-hand in the work of their enemies were preparing the, rough food of the trail. But she was beyond all such concern.

Far out on every hand lay the amazing panorama of the splendid valley, but she saw none of it. The mighty frozen waterway, the depths of virgin snow, the far-reaching woodlands its gaping lips embraced; they were things of frigid beauty for her eyes to gaze upon, but their meaning was lost upon a mind tortured with the vivid, hateful pictures it was powerless to escape.

From the moment of that dreadful night when she had witnessed the ruthless climax of the work to which she had given herself she had known no peace. It was no thought of her failure, her capture, that inspired her trouble. She could have been thankful enough for that. It was the only mercy, she felt, that had been vouchsafed to her.

No, long before her capture, a deep undermining of regret had set in. She had been without realisation of it, perhaps. But it had been there. In yielding to the demands of those she served, in her self-confidence she had forgotten the woman in her. She had forgotten everything but the crazy ambition which had blinded her to all consequences. Yes, even in the excitement of the work itself she had forgotten everything but the achievement she desired. But through it all, under it all, the woman in her had been slowly awakening, and an unadmitted regret at the destruction of work which meant the whole life of another had been stirring. Then, when the leading tongues of the guns had flashed out, and human life, even the life of dogs, had yielded to the demand of her cause, the last vestige of her dreaming had been swept away, and she told herself it was murder, *murder at her bidding*!

Now her soul was afire with the bitterness of repentance, with passionate self-accusation. Murder had been done through her. Murder!

The horror of it all had driven her well-nigh demented when she gazed from the distance while the two men disposed of Arden Laval's body under the snow. The dogs? They had been left where they fell. The living had been cut loose from their trappings to roam the forests at their will, while the dead had remained to satisfy the fierce hunger of the savage forest creatures. Even the sled had been destroyed, and its wood used to make fire that the living might endure on those pitiless northern heights. The memory of it all was days old now, but its horror showed no abatement. The agony was still with her. She felt that never again could she know peace.

So she had moved away out from camp, as she had done at every stopping they had made on the long journey from the highlands down to Sachigo. Somehow it seemed to her impossible to do otherwise. She felt she must hide herself from the sight of those others who were her captors, and who, in their hearts, she felt, must deeply abhor the presence of so vile a creature in their camp.

How long she had been standing there, while the men prepared the mid-day meal, she did not know. It was a matter of no sort of consequence to her anyway. Nothing really seemed of any consequence now. Her jaded mind was obsessed by a horror she could not shake off. There was nothing, nothing in the world to do but nurse the anguish driving her.

"You'll come right along and eat, Nancy?"

The girl almost jumped at the gentle tones of the man's voice, and glanced round at Bull Sternford in an agony of sudden terror.

"I—I—" she stammered. Then composure returned to her. "If you wish it," she said submissively. "But I don't need food."

Bull regarded the averted face for moments. Sympathy and love were in his clear gazing eyes. He understood something of the thing she was enduring, and the tone of his voice had been a real expression of his feelings. This girl, with the courage of twenty men, with her radiant beauty, and in her pitiful, heartbroken condition, was far more precious to him than any victory he had set himself to achieve. He knew that the world held nothing half so precious.

He came a step nearer.

"I wonder if you'll listen to me, Nancy," he said, with a hesitation and doubt utterly foreign, to him. "You know, for all that's happened, for all we're mixed up against each other in this war, I'm the same man you found me on the *Myra* and in Quebec. I—"

"Don't."

The girl flung out her hands in a piteous appeal. And Bull recognised the hysteria lying behind the movement.

"I know," she cried. "Oh, I know. But—don't you understand? You must know what I am. It's my doing that Laval has gone to his death. I'm responsible, just as surely as if I'd fired the gun that robbed him of his life. Oh, why, why didn't I refuse the work? Why did they send me? And those dogs. Those poor helpless dogs. They, too. I must have been mad—mad. How can you come near me? How can you stand there summoning me to eat food—with you? It's useless. It's—I who sent that man to his death—I who—"

"Why, I thought it was Gouter."

Bull's manner had suddenly changed. The danger signal in the girl's eyes had determined him. So he smiled, and there was laughter in his challenge.

"Say," he went on rapidly, "if you told that to Gouter he'd be crazy mad. He's the boss running shot on Labrador, and if you claimed responsibility for the killing of Laval you'd be dead up against it with him." He shook his head. "No, he's sort of grieved he didn't drop him plumb on the instant as it is. It won't do you talking that way with him around."

He watched for the effect of his words and realised a slight relaxing of the strained look in the hazel eyes. Forthwith he plunged into the thing he contemplated.

"I'm going to make a big talk with you before we eat," he said. "You see, I've wanted to right along, Nancy, but—Well, I want to tell you you're no more responsible for Laval's life, and the lives of those dogs, than I am. We're each playing our little parts in the things of life like the puppets we are. Our hands are clean enough, but it's not that way with the skunks that could send you, a girl, almost a child, to do the work, and live the life that boys like Gouter hardly know how to get through. That man, Peterman, is going to get it one day from me if I have luck. And I won't call it murder when I get my hands on his dirty alien throat. But never mind that. I want to ease that poor aching head of yours. I want to try and get you some peace of mind. That's why I tell you you've nothing to chide yourself for, nothing at all. It's true. You've played the game like the loyal adversary you are. And, for the moment, I'm top dog. You've handed me a bad nightmare by the wonderful courage and grit you've well-nigh shamed me, as a man, with. True, true you haven't a thing to blame yourself with. You've fought a mighty big fight I'd have been pleased to fight. It's just circumstances pitched you into the muss up, and let you see the thing your folks have brought about. It's that that's worrying. Think, Nancy, think hard. This is their fight. Not yours. The blood of Laval is on Elas Peterman's head. His, and those other creatures who are ready to commit any crime to steal our country from us. Oh, I'm not preaching just my side. It's true, true. We at Sachigo were content to compete openly, honestly. Peterman and those others saw disaster in our competition. And so they got ready to murder—if necessary. It's the soulless crime of a gang of unscrupulous foreigners, and those hounds of hell have left you to suffer for it just as sure as if they'd seared your poor gentle heart with a red hot iron. Say, Nancy," he went on, with persuasive earnestness, "put it all out of your mind. Forget it all. You're out of the fight now. And it just hurts me to see your eyes troubled, and that poor tender heart of yours all broken up. Won't you?"

The girl had turned away to the gaping valley again. But she answered him. And her tone was less dull, and it was without the dreadful passion of moments ago.

"I—I've tried to tell myself something of that," she said, with the pathetic helplessness of a child.

"Then try some more."

Bull had drawn nearer. He laid one hand gently on her shoulder. It moved down and took possession of the soft arm under her furs. Nancy shook her head. But there was no decision in the movement.

"Oh, I wish—" she began.

But she could get no further. Suddenly she buried her face in her hands, and broke into a passion of weeping.

Bull stood helplessly by. He gazed upon the shaking woman while great sobs racked her whole body. There was nothing he could do, nothing he dared do. He knew that. His impulse was to take her in his arms and protect her with his body against the things which gave her pain. But—somehow he felt that perhaps it was good for her to weep. Perhaps it would help her. So he waited.

Slowly the violence of the girl's grief subsided. And after a while she turned to him and gazed at him through her tears.

"I'm—I'm—"

But Bull shook his head.

"Come. Shall we go and eat?"

He still retained his hold upon her arm. And as he spoke he led her unresistingly away towards the camp.

CHAPTER XXI
THE MAN IN THE TWILIGHT

Bat Harker passed out of the house on the hillside. Muffled in heavy furs he stood for a moment filling up the storm doorway, gazing out over a desolate prospect, a scene of grave-like, significant stillness.

The mills he loved were completely idle. But that was not all. He knew them to be at the mercy of an army of men who had abandoned their work at the call of wanton political and commercial agitators. It was disaster, grievous disaster. And he told himself he was about to beat a retreat like some hard-pressed general, hastily retiring in face of the enemy from a position no longer tenable.

There was no yielding in the lumberman. But to a man of his forcefulness and headstrong courage the thought of retreat was maddening. He was yearning to fight in any and every way that offered. He knew that he was going to fight this thing out, that his present retreat was purely strategic. He knew that the whole campaign was only just beginning. But it galled his spirit that his first move must be a—retreat.

The late winter day was fiercely threatening, fit setting for the disaster that had befallen. The cold was bitterly intense, but no more bitter than the lumberman's present mood. There down below were the deserted quays with their mountains of baled wood-pulp buried deep under white drifts of snow. And the voiceless mills were similarly half buried. Look where he would the scene was dead and deserted. There was not one single stirring human figure to break up the desolation of it all.

It was a sad, white, desolate world, which for over fifteen years he had known only as a busy hive. Roadways should have been clear. Traffic should have been speeding, every service, even in the depth of winter, should have been in full running. The mills—those wonderful mills—should have been droning out their chorus of human achievement in a world set out for Nature's fiercest battle ground.

From the moment of that first encounter in the recreation hall Bat had known the strike to be inevitable. Bull's swift action at the outset had had its effect. For the moment it had checked the movement, and reduced it to a simmer. Heat and power had been restored, and work had been resumed, and outwardly there had been peace. But it was artificial, and the lumberman and the engineer had been aware that this was so.

Brief as was the respite it was valuable time to the men in control, and they used it to the uttermost. The leaders of the strike had been robbed of the advantage they had sought from a lightning strike. But they were by no means defeated. It was only that they had lost a move in the game they had prepared.

At the end of a week Bat awoke one morning to find the mills and all traffic at a standstill, and the workers skulking within the shelter of their own homes.

Then it was that the benefit of a week's respite was made plain. Every plan that had been prepared was forthwith put into operation. Power and heat were again cut off. The loyalists, which included a large number of the engineering staff, and the staff of the executive offices, were equipped with such weapons as would serve, and set guard over the food and liquor stores, and the essentials of the mills. And the power house was fortified for siege.

But the strikers gave no sign. There was no attempt at violence. There was no picketing, and no apparent attempt at coercion of the loyalists. It almost seemed as if the objects of the leaders had been achieved by the simple cessation of work.

This silent condition of the strike had gone on for days with exasperating effect upon the defenders. Bat endeavoured by every means in his power to bring the leaders of the movement into the open to discuss the situation. But every effort ended negatively. The men would not contemplate the conference table, and finally, in headlong mood, the lumberman had committed the grave mistake of provocation. He threatened to cut off food supplies if the leaders continued in their refusal to confer.

Two weeks elapsed before his threat reacted. Two weeks of continued silence and apparent inaction by the strike leaders. The men's first terror at the loss of heat and power seemed to have passed. As Bull had suggested they had resorted to the methods of the trail, and day and night mighty beacon fires burned along the fore-shores of the cove upon which their homes were built. The men and women came and went peaceably but silently between the food stores and their homes, purchasing such provisions as they needed. And the manner of it all, the cold silence, should have served a warning of the iron hand in exercise behind the strike.

The bombshell came at the end of the third week. It came in the form of a message crouched in the flamboyant phraseology beloved of the Communist fraternity. It was conveyed by a small youth some ten years of age, as though its authors were fearful lest a full grown bearer should be made to suffer for the temerity.

Bat had received it at the office, and his manner had been characteristic.

"Fer me, laddie?" he had said, as he took possession of the official-looking envelope. Then he gently patted the boy's shoulder. "All right, sonny," he added. "You get right back to your folks. Pore little bit."

With the boy's departure he had lost no time in reading the ultimatum the message contained.

> "A Soviet has been formed. The Workers will not submit to inteference with the food supplies of the people such as has been threatened by men who have no right over the life and death of their fellows. In view of this threat, the Soviet of the Workers has determined to possess itself of the mills and all properties pertaining thereto. The whole territories and properties hither controlled under a capitalist organisation will in future be administered by the Soviet or the Workers. You are required, therefore, to hand over forthwith all accountings, administration, and all funds, all legal documentary titles such as are held by you of freeholds and forestry rights relating to Sachigo. Furthermore, it is required of you to restore intact the machinery of the new power station, and to hand over the whole premises in full running order. One week's grace will be permitted for the execution of this order. Failing absolute compliance, the ruling Soviet of the Workers reserves to itself the right of adopting such measures to enforce the Will of the Workers as it may deem necessary.
>
> "On behalf of the Soviet of the Workers,
>
> "LEO MURKO,
>
> "Chief Commissionary."

At the finish of his reading Bat had looked up into the dark face of Pete Loale who was standing by.

"Leo Murko?" he said, in an ominously restrained tone. "Ther' ain't no guy o' that name on our pay-roll. Guess he'll be that feller Bull dropped out into the snow." Then with a sudden explosive force: "In God's name why in hell didn't he break that skunk's neck?"

The week's grace had expired. It had been a week of further hasty preparations. Every day had been used to the uttermost, and even far into the night the work had gone on. The office on the hill, as well as the executive offices down at the mill, had been cleared out. Documents, cash, books, safe. Everything of real importance had been removed to the citadel power house. The mining of the penstocks had been completed, and left ready to be blown sky high at a moment's notice. Whatever befell, the men who had given their lives to the building of the mills were determined that only a useless husk should fall into the hands of the strikers.

Now had come the Communists' final declaration of war. The message had been brought less than an hour ago by the same youth, who had again departed with Bat's smiling expression of pity. The letter was ominously brief.

> "The Order of the Soviet of the Workers will be enforced forthwith. No mercy will be shown in the event of resistance."

Bat's fury had blazed as he read the message. Again it was signed "Leo Murko." How he hated that name. He had been alone in the office when the letter came, and had seized the 'phone and called up the engineer at the power house, and read the message to him. Skert Lawton's reply was as instant as it was characteristic.

"That's all right," he said. "We're fixed for the scrap. Just come right over."

It was this last act that Bat contemplated now. And he hated it. He knew well enough he must go. There was no sane alternative. The power station was the prepared fortress. It had everything in it that must be guarded and fought for. But his fierce regret was none the less for the knowledge.

Then, too, his regret was for something else. It was at the absence of Bull Sternford. This was no expression of weakness. It was simply he desired the man's companionship. They had worked together. They had planned and built together. And, now, in the moment of battle, it seemed to him they should still be together.

But he knew that was impossible. When Bull's call to the forest had come in the night there had been no opportunity for explanation. He, Bat, had been engaged down at the mill, and the other had been rushed in his preparations. Bull had made his farewell to him in a great hurry. He had outlined briefly the thing happening in the forests. That had been all. That and a few words on the affairs of the mill.

How the news had reached Bull, and who the messenger, had never transpired between them. Perhaps Bull had forgotten to mention it. Perhaps, in the hurry of it all, Bat had forgotten to ask. Perhaps, even, the messenger himself had impressed secrecy for his visit, which had been timed for the dead of night. At any rate Bat knew none of these things, and was in no way concerned for them. All he was concerned for was the absence of the man who was something more to him than a mere partner.

Thinking of him now Bat remembered the other's final words, and the memory stirred him deeply.

"Remember, old friend," he had said, "young Ray Birchall will be over from England at the break of winter. On his report to his people depends the whole thing we've built up. We've got to have these mills running full when that boy gets around. There's not a darn thing else matters."

It was the final spur. The mills running full. Bat spat out his chew, and turned and locked the door behind him. Then he moved away hurriedly, gazing straight in front of him as though he dared not even think of the place he was leaving.

On the foreshore of the Cove, out towards the guarding headlands, half a hundred fires were burning. They were immense beacon fires of monstrous proportions. Belching columns of smoke clouded the whole region till the water-front looked to be in the grip of a forest fire.

Men, and women, and children were gathered about them. They were basking in a moderation of temperature such as their homes could no longer afford them. But it was a curious, silent gathering, indifferent to everything but the feeding of the fires on which they felt their very existence depended.

The forests which supplied the fuel came down to the edge of the now idle trolley track. Already acres and acres had been felled to feed the insatiable fires. The woodland decimated, and the devastation was going on in every direction.

About the houses there were others engaged in homely chores. There were men, and women, too, clad heavily in the thick sheepskin clothing which alone could defeat the fierce breath of winter. Here again was silence and gloom, and even the children refrained from their accustomed pastimes.

A tall, fur-clad figure was moving through the settlement. His feet were encased in moccasins, and thick felt leggings reached up just below his knees. For the rest his nether garments were loose fur trousers, and his body was covered by a tunic reaching just below his middle, with a capacious hood attached to it almost completely enveloping his head.

He moved slowly and without any seeming object. He passed along, and paused when he encountered either man, woman, or child. With the men he spoke longest. But the women claimed him, too. And generally he left behind him a change of expression for the better in those with whom he talked.

He paused beside a small party of elderly men. They were at work upon a prone tree trunk of vast girth. They were cutting and splitting it, fresh feed for the fires which must never be permitted to die down.

The men had ceased work on his approach. But they went on almost immediately, all except one. He was a grizzled veteran, a man just past middle life. His face was deeply lined, and a scrub of whisker protected it from the cold. He had been seated on the log, but he stood up as the tall man addressed him by name.

"You'll be there, Michael," he said, brushing the frost from his darkly whiskered face, and breaking the icicles hanging from his fur hood where it almost closed over his mouth.

The man's grey eyes were smiling as they looked into the wide black eyes so mildly encouraging.

"Sure, Father," came his prompt reply. "We got to be ther' anyway. That don't matter. But we're for your lead, an' we'll stand by it, sure. There's going to be no sort of damn fool mistake this time."

The tall man nodded.

"There must be no mistake this time," he said keenly. "Say, how many years is it since I sent you along here with a promise of good work and better wages, and a square deal?"

"Nigh five years, Father."

"And you got all—those things?"

"Sure. More."

Father Adam nodded.

"And those are the things a man's entitled to. Just those," he said. "If a man wants more it's up to him. He must earn it in competition with the rest of his fellows. If he can't earn it he must do without, or quit the honesty that entitles him to hold his head up in the world. There's no honesty in the things these men propose."

"That's so, Father."

There was decision in the man's agreement. But even as he spoke his gaze wandered in the direction of two small children, like bundles of fur, playing in the snow.

"Poor little kids," he said. "Say, it's hell for them with heat cut off."

Again the tall man nodded as he followed the other's gaze.

"That's so. But I don't blame the mill-bosses. This gang is trying to steal from the men who've always handed out a straight deal. Do you blame them for defending themselves?"

Michael shook his head.

"I don't see I can. After all—"

"No. Listen. You boys have it in your own hands. These crooks from the Skandinavia got a strangle holt on the youngsters of this outfit who've no kiddies like those. You older boys let 'em get it. You weren't awake. Now you find yourselves caught in the tide. We've got to make a break for it. There'll be heat in plenty when you break free. Seven o'clock. That's the time your masters ordered the meeting for. Seven o'clock. That's the time they intend to commit their great crime—with you helping them."

Father Adam smiled as he drove his satire home.

"Not on your life!" The man's grey eyes were fierce. "Give us the lead, Father," he cried. "We—we just got to have that. Ther' ain't a real lumberjack in these forests won't follow it. It'll be a scrap. A hell of a scrap. Oh, I know. Maybe some of us'll never see the light of another day. But sure it's got to be. We ought to've gone over from the start, and stood by our jobs. But I guess none of us with wives and kiddies had the guts. They threatened our women and children, an' we weakened. But it's different now, sure. We've learned our lesson. It's themselves they're out for, an' we'll be their dogs to be kicked and bullied as they see fit. We'll follow your lead, Father, an' it don't matter a cuss when the scrap comes."

Father Adam nodded. His dark eyes were alight with something more than the smile shining in them.

"Good," he said. "I shall be there."

He moved away and Michael rejoined his companions. They talked together for a moment or two while their eyes followed the receding figure.

They saw it stop and speak to one of their wives. She had a small child with her. They saw it bend down into a squatting attitude and draw the child towards it. Then they saw a lean hand draw out of its mit and proceed to touch a swelling on the little mite's neck. They understood. And when the figure finally passed on out of sight, they returned to their work, each man absorbed in his own thought, each man with a surge of deep feeling for that lonely figure. For they were all men who knew, and understood the man who lived in the twilight of the forests.

The recreation room was packed to suffocation, packed from end to end with a human freight. The benches were crowded, and the tables groaned under the weight of as many rough-clad creatures as could crowd themselves thereon. Every inch of floor space was occupied, and even the recesses in the log walls which contained the windows were utilised as sitting places for the audience which had gathered at the imperative order of the Soviet of the Workers.

Kerosene lamps had replaced the brilliant electric light to which the men were accustomed. A haze of tobacco smoke created a sort of fog throughout the length of the building, and contrived to soften the harsh lines of the sea of human faces turned towards the raised platform whereon sat the members of the ruling Soviet. The temperature of the room was cold for all the warming influence of the human gathering, and every man wore his fur-lined pea-jacket closely buttoned.

Once, in a light moment, Bull Sternford had declared that male human nature in the "bunch" was the ugliest thing in the world. Had he witnessed that sea of faces, so intently, so anxiously turned towards the leaders they had presumably elected, he must have been well satisfied with the truth of his conviction.

Such was the ascendancy and power the Bolshevist leaders had gained in the brief month since the first rumble of industrial war had been heard in Sachigo, that there were few who had failed to obey their summons. Not only was the hall crowded but a gathering of many hundreds waited outside. It was the hour of Fate for all. They understood that. It was the hour of that Fate which had been decreed by men, who, under the guise of democratic selection had usurped a power over the rest of the community such as no elected parliament of the world had ever been entrusted with.

It was doubtful if the majority fully realised the significance of what was being done. It is certain that a feeling of deep regret stirred voicelessly in many hearts. But every man there was a simple wage earner whose horizon was bounded by that which his wage opened up. For the rest he was left guessing, but more often fearing. So, with his muscles of iron, his human desires, and his reluctance to apply such untrained reasoning as he possessed, he was ripe subject for fluent, unscrupulous, political agitators, and ready to sweep along with any tide that set in.

The leaders on the platform understood this well enough. It was their business to understand it. The others, the leaders' immediate supporters, were men of fiery youth, or those whose work it was to wreck at all costs, and snatch to themselves, in addition to pay for their fell work, such loot as the wreckage afforded them.

The hum of talk snuffed right out as the leader rose to address the meeting. It was Leo Murko, the same man, a hard-faced, foreign-looking Hebrew whom a month before Bull's great arms flung through the broken window into the snowdrift beyond. His position now, however, was far different from that which it had been when his endeavours had been concentrated upon enrolling a Communist following. All that had been achieved or sufficiently so. Now he was the dictator whose orders could be backed by an irresistible force. His whole manner had changed. The velvet glove of persuasion had been discarded, and he hurled his commands with deep-throated authority, and the smile of encouragement and persuasion was completely abandoned.

His preliminary was brief. A phrase or two of flattery and acknowledgment to those on the platform supporting him dismissed that. Then he passed on to the objects in view. In five minutes he had dismissed also the ultimate destiny of the mills, and the manner in which the Workers were to benefit by its administration. Then he flung himself into a fiery denunciation of all capitalists, and particularly those who had dared to employ his audience on good wages for something like fifteen years. That completed he passed on to the plans for taking over the mills forthwith.

During the earlier part of his address the audience listened with grave attention. Here and there little outbursts of applause punctuated his sentences. But when he came to the task which had been set for that night a deathly silence prevailed everywhere. The intensity was added to rather than broken by the harsh clearing of throats that came from almost every part of the hall.

"The whole thing needs cleaning up before daylight," he hurled at them. "Our organisation is complete. Here," and he indicated the table nearby littered with papers and surrounded by four or five men who were members of the elected Soviet, "we have the lists of the names of every comrade, and the numbers of men to be used in every detail of the work before us. They have been carefully drawn up with a view to the task required to be put through. Some tasks will be simple. Some will be less so." A grim light that was almost a smile shone in his black eyes. "But we have carefully discriminated in our personnel. That is as it should be. There will be certain bloodshed. Knowing the temperament and preparations of your late masters this seems to be inevitable. But again we have provided. Our greatest and most important task is the possession of the power station, and for the capture of that we have machine guns which will quickly reduce the enemy to capitulation. The strength of the enemy we know to the last fraction—"

"Do you?"

The challenge came from the back of the hall. It came in a quiet, refined voice that swept through the hall with the cold cut of a knife. Someone had risen from a sitting position on a table. He stood up. It was the tall, dark figure of Father Adam clad in a garment which enveloped him from head to foot like the black cassock of a priest.

"Do you?" he cried again, as the startled leader stared stupidly at the interrupter.

Every eye turned to the back of the hall on the instant. The men on the platform looked up from their work to witness the daring of one who could interrupt the elected leader of the people. One man, slight, foreign-looking, who had been seated at the back of the platform stood up and leant against the wall.

"You know nothing of these people you are determined to destroy with machine guns," Father Adam went on. "You know nothing of the men with whom you are dealing, either the owners of the mill, or the men who have found an ample livelihood under their organisation. How can you know them? You are dastardly agents of an alien company, sent and paid to wreck a wholly Canadian enterprise. This is your first object. Your second is even more sinister, for you are the agents of that mad Leninism which has destroyed a whole race of workers in a vast country like Russia. You are a supreme pestilence seeking to destroy such human nature as will listen to your vile doctrines. It is I, I, Father Adam, tell you so. The men here to-night, whom you are inciting to theft and brutal murder, know me. They know me as their servant, as their loyal comrade and helper, ready to answer their call when trouble overtakes them, ready to yield them of my best service in the day of prosperity or the night of their woe. And as it is with them so it is with their women and their babes. That's the reason I am here to-night, the black night of their woe. And so I ask them to listen to me now as they have listened many times before in the woods and the mills, which is the world to which we all belong. If they do that, if only reason asserts itself, they'll here and now turn on you, and rend you, you and your wretched gang. They'll cast you out of their midst, and fling off a foreign yoke, as they would cast out any other unclean pestilence for the purification of their homes. They'll pack you out into the northern night where no foul germs can exist. Are they to become thieves at your bidding? Are they to become murderers because your foreign money has bought them machine guns? Would they go back to their women, and their innocent babes, wiping their blood-stained hands to ask them to rejoice in the brutal crime committed in the name of brotherhood and fellowship? No, sir. I know them. You don't—"

The Bolshevist flung out a denouncing hand and bellowed in his seething wrath:

"Traitor! He is of the Cap—"

But immediate uproar drowned his denunciation and a great voice shouted in the din.

"Let him speak."

A dozen other voices strove to make themselves heard, and a wild pandemonium was rising when clear and sharp Father Adam's voice rang out again above it.

"I tell you they'll have no more of you," he cried as the leader dropped back to his seat, and the dark man at the back of the platform further bestirred himself. "Order them now to man your machine guns and murder the men in the power house! Give your orders here and now! Read out your list of names and see—"

A shot rang out. The flame of a gun leapt somewhere at the back of the platform, to be followed by complete, utter silence.

Then came a sound. It was a hardly-suppressed moan. Father Adam reeled slowly. He half turned about. Then he crumpled and dropped to his knees and fell forward into hands outstretched to catch him.

Paralysis seemed to grip that dense-packed human throng. But it was only for a second. Then the avalanche leapt for the abyss.

"Father! Father Adam!"

The cry went up seemingly from a thousand throats. And with a roar the crowd surged forward. It hurled itself at the platform.

Bull stared up at the house. He moved away and glanced over the windows. Then his eyes turned to the valley below, and his gaze settled itself on the great fires burning on the northern foreshore of the Cove.

For some moments he stood contemplating the thing he beheld. Then, at last, he turned back to the locked door of his office. Without a word he raised one foot, and, with all his force, crashed its sole against the lock.

The lock gave and the door fell back into the pitch darkness beyond. He passed within. After a while a light appeared in the office window. It passed. Then it reappeared in each window of the building in succession. Presently it remained stationary and fresh lights appeared in several of the windows. Minutes later he reappeared in the doorway.

He stepped out into the snow and came over to the waiting dog train.

"It's a cold sort of welcome," he said quietly. "But—will you please come right in, and I'll see how I can fix you up for comfort. I guess things have happened since I've been away. They've turned off heat. However—"

Nancy McDonald rose from her place in the sled. She flung back the wealth of furs under which she had been well-nigh buried and stepped out. She made no reply, but stood waiting while Bull gave orders to his driver.

"Get those dogs fixed, Gouter," he said. "Then come right along back here. You'll need to gather fuel and set those stoves going."

A great fire was roaring in the wood stove in the office. Nancy and Bull were standing before it seeking to drive out the cold which seemed to have eaten into their bones. Bull had drawn up his own rocker-chair for the girl but she had not availed herself of it.

"You are not going to keep me here, prisoner in—your house?"

The girl spoke in a low, hushed tone. In the indifferent lamp-light she looked ghastly pale and utterly weary-eyed. She had removed her furs, revealing herself clad in the heavy clothing which alone could have served on her desperate journey through the camps. It robbed her figure of much of its usual grace.

"I'm afraid I am." Bull smiled gently, for all the decision of his words. "You see, Nancy, we're still at war. Still fighting the battle that others have forced on us."

Nancy inclined her head.

"I'd forgotten," she said almost humbly. "But you have no women folk around you," she went on urgently a moment later. "Does war mean that—that I must submit even—to that?"

It was the woman in her that had taken alarm. Her hands were pressed together as she held them over the stove. The man understood. She moved away to the window, over which the curtains had not been drawn, and Bull watched her.

"Every respect will be paid you," he said. "You've nothing to fear. When Gouter returns he'll get food, and we'll make the best preparations we can. I've to consider others with more at stake than even I."

"Look!"

The girl had turned. Her eyes were wide with terror. She was pointing at the window, and Bull hurried to her side.

A great fire was raging on the north shore of the Cove. It was the recreation room, that room which Bat had so bitterly come to hate. It was ablaze from end to end, and lit up its neighbourhood so that the scene was of daylight clearness. A horde of human figures were gathered about it, in a struggling, seething mass, and the man realised that a battle was raging, a human battle, whilst the demon of fire was left to work its will.

He stood there, held speechless by the thing he beheld.

"What is it? What does it mean?"

Panic drove the questions to the girl's lips. And she turned in an agony of appeal to the man beside her.

"It means the work of the Skandinavia has been well and truly done."

CHAPTER XXII
DAWN

The hush of dawn was unbroken. The shadows of night receded slowly, reluctantly renouncing their long reign in favour of the brief winter daylight. The shores of the Cove lay hidden under a haze of fog.

There were no sounds of life. The world was desperately still. No cry of wild fowl rose to greet the day. There was not even the doleful cry of belated wolf, or the snapping bark of foraging coyote to indicate those conditions of life which never change in the northern wilderness. It was as if the world of snow and ice were waking to a day of complete mourning, a day of bitter reckoning for the tumult of furious human passions, which, under the cloak of night, had been loosed to work the evil of men's will.

With the first gleam of the rising sun a breeze leapt out of the east. It came with an edge like the keenest knife, and ripped the fog to ribbons. It churned and tangled it. Then it flung it clear of its path, leaving bare the scene of wreckage which the rage of battle had produced.

It was a scene for pity and regret. Gone was the building which had been set up for the workers' recreation. Only a smoking ruin remained in its place. A dozen other buildings in the neighbourhood bore the scars of fire, which they would doubtless carry for all time of their service. The mill, however, was safe. The work of more than fifteen years remaining intact. But it had been so near, so very near to complete destruction.

With the passing of the fog further disaster was revealed. It was the wreck of human life which the night had produced. Daylight had made it possible to deal with the injured and those beyond all human aid. And the work was going forward in the almost voiceless fashion which the presence of death ever imposes on the living.

Viewed even from a distance there could be no mistaking the meaning, the hideous significance of it all. And Nancy, gazing from a window in the house on the hill, shrank in terror before that which she believed to be the result of the cruel work to which she had lent herself.

It had been a dreary, heartbreaking night of sleepless watching and poignant feeling. Nancy was alone in her prison, a beautiful apartment, the best in the house. Bull Sternford had conducted her thither personally, and, in doing so, had told her the thing he was doing, and of his real desire to save her unnecessary distress.

"You see," he had explained, with a gentleness which Nancy felt she had no right to expect, "there's just about the best of everything right here. It's as it was left by the feller who designed and decorated it for the woman he loved better than anything in life. No one's ever used it since. I'd be glad for you to have it. We've only a Chink servant to wait around on us, and a rough choreman, and I guess they don't know a thing about fixing things for a woman. But they've kept it clean and wholesome, and that's all I can say. Can you make out in it to-night?"

He smiled. Then his steady eyes had turned away to the window where the light of the raging fire could be seen. And after a moment he went on.

"You're a prisoner. I can't help that. That's got to be. But no lock or bolt will be set to keep you here. You're free to come and go as you choose. You can make the doors of the room fast against intrusion, if you feel that way. But there'll be none. To-night you'll just be dead alone in the place. You see, I've got to get out and pull my weight down there."

So he had left her. He had left her to a punishment more desperate than anything he could have designed. Her windows looked out over the mill. And a subtle force attracted her thereto, and held her sleepless and despairing the whole night long. She had been forced to sit there watching the tragedy being enacted. A tragedy with which she knew she was connected, and for which, in her exaggerated self-condemnation, she believed herself responsible.

The agony of that prolonged vigil would never be forgotten. Fascinated, dreading, every act of it seared the girl's soul as with a red hot brand. It was the Skandinavia's work. The agents of the Skandinavia. And she knew that she, perhaps, was their principal agent. The rattle of machine guns. The human slaughter. She had witnessed the terror of it all in the fierce light of the conflagration which looked to be devouring the whole world of the mills. She could never forget it. She could never forgive herself her share in the ghastly plans for that hideous destruction. But more than all she knew she could never forgive, or again associate herself with those who had designed the inhuman work of it all and plunged her into the maelstrom of its execution.

Now, in the daylight, she was still at the window. There was no relief. On the contrary. With the smoke cleared from the smouldering ruins she saw the full extent of the wreckage. It was sprawling everywhere, human and material. An army of men, it seemed, was searching the battlefield. It was searching and collecting amongst the ruins. And she watched the bearing away on improvised stretchers, of still, helpless, human burdens which none could mistake. She could bear no more of it. She shut out the sight and fled from the window, covering her eyes with her hands.

But she was recalled almost instantly. The sound of men's rough voices startled her. Whence came the sound she could not judge. But it seemed to her it was from somewhere outside. So she stealthily peered out. It was a small group of fur-clad figures. They were approaching the house over the snowy trail that came up from the mill.

New terror leapt. They were supporting a prone, human body! They were bringing it up to the house! Who—who could they be bringing up to that house, which was the home and the office of the master of the mill? In that supreme moment all that which had gone before was completely forgotten. She stood clutching at the window casing, in a desperate effort to steady herself.

She knew. Oh, yes, it could be no other. It must be Bull Sternford they were bringing up. Bull Sternford—the man who—The agents of the Skandinavia had done him to death! The agents of the Skandinavia!

Bat Harker was standing at the window of the office on the hill. His hard, grey eyes were searching the distance below, and his square jaws were busy on their usual occupation. Bull was sitting in a rocker-chair. He was leaning forward, gazing down at the thickly carpeted floor, and his hands were clasped between his outspread knees. Both men were dishevelled. Their clothing was stained, and their hands and faces were begrimed as a result of the fierce work of the night.

Bat suddenly turned from his silent scrutiny.

"He'll pull around? You think so?" he demanded.

There was an appeal in his harsh voice such as Bull had never heard in it before, and he looked up with a start.

"That's how Jason reckoned," he said.

"Oh, to hell with Jason!" Bat's retort was fiercely uncompromising. "Who's Jason anyway? A medical student who hadn't the guts for his job. Leastways he got on the crook. It's the thing you reckon I want to know."

"I reckon he'll pull around," Bull returned quietly. Then he stirred wearily. "But you're hard on young Jason, Bat. He's bright enough. I like the way he handles his job. And anyway he's the only feller around this layout with any knowledge of a sick man. He's qualified you know. He wasn't just a student. He practised before he went down and out and took to the forests. We've got to rely on him till we get a man up from Montreal, which won't be for weeks. He'll be through along from fixing him in a while. Then we can hear the thing he's got to say. Maybe we'll be able to judge better then."

"I wired Montreal," Bat said sharply.

"Good."

The lumberman turned again to his window, and Bull continued to regard the carpet which had no interest for him. Both were weary, utterly weary in body as well as mind.

It was full, broad daylight now, with the low, northern sun gleaming athwart the scene which these men had so recently left. They were conscious of the victory gained. They rejoiced in the complete defeat of an enemy who had come so near to defeating all their plans. But the cost appalled them They had both faced the play of machine guns. They had seen their men fall to the scythe-like mowing of a cruel weapon of which its victims had no understanding. Then, when the machine guns had been silenced, they had witnessed the rage with which these hard-living jacks had meted out their ideas of just punishment upon the murderers of their comrades.

The wanton inhumanity of the whole thing had sickened them both Both knew and were indifferent to the roughness of the fierce northland But the ordeal through which they had passed was something far beyond the darkest vision of conflict they had ever contemplated.

Neither had been present to witness the shooting of Father Adam. Bu both had been there within minutes of the beginning of the battle which i had started. From the power house Bat had discovered the thing happening just as Bull had seen from the window of his office the leaping flames which had threatened the mill. It had been largely due to their timely leadership that ultimate victory had been snatched. But the work of it had been terrible.

Now they had returned to their quarters, their night's work completed. Down below comrade was attending to comrade in such fashion as lay to hand, and those beyond earthly aid were being disposed to their last rest. Thus these men had been left free to succour the wounded creature whose timely lead had made possible the defeat that had been inflicted.

Bat had but one concern just now. Father Adam. The man whose secret he held. The man who counted for everything in his rugged life. He raised his blood-shot eyes to his companion's face.

"If—Father Adam—passes, I'm done with Sachigo, Bull," he declared almost desperately. "It 'ud break me to death. You can't know the thing that feller means to me. You know him for the sort of missioner all these folks guess he is. That's how he'd have you know him. And it goes with me all the time. But I know him just as he is."

Bull nodded. He made no reply. He knew the lumberman was well-nigh beside himself, and he gazed back into the hot eyes and wondered.

But Bat had nothing more to say. He even felt he had said more than he had any right to say. So he turned again to the window.

A few moments later the door communicating with the house was unceremoniously thrust open. The two men looked round. It was a youngish man dressed in the overalls of an engineer who hurried in. He was alert and full of business; a condition which he seemed to appreciate.

"It's all right, boss," he cried cheerfully, addressing himself to Bat. "Guess the good Father'll get away with it. He's out of his dope an' smiling plenty. I jerked that darn plug that holed him right out, an' it's a soft-nosed swine. I left it back there for you to see. The feller who dropped him deserves rat poison. I hope to God they got him. Anyway I got the wound cleaned up and fixed things. Now we just got to keep it clean and open, and watch his temperature. Then we don't need to worry a thing. I'll do that. But someone'll have to sit around and nurse him. I'll have to get along down. There's nigh a hundred needin' me. Gee I An' after all these years, too. It makes me wonder."

There was a smile of keen appreciation in the eyes that looked into those of the lumberman. And the look deepened when Bat thrust out a large and dirty hand at him.

"Thanks, boy," he said, in obvious relief. "I'm goin' to nurse that pore feller. Maybe I ain't much in that line. But I'll promise he don't lack a thing I can hand him. Here, shake. You'll be along to fix him again?"

"Right on time," was the quick rejoinder.

Jason had readily enough gripped the outstretched hand. Then he hurried away. And neither of the men begrudged him the obvious vanity which his momentary importance had inflamed.

With the man's going Bull passed a hand back over his ample hair.

"God!" he exclaimed wearily. "It's been a tough night."

"Tough?"

Bat's response spoke a whole world of feeling. He moved from his window and flung himself into a chair.

"He saved us," he went on. "Father Adam. He saved the whole of our darn outfit. How he did it I don't just know. Maybe I'll never know. He don't talk a lot. I gathered something of it from the boys. But there wasn't time for talk." He shook his grizzled head. "You see, I didn't even know he was around. And you never told me it was him brought you word from the camps. He must have been at work around from the start. He must have got hold of a bunch of the boys he knew. And when he got 'em right, why—Say, I'd have given a thousand dollars to have heard him fire his dope at that lousy gang. It must have been pretty. But they got him. And I guess that was the craziest thing they did. The fool man who could shoot up Father Adam in face of the forest-boys could only be fit for the bughouse."

He sighed. It was not for the man's madness in shooting, but for the hurt inflicted. Then a grim, vengeful smile lit his eyes.

"Why, I guess there ain't a single agent of the Skandinavia down there left with a puff of wind in his rotten carcase. The boys were plumb crazed for their blood an' got right up to their necks in it. I'm glad. I'm—"

"Oh, forget it, man." Bull spoke sharply. "There's things we can take a joy in remembering. But this isn't one of 'em. No. The thing for us now is work. Plenty of work. The mill needs to be in full work inside a week. We haven't an hour to lose, with young Birchall coming along over. Skert's promised us power in twenty-four hours. He's at it right now. The camps on the river'll be working full, and making up lost time. The rest's up to us right here. But—but," he added, passing a hand nervously across his forehead, "I've got to get sleep or I'll go stark crazy."

Bat eyed the younger man seriously. It was the first time he had realised his condition. His sympathy found the rough expression of a nod.

"You had a hell of a time up there," he said.

Bull laughed. There was no mirth in his laugh.

"It was tough all right. I wonder if you'd guess how tough." He shook his head. "No. You wouldn't. You reckon Father Adam's a pretty good man, but I tell you right here you don't know how good, or the thing he did for us single-handed. I know—now. He set me wise to it all, and didn't leave me a thing to do but make the trail he'd set for me. It was an easy play dealing with the fool forest-jacks who'd swallowed the Skandinavia's dope. Yes. That was easy," he added thoughtfully. "But that was just the start of the game. Father Adam had located the trail of the outfit the Skandinavia had sent and it was my job to come right up with 'em and silence 'em."

He broke off and sat staring straight in front of him. His fine eyes were half smiling for all the weariness he complained of. He yawned.

"Well, I hit that trail," he went on presently. "I hit it, and hung to it like a she-wolf out for offal. I just never quit. It was that way I forgot sleep. It wasn't till between No. 10 and 11 Camps we got sight. We were out in the open, up on the high land. We'd a run of fifty mile ahead of the dogs. When we got sight that boy Gouter was after 'em like a red-hot devil. Drive? Gee, how he drove!"

Again came the man's mirthless laugh.

"There's things in life seem mighty queer at times. It was that way then. There was a man I wanted to kill once bad. Guess I've never quit wanting to kill him, though I'm glad Father Adam saved me from doing it. He was Laval—Arden Laval, one of the Skandinavia's camp-bosses. Well, I saw him killed on that trip, and I helped bury him in the snow. Gouter drew on him on the dead run at fifty yards. He dropped him cold, and wrecked the outfit the feller was driving. There were two in the bunch that the Skandinavia sent there to raise trouble for us. Laval and another. Laval's dead, and the other we brought right along as prisoner. That other's here in this—"

A light knock interrupted the story. Bull turned with a start. Then he sprang to his feet, every sign of weariness gone. He stood for a moment as though in doubt. And the lumberman, watching him, remarked the complete transformation that had taken place. He was smiling. His straining eyes had softened to a tenderness the onlooker failed to understand.

He moved swiftly across the room and flung open the door.

"Will you come right in?"

The lumberman heard the invitation. The tone was deep with a gentleness he had never before discovered in it. And in his wonder he craned to see who it was who had inspired it.

Bull moved aside.

It was then that Bat started up from his chair, and a sharp ejaculation broke from him. Nancy McDonald was standing framed in the doorway.

CHAPTER XXIII
NANCY

Bat was hurrying down the woodland trail. For once in his hard life he knew the meaning of rank cowardice. The sight of Nancy McDonald had completely robbed him of the last vestige of courage. The atmosphere of the office, that room so crowded with absorbing memories for him, had suddenly seemed to threaten suffocation. He felt he must get out. He must seek the cold, crisp air of the world he knew and understood. So he had fled.

Now he was alone with a riot of thought that was almost chaotic. There was only one thing that stood out clearly, definitely, in his mind. It was the Nemesis of the thing that had happened. It was Nemesis with a vengeance.

His busy jaws worked furiously under his emotion. He spat, and spat again, into the soft white snow. Once he stopped abruptly and gazed back over the circuitous trail. It was as though he must look again upon the thing that had so deeply stirred him, as though he must look upon it to reassure himself that he was not dreaming. That the thing had driven him headlong was real, and not some troublesome hallucination.

Nancy McDonald! The beautiful stepdaughter of Leslie Standing, with her red hair and pretty eyes, was the agent of the Skandinavia, paid to wreck the great work he and Leslie had set up. She was paid to achieve the destruction at—any cost.

It was amazing. It was overwhelming. It was even—terrible.

He pursued his way with hurried steps. And as he went his mind leapt back to the time when he had made his great appeal for the poor, deserted child shut up in the coldly correct halls of Marypoint College. What an irony it all seemed now. Then he remembered her first coming to Sachigo, and the mystery of the letter from Father Adam heralding her arrival. He had understood the moment Nancy had announced her name to him on the quay. He had understood the thought, the hope which had inspired the letter.

In his rugged heart he had welcomed the letter which Father Adam had written. He had welcomed the girl's first coming to the place he felt should be her inheritance. He had seen in those things the promise of the belated justice for which years ago he had appealed. Father Adam had asked Bull to receive her well. Why? There was only one answer to that in the lumberman's mind. Father Adam had seen her. He understood her beauty, and had fallen for it. What more reasonable then that Bull should do the same.

But that was all past and done with now. All the things he had dreamed of, and so ardently desired, had been lost through a mischievous Fate. The neglected stepdaughter of Leslie Standing was body and soul part of their enemy's armament of offence. It was all too crazy. It was all too devilish for calm contemplation.

The sight of the girl's pathetic eyes, so weary, so troubled, had been sufficient. Bat could not have remained in that room another minute. No. Down at the mill were the things he understood. They were the things he was bred to, and could deal with. These others were something that left him hopeless and helpless. So he went, determined to lay the ghost of the thing behind him in the tremendous effort the necessities of the mill demanded he should put forth.

Bull's emotions were deeply stirred. He gazed into the tired eyes of the girl, so beautiful for all their complete dejection. He marked the cold pallor of her cheeks, and realised the dishevelled condition of her glorious masses of hair. An intense pity left him gravely troubled.

As Nancy stood gazing up at the man, complete hopelessness oppressed her. She remembered well enough the declaration of war between them. She remembered, too, that it had meant nothing personal when it was made. At the time she had had no inkling of the terrible thing it could mean, or how nearly it could bring them into real, personal conflict.

She had been wholly unprepared for the demand that had been thrust upon her by the man, Peterman. It had frightened her at first. She had shrunk from it. Then, finally, she had accepted it as her duty, under pressure. Peterman had made it appear so trifling. A journey, a trying journey, perhaps, but one to be made with all the comfort he could provide. And then to preach to those ignorant forest-men the disaster towards which their employers were heading. As Peterman had put it, it had almost seemed a legitimate thing to do. Convinced as she had been of the disaster about to fall on Sachigo, it had seemed as if she were even doing them a service.

Had she been able to search Peterman's mind she would never have taken part in the dastardly thing he had planned. Had she been able to read him she would have quickly discovered the real motive he had in sending her. She would have discovered the furious jealousy and wounded vanity which meant her to be a prime instrument in the wrecking of Bull Sternford and his mills. She would have realised the devilish ingenuity with which he intended to wreck her friendship with another man so that he might the more truly claim her for himself. But she had no suspicion, and had blindly yielded herself to the duty she believed to be hers.

After Bat's hurried departure Bull cast about in his mind for the thing to say to her. And somehow, without realising it, the right words sprang to his lips.

"We won!" he said. And the smile accompanying his words was one of gentle raillery, and suggested nothing of the real tragedy of the thing that had happened.

The girl's eyes widened. She strove to understand the dreadful lightness with which Bull spoke. Victory? Defeat? At that moment they were the two things furthest from her mind.

Bull drew forward a chair, and gently insisted. And Nancy, accepting it, realised in a dull sort of way that it was the chair she had occupied at the time of her first visit, which now seemed so far, far back in her memory. Bull sat again in his rocker. He leant forward.

"Sure," he went on, "we've won out. Your Skandinavia's beaten. Beaten a mile. We've won, too, at less cost than I hoped. Does it grieve you?"

There was no softness or yielding in his tone. It was as he intended; the tone of a man who cares only that victory has been won. Nancy shook her head.

"I'm—I'm glad," she said desperately.

"Glad?" Bull was startled.

The girl made a little involuntary movement. She averted her gaze to the window through which the wintry sunlight was pouring.

"Oh, don't you understand? Can't you? Is the victory so much to you that you have no thought, no feeling, for the suffering it has brought? Are you so hard set on your purpose of achievement that nothing else matters? Oh, it's all dreadful. I used to feel that way. I counted no cost. Achievement? It was everything to me. And now, now that I know the thing it means I feel I—I want to die."

Bull took a strong hold upon himself.

"I know," he said slowly. "You see, Nancy, you're just a woman. You're just as tender and gentle—and—womanly, as God made you to be. He gave you a beautiful woman's heart, and a courage that was quite wonderful till it came into conflict with your heart. You had no right to be flung into this thing. And only a man of Peterman's lack of scruple could have done such a thing. Well, I'm not going to preach a long sermon, but I want to tell you some of the things I've got in my mind before I get the sleep I need. God knows that none of this thing you're blaming yourself for lies at your door. It would all have happened without you. Peterman designed it, and put it through for all he was worth. Now I want to say I'm glad—glad of it all. I've no pity for the Bolshevic dregs of Europe he employed. They were out for loot, they were out to grab the things and the power that other folks set up. Any old death that hit them they amply deserved. As for our folk who've gone under—well, we mustn't think too deeply that way. We all took our chances, and some had to go. I was ready to go. So was Bat. So were we all. We wanted victory, and we wanted it for those who survived. We honour our dead, but our lives must not be clouded by their going. It's war—human war. And just as long as the world lasts that war will always be. Good and bad men will die, and good and bad women will suffer at the sight. But for God's sake have done with the notion that you—you have anything to take to yourself, except that you've fought a good fight, and—lost. It sounds like the devil talking, doesn't it? Maybe you'll think me a monster of heartlessness. I'm not."

"Oh, I wish I could feel all that," Nancy exclaimed with an impulse which a few moments before must have been impossible.

"You can." Bull nodded. "You will."

"You think so?" Nancy sighed. "I wish I could." Suddenly she spread out her hands in a little pathetic gesture. "Oh, it all seems wrong. Everything. What am I to do? What can I do? I—I can't even think. Whichever way I look it all seems so black and hopeless. You think I can—will?"

Bull's sympathy would no longer be denied. He rose from his chair and moved to the window. His face was hidden from the troubled eyes that watched him. But his voice came back infinite in its gentleness.

"You want to do something," he said. "You want to give expression to the woman in you. And when that has happened it'll make you feel—better. I know."

He nodded. Suddenly he turned back to her, and stood smiling down into her anxious eyes.

"Tell me," he went on, "what is it you want to do? You're no prisoner now. The war's finished. You're just as free as air to come and go as you please. You can return to Quebec the moment you desire, and the *Myra* comes along up. And everything I can possibly arrange shall be done for your happiness and comfort. When would you like to go?"

The girl shook her head.

"I wasn't thinking of that."

"I knew that," Bull smiled.

"Father Adam. He's in the house there sick and wounded," Nancy hurried on. "I know him. I—may I nurse him back to health and strength. May I try that way to teach myself I'm not the thing I think and feel. Oh, let me be of use. Let me help to undo the thing I've done so much to bring about."

The girl's hands were thrust out, and her eyes were shining. Never in his life had Bull experienced such an appeal. Never in his life had he been so near to reckless disregard for all restraint. He came nearer to her.

"Surely you may do that," he said. "And I just want to thank you from the bottom of my unfeeling heart for the thought that prompts you. We haven't a soul here to do it right—to do it as you can. And Father Adam is a mighty precious life to us all—in Sachigo."

CHAPTER XXIV
THE COMING OF SPRING

It had been a hard day. Bull Sternford had spent it dealing with complicated financial schedules, an amazing, turbulent sea of figures, until his powers and patience had temporarily exhausted themselves.

In a final fit of irritation he had flung his work aside, and risen from his desk. The insufferable heat of the room, and the reek of his own pipe disgusted him. So he had moved over to the window where the cold air of early spring drifted in through the open ventilating slot in the storm sash.

His gaze was on the Cove below, where the snow-laden ice was discoloured by the moist slush of thaw, and the open waters, far down towards the distant headlands, had so deeply encroached upon the claims of winter.

A great, premature thaw had set in. It was the real spring thaw a month or more early. Skert Lawton, who controlled the water power of the mill, had warned him of its coming. Bat too had spoken out of his years of experience of the moods of Labrador's seasons. But somehow the sight of it all gave him none of the joy with which it had inspired the others.

The evil night of threatened disaster had become only a memory. Nearly six weeks had passed since Nancy McDonald had craved the privilege of caring for the man who had so nearly given his life in the saving of the mill and all the great purpose it represented. Now he was mercifully returned to health and strength under the devoted care that had been bestowed upon him. The mill was again in full work. And the human army it employed had returned to their peace-time labours in the full determination to undo the grievous hurt which the mischief of the Skandinavia's agents and their own folly had inflicted. In the relief of reaction, they, no less than their employers, had redoubled their efforts.

All outward sign of the trouble through which the mill had passed had long since been cleared away under the driving power of the forceful Bat Harker. The scars of fire remained here and there. But they were no more than a reminder for those who were ready to forget the folly they had once committed.

Everything was moving on now as Bull and his comrades would have had it. Only that morning word had come through that Ray Birchall was on his way from London for the purpose of his report, and expected to reach Sachigo in three weeks' time. Could anything, then, be better than this early thaw? It was a veritable act of Providence that the London man's inspection of the mills, and all the property involved would take place under the most active conditions.

It should have been a time of rejoicing and mental ease. It should have been a time of stirring hope. A moment for complaisant contemplation of a great purpose achieved. But the man at the window regarded the thing he looked upon without any display of pleasurable feeling. The sight of it literally seemed to deepen the unease which looked out of his eyes.

In the midst of Bull's pre-occupation the door from the outer office was thrust open, and Bat Harker's harsh voice jarred the silence of the room.

"Gettin' a peek at things," he cried, stumping heavily across the thick carpet. "Well, it looks good to me, too. Say, if this lasts just one week we'll be as clear of snow as hell's sidewalks." Then he flung open his rough pea-jacket and pushed his cap back from his lined forehead. "Gee, it's hot!"

The lumberman was standing at Bull's side, and his deep-set eyes were following the other's gaze with twinkling satisfaction. Bull nodded and moved away.

"Yep," he ejaculated. "It should be good for us."

He passed over to the radiators and shut them off. Then he went over to the wood-stove and closed down the dampers. Then, with a curious absent-mindedness, he stood up and held out his hands to the warmth radiating from the stove.

Bat was watching him interestedly. And at sight of his final attitude he broke into one of his infrequent chuckles and flung himself into a chair.

"Say, what in—? Feeling cold?" he demanded.

Bull's hands were promptly withdrawn, and, in spite of his mood, a half smile at his own expense lit his troubled eyes.

"That's all right," he said. "It's on me, sure. I guess my head must be full of those figures still."

He returned to the window and stood with his back to his companion. Bat watched him for some moments.

Bull had changed considerably in the last few weeks. The lumberman had been swift to observe it. Somehow the old enthusiasm had faded out.

The keen fighting nature he had become accustomed to, with its tendency to swift, almost reckless action, had become less marked. The man was altogether less buoyant.

At first it had seemed to Bat's searching mind as if the effects of that desperate trip through the forests, and the subsequent battle down at the mill, had left its mark upon him, had somehow wrought one of those curious, weakening changes in the spirit of the man which seemed so unaccountable. Later, however, he dismissed the idea for a shrewder and better understanding.

He helped himself to a chew of tobacco and kicked a cuspidore within his reach.

"The fire-bugs are out," he said. "The last of 'em. I jest got word through. It's the seventh. An' it's the tally."

It was a sharp, matter-of-fact statement. He was telling of a human killing, and there was no softening.

Bull nodded. He glanced over his shoulder.

"You mean—?"

"They shot five of 'em to death. The last two they hanged." A grim set of the jaws, as Bat made the announcement, was his only expression of feeling.

"Makes you wonder," he went on, after a pause. "Makes you think of the days when locomotives didn't run. Makes you think of the days when life was just a pretty mean gamble with most of the odds dead against you. It don't sound like these Sunday School days when the world sits around, framed in a fancy-coloured halo, that couldn't stand for any wash-tub, talkin' brotherhood an' human sympathy. It's tough when you think of the bunch that sent those boys to fire our limits. They knew the full crime of it, and knew the thing it would mean if we got hands on 'em. Well, there it is. We got 'em. An' now ther' ain't a mother's son of 'em left alive to tell the yarn of it all. It's been just cold, bloody murder. An' the murder ain't on us. No, I guess the darn savage eatin' hashed missioner ain't as bad a proposition as the civilised guys who paid the price to get those toughs killed up in our forests. I can't feel no sort of regret. It won't hand me a half-hour nightmare. But it makes me wonder. It surely does."

He spat accurately into the cuspidore.

"Does the report hand you anything else?" Bull asked, without turning. The other noticed the complete lack of real interest. He shrugged.

"The camps are all in full cut. They're not a cord behind."

Bat looked for a word, the lighting of an eye. There was none. And he stirred in his chair, and exasperation drove him.

"Don't it make you feel good?" he demanded sharply. "It's the last guess answered, unless there's a guess when that boy, Birchall, comes along. Anyway, you don't figger ther's much guess to that, with the mill runnin' full, an' every boom crashed full of logs. No. Here, Bull!" he cried, with sudden vehemence. "Turn around, man. Turn right around an' get a grip on it all. The game's won to the last detail. Can't you feel good? Can't you feel like a feller gettin' out into the light after years of the darkest hell? Don't it make you want to holler? Ain't there a thing I can say to boost you? The boys down at the mill are hoggin' work. The groundwood's on the quays like mountains. The mills are roaring like blast furnaces. Can you beat it? Spring. The flies an' skitters, an' shipping. Why, in a week I guess Father Adam'll be hittin the trail for the forests, an'—"

"Nancy McDonald will be sailing for Quebec."

Bat was no longer gazing on the other's broad back and the mane of hair which did its best to conceal his massive neck. Bull had turned. His strong face was flushed. His fine eyes were hot. There could be no mistaking the passionate emotion which the other had stirred.

The two men gazed into each other's eyes. Then with a curiously expressive gesture of his great hands Bull turned to the chair standing near, and flung himself into it.

The lumberman's eyes twinkled. He had done the thing he desired. "An' you don't want her to?" he said deliberately.

Just for a moment it looked as though a headlong outburst was about to reply to him. Then, quite suddenly, the hot light in Bull's eyes died out and he smiled. He shook his head.

"No," he said in simple denial. "If she goes it means the end of Sachigo for me."

"You reckon you'll quit?"

In a moment the lumberman remembered a scene which had been enacted years ago on the high ground on the north shore of the Cove. He would never forget it. It had been the final decision of another to quit Sachigo. And the reason had been not dissimilar.

There was no reply. Bull sat staring blankly in front of him. His eyes were on the wintry sky which was still broad with the light of day beyond the window.

Presently his gaze lost its abstraction and came again to the strong, lined face of the older man.

"Yes, Bat," he said calmly, almost coldly, "I'd have to quit. I just couldn't stand for it. Nancy's got right into my life. She's the only thing I can see—now."

"Fer all she's a kind of prisoner right here, caught red-hand doin' the damnedest she knows to break us in favour of the outfit that pays her?"

Bat smiled as he flung his challenge. But his tone, his words, were no indication of his mood, or of the rapid thought passing behind his shrewd eyes. A great sense of pleasure was asurge within him. He wanted to tell of it. He wanted to reach out and grip the other's hand, and tell him all that his words meant to him. But he refrained. Another man's secret was involved, and that was sufficient. His lips were sealed.

Bull stirred restlessly.

"Oh, psha!" he cried at last, with a force that displayed the tremendous feeling he could no longer deny. "I know what you think, Bat. I'm crazy. Well, maybe I am. Most men get crazy one time in their lives when a woman gets around. It's no use. I just can't help it. I know all you're thinking. Nancy McDonald belongs to our enemies. As you say she's done her damnedest to break us. Maybe you reckon I ought to feel for her like the devil does about holy water. Well, I don't. I'm plumb crazy for her, and when spring clears up the waters of the Cove, and the *Myra* comes alongside, she's going right aboard, and will pass out of Labrador and out of my life. I'm never going to get another sight of her. I'm never going to get another sound of her dandy voice, or a sight of her pretty eyes, and—Hell! What's the use. Oh, I know it all. You've no need to tell me. We've made good. We've fought and won out. My contract's complete, and everything's looking just as good for us as it knows how—now. This mill. It's ours. Yours, and mine, and that other's, who I don't know about. All I've to do is to sit around with the plums lying in my lap. Well, I don't want those plums without Nancy. That's all. I don't want a thing—without Nancy. All the dollars in America can burn in hell for all I care, and as for groundwood pulp it's a damp mess of fool stuff that don't signify to me if it finds its way to the bottom of the North Atlantic. An added month of open season? What does it mean to me? Work. Only work, and flies, and skitters. An added month of 'em. Father Adam's a whole man again now, thanks to that dandy child. He'll pull right out to the forests again, and—she'll pull out too. I—"

"That's all right," Bat broke in drily. "I get all that. But why not marry the gal? Marry her an' quit all this darn argument. I guess this mill's goin' to hand you all you need to keep a wife on. That seems to me the natural answer to the stuff that's worryin' you."

His eyes twinkled as he regarded the other's troubled face.

"Is it?"

Bull was on his feet. Hot, desperate irritation lay behind the retort which Bat's gentle sarcasm had drawn forth. His eyes were alight, and he passed an unsteady hand across his forehead in a superlatively impatient gesture.

"Marry her?" he exploded. "Say, are you every sort of darn fool on God's earth, man? How can I hope to marry her? What sort of use can a girl like that have for the man who's beat her right out of everything she ever hoped to achieve? I've had to treat her like any old criminal, and hold her prisoner. I've brought her right down here leaving her in a man's household without another woman in sight. Say, these cursed mills have made it so I've had to commit every sort of rotten act a man can commit against a high-spirited girl. And you ask me why I don't marry her? You've been too long in the forests, Bat. Guess you've lost your perspective. Nancy McDonald's no sort of chattel to be dealt with any way we fancy. Get sense, man, an' talk it."

Bat's regard was unwavering before the other's angry eyes.

"Sense is a hell of a good thing to have an' talk," he said quietly. "I most generally notice the feller yearnin' for someone else to get it an' talk that way, mostly has least use for the thing he's preachin'. Maybe Nancy feels the way you reckon. But that don't seem to me to worry a deal. Still, maybe things have changed around since the days when I hadn't sense to keep out of gunshot of a pair of dandy eyes. And anyway I don't seem to remember the boys bein' worried with the sort of argument you're handing out. If my memory's as good as I reckon, the boys most gener'ly married the gal first, an' got busy wonderin' about things after. All of which seems like so much hoss sense, seem' the natur' of things is that most gals needs their minds made up for 'em. You see, Bull, I kind o' fancy womenfolk ain't just ord'nary. They got a bug that makes 'em think queer wher' men are concerned. Now Nancy's all sorts of a gal, an' that bein' so I don't reckon she sees the hell-fire crimes you've committed against her just the way you see 'em. I allow they're pretty darn tough. Shootin' up her outfit an' dumpin' her into a snowdrift up on Labrador's mighty hard sort of courtin'. Grabbin' her up an' settin' her hospital nurse to her enemies, in a house full of a bunch of tough men don't seem the surest way to make her smile on the feller that did it. Then most generally beatin' the game she set out to play looks like makin' fer trouble plenty. It sure seems that way. But you never can tell with a woman, Bull. You just can't."

Bat shook his grizzled head in solemn denial, but his eyes were laughing. Bull smothered his resentment. He, too, shook his head, and somehow caught the infection of the other's smile.

"But she's ambitious," he said. "And she isn't the sort of girl to take that easily. No."

Bat nodded and rose from his chair. Something of his purpose had been achieved and he was satisfied. He felt he had said all that was needed for the moment. So he prepared to take his departure.

"Maybe that's so, boy," he agreed readily. "But ambition's a thing that changes with most every wind. That don't worry me a thing. Say, you've sort of opened out about this thing to me, an' I ain't sure why. But I kind of feel good about it. You're younger than me by years I don't fancy reckonin'. I feel like I was an elder brother, an' I'm glad. Well, that bein' so, I'd like to say right here ther's just one ambition in a woman's life that counts. And she mostly gits it when she hits up against the feller that's got the guts to make her think his way. When that happens I guess you can roll up every other old schedule, an' pass it into the beater to make new paper. It's the only use for it. See? But I 'low I don't know women like I do groundwood, which was the stuff that fetched me here right now. You see, I was feelin' good about things, an' I fancied handin' you the news of them 'fire-bugs' myself. Guess it hasn't handed you any sort of delirium so far, Bull, but it will later. I allow ther' ain't room for two fevers at the same time in a man's body. When you've set Nancy McDonald figgerin' your way, your temperature's liable to go up on the other. So long, boy."

CHAPTER XXV
NANCY'S DECISION

With the lengthening days the world of Labrador was already donning its brief, annual smile. But the passing of winter was no easy thing. There had been rain and "freeze-up," and rain again. And the whole countryside was a dripping, melting sea of wintry slush. The sun was rising higher in the steely heavens with each passing day, but winter was still reluctant. It passed on to its dissolution only under irresistible pressure.

Nancy, no less than Father Adam and those others, to whom the early thaw meant so much, watched the passing of winter with the closest interest. But her interest owed its origin to a far different inspiration. She knew it meant that her time at Sachigo was nearing its end, and the future with all its barrenness was staring at her.

She moved restlessly about the large kitchen while the Chinaman, Won-Li, was preparing toast over the cook stove. She stood awhile at the window and watched the winging of a seemingly endless flight of early geese passing up from the South. Then she turned away and glanced about the scrupulously clean and neat apartment. It was so very different from the place she had first discovered weeks ago.

After awhile she took up her position against the kitchen table, and stood there with her gaze upon the bent figure of the cook in its long, blue blouse. But she was scarcely interested in the man's labours. She was not even waiting for him to complete them. She was just thinking, filled with apprehension and without confidence. Her mind was made up to a definite purpose whose seeming immensity left her staggered.

Nancy was no longer the distraught creature who had witnessed the terrible night of fire and battle down at the mill. Many weeks had passed since then. Weeks full of mental, bodily, and spiritual effort. From the first dark moments when she had begged the privilege of nursing the wounded missionary, broken in spirit, a beautiful creature well-nigh demented with the horror of the thing she believed herself to be, the woman soul of her had found a measure of peace.

It had been slow in coming. There had been moments when she had nearly broken under the burden of conscience. There had been moments when the weight of unutterable depression, and the sense of guilt, had come near to robbing her of her last shred of mental balance. But the woman's mission of nursing had saved her in the end. That, and the physical effort to which she had applied herself.

It was all so single-minded and simple. It was all so beautifully pathetic. Nancy had found a careless household rapidly decaying through mannish indifference to comfort. She understood. These men were completely absorbed in the service of the great mills, and nothing else mattered to them. Oh, yes, that was understandable. She knew the feeling. She knew how it robbed its victim of every other consideration in life. So she had flung herself into the task of re-ordering the household of which she had been forced to become a part, that she might yield them comfort in their labours and help herself in her own effort to obtain peace of mind.

She had transformed an untidy, uncared-for bachelor habitation into a wholesome, clean establishment of well-ordered life. She had lifted a lazy Chinaman into a reasonable specimen of comparative energy, and saw to it that meals were well and carefully served, and partaken of at regular hours by men who quickly discovered the futility of protest.

But her work by no means ended there. From one end to the other the house was swept and garnished, and the neglect of years disposed of. Bedrooms were transformed from mere sleeping places to luxury. Linen was duly laundered, and clothing was brushed, and folded, and mended in a fashion such as its owners had never thought possible. She was utterly untiring in her labours, and in the process of them she steadily moved on towards the thing she craved for herself.

The men realised the tremendous effort of it all. And Bull Sternford, for all his absorption in his work, had watched with troubled feelings. His love for Nancy had perhaps robbed him of that vision which should have told him of the necessity, in her own interests, for that which the girl was doing. So there were times when he had protested, times when he felt that simple humanity demanded that she should not be permitted to submit herself to so rough a slavery. But Nancy had countered every protest with an irresistible appeal.

"Please, please don't stop me," she had cried, almost tearfully. "It's just all I can do. It's my only hope. Always, till now, I've lived for myself and ambitions. You know where they have led me—Ah, no. Let me go on in my own way. Let me nurse him back to health. Let me do these things. However little I'm able to do there's some measure of peace in the doing of it."

So the days and weeks had dragged on, and now the time of Nancy's imprisonment was drawing to its inevitable close. With Spring, and the coming of the *Myra*, she would have to accept her freedom and all it meant. She would be expected to return to her home in Quebec, and to those who had employed her and sent her on her godless mission. She understood that. But she had no intention of returning to Quebec. She had no intention of returning to the Skandinavia.

During the long hours of her labours she had searched deeply for the thing the future must hold for her. It was the old process over again. That great searching she had once done at Marypoint. But now it was all different. There had been no sense of guilt then, and the only man who had been concerned in her life had been that unknown stepfather, whom, in her child's heart, she had learned to hate. It had been simple enough then. Now—now—

But she had faced the task with all the splendid, impetuous courage that was hers. There was no shrinking. Her mind was swiftly and irrevocably made up. She would abandon the Skandinavia for ever. She would abandon everything and follow those dictates which had prompted her so often in the past. Father Adam's self-sacrificing example was always before her. The forests. Those submerged legions which peopled them. Was there not some means by which she could join in the work of rescue? She would talk to Father Adam. She felt he would help her. She wanted nothing for herself. If only the rest of her life could be translated into some small imitation of the life of that good man, then, indeed, she felt her atonement might be counted as something commensurate.

It was not until her decision had been taken that she permitted herself to seek beyond it. But once it was taken the crushing sense of added desolation well-nigh paralysed her. Somehow, never before had she understood. But now—now the sacrifice of it all swept upon her with an overwhelming rush. Bull Sternford. Bull Sternford, the man whom with all her power she had striven to defeat, the man whose strength and force of character had so appealed to her, the man who must hate her as any clean-minded man must hate a loathsome reptile, she would never see him again.

Oh, she knew now. She made no attempt at denial. It would have been quite useless. She loved him. From the moment she had looked into his honest eyes, and realised his kindly purpose on her behalf at their first meeting, she had loved him. She must cut him out of her life. It was the penalty she must pay for her crimes.

And now the moment had arrived when she must put her plans into operation. Time was pressing. The season was advancing. So she had chosen the hour at which she served tea to Father Adam as the best in which to seek his advice and support.

The light tap on Father Adam's door was answered instantly. Nancy passed into the room with trepidation in her heart, but the hand bearing the tea tray was without a tremor.

The man whose life belonged to the twilight of the northern forests was seated in a deep rocker-chair under the window through which the setting sun was pouring its pleasant spring light. He had been reading. But his book was laid aside instantly, and he stood up and smiled the thanks which his words hastily poured forth.

"You know, Nancy, you're completely spoiling me," he said. "I'm going to hate my forest coffee out of a rusty pannikin. I don't know how I'm going on when I pull my freight out of here."

The girl's responsive smile faded abruptly as she set the tray on the table beside the chair.

"When are you going to—pull your freight?" she asked, with a curious, nervous abruptness.

For a moment the man's eyes were averted. Then he straightened up his tall, somewhat stooping figure. He flung his lean shoulders back, and opened his arms wide. And as he did so he laughed in the pleasant fashion which Nancy had grown accustomed to.

He was the picture of complete health. His dark face was pale. His black hair and sparse beard were untouched by any sign of the passage of years. There was not an ounce of superfluous flesh under the curiously clerical garments he lived in.

"Why, right away, child," he said, with simple confidence. "I'll just need to wait for a brief 'freeze-up' to get through the mud around Sachigo. Once on the highlands inside there'll be snow and ice for six weeks or more. I told Sternford this morning I was ready to pull out. You see, thanks to you I've cheated the folk who reckoned to silence me. I'm well, and strong, and the boys of the forest are—needing me. Every day I remain now I'll be getting soft under the unfailing kindness of my nurse."

Nancy poured out the tea. There were two cups on the tray and the man was swift to notice it. She smiled up at him.

"Won't you sit down?" she urged. "You see, I've brought a cup for myself. I—I want to have a long talk with you. I, too, have got to 'pull my freight.'"

Father Adam obeyed. His dark eyes were deeply observant as he surveyed the pretty face with its red glory of hair. That which was passing in his mind found no betrayal. But his thought had suddenly leapt, and he waited.

Nancy passed him his cup and set the toast within his reach. Then she pulled up a chair for herself and sat down before the tea tray.

"Yes," she went on, "that's why I brought my cup. I must get away." She smiled a little wistfully. "My imprisonment is over. Mr. Sternford set me free long ago, but—well, anyway I'm going now, and that's why I wanted to talk to you."

She seemed to find the whole thing an effort. But as the man's dark eyes remained regarding her, and no word of his came to help her, she was forced to go on.

"You know my story," she said. "You've heard it all from Mr. Sternford. I know that. You told me so, didn't you?"

The man inclined his dark head.

"Yes," he said. "I know your story—all of it."

"Yes." The girl's tea remained untouched. Suddenly she raised one delicate hand and passed her finger tips across her forehead. It was a gesture of uncertainty. Then, quite suddenly, it fell back into her lap, and, in a moment, her hands were tightly clasped. "Oh, I best tell you at once. Never, never, never as long as I live can I go back to the Skandinavia. All the years I've been with them I've just been lost in a sort of dream world of ambition. I haven't seen a thing outside it. I've just been a blind, selfish woman who believed in everybody, and most of all in herself and her selfish aims. Can you understand? Will you? Oh, now I know all it meant. Now I know the crime of it. And the horror of the thing I've done, and been, has well-nigh broken my heart. Oh, I'm not really bad, indeed I'm not. I didn't know. I didn't understand. I can never forgive myself. Never, never! And when I think of the blood that has been shed as the result of my work—"

"No." The man's voice broke in sharply. "Put that right out of your mind, child. None of the blood shed is your doing. None of it lies at your door. It lies at the door of others. It lies at the door of two men only. The man who first set up this great mill at Sachigo, and the man whose hate of him desired its destruction. The rest, you, those others, Bull Sternford and Harker, here, are simply the pawns in the battle which owes its inception to those things that happened years ago. I tell you solemnly, child, no living soul but those two, and chiefly the first of the two, are to blame for the things that have happened to-day. Set your mind easy. No one blames you.

No one ever will blame you. Not even the great God to whom we all have to answer. I know the whole story of it. It is my life to know the story of these forests. Set your mind at rest."

"Oh, I wish I could think so. I wish I could believe. I feel, I feel you are telling me this to comfort me. But you wouldn't just do that?"

The man shook his head.

"It's the simple truth," he said. Then he reached for his tea and drank it quickly. "But tell me. You will never go back to the Skandinavia? I—am glad. What will you do?"

"That's why I've come to you now."

The tension had eased. Nancy's distress gave way before the man's strong words of comfort. She, too, drank her tea. Then she went on.

"You know, Father—"

The man stirred in his chair. It was a movement of sudden restlessness as if that appellation on her lips disturbed him.

"—I want to—I want to—Oh, how can I tell you? You are doing the thing I want to help in. All my life I felt the time would come when I must devote myself to the service and welfare of others. I think it's bred in me. My father, my real father, he, too, gave up his life to those who could not help themselves. Well, I want to do the same in however humble fashion. These men, these wonderful men of the forests whom you spend your life in succouring. Can I not serve them, too? Is there no place for me under your leadership? Can I not go out into the forests? I am strong. I am strong to face anything, any hardship. I have no fear. The call of these forests has got right into my blood. Don't deny me," she appealed. "Don't tell me I'm just a woman with no strength to withstand the rigours of the winter. I couldn't stand that. I have the strength, and I have the will. Can you? Will you help me?"

The girl's appeal was spoken with all the ardour of youthful passion. There was no sham in it. No hysterical impulse. It was irresistibly real.

The man's eyes were deeply regarding her. But he was thinking far less of her words than of the girl herself. Her amazing beauty, the passionate youth and strength. The perfection of her splendid womanhood. These things held him, and his mind travelled swiftly back over years to other scenes and other emotions.

When at last he spoke his words came slowly and were carefully considered.

"I think, perhaps, I can help you," he said. "You are determined? You want to help those who need help? The men of the forests?" He shook his head. "I don't see why you shouldn't help the men of these forests who—need your help."

Nancy drew a deep breath. A wonderful smile sprang into her pretty eyes. It was a glad smile of thanks such as no words of hers could have expressed.

"Oh, thank you, Father—thank you."

Again came the man's restless movement at the word "Father." He abruptly leant forward and held his cup out for replenishment.

"May I?" he asked. Then his smile broke out again. "But tell me," he went on. "What have you done about the Skandinavia?"

"Nothing."

Nancy returned him his cup with an unsteady hand.

"Nothing? But you must communicate with them. You should write and tell them of your decision. You should tell them you don't intend to return to them."

Father Adam sipped his tea. He was watching intently but unobtrusively the transparent display of emotions which his words had conjured.

"I hadn't thought about it," Nancy said at last, not without some disappointment. "Do you really think I should write? But it will take so long to reach them. I can't wait for that. It—"

"Wire."

"Yes. I suppose I could—wire."

"Sternford will have it sent for you."

In a moment the light of hope died out of the girl's eyes. The excited flush on her cheeks paled. And the man saw, and read the sign he beheld.

He waited. But Nancy remained silent, crushed under the feeling of utter desolation to which the mention of Bull Sternford's name had reduced her.

Father Adam set his cup down.

"Don't let the sending of that message worry, child," he said quickly. "These people deserve no better treatment after the thing they've done to you. All you need say is, 'You will accept my resignation forthwith.'" Write that out on a piece of paper, and sign it. Then take it along to Mr. Sternford.

Tell him of your decision, and ask him to have it sent by the wireless. He'll do it, my dear. And after that—why, after that, if you still feel the same about things, and want to turn missionary in the lumber camps, come right back to me here, and I'll do for you as you ask. It's a great thought, Nancy, and I honour you for it. It's a hard, desperate sort of life, without comfort or earthly reward. Once the twilight of the forest claims you, and its people know you, there's nothing to do but to go on and on to the end. Will you go—and send just that message?"

Nancy inclined her head.

"Yes. I'll go right away, just as soon as I've taken this tray back."

She rose abruptly. She gathered the remains of the meal on to the tray and picked it up. And the manner of her movements betrayed her. She stood for a moment, and the man saw the struggle for composure that was going on behind her pretty eyes.

"Father," she said at last, and the man abruptly rose from his chair and moved away, "I just can't thank you—for this. It's given me fresh hope. A hope I never thought would be mine. Some day—"

Her voice broke and the man turned at once. He was smiling again.

"Don't say a word, my dear. Not a word. Go and write that message, and take it to Sternford. And then—why—"

He moved over to the door and held it open for her. As she passed out he nodded kindly, and looked after her till she vanished into the kitchen at the end of the passage.

Father Adam was alone again in the room that had been his for so many weeks. The door was closed and he stood at the window gazing out at the dreary world beyond. But he saw nothing of it. He was thinking with the speed of a mind chafing at delay. He was wondering and hoping, and—fearing.

CHAPTER XXVI
THE MESSAGE

It was a woman of desperately fortified resolve who turned the handle of the office door in response to Bull Sternford's peremptory summons. The thought of the coming interview terrified Nancy, and her terror had nothing whatever to do with the sending of her message.

Bull failed to look up from the mass of papers that littered his desk. His sharp "Well," as Nancy approached him, was utterly impatient at the interruption. And its effect was crushing upon the girl in her present dispirited mood. She felt like headlong flight. She stood her ground, however, and the sound of her little nervous clearing of the throat came to the man at the table.

Bull looked up. In an instant his whole attitude underwent a complete change. His eyes lit, and he sprang from his seat behind the desk. He came towards the shrinking girl, eager and smiling with the welcome his love inspired.

"Why, say, Nancy," he cried. "I just hadn't a notion it was you. I was up to my neck in all this stuff," he said, indicating the litter on his desk, "and I hadn't a thought but it was the darn Chink come to worry with food." He laughed. "You certainly have handed me some scare since you got a grip on our crazy household. I've got a nightmare all the time I've got to eat. And the trouble is I'd hate to miss any of it. Will you come right over to the window and sit? There's daylight enough still. We don't need to use Skert's electric juice till we have to. I'm real glad you came along."

The man's delight was transparent. Nancy remained unresponsive, however. She was blind to everything but the thing she had come to do, and the hopelessness that weighed so heavily upon her.

"I'm sorry," she said simply, accepting the chair he set for her. "I didn't think you'd—you see, I waited till I guessed you'd be through. But I won't keep you. It's just a small favour, that's all."

Bull observed her closely. She was so amazingly and completely charming. She was no longer clad in the rough, warm garments of the trail. Even the cotton overall she used in the work of the house had been removed. Now a dainty frock, that had no relation to the rigours of Labrador, displayed the delicate beauty of her figure, and perfectly harmonised with the colouring of her wonderful hair. Somehow it seemed to the man her beauty had intensified in its appeal since the day of her supreme confidence in the cause for which she had so devotedly fought.

"A favour?" he laughed. "Why, I'm just glad."

Even while he spoke Bull remembered his talk with Bat Harker when he had listened to a wealth of pitying comment upon the feelings and opinions he had then laid bare. The girl's unsmiling eyes troubled him.

"What's the favour?" he asked simply, as Nancy remained silent.

The girl started. She had turned to the evening light pouring in through the window. Her thought had wandered to that grim, dark future when the twilit forests would close about her, and the strong tones of this man's voice would never again be able to reach her.

She drew a folded paper from the bosom of her frock.

"Would you let them send it for me—wireless?" she asked timidly. "It's—it's to Mr. Peterman."

All Bull's desire to smile had passed. He nodded.

"Yes," he said. "If you wish it. It shall be sent right off."

His tone had suddenly lost its warmth. It seemed as if the mention of Peterman's name had destroyed his goodwill.

Nancy searched his face anxiously. The man's brows had depressed and his strong jaws had become set. She knew that expression. Usually it was the prelude to uncompromising action.

She drew a deep breath.

"Oh, I know," she cried. "I know the thing you're thinking. You're reminding yourself of all I've done, and of the injury I've striven to inflict on you. You're wondering at my temerity in asking you to help me communicate with your enemies. But please, please don't think worse of me than you can help. I'm not just trying to use you. It's not that. Will you read the message? Maybe it'll tell you better than any words of mine."

The paper was held out to him in an unsteady hand. Bull ignored it. He shook his head.

"No," he said.

Nancy sprang to her feet.

"But you must read it," she cried. "If you don't I—oh, I won't send it. I couldn't. Don't make me sorry I asked this favour. It is so little to you, and—and it means so much to me."

She stood waiting, but Bull showed no sign of yielding. He was thinking of the man, Peterman. He remembered his good-looking Teutonic face, and the favour with which Nancy had seemed to regard him. A smouldering jealousy had suddenly blazed up within him.

Nancy turned away in desperation. She moved to depart.

"I'm sorry," she said. And even in her trouble there was a coldness in her tone no less than his.

Bull choked down his feelings.

"Please don't go," he cried, urgently. "It would please me very much to have that message sent. Say, I wasn't thinking the way you reckoned. I wasn't thinking of the message at all."

"Then you will read it?" The girl came back readily.

"Why should I?" Bull asked smilingly. "Say, a friend asking me to send a message for him, a message no concern of mine, what would you think, what would he feel, if I demanded to read its contents?"

He ran the fingers of one hand through his mane of hair and stood smiling down into the girl's pretty eyes.

"You know this thing makes me want to talk. I've just got to talk. The position's sort of impossible as it stands. Maybe you don't guess the thing I'm feeling, and maybe I don't just know how it is with you. We've got to talk right out and show down our hands. If we don't—"

He turned away and glanced out of window. Then his eyes came back claimed by the magnetism which the girl exercised.

"You know, Nancy, our war is over. The war between you and me. We declared war, didn't we? We declared it in Quebec, and we both promised to do our best, or—worst. It was a sort of compact. We made it meaning it, and understanding the meaning of it. If you got the drop on me you were to use it. The same with me. It was one of those friendly things, between friends, which might easily mean life or death. We knew that, and were ready to stand just for whatever came along. Well, we fought our battle. It's over. It's done. Now for God's sake let's forget it. It's easy for me. You see, I'm a rough, hard sort of product of these forests that doesn't worry with scruples and things. I'm not a woman who's full of the notions belonging to her sex. I can wipe the whole thing out of my mind. I can feel glad for the scrap you put up. I can think one hell of a great piece of you for it. Maybe it's different with you, being a woman. I guess it's not going to be easy forgiving the way I had to handle you back out there on the trail. Or the way you were forced to live our camp life on the way down here. Or how I've had to hold you prisoner in a rough household of rougher men. I get all that. I know the thing it is to a woman. All it means. Still, it must have been plain to you the chances of that sort of thing before you started in. That is if I was worth my salt as a fighter. Well, can you kind of forgive it? Can't you try to forget? Can't you figger the whole darn thing's past and done with, and we're back at where we were in those days in Quebec, when you didn't hate me to death, and felt good taking dinner in my company? Say, do you remember the old *Myra* you'll soon be boarding again? You remember our talk on the deck, when the howling gale hit us? We were talking of the sense of things in Nature, and how she mussed them up. And how we'd have done a heap better if the job had been ours. Well?" His smile deepened. "Here we are standing in the sort of fool position of—what'll I call it? Antagonism? Anyway we agreed to fight, and stand for all it means to us, and we're both feeling all broken up at the way we had to act to hurt each other most." He shook his head. "Where's our boasted sense of things? We ought to be sitting right here talking it over, and laughing to beat the band, that I had to treat you like a dangerous bunch of goods li'ble to get me by the throat, and choke the life out of me, while you were chasing every old notion folks could stuff into your dandy head to set me broke and busted so I wouldn't know where to collect a square feed once a week. That's what we ought to be doing, if we had the sense we guess. Instead of that you're feeling badly at me for the things I had to do to you. And I'm worried to death I'll never get a laugh from you for the fool talk I don't know better than to make. You need me to send that message to Peterman. Why, sure I'll send it, even if it's to tell him how mighty glad you are to be quitting the prison I'd condemned you to, and the joy it's going to hand you to see his darnation Teuton face again. Sure I'll send it. It's the least I can do to make up to you for those things I've done to you. But—but for God's sake don't ask me to read it."

The man concluded with a gesture that betrayed his real feelings. He was in desperate earnest for all his attempt at lightness. His words came swiftly, in that headlong fashion so characteristic of his most earnest mood. And Nancy listening to him, caught something of that which lay behind them. The faintest shadow of a smile struggled into her eyes. She shook her head.

"I haven't a thought in my head about you—that way," she said. "It's not been that way with me. No." She averted her gaze from the eager eyes before her. "It's the thing I've done and been. It's the thing you, and every other honest creature, must feel about me. Oh, don't you see? The killing, the bloodshed and suffering—But I can't talk about it even now. It's all too dreadful still. I'm quitting when Father Adam goes, and—and—But believe me no judgment you can pass on me can begin to express the thing I feel about myself. Please don't think I bear one single hard thought against you."

The man laughed outright. The buoyancy of that moment was supreme. Bat Harker was again in his mind. Bat, with all his quaint, crude philosophy.

"Say, that beats everything," Bull cried. "My judgment of you. And all this time I've been guessing—Oh, hell! Say, do you know, it gets me bad when I think of you going back to Peterman and his crew? It sets me well-nigh crazy. Oh, I know. I've no right. None at all. But it don't make me feel any better. Here, I'll tell you about it. I'm not going to take to myself virtues I don't possess, and have no right to anyway. I wanted to win out in the fight against the Skandinavia because I'm a bit of a fighting machine. I wanted to win out for the dollars I'm going to help myself to. But I also wanted to win out because of the great big purpose that lies behind these mills of Sachigo. I want you to get right inside my mind on that thing so you'll know one of the reasons why I hate that you're sending word to Peterman. You'll maybe understand then the thing that made me fight you, a woman, as well as the others, and treat you in a fashion that's made me hate myself ever since. I'm going to say it as bluntly as I know how. It'll be like beating you, a helpless victim, right over the head with a club. I've acted the brute right along to you, an' I s'pose I best finish up that way. You were doing your best to sell your birthright, my birthright, to the foreigner. You were helping the alien, Peterman, and his gang, to snatch the wealth of our forests. Why? You didn't think. You didn't know. There was no one to tell you. You simply didn't know the thing you were doing.

"This man Peterman was good to you. He held out prospects that glittered. It was good enough. And all the time he was looking to steal your birthright. The birthright of every Canadian. That makes you feel bad. Sure it does. I can see it. But I got to tell it that way, because—Here, I'm on the other side. It was chance, not virtue set me there. But once there the notion got me good. Sachigo was built to defend the great Canadian forests against the foreigner. That slogan got a grip on me. Yes, it got me good. I could scrap with every breath in my body for that. Well, now we've got the Skandinavia beat, and in a year or so they'll be on the scrap heap, ready to sell at scrap price. That's so. I know. Sachigo will be the biggest thing of its kind in the world next year, and there won't be any room for the Skandinavia. That's a reason I hate for you to go back to Peterman—one reason."

"But I'm not going back," Nancy cried vehemently.

Bull stared wide-eyed.

"You're not going back?" he echoed stupidly. Then of a sudden he held out his hand. "Say, pass that message right over. Why in—Guess I'm crazy to read it—now."

Nancy held the paper out to him. There was something so amazingly headlong in his manner. All the girl's apprehensions, all her depression, were swept away, and a rising excitement replaced them. A surge of thankfulness rose up in her. At least he would learn that she had no intention of further treachery to the land of her birth.

"Accept my resignation forthwith."

Bull read the brief message aloud. It was addressed to Peterman, and it was signed "Nancy McDonald." The force, the coldness of the words were implacable. He revelled in the phrasing. He revelled in the thing they conveyed. He looked up. The girl was smiling. She had forgotten everything but the approval she saw shining in his eyes.

Suddenly he reached out and his great hands came gently down upon her softly rounded shoulders. It was a wonderful caress. They held her firmly while he gazed into her eyes.

"Say, Nancy," he cried, in a voice that was deep with emotion. "You mean that? Those words? You've quit the Skandinavia? What—what are you going to do?"

"I—I'm going to the forests with Father Adam. I'm going to help the boys we've so often talked about. I'm—"

"Not on your life!"

The man's denial rang out with all the force of his virile nature.

"Say, listen right here. You've quit them. You've quit Peterman. And you reckon from one fool play you're going right over to another. No, sir, not on your life. It's my chance now, and by God I don't pass it. I'm kind of a rough citizen and don't know the way a feller should say this sort of stuff. But I'm crazy to marry you and have been that way ever since you came along, and sat right in this office, and invited me to take tea in the parlour of that darnation bug, Peterman. Do you know all that means, Nancy? It means I'm just daft with love for you, and have been ever since I set eyes on you, for all I had to treat you worse than a 'hold-up.' Say, my dear, will you give me the chance to show you? Can you forget it all? Can you? I'll raise every sort of hell to fix you good and happy. And you and me, together, we'll just send this great Sachigo of ours booming sky high, and in a year I promise to hand you the wreckage that was once the Skandinavia. Marry me, dear, and I'll show you the thing a man can be and do. And I'll make you forget the ruffian I've had to act towards you. Will you let me help you to forget? Will you—?"

Nancy's eyes were frankly raised to the passionate gaze which revealed the depths of the man's great heart.

"I have," she said in a low voice. "I've forgotten everything but—but—you."

She moved as she spoke. There was no hesitation. All her soul was shining in her eyes, and she yielded to the impulse she was powerless to deny. She came to him, releasing herself from the great hands that held her shoulders. She reached up and placed her soft arms about the neck that rose trunk-like above his shoulders. In a moment she was caught and crushed in his arms.

"Why—that's just fine!"

The exclamation broke from the man out of sheer delight and happiness. And the while he bent down and kissed the smiling upturned face, and permitted one hand to wander caressingly over the girl's wealth of beautiful hair.

CHAPTER XXVII
LOST IN THE TWILIGHT

A fierce wind swept down off the hills. So it had blown all night and all the day before. The sky was overcast, and the thermometer had dropped below zero. It was one of those brief "freeze-ups" such as Father Adam had awaited, and it might last two or three days. Then would come prompt reaction, and the rapidity of the thaw would be an hundred-fold increased.

The sun was hidden, and the sky looked to be heavily burdened with snow. The earth was frozen solid, and the wide flung forests were white with the hoar frosts of Spring.

Father Adam was standing beside the crouching team of dogs. There were five of them; great huskies, shaggy of coat and fiercely wolfish. They were fat and soft from idleness. But they would serve, for the sled was light, and a few days' run would swiftly harden them.

The outfit was waiting just beyond the kitchen door of the house on the hill, and the view of the busy Cove below was completely shut out. The position for the waiting sled had not been calculated by the man who owned it, but by the shrewd, troubled mind of Bat Harker.

He was standing beside the tall figure of the missionary now, squat and sturdy, looking on with half-angry, wholly anxious eyes. His expression was characteristic of the man when he was disturbed. Father Adam's dark eyes were surveying his outfit. There was no emotion in them. They were calm, and simply searching, in the fashion of the practised trail man.

"Say, Les, this is just the craziest thing of all your crazy life," Bat said at last, in a tone kept low for all the feeling that lay behind it. "I tell you they're waiting on you. They've got you set. Just as sure as God this'll be your last trip. It's kind of useless talkin' it again out here, I know. We've talked an' talked it in that darn sick room of yours till I'm sick to death trying to git sense into you. We know the game from A to the hindmost letter of the darn alphabet. We haven't shouted it, you an' me, because there wasn't need. But Idepski's been right here since ever he got his nose on your trail. It was his gun that took you weeks back, an' sent you sick. If I know a thing he meant just to wing you, and leave you kind of helpless, so he could get hands on you when he fancied. He wants you alive, and he's goin' to git you. Ther's word got round you're pulling out. It's clear to me. A bunch of boys hit the trail out of here three nights gone, and I've a notion Idepski went with 'em. Are they wise you're pulling out? Sure they are. Why, in God's name, don't you quit it?"

The man whom the forest world knew as Father Adam, but whom Bat knew as Leslie Standing, shrugged his shoulders.

"Why should I?" he said, his dark eyes mildly enquiring, "you can't tell me a thing I don't know about Idepski. I knew it was he who dropped me. I saw him that night down there and knew him right away. Maybe he can fool you with his disguises. He can't fool me. I'd been watching him days before that."

"Why didn't you show yourself? Why didn't you say?"

Bat spoke fiercely in his exasperation.

The missionary smiled.

"You'd have had him shot up," he said. "I know. No. If you'd known I was around it would have queered the hand I was playing. Here, Bat, let's get this thing right. You could shoot up a dozen Idepskis, and there'd be others to replace 'em. Hellbeam's dogs'll never let up." He shook his head. "It's a play that'll go on to the—end. I know that. I tell you I've got past caring a curse about things. When the end comes, what does it matter! Not a thing. It's useless talking, old friend," he said, as Bat attempted to break in, "quite useless. But don't reckon I'm a willing quitter. I'll play the game till it can't be played longer. And when I've got to I'll throw my hands up. Not before. But Idepski can't follow my trail."

"But he ken cut it," Bat cried, desperation finding expression in a clenched, out-held fist.

"Can he?"

The missionary smiled confidently. And Bat suddenly flung out both hands.

"Say, Les," he cried, "do you think I want to see my partner, and best friend, hounded to a life of hell by that swine, Hellbeam? It breaks me to death the thought of it. Man, man, it sets me nigh crazed thinking that way. Don't I count with you? Don't the others you came along to help count? That dandy gal I've heard you wish was your own daughter? Don't she count? Say, we're all for you, Bull an' Nancy, an' me, just the same as the rest of the folk of the forest. Stop right here, man. Take your place again, an' we'll fight Hellbeam as we've fought his Skandinavia. Say, we'll fight for you as we've never fought before. We'll fight him, and beat him, and keep you safe from that hell he's got waitin' for you. Just say the word, and stop right here. And I'll swear before God—"

Leslie Standing raised a protesting hand. His eyes were unsmiling.

"It's useless, old friend," he said with irrevocable decision. "You don't know the thing you're trying to pledge yourself to. You think me a crazy man. You think I'm just asking for the trouble Hellbeam figures to hand out to me. I'm not. I've got the full measure of the whole thing. And I know the thing I'm doing doesn't matter. I'm not going to change the plan of life I've laid down. I've learnt happiness in the forests. The twilight of it all has been my salvation. Time was when I had other desires, other delights. They've long since passed. Now there's only one appeal to me in life. It's the boys, the scallawags, who haunt the forest like I do. I love them. And my life's theirs as long as Hellbeam leaves it to me. Get just that into your thick, old head, Bat, and for our last five minutes together we can talk of things more pleasant than Hellbeam."

The missionary smiled down into the strong face of his companion. And the lumberman realised the uselessness of further protest. He yielded grudgingly. He yielded because he knew and loved the man. By a great effort he turned his mind from the dread haunting it.

"You've got me beat, Les," he growled. Then he spat in his disgust.

The missionary nodded, and, with a gesture of the hand, he indicated the hidden mills below them.

"It's queer the way the whole thing's completed itself as I hoped and dreamed so long ago," he said thoughtfully. "You know, Bat, that yellow streak in me was a better thing than either of us knew. If I hadn't had it I'd have stood my ground. I'd have fought to the end, and I'd have been beaten, and Sachigo would have crashed. Do you see that? No. That's because you look at things with the obstinate eyes of great courage. While I, through fear, see things as they are. We won't debate it now. The accomplished fact is the thing. You've set Sachigo on top. Sachigo will rule the Canadian forest industry. The foreigner is on the scrap heap. We've helped to build something for this great old Empire of ours, and so our lives haven't been wholly wasted. It's good to feel that when the time comes to pay our debts.

That boy Sternford's a great feller. I'm glad about him. Say, I felt I could cry last night when he and Nancy came along like two school-kids to tell me of the thing they'd fixed. I felt like handing them my story and claiming my place as Nancy's stepfather. But I didn't. You see, she's glad about me as Father Adam, a dopey missionary. But I can see her eyes blaze up red-hot with anger at the man who took her mother from her, and denied her existence. No, it's best that way. She's found the man I could have chosen for her, and I'm glad. She's a great lass. She's all her mother—and more."

Bat inclined his stubborn head. He was still thinking of the dogs, and the sled, and all they meant to him just now.

"Does she know about her share in the mills?" he asked brusquely.

The other shook his head.

"Not yet. But I've sent word to Charlie Nisson. He'll be along up on the *Myra*. And when he comes she'll know." He laughed quietly. "Say, I'd be glad to see them when they know about it—she and Bull. They're going to be married right after Birchall's been along and finally fixed things. It'll be a great day. I wonder. You know, Bat, I'd like to think Nancy—my Nancy—knows all about this. I wonder if she does. Do you think so?"

Bat turned away. His eyes were on the surrounding forest, and the white gossamer of the hoar-frost clinging to the dark foliage. He dared not trust himself to reply.

Again came the missionary's quiet laugh.

"I wonder," he said. Then, in a moment, a curious flicker marred the calm of his eyes. "Bat, old friend," he went on, after a pause, "there's just one thing I'm going to ask you before I pull out. It's a promise I want. When the time comes for me to pay, will you tell her? Will you tell them both? If I'm gone will you tell them the thing you know—all of it? Don't make me out to be any old angel I guess you'd like to paint me. Just hand 'em the story of the white-livered creature I am, without the nerve of a jack-rabbit. Will you do that?"

He held out a hand from which he removed his fur mitt. Bat turned. He saw the hand, and disregarded it in a surge of feeling.

"Tell 'em? Tell 'em?" he cried. "Say, Les, for God Almighty's sake don't you pull out. You're my friend. You're the one feller in the world that matters a curse to me. Quit boy. Stop right here, an'—"

"Will you tell 'em?"

The hand was thrust further towards the lumberman so that he could no longer ignore it.

"Hell! Yes!" he cried, in fierce mental anguish. I'll tell 'em—if I have to." He seized the outstretched hand in both of his and gripped it with crushing force. "You're goin'—now?"

"Sure."

Their hands fell apart. Bat's dropped to his side like leaden weights.

"So long," he said dully, as the other took his place in the sled. Then he added, "So long, Les."

The sled needed breaking out, and the lumberman watched the operation of it without a word. His emotions were too real, to deep for anything more. He looked on while the first sharp order was flung at the dogs. He watched them leap to their feet and stand ready, great, powerful, untamed souls eager for their, task. Then the man in the sled looked round as he strung out the long lash of his short-stocked whip.

"So long, Bat," he cried smilingly. And his farewell was instantly followed by the sharp command to "mush."

Far out on the desolate highlands the dogs broke trail over a waste of virgin snow. The cold had abated, and the flurry of snow that rose up under their feet was wet and melting. The way lay through the maze of woodland bluffs which lined the upper slopes of the course of the Beaver River. Beyond them, northward, lay the windswept barrens of the highlands.

Father Adam knew the trail by heart. The maze of bluffs through which he was passing afforded him no difficulties or anxieties. He read them with the certainty of wide and long experience. There was nothing new that Labrador had to show him. He knew it all, and revelled in the wide freedom its fierce territory afforded. The moods of the country concerned him not at all. Furious or gentle, tearful or hard with the bitterness of desperate winter, it was all one to him. He loved the twilight of its mysterious, fickle heart. It was as much his home as any place on earth.

The dogs swept on at a steady gait. The cruel whip played over furry backs, a never-ceasing threat. And so the miles were hungrily devoured. It was the first day of freedom for dogs and man alike, and each moment of it yielded a sense of almost fierce joy.

The bluffs narrowed in, and the softer snow slowed the going. Instantly a sharp command hurled the leading dog heading for the open where the surface was hard and dry. The team swung away behind him and the sled pursued. Then the silence broke.

A shot rang out. It came from the shelter of a bluff directly ahead. The leading dog floundered. Then the brute fell with a fierce yelp, and sprawled in the snow while the others swept over his inert body. The man in the sled strove to brake the sled with the "gee-pole" which he snatched to his aid. There was a moment of desperate struggle. Then the sled flung tail up in the air and the man was hurled headlong amidst his dogs.

Father Adam stood with mitted hands thrust up above his head. He was gazing into the smiling eyes of a man no less dark than himself. There were three others confronting him, and each was armed with a stubby, automatic pistol which covered his body.

"Guess Hellbeam's waiting for you over the other side, Mr. Leslie Martin, or Standing, or Father Adam, as you choose to call yourself. He's waited a long time. But you ain't tired him out. Guess your game's up."

"Oh, yes?"

The missionary smiled back into Idepski's derisive eyes.

"You can drop your hands," the agent went on. "We've got your gun. And I guess you'll be kind of tired before we get you to the coast. You're going to find things a heap tougher than No. 10 Camp—where you sent me. You surely are."

"The coast?"

The missionary was startled.

"Yep. There's going to be no play game this time. Hellbeam's yacht's waiting on you. You'll take the sea trip. It's safer that way."

"Yes."

The mitted hands had dropped to the missionary's sides. He moistened his lips, which seemed to have become curiously dry. Once, and once only, there was a flicker of the eyes as he looked into the face of his captor. Otherwise he gave no sign. His time had come. He knew that. He had always known it would come. There was neither heat nor resentment in him against these men who had finally hunted him down.

"How do we travel?" he asked quietly. "You've shot up my leader."

The other nodded. He understood the tone of complaint and regret in which the trail man spoke of his dog. He grinned maliciously.

"We'll shoot up the rest for you. They'd only feed the wolves if we left 'em. We've two dog trains with us. Don't let that worry. You best get your kit loosed from your sled."

The prisoner turned to obey, but the agent changed his mind. He laughed.

"No. Guess the boys can fix that. It's safer that way. You move right on into yonder bluff. And you best not try making any break. There ain't only Hellbeam in this. I haven't forgotten—No. 10 Camp. Your game's plumb up."

"Yes, plumb up."

Father Adam obeyed. He moved away, followed closely by the man who had hunted him for so many years. There was no escape. He knew that. The reckoning he had always foreseen had overtaken him. So, without a word of protest, he passed for the last time into the twilight of the woods.